Rosie Goodwin has worked in social services for many years. She has children, and lives in Nuneaton with her husband, Trevor, and their four dogs.

Praise for Rosie Goodwin's previous novels:

'Goodwin is a fabulous writer and surely has a bright future. She reels the reader in surprisingly quickly and her style involves lots of twists and turns that are in no way predictable'
Worcester Evening News

A good tear-jerker . . . compelling' *Reading Evening Post*

'Goodwin is a born author' *Lancashire Evening Telegraph*

'A lovely story of two women finding their own way in life – very enjoyable . . . It's a real page-turner' *Yours*

'Brilliant, a real tissue box tale, heartrending'
Daily Echo, Bournemouth

'A beautifully woven tale of tangled lives . . . An author able to balance emotions, especially love, with skill and wise involvement' *Coventry Evening Telegraph*

'One to make you laugh and cry' *Our Time*, Cambridge

'Her stories are now eagerly awaited by readers the length and breadth of the country' *Heartland Evening News*

'A promising and well-drawn debut' *Lancashire Evening Post*

'A story of adversity and survival' *Huddersfield Daily Examiner*

MOONLIGHT AND ASHES

ROSIE GOODWIN

headline

First published in Great Britain in 2006
by HEADLINE PUBLISHING GROUP

First published in paperback in Great Britain in 2007
by HEADLINE PUBLISHING GROUP

1

ISBN 978 0 7553 2986 1

Typeset in Calisto by Palimpsest Book Production Limited,
Grangemouth, Stirlingshire

Printed and bound in Great Britain by
Clays Ltd, St Ives plc

Headline's policy is to use papers that are natural, renewable
and recyclable products and made from wood grown in sustainable forests.
The logging and manufacturing processes are expected to conform to the
environmental regulations of the country of origin.

HEADLINE PUBLISHING GROUP
A division of Hachette Livre UK Ltd
338 Euston Road
London NW1 3BH

www.headline.co.uk
www.hodderheadline.com

*I dedicate this book to my friend, Ronnie Schwartz,
the 'real' Soho Gus, and also to Betty, with gratitude for
your never-ending faith in me
with all my love xx*

Acknowledgements

Special thanks to Flora, Poppy, Helena, Jane, Joan and the wonderful team at Headline. When Flora, my editor first commissioned me to write this book I was very apprehensive about it, but once I began I loved writing it and hope my readers will love it too.

Also thanks to Philip Patterson, my agent, and Kate and the Babe's for all their love and support.

During the research for this novel I was privileged to speak to many people who had lived and fought through the Second World War. Their bravery and courage made me feel very humble, and I would like to pay tribute to them and also to the people who died fighting for our country.

Part One

Prologue

Coventry, September 1939

'Do you think there really *will* be a war?' Maggie Bright asked as she cradled Lucy, her nine-month-old baby daughter, to her chest.

Her husband, Sam, glanced at her scornfully across the top of his newspaper.

'Don't see how it can be avoided now, accordin' to Chamberlain. They've startin' evacuatin' the kids already. Happen we should think o' getting them pair upstairs away.' When he thumbed towards the stairs door, Maggie visibly paled.

'No, we can't. Not with them both covered in chickenpox.' Her voice betrayed her deep fear.

He snorted derisively. 'If they didn't have chickenpox you'd come up wi' some other excuse to keep 'em with yer. If we'd lived in London you wouldn't have had a choice. They'll turn into a right pair o' cissies, the way you mammy pamper 'em. To hear you goin' on, anyone would think they were still babies instead of eight year olds.'

Maggie swallowed the hasty denial that sprang to her lips and lowered the baby, who was now fast asleep, into the wooden crib at the side of the fireplace.

It was a relief when, minutes later, Sam rose from his seat and snatched his jacket and flat cap from the back of the door. 'I'm off to the pub fer a few bevvies. Don't wait up fer me,' he told her shortly.

Maggie nodded, and once the door had closed behind him, she sank down at the kitchen table and buried her face in her hands. What would she do if there was a war and she *had* to send her twins away? She knew that she would get to keep Lucy with her, for it seemed that they were only evacuating children of school age as yet. But how would Lizzie and Danny cope with being away from her – or worse still, away from each other? The fact that they were twins and as close as could be was no guarantee that they would be placed together. Only that very morning she'd heard Mrs Marshall from Bird Street telling someone in the butcher's shop how her three children had all been placed in separate houses somewhere in the Lake District. Oh, admittedly, it sounded like the children were having a whale of a time, but she doubted Lizzie and Danny would if they were apart.

She thought of them lying upstairs, probably tucked into the same bed. In looks, they were like two peas in a pod, with their fair hair and deep blue eyes, and yet in every other way they were as different as chalk from cheese. Lizzie tended to be timid and shy, whereas Danny, the older by eight minutes, was extrovert and full of mischief. Even so, there was some unseen bond between them that sometimes shocked their mother to her very roots. They were so close that sometimes Danny would finish Lizzie's sentence for her – and woe betide anyone who so much as looked at her the wrong way. Maggie had lost count of the number of times she'd been called to the school to sort out his skirmishes, and yet she could never be angry with him for long. In fact, she found the way he stood up for his sister strangely

4

touching. Her frown deepened. The thought of being separated from them hardly bore thinking about, for her children were her whole world.

Clasping her hands together, she prayed for peace.

Chapter One

'Why is Mam crying?' Lizzie whispered as she leaned against Danny.

'Sshh,' Danny whispered back.

They were crouched at the top of the narrow staircase, and downstairs in the kitchen they could faintly hear the wireless and their mother's sobs.

'Seems like that bloke on the nine o'clock news has just declared we're at war,' Danny told her solemnly.

'But what does that mean? An' why is Mam cryin' about it?'

Danny shrugged his slight shoulders. 'Don't really know. I do know though that war is a bad thing, so perhaps that's why she's cryin'.'

'What do you mean, a bad thing?'

'Well . . .' Her brother struggled to explain his concept of war. 'I reckon the Germans drop bombs an' shoot people an' that.'

Lizzie paled as her eyes almost started from her head, but the debate was stopped from going any further when they heard the sound of a chair being scraped away from the table. Grasping his sister's hand, Danny hauled her past their parents' bedroom to the privacy of the room they shared. It was a small room, with just enough space for two single beds, a single wardrobe and a chest of drawers, but Maggie had brightened it with cheap pictures and posters on the walls. Now, as their father's heavy tread sounded on the stairs, the twins leaped into their narrow beds and pulled the blankets up to their chins. They should have been asleep a couple of hours ago; their dad would go mad if he found them still awake and, worse still, out of bed!

They waited until they had heard their parents' bedroom door open and shut, then Danny crept across the linoleum-covered floor and slipped in at the side of Lizzie. Shivering, she snuggled into the safety of his arms. She was frightened without really knowing why, but Danny would make everything all right; he always did.

Downstairs, their mother was pottering about as she made up the fire and locked the doors, then seconds later, their bedroom door creaked open and she peeped in. She grinned when she saw them tucked in together.

'I don't know why I bothered buying you a bed each,' she scolded, but her eyes were twinkling.

Instantly, Lizzie felt brighter. Their mam was lovely – kind and gentle, and pretty too, with her fair hair and blue eyes. Grandma Sharp, who lived just across the road from them in Clay Lane, had always told Lizzie that their mam had looked just like Lizzie did now when she was a little girl, but Lizzie had always found that hard to imagine, until Grandma had shown her some photographs of her mother as a child. Then Lizzie could see that they did look remarkably alike. It was strange to imagine that her mam had ever been a little girl, though. After all, she was their mam – and the best mam in the whole wide world, as far as Lizzie Bright was concerned.

When Maggie went over to tuck the blankets more tightly around them, Lizzie whispered, 'Why've you been crying, Mam?'

Maggie struggled to find the right words to answer. Eventually she told her, 'I heard something sad on the wireless.' There was no point in lying to them; they would find out about it at school.

'What did you hear?' It was Danny's turn to ask questions now.

Taking a deep breath, Maggie replied, 'I heard that England is now at war.'

'But why?'

Smoothing an imaginary crease from the candlewick bedspread, Maggie straightened and hurried towards the chink of light that was peeping through a small gap in the curtains. Closing them, she sighed, 'Because people can't always live together without fighting.'

'Like you an' Dad, you mean?' Danny said innocently.

Maggie bent swiftly to peck them both on their cheeks. 'Me and your dad don't fight,' she said, none too convincingly, then she turned and made for the door so that they wouldn't see the fresh tears that were ready to fall at any second. Feeling their frightened eyes boring into her back, she turned just once more to smile at them reassuringly. 'Don't you two get worrying now. It will probably all be over in no time. We'll be just fine, you'll see. Now go off to sleep else you'll never get better.'

Her heart swelled with love as she looked at them. They were both covered in Calamine lotion from head to foot to stop them itching, and looked like two little ghosts. They stared back at her, and once the door had closed behind her they snuggled further down into the bed.

Lizzie was trembling and Danny held her protectively against him.

'Don't worry,' his soft voice sliced through the darkness. 'If Mam says it'll be all right, then it will be.'

Comforted, Lizzie yawned and closed her eyes. Soon, their gentle snores echoed around the room.

'Vera Hodges' son joined up today,' Maggie remarked as she slid a slice of bacon onto a sturdy white dinner-plate.

Sam glanced up briefly from the newspaper he was reading. 'Him an' a few dozen more, from what the blokes at work were sayin' today,' he grunted.

Danny and Lizzie, who were sitting at the opposite side of the table to their father, exchanged a worried glance. Since the beginning of the war, lots of people they knew had gone away to fight, and it disturbed them. They sat silent until at last their mam had finished putting out the dinner and joined them at the table.

After folding his newspaper and lifting his knife and fork, their father grimaced. 'Call *this* a dinner?' He glared at Maggie. 'One bloody strip o' bacon an' one sausage? How's a workin' man supposed to keep his strength up on this – an' where's me fried egg, eh?'

Hastily, Maggie slid her sausage onto his plate. 'Sorry, Sam. It's all this talk about rationin'. I'm doin' the best I can. Everybody seems to be panicking and grabbing everything they can. I had to queue up at the butcher's for over an hour just to get this. As for eggs – well, at the minute they're harder to get hold of than snow in summertime.'

'Huh!' Grunting his disapproval, Sam began to shovel the food into his mouth at an alarming rate. It was at that moment that Lucy woke up and began to cry.

Maggie hurried over to the crib at the side of the fire-place and lifted her out.

'You have my dinner an' all,' she told her husband. 'This one needs feedin', an' by the time I'm done it'll be stone cold anyway.'

Without so much as a word, Sam scraped her dinner onto his plate. Maggie crossed to the walk-in pantry at the side of the room and removed a glass feeding bottle full of milk formula that she had prepared earlier.

Settling into the fireside chair, she began to feed the baby, who gulped at the milk greedily. The twins grinned at each other. They still hadn't got over the novelty of having a baby sister, and treated her like a little doll. Lucy was dark like her father, with chocolate-brown eyes that melted the heart of anyone who saw her. Their grins vanished, however, as they saw their mother's meal disappearing into their father's mouth, and without a word being uttered they both knew exactly what the other was thinking. Their mother was losing weight and had dark circles beneath her eyes that told of the sleepless nights she was having. Lucy was teething, and often they would get up in the mornings to find their mother pacing the floor of the small kitchen-cum-sitting room with the baby in her arms.

Their father rose from the table, snapped his braces off his broad arms and swiped a lock of dark hair from his forehead.

'Going out, are you, Sam?' their mother asked timidly.

He snorted. 'O' course I am. It's Friday night, ain't it? A bloke's entitled to a few bevvies down at the pub wi' his mates after a hard week's graft, ain't he?'

'Yes, yes, of course he is,' Maggie hastened to agree with him. 'Just let me settle Lucy back down an' I'll fetch the bath in and fill it for you.'

'Huh, it'll be quicker to fetch it in meself. That little madam's rulin' the roost, from what I can see of it. I don't know why yer don't just put her down an' let her howl. She'd soon learn to belt up if yer didn't pander to her.'

10

'She can't help it, Sam,' Maggie pointed out. 'The poor little mite's in pain with her teeth, that's why she's cryin' all the time.'

Impatiently, he strode across the room and flung open the back door that led onto the shared yard. Seconds later, he returned with a tin bath that had been hanging on a nail outside.

'Any hot water in the tap?' he asked roughly.

'There should be, I've had the fire roarin' up the chimney as much as I dare,' Maggie said.

Soon all four of them were traipsing back and forwards from the sink with hot water in kettles, saucepans and anything else that would hold water. It was a Friday-night ritual that they were all used to, and soon the bath was steaming in front of the fire.

'You two pop upstairs an' read your books while yer dad has his bath,' Maggie told the twins, and obediently they turned and made their way up the steep narrow staircase.

At the top they hurried along to their room and slipped inside. Sinking onto her bed, Lizzie lifted her Enid Blyton book as Danny approached the one sashcord window that the room boasted.

'Don't let any light show,' Lizzie warned him fearfully. Recently, their mother had gone out and bought black-out material that she'd stitched to the back of every single pair of curtains in the house, and the little girl knew that it would be more than their life was worth if they let any light spill out onto the pavement. Only last week, Danny had stood gazing down into the street below, forgetting to close the curtains properly, which had resulted in a visit and a stern reprimand from Mr Hutton, the ARP warden. When he had gone, their father had threatened the boy with his belt, should he ever do such a thing again.

'I ain't *totally* thick, yer know,' Danny sniffed indignantly, and instantly contrite, Lizzie threw down her book and crossed to stand beside him.

'Why does it matter so much if a bit of light *does* show?' she enquired.

'It's 'cos if there's any planes wi' bombs in 'em flyin' over Coventry an' they see a light, they could drop 'em on us,' her brother explained.

Lizzie shuddered. The twins could only hope that this war would soon be over, as their mam had promised, so that their lives could get back to normal. Many of their friends had already been sent away, and their class was almost empty. Just the thought of leaving their mother struck terror into their young hearts, but thankfully up to now Maggie had stood up to their father and refused to let them go, saying that she wanted the family to be together for Christmas.

It was almost half an hour later when they heard the back door slam, and then their mother's voice floated up the stairs to them. 'Come on, you two. It's time for your baths.'

Danny sighed. He hated bath nights, but all the same he slid off the bed and followed his sister downstairs. Their mother's face was flushed from her many journeys to and from the sink with kettles of hot water but she smiled at them as they tumbled back into the room.

'Right – you first, Lizzie. Then I can be putting your rags in while Danny has his.'

Lizzie groaned inwardly. Every bath night, once she was washed, her mother would sit and painstakingly twist strips of rag into her wet hair, which would ensure she got up the next morning looking like Shirley Temple. She hated it, but loved her mam too much to tell her so. At eight, she considered she was too old for ringlets –

especially when Susan Warren at school made fun of her.

In no time at all she was immersed in the hot water and she sat quietly while her mam rubbed a mix of camomile powder and warm water into her hair, then tipped jug after jug of warm water over her head until she was sure she was clean. The girl rubbed herself dry with a big towel whilst Danny underwent the same procedure. Then she sat patiently as the rags were twisted into her wet hair, ouching occasionally as the wooden hairbrush caught on a knot.

An hour later, as Maggie was just emptying the last of the bathwater down the deep stone sink, a knock came on the back door and both children grinned. That would be their Uncle David. He always popped in on a Friday night, and he usually came bearing treats tucked down deep in his pockets.

Hopping off his seat, Danny flew to the door and flung it open. 'Hello, Uncle David.'

A tall man who was the double of their father stepped into the room and ruffled his nephew's hair as he flashed a wink at Lizzie. 'Hello, young man. Been good this week, have you?' His chocolate-brown eyes twinkled.

'I've been *very* good,' Danny hastened to tell him as their uncle took his coat off and draped it over the back of a chair.

'Good. I might find something nice for you then. But first I'll get this bath outside for your mam, eh?'

As he lifted the tin bath effortlessly, Maggie bustled away to put the kettle on. Soon they were all seated at the table sipping mugs of steaming cocoa and helping themselves from the biscuit barrel, and not for the first time, Danny felt a pang of regret that his uncle wasn't his father. David and Sam were twins, just like him and

13

Lizzie, and to look at they were almost identical, except that his uncle had a dimple in his left cheek whilst his father had a dimple in his right. There, any similarity between the two men ended, for Uncle David was kind and funny, whilst his father was fed up and angry for most of the time.

Lizzie was thinking much the same thing as their uncle delved into his coat pocket and produced two bars of Fry's Five Boys chocolate as if by magic.

'Now don't go getting it all over your clean night-clothes, else you'll get me into bother with your mam,' he warned.

'Ta, Uncle David,' they chorused, and in seconds they'd ripped the wrappers off and were eating the chocolate as if they'd never tasted it before.

Maggie smiled indulgently, but just then Lucy let out a lusty wail and she rose from the table. 'No peace for the wicked,' she sighed. 'I reckon this one is overdue for her bottle.'

'I'll warm it up for you,' David offered as the baby's cries grew louder. They stopped immediately Maggie inserted the rubber teat between her rosebud lips, and they all sighed with relief. Lucy might only be small but she could certainly make her presence known. She drained the bottle in seconds, then lay placidly as Maggie removed her nappy, dropped it into the enamel bucket to soak and then fastened the safety pins into her clean one.

'There, little lady. That's better, isn't it?' Maggie said, her face alight with love. Lucy gurgled contentedly, and not for the first time a wave of envy swept through David. How could his brother have so much while *he* had nothing? If Maggie and the children had been his, then they would have had to crowbar him away from them, yet Sam escaped to the pub every chance he got. He supposed his love for Maggie had started the very first time he'd clapped eyes on her, but it was too late for regrets now. She had made her choice when she married Sam and there was nothing he could do about it.

Without being smug, David knew that there were plenty of women who would be more than willing to become his partner, but none of them ever quite measured up to Maggie in his eyes.

Seeing him become morose, Maggie's eyes creased with concern. 'Is something wrong, David?' she asked anxiously.

Aware of the children's eyes on him he forced a smile to his face. 'No, no, course not. Though there is something I need to tell you when the children have gone to bed. Nothing for any of you to worry about though,' he added hastily to his nephew and niece.

'Right, well, speaking of bed, I think it's about time you two skipped off and got tucked in, don't you?'

'Aw, Mam. Can't we have just another half hour?' Danny beseeched.

Normally, Maggie would have relented, but tonight for some reason a sense of foreboding had settled around her like a cloud. Now that she came to think about it, David hadn't quite been his normal cheery self since the minute he set foot through the door, and she had an awful feeling that she wasn't going to like what he was going to tell her.

'No, you cannot,' she retorted in a manner that brooked no argument. 'Now come on, the pair of you, else you'll have bags under your eyes in the morning.'

Reluctantly, the twins slid off their seats, offered their cheeks for a goodnight kiss and then trooped away up the stairs. The second Maggie heard their bedroom door close behind them she turned to David. 'All right then – what is it you have to tell me that's so important?'

'Never mind about that for now. How did you do that?' He stabbed his finger towards a bruise that was just fading on her cheek.

Maggie flushed and covered it self-consciously with her hand. 'Oh, I er . . . I bumped it on the cupboard door the other day. I must be getting clumsy in my old age.'

Ignoring her light tone, he said, 'He's been at his tricks again, hasn't he, the lousy bastard.'

'Of course he hasn't. I told you – I bumped it on the door, and you shouldn't talk about your brother that way.'

'Huh! Just because he's my brother doesn't mean I have to like him. Sometimes I can hardly believe we ever lay in the same womb together.'

Finding no answer, Maggie lowered her eyes and began to play with the fringe on the chenille tablecloth. Eventually she said, 'So – are you going to tell me what's going on or what then?'

The anger seemed to leave him in a flash and now it was his turn to be sheepish. 'Well, the thing is, I've er . . . I've decided to join up.'

'*You've what?*' Panic gripped her. 'But you can't!'

'Why can't I? Would you really care?'

Maggie stared into the depths of the fire, her heart fluttering with shock. There was so much she wanted to say, but she and David had missed their chance many years ago, and now it was too late. Perhaps it would be better if he did leave, for being so near him and seeing him so often was almost painful.

'I'm just worried that you might get hurt, that's all,' she muttered, and her heart was breaking as she saw the hope in his eyes die.

'If everyone thought like that, no one would go. Anyway,

if things carry on the way they are, no one will have a choice. The Germans have already invaded Poland and I reckon it won't be long before they start on us.'

'I suppose you're right,' she said dully, and they lapsed into silence as she tried to imagine her life without him.

Chapter Two

November 1939

From their place at the kitchen table the twins sat watching their father. He was standing in front of the mirror above the mantelpiece smoothing Brylcreem onto his jet-black hair. When he was ready, he stepped towards the door. 'Best behaviour for your mother then, else it'll be a taste o' me belt fer you pair when I get back in,' he warned, then without so much as another word he opened the back door and stepped outside. The fire flickered and spat in the draught, and then he was gone. Maggie hurried to place the black-out curtain back over the door.

'Wouldn't be surprised if it didn't snow tonight,' she commented.

'Cor, that would be smashin',' Danny said, excited. 'We could go sledgin' in the park, Lizzie.'

His sister was just about to reply when a tap came on the back door and seconds later, Mrs Massey, their neighbour, popped her head round it.

'Is it all clear?' she asked.

Maggie grinned. 'If you mean, has Sam gone to the pub yet, yes he has.'

'Good.' Mrs Massey barged into the room slamming the door behind her against the increasingly bitter night. Waving a bottle of stout in the air, she announced, 'My Fred treated me afore he went out an' I thought you might like to share a sup wi' me. I've got half a dozen Woodbines an' all so we're all set fer a good Friday night, by the looks of it.' Peering at Lucy, who was by now fast asleep in her crib again, she settled herself into the fireside chair.

Danny and Lizzie exchanged an amused glance. They thought the Masseys were a very funny couple. Mrs Massey was huge, with chins that wobbled when she laughed and a backside that she had to squeeze into a chair, whilst Mr Massey was a tiny little man, stick-thin, who only reached up to his wife's shoulder. Even so, they seemed happy and had produced five children. The two oldest girls were married, the oldest boy had just joined up, and the two younger children, Carol and Tony, had recently been evacuated.

It was these two that Maggie asked after now as she set two glasses on the table. 'Any news of the kids?'

The big woman's lower lip quivered. 'Matter o'fact, I had a letter from both of 'em just this mornin'. Seems they're in a village somewhere on the outskirts o' Nuneaton, but they ain't livin' together. Tony is with a farmer an' his wife, an' havin' the time of his life if his letter is owt to go by. Carol is with a childless couple an' sounded a bit homesick in the letter.'

Maggie squeezed her hand sympathetically. 'You must miss them.'

'Yes, I do,' Mrs Massey admitted. 'Though God knows why. The little buggers were allus up to some mischief or another at home, but it ain't the same wi'out 'em an' Lord only knows how we'll feel at Christmas.' She looked across at the twins, clean and ready for bed after their Friday-night baths. Danny was sketching on a large pad and Lizzie had settled down at the table to do a jigsaw. 'Yer really should be thinkin' o' gettin' them pair somewhere safe an' all,' she advised. 'You'd never forgive yourself if there were any bombin' an' any harm come to 'em. They've had no choice but to send the kids out of London, an' they reckon that soon we won't have a choice either.'

'Oh, I don't think there's much chance of that,' Maggie said quickly, eager to change the conversation in front of the twins.

Mrs Massey sniffed, and hitching up her huge breasts, she took a slurp from her glass and stared into the flickering fire.

Half an hour later, when the twins were in bed, she resumed the earlier conversation almost immediately.

'You'll have to let 'em go soon, love, so yer may as well make yer mind up to it,' she said gently. 'Only reason they weren't sent off wi' mine was 'cos they had the chickenpox an' were too bad to go. But it'll be different now they're well. They could well decide to evacuate 'em any day now.'

'*No!*' Maggie flushed as she realised that she had raised her voice. She couldn't pretend that her marriage had been made in heaven, but she could just about endure it while she had her children around her. God knows what she'd do if the twins weren't there. Suddenly tired, she sank down onto the old settee. 'I'd just like to keep the family together until after Christmas,' she muttered, and her neighbour's kind heart went out to her.

'I know yer would, love, an' God willin', yer shall. I'm only warnin' yer 'cos this bloody war is goin' from bad to worse. The first bombs could be dropped on London any day now, an' then it's only a matter o' time till they start to really target Coventry. Think of it – most o' the car factories in the city are turning out ammunition, tanks an' aircraft parts already, so it's obvious the

Germans are gonna take a pot at them. I ain't sayin' it to frighten yer. This ain't easy fer none of us. There's my Will out there somewhere, bless him. I ain't heard hide nor hair of him since he joined up last month, an' who knows how long it will be till I see him again? They could send him anywhere. Could have already, fer all I know. An' then there's my Fred – he's already put hisself up for fire watch, should he be needed.'

'I know how you feel,' Maggie replied. 'David has gone off to camp too, but as yet he hasn't let us know where he is.' Swallowing the lump that had formed in her throat, she patted her neighbour's hand. Mrs Massey was a big woman with a big mouth at times. But for all that she had a big heart too, and during the years that Maggie had lived next door to her, she had proved herself to be a good friend and neighbour time and time again.

'We'll get through this together,' Maggie said now.

Mrs Massey nodded. 'Aye, happen we will, love. By the way, word has it that they're startin' to put the Anderson shelters up in Swanshill next week, so be prepared.'

Maggie gulped deep in her throat – it was all so much to take in.

Upstairs, the twins plopped miserably onto the side of Lizzie's bed. Friday nights weren't the same any more without Uncle David's visits. Only last week, he had called round whilst their father was at work to tell them that he would be going away. He had looked very smart, but different somehow in his Army uniform. Their mum had sobbed and clung on to him as if she might never see him again, and that had brought tears to Lizzie's eyes too.

Their mother had told them that now Uncle David

had gone, he might be away for a very long time. The thought made the sides of Lizzie's mouth droop. They all missed him already. All except her father, that was. He and her Uncle David didn't get on, for some reason.

The twins had lost count of the number of times they had heard the two men rowing. It was usually following one of their mother's accidents. Maggie always seemed to have a black eye or a split lip or something, but whenever they asked her what she'd done, she said she had just slipped or bumped herself somehow. And with that, the twins had to be content, although at eight years old they were beginning to notice that the accidents always seemed to happen after they had heard their father shouting while they lay in bed.

'It won't be the same without Uncle David here fer Christmas,' Lizzie reflected sadly as she lounged on her candlewick bedspread, the rags in her hair dancing like snakes. 'Where do yer reckon he's gone?'

'I heard Mam tellin' Dad as he'd gone somewhere up North fer trainin',' Danny replied gloomily.

Dropping onto the bed beside her, their fingers entwined as they sat thinking of their uncle, but then their mother's voice interrupted their melancholy thoughts.

'I hope you two are in bed?' she called. 'I shall be up to check in a minute, and make sure you have that light out else we'll have Mr Hutton hammering on the door.'

Guiltily, Danny clicked off the light and side-by-side they clambered into Lizzie's bed.

'Ooh, it's freezin',' Lizzie complained as the cold sheets settled around her thin legs. 'Mam's forgot to put the hot bottle in to take the chill off.'

'Never mind. Cuddle up to me an' you'll soon get warm,' Danny told her reassuringly.

They lay in silence for some time until eventually

Lizzie asked, 'You don't think Mam will send us away, do yer, Danny?'

He shrugged in the darkness. 'Shouldn't think so. It's London they're bombin', not Coventry. I reckon we're as safe as houses.'

On that optimistic note they drifted off to sleep.

It was some time later when the sound of the back door slamming brought Danny springing awake. Knuckling the sleep from his eyes, he eased his other arm from around Lizzie and inched towards the edge of the bed. Then, very carefully, so as not to disturb his sister, he swung his legs down onto the cold lino and crept towards the door.

'Ah, bin cryin' again, have yer?' he heard his father jeer. 'Missin' that brother o' mine, are yer?'

'Of course I'm not,' his mother said hotly. 'I'm just a bit low, that's all, worrying about what's going to happen to us. And keep your voice down. You'll wake the children.'

Silent as a little mouse, Danny tiptoed to the top of the stairs and listened.

'Huh! The children. It's always the bloody children,' his father exploded. 'Sometimes I reckon you'd be happier if I were to join up an' all!'

Danny waited for his mother to deny it, and when no response was forthcoming he frowned into the darkness. Why were his mam and dad always shouting at each other? He'd never heard his mam shout at Uncle David. But then Uncle David was different to his dad. He'd always made time for them, whereas his dad just made them feel that they were nothing but nuisances and always in the way.

'I don't want this to turn into an argument, Sam,'

Maggie said wearily. 'I've got enough on my plate at the minute. I've got to take the children to get their gas masks and identity discs next week, and on top of that, the men are coming to fit the Anderson shelter out the back.'

'I don't know why yer don't just let the kids go with the next lot of evacuees,' Sam told her gruffly.

Danny heard her horrified gasp. 'How can you say that? They're your children as well, Sam!'

'That's as may be. But go on – admit it – don't yer just wish they weren't, eh? If they'd been *David's* kids yer could all have lived happy ever after, couldn't yer? It's as plain as the nose on yer face that you all think more o' him than me.'

'That's a terrible thing to say!' Maggie cried, but even Danny didn't find her words convincing.

A funny fluttery feeling started in the pit of his stomach as he heard something overturn and crash to the floor. Then he heard his mother cry out, and unable to bear it, he fled down the stairs and threw the kitchen door open. His father was grasping Maggie's arm, his fist raised. There was blood trickling from her nose and she was crying, but the second she saw Danny she forced a smile to her face.

'Hello, love, what are you doing out of bed? I just knocked the chair over and your dad was helping me pick it up.' She shook Sam's hand from her arm and glared at him as she righted the chair, then crossing to Danny she gently herded him back towards the stairs door. 'Come on now, pet. It's very late. You get back up to bed, eh?'

Danny glanced at his father, who had lit a cigarette and was standing in a cloud of smoke. His face was very red, and the boy could smell the beer on his breath even from across the room.

'Go on, yer nosy little bugger,' the man belched. 'Do as yer mam tells yer, or do yer need me to help yer up the stairs?'

As Sam's hand shifted to his belt and he swayed unsteadily towards him, Danny turned and sprinted away to the safety of his room, taking the steep stairs two at a time. Once there, he leaned heavily against the door as his heart settled back into some sort of normal rhythm. What had his dad meant about their mam wishing Uncle David had been their dad? It was all very confusing. He was relieved to see that Lizzie was still fast asleep, her thumb jammed tight in her mouth. And what had his mam meant when she said that he and Lizzie were to be issued with gas masks and identity discs? Danny knew what they were; he had seen them on children in the *Pathé News* at the pictures at the Saturday-morning matinées. All the children in London had them, but why would they need them in Coventry? They were safe here. It was London that was being bombed.

For once he passed Lizzie's bed and, creeping over to his own, he slithered inside, gasping as he thrust his feet down into the cold sheets. Apart from the fact that half his classmates had been sent to the country and there wasn't so much food in the shops, life in Coventry seemed to be pretty much as it had been before the war, so why was everyone so worried?

Straining his ears into the blackness he was relieved to hear that all was quiet, so turning on his side, he shut his eyes tight and soon slipped into an uneasy sleep.

The following Monday, as the twins walked home from school, they were shocked to see huge open-backed lorries lined up the length of Clay Lane. Piled high on the backs of them were huge sheets of corrugated iron that workmen were throwing onto the ground.

'What's going on?' asked Lizzie, totally bewildered.

'These must be for the Anderson shelters Mam were on about,' Danny replied wisely. 'I reckon we're going to get one in our back yard.'

'But why? What are they for?'

'You go an' shelter in 'em if any bombs get dropped, from what I can gather.' Danny dodged a workman who was trying to manoeuvre one of the shiny sheets up a narrow entry. The air was ringing with the sound of the sheets as they hit the ground and the workmen's shouts.

All along the rows of terraced houses, women in headscarves twisted into turbans were standing, arms folded across their wrap-around pinafores, shivering but watching the proceedings with interest.

Soon the twins' house came into view. Just as Danny had predicted, a lorry was parked outside. Their mother was standing on the doorstep with Lucy, who was now almost a year old, perched on her hip. She waved when she saw them and the twins broke into a trot.

'What do you make of this then?' she smiled, deliberately keeping her voice light.

'Danny says we'll have to shelter inside these things they're building if we get bombed, but we *won't* get bombed, will we, Mam?'

Hearing the fear in the child's voice, Maggie hugged Lizzie to her with her free arm. 'Hopefully not, sweetheart. But it'll be nice to know it's there, just in case. Now come on in out of the cold. I've got your tea all ready for you, and Grandma's here. She's baked you a cake.'

The children trudged past her into the smart front

room that was kept for high days and holidays, and on into the kitchen.

Ellen Sharp beamed as they flew into her arms. 'Hello, me darlin's. Had a good day at school, have you?'

She had to shout to make herself heard above the noise coming from the yard. Crossing to the window, Danny lifted the net curtain to see what was going on. Their shelter was almost done and looked strangely out of place next door to the coalhouse and the outside lav.

'Ain't left much room fer us to play, has it?' he remarked as his mother came to stand beside him.

'Well, that won't matter, will it? You can play inside it,' she pointed out. 'Now wash your hands and come to the table.'

Minutes later, they were all seated and their grandma began to slice a big crusty loaf, which she then smeared sparingly with butter.

'There seems to be a shortage of everythin',' she complained. 'I just wonder what we'll end up with for us Christmas dinner this year. The shelves in the food shops are half-empty already, an' the rationin' ain't even officially begun yet.'

Maggie spread the bread with jam and passed a slice to Lizzie. 'Well, at least we're all still together.'

'There is that in it, but for how much longer?' her mother asked. Instantly Maggie's appetite fled. 'An' have you heard from David?'

The children's ears pricked up as Maggie lifted Lucy into her wooden highchair. 'I got a brief note but he didn't say much,' she said quietly. 'Just that he was OK and that he was up North doing his training.'

'Whereabouts up North?'

Maggie shrugged. 'He didn't say. I don't suppose he was allowed to.'

'Huh! Damn war,' Grandma grunted. 'Let's just pray as Him Upstairs keeps an eye out for David an' all the other young men that are out there fightin' fer their country.'

The room became silent, save for the sound of hammering outside, as the workmen put the finishing touches to the Anderson shelter.

Chapter Three

Three days later, the twins set off for school with their new gas masks slung across their shoulders in little cardboard boxes. Danny was far from happy about it.

'Fancy havin' to lump these about everywhere,' he grumbled. 'It's goin' to be a right pain in the arse.'

'You'll have a pain in the arse all right if Mam catches yer swearin',' Lizzie warned him as she fingered the new identity disc that was tied around her wrist. She quite liked hers because it was all shiny and new and looked like a bracelet. Danny on the other hand hated his as much as his gas mask, and had chosen to wear it round his neck where it wouldn't be seen.

'Can't see the point in 'em,' he stated as he kicked at a stone. It was a bitterly cold, frosty morning and the pavements sparkled like diamonds in the weak morning sun. 'T'ain't as if we're goin' to get bombed now, is it? The Jerries are droppin' all the bombs on London.'

'Well, Mam says they're just in case,' Lizzie told him sensibly and they hurried on, intent on getting out of the cold.

As they passed Swanswell Pool, Danny was delighted to see that it was frozen over. 'We could have a skate on that on the way home,' he remarked joyously, his complaints suddenly forgotten.

Lizzie's head wagged from side-to-side. 'Don't yer remember what happened to Jimmy Nailer last year? He went through the ice in the middle an' they had to get the firemen to pull him out. He got pneumonia an' ended up in hospital fer Christmas.'

'Spoilsport,' muttered Danny, and they continued on their way, their breath hanging on the air in front of them like white lace.

When they emerged from school that afternoon, the twins were shocked to see huge silver barrage balloons suspended on thick metal wires floating above the city. The spire of the magnificent Cathedral looked strangely at odds amongst them.

'What are they for?' Lizzie whispered in awe.

'I know,' Danny told her proudly. 'They're so as if the enemy planes did come to drop bombs an' tried to fly too low, they'd get tangled up in 'em an' crash.'

'Ugh!' Lizzie shuddered at the image he had conjured up.

Although it was only four o'clock, it was almost dark by the time the children turned into Clay Lane. It was the first week in December, and normally they would be passing brightly lit Christmas trees in people's front windows, but this year no one seemed to have the heart for it.

The Lane now looked as it normally did, thanks to the womenfolk who had set to and cleaned up all the mess left by the gangs of men who had erected the Anderson shelters. The rows of back-to-back terraced houses all looked the same, apart from the curtains that hung at the windows, but once they were drawn against the cold winter night, then they became indistinguishable one from another, thanks to the blackout curtains that everyone had now been forced to use.

The children arrived home in a sombre mood, but the second they set foot through the door, their faces lit up.

'Uncle David!' they shrieked.

He was sitting in the chair at the side of the fire bouncing Lucy, who was giggling with glee, up and down on his knee.

'Hello, kids.' Slinging their gas masks down, they flew across and wrapped their arms around him.

'Oh, we've missed you *so* much!' Lizzie was so excited she was hopping from foot to foot. 'How long are you home for?'

'Will you be here fer Christmas?' This from Danny.

'When did you get back?' Lizzie asked.

'Whoa, hold on there. One question at a time, eh? But first let's see what I have in my pockets.' Laughing, he placed Lucy down on the rug in front of the fire and checked that the guard was in place. The little girl was crawling now, and would soon be walking.

Lizzie thought her uncle looked very handsome in his uniform, and she was fascinated by the shiny buttons on his jacket.

David proceeded to delve into his pockets and unload all sorts of treats onto the table. The twins eyed them greedily. There were gobstoppers, toffee pincushions, sherbet dabs, farthing chews, and a packet of liquorice bootlaces – the twins' favourite.

'But not before your tea, mind,' their mam warned, though her eyes were shining. Lifting the knitted tea cosy from the pot she poured them each a cup of tea in her best china cups.

'Cor, Mam, it ain't often these come out o' the china cabinet.' Danny remarked, almost afraid to lift his in case he dropped and broke it.

'Yes, well, it's a special occasion, isn't it? Uncle David

being home, I mean.' Lizzie noted that their mam had turned a pretty pink colour as she said it and wondered why. But she didn't have long to dwell on it because Danny started firing questions at him again.

'Have yer killed anyone yet?'

'No, Danny, I haven't. And I sincerely hope I never have to.' Uncle David was solemn again now. 'I've been doing my training. And in answer to your earlier questions, no, I won't be here for Christmas, unfortunately. They've just allowed me a couple of days' leave before they ship me out.'

Danny's face fell a foot. 'Where will they be sending you to?'

David sipped at his tea before answering. 'I don't know. None of us do. We just have to go wherever they send us, but I have an idea they'll be taking us over to France.'

Lizzie noted that all colour had now drained from their mother's face. She didn't like the sound of their uncle being sent to France. Wasn't that where all the fighting was going on? She'd seen newsreels of the soldiers there, and it didn't look very nice at all.

All the time they were talking, Lucy was clinging onto the edges of a chair, but suddenly she let go, and on very unsteady feet she took her first two steps.

Everyone's mouths fell open with amazement as Lucy beamed at them, as if aware of what a great milestone she had just passed. Uncle David swooped towards her and snatched her up just as she was about to fall forward, and everyone laughed as the tense mood was broken.

'Well, I'll be!' Uncle David's eyes were moist as he kissed the downy hair, so like his own and his twin brother's. 'No matter where they send me now I'll have this to remember.' He and Maggie exchanged a funny look, which didn't go unnoticed by the twins, but before they could say anything, the back door suddenly flew open and Grandma Sharp burst in carrying a large dish covered with a crisp white tea-towel.

'Why, David lad – I didn't know you were back. How long are yer home for? My, it's good to see yer all safe an' sound.'

Dropping the dish onto the table she caught David to her in a great hug and the twins giggled as he blushed a deep crimson.

They chatted for a few moments until Grandma said to Maggie: 'Pop that in the oven to keep warm, love. I queued up an' got a load of mince today so I thought I'd do you all a cottage pie while I were makin' ours. No sense in it goin' to waste, is there?'

'Thanks, Mam. That'll go down a treat.' When Maggie glanced nervously at the wooden clock on the mantelpiece and then back at David, an unspoken message passed between them and he hastily rose from his seat and started to shrug his long arms into a khaki-coloured overcoat.

'It's time I were off,' he stated. 'Sam will be home from work in a minute an' he won't take kindly to findin' me here delayin' your dinners.'

'Aw, do yer have to go, Uncle David?' Lizzie's eyes filled with tears as he strode towards the door. He stopped to tousle her shining ringlets and tweak her ribbons.

''Fraid so, Lizzie. Your other grandma will have my guts for garters if I'm late for my tea. But I'll tell you what – I'll go sniffin' round to see if I can't find you a Christmas tree tomorrow, an' if I do I'll drop it in when you get in from school. How would that do?'

'Ooh, yes, please.' Happy again, Lizzie watched him leave, closing the door behind him.

His footsteps had barely finished echoing in the entry when Grandma Sharp sighed and glanced meaningfully at Maggie. 'Bloody shame if you were to ask me,' she said.

Maggie flushed and hissed, 'That's enough o' that, Mam. Especially in front of the children.'

Danny raised his eyebrows at Lizzie in exasperation. Sometimes grown-ups were very hard to understand.

Later that evening, as the children sat at the kitchen table doing a jigsaw, Danny suddenly remembered the treats his uncle had brought them.

'Can we have a few of the sweets Uncle brought us, Mam?' he asked innocently.

His father, who was reading the newspaper in the fire-side chair, instantly looked up. 'An' what uncle would that be then?'

'Uncle David,' Lizzie piped up brightly. 'He's home on leave fer a couple o' days an' he popped round to see us.'

'*Did* he now!' When Sam's head snapped round to glare at Maggie, who was sitting opposite to him, she tensed and her knitting needles seemed to click even faster.

'Oh yes. I er . . . forgot to mention it, what with getting the dinner out an' seein' to Lucy, an' one thing an' another.'

'It's time you pair were in bed,' their father suddenly said, turning his attention back to the twins.

'But Dad, it's only just gone seven,' Danny protested.

'I don't care if it's only just gone six. I said bed. Now get up them stairs if yer know what's good fer yer.'

When their dad used that tone of voice the twins knew better than to argue. They hastily washed in the cold water that stood on the washstand in their unheated bedroom, then changed into their night clothes and clambered into Lizzie's bed. Almost immediately, the sound of raised voices came up the stairs to them, and Lizzie began to cry.

Danny cuddled her close. 'Don't cry, Lizzie. Happen Dad just got out o' bed the wrong side this mornin', eh? Or perhaps he's tired. They're makin' parts fer tanks an' all manner o' things at the Dunlop now, yer know. They don't keep the parts in the factory though. Once they're made they send 'em to what they call shadow factories on the outskirts o' the city.'

'How do you know all this, an' why do they send 'em away?' asked Lizzie, greatly impressed with her twin's knowledge.

'I know 'cos I heard Mr Massey tellin' one o' the other neighbours about it. They do it to stop houses with people in 'em from gettin' bombed.'

While both children tried to puzzle this out, they eventually went to sleep with the sound of their parents' raised voices in the background of their dreams.

The following day brought the first snow – and cries of delight from Danny when he got up and drew aside the bedroom curtains.

'Hey, Liz, come an' look at this. Everywhere looks brand new.'

Lizzie yawned and stretched before reluctantly leaving the warmth of the bed to join him at the window, where she peered out into the eerie grey light. The rows of sooty rooftops were sparkling white and everywhere looked clean and bright.

After quickly washing and struggling into their school clothes they hurried down the stairs to find their mam stirring a big pan of porridge on the stove. Bursting into the room, Danny asked, 'Mam, have yer seen the—' He stopped abruptly when he caught sight of the big purple bruise that covered the whole of her left eye.

Seeing his horrified reaction she self-consciously raised her hand to cover it. 'Clumsy Clogs has been at it again,' she smiled. 'I reckon I'm becoming a walking disaster.'

'How did you do it?' Danny asked as Lizzie looked on in silent horror.

'Never mind that now. Your breakfast is ready, so come to the table and get it, else you'll be late for school.'

Hearing the note of impatience in her voice, the twins silently did as they were told. Breakfast was a quiet affair and they were almost glad when they set off for school in their shiny Wellington boots. But somehow the snow-fall didn't seem quite so important now.

It was almost lunchtime when Maggie's back door opened and David appeared, clutching a rather bedraggled Christmas tree.

'It looks as if it's taken a bit of a bashin', I'm afraid, but there aren't that many to . . .' The words died on his lips when he saw her eye. 'Looks like you have, an' all. Just how the bloody hell did you get *that* – as if I need to ask.' He was lit up with anger like a beacon.

'David, I think you'd better sit down. We need to talk,' Maggie told him wearily.

Without a word, he sat down on the hard-backed chair at the kitchen table, but never once did his eyes leave her face.

'David . . .' She struggled to find the right words. 'It has to end.'

'What has to end?'

'You know exactly what. Look at this,' she stabbed a

finger towards her eye. 'Can you really blame Sam for feeling as he does, given the circumstances? He's as trapped in this marriage as I am.'

'Rubbish!' The word exploded from David's lips like a bullet from a gun before he even had time to think about it. 'He was always the same, right from when we were kids. Anything I had, he wanted – and that included you.'

'But you never really did have me, did you?' she said softly. 'What I mean is, we weren't engaged or anything. We hadn't even been going out together for all that long when I—'

'When my brother got you drunk and into bed and pregnant – is *that* what you're trying to say?' All the pent-up rage and resentment that he had locked inside for years spewed out of him now as she hung her head in shame.

'Maggie, admit it. He tricked you. We loved each other and you would never have gone to bed with him if you hadn't thought he was me.'

'It doesn't really matter now, does it?' Her voice was tired. 'I did get pregnant by him and he did the honourable thing by marrying me. The trouble is, he's never forgiven me for loving you, and while you're still on the scene we'll never be a proper family. The children are getting older now and it's not fair for them to see this all the time. He's eaten up with jealousy. So, if you *do* still love me, then you have to let me go. He deserves a chance. It's time you and I put the past behind us.'

Shock registered on his face as he stared back at her. 'Maggie, you know I would still have married you, even when you found out it wasn't me that you'd slept with. Why did you have to go and marry that bastard?'

'Because it wasn't right that you'd be bringing up his children,' she told him dully.

David could hardly believe what he was hearing, and yet somehow he knew that she meant every single word. This was the end. The end of all the years he had hoped she would leave Sam and come back to him.

'It doesn't have to be like this, you know.' He took her hands in his and gently shook them up and down. 'Just say the word and I'll take you and the children somewhere safe until this bloody war is over. Then when I come back we can start again.'

She smiled at him sadly through a haze of tears. 'If this were a fairy story then it might work. But this is real life. It's got to stop – now, David – and we both know it, deep down.'

His wonderful brown eyes filled with tears and he dropped her hands. 'Are you quite sure about this?'

She nodded. 'He deserves a chance.'

Collecting his hat, he walked towards the door and turned the handle feeling as if the bottom had dropped out of his world.

'David?'

He turned, locking the sight of her away in his memory.

'May God go with you and keep you safe.'

Slipping through the door, he closed it quietly behind him.

Chapter Four

As Ellen looked across at her daughter, her eyes were full of concern. Maggie looked awful, though now she came to think of it, none of them looked at their best. Christmas had been a sombre affair this year and so was New Year. Usually the New Year would get off to a fine start, with neighbours in and out of each other's houses, and wine and beer flowing like water. But this year no one seemed to have the heart for it, and the black-out restrictions hadn't helped.

But there was more to Maggie's haggard appearance than that, her mother was sure of it. She hadn't seemed herself since David had returned to his base. Perhaps it was a good thing that he had gone, Ellen Sharp thought privately. Sam seemed a lot more relaxed since his twin had left and she'd noticed that Maggie hadn't had a black eye or a split lip for a while.

Ellen had always been a great believer that everything happened for a reason, and she could only pray that things would work out for them. Sighing, she lifted the newspaper and the headlines leaped out at her:

Jan 1st London – Two million 19 to 27 year olds called up.

'Don't bear thinkin' about, does it?' she commented.

Maggie shook her head in reply. 'No, it doesn't. I just wonder how long it will be before the men in Coventry start getting their call-up papers?'

'Not long, the way things are goin'.' Ellen shuddered at the thought, grateful that her old man was too old.

Just then, the twins burst into the room like a breath of fresh air. They had been out playing in the snow and their dimpled cheeks were rosy. They were due back at school in a few days' time and intended to make the most of every second of their freedom.

'We just saw Mrs Massey an' she reckons as she's going to have a big surprise fer us later on,' Danny informed the two women excitedly. 'What do yer think it will be, Mam?'

Maggie winked at her mother. She knew exactly what the surprise was but had no intention of spoiling it for them.

'Happen you'll know soon enough,' she teased.

Danny pouted, and crossing to his grandma, who already had Lizzie on her lap and Lucy playing with her wooden bricks at her feet, he planted a wet kiss on her wrinkled cheek.

'Do you know what the surprise is, Gran?'

She laughed. 'I might. But as yer mam says, you'll know soon enough an' if we tell yer it won't be a surprise, will it?'

'Aww . . .' Peeling his wet coat off, Danny flung it across the back of a chair and held his hands out to the fire. Grown-ups could be no fun at all sometimes!

Turning her attention back to Maggie, Ellen asked, 'So what do yer think to the rationin' then?'

'From what I've heard we're going to be issued with ration books for butter, sugar, bacon and ham, though to be honest they've been in short supply for some time now. Half the boxes on the shelves in the corner shop are empty already.'

'Don't I know it,' Ellen muttered, disgruntled. 'Beats me how you manage to feed this brood. It ain't so bad for me wi' just the two of us to worry about. Don't get frettin' though. I dare say me an' yer dad will have a bit goin' spare so don't struggle. Just shout up if yer runnin' short of owt.'

'I will, Mam, thanks.'

Lifting Lizzie from her lap, Ellen rose from the table and stretched painfully. 'Ooh, I don't mind tellin' yer, this bloody snow don't do nothin' fer me arthritis. Still, complainin' ain't goin' to make any difference, is it? An' sittin' here won't get yer dad's dinner cooked either so I'd best be off.' Crossing to the door she began to pull on her fur-lined boots. They'd been a Christmas present from Maggie and she loved them. Then came the thick red coat that she had bought for a snip from the rummage sale not long ago. Finally she tied a warm woollen head square under her chin and began the ritual of kissing the children goodbye.

'Right now, you lot – be good fer yer mam. An' be sure to pop over an' tell me what Mrs Massey's surprise was later, eh?'

The twins nodded in unison as she let herself out into the bitterly cold yard, cursing loudly as a fall of snow slid off the sloping kitchen roof and landed on her head. They were still laughing as they heard her clomping off down the entry.

'Anyone would think me gran were goin' to the North Pole instead of just across the Lane, the way she dressed up,' Danny giggled.

'That's because she's old, an' old people have to keep warm. Miss Timpson at school told us that,' Lizzie said importantly. Miss Timpson was Lizzie's teacher, a pretty young woman with huge dark eyes and a mass of curly black hair, who wore lovely red lipstick. Lizzie adored her and believed every word she said.

Maggie now suggested, 'Why don't you two read your comics for a bit now and get warm while I put the dinner on?'

The twins nodded and soon were lost in the adventures of Desperate Dan and the Bash Street Kids.

Sam arrived home in a very black mood that night. 'This bloody war is goin' from bad to worse,' he grumbled as he took off his coat and hung it on a hook on the back of the kitchen door. 'Word has it that the *Union Castle* liner has been sunk off the south-east coast by a mine. They reckon a hundred and fifty-two men are missin', feared dead.'

Maggie shuddered as she strained the cabbage into a colander in the sink. How must they be feeling, the women they had left behind? Each of those poor men, some of them little more than boys, was someone's husband, brother, son, friend or lover. It hardly bore thinking about. Every day the newspapers were full of horror stories about the bombings in London and the lives that were being lost there too. But she didn't have long to dwell on the fact, for suddenly a tap came on the door and Mrs Massey, her face wreathed in smiles, popped her head into the room. Behind her were Carol and Tony.

Danny squealed with delight as he leaped off the chair and rushed across to his friend, whom he had missed dreadfully. '*Tony!* What you doin' back here?'

Mrs Massey answered for him. 'Couldn't see the point in keepin' 'em away from home any longer. Seems like London's the target fer the bombs, not us, thank the Lord.

So I thought, Ah, sod it. Let the poor little buggers come back where they belong. I ain't the only one thinkin' that way either. There's quite a few gradually creepin' back home. Happen we were a bit too hasty sendin' 'em away in the first place. Christmas made me mind up. It were like a bloody morgue round there wi'out these pair.' As she spoke she ruffled Tony's hair and he grinned up at her as Carol snuggled into her mother's side and smiled shyly at Lizzie.

The boys were already chattering away ten to the dozen, but seeing that Sam was looking irritable, and Maggie was in the middle of putting the dinner out, her neighbour didn't want to impose.

'Come on, you two. I suppose I'd better think about feedin' you an' all.' When Tony and Danny groaned she chuckled. 'Never mind, lads. Yer can get together tomorrow.'

'Yes, an' I'll show you our Anderson shelter,' Danny piped up. 'Mam's made it like a little house inside, wi' beds and chairs an' everythin'. We ain't had to sleep in it yet though.'

'God willin' yer never will,' Mrs Massey said, and herding the children back towards the door she disappeared the way they had come.

'So *that* were the surprise Grandma Sharp were on about, was it?' Danny's whole face was alight as Maggie nodded.

'Yes, it was. But never mind that for now. Get those comics and that sketching-pad off the table an' let's get the cloth on and the dinner out before it gets cold, eh? Lizzie, you fetch the cruet, and Danny, you put the knives and forks out. Sam, love, will you put Lucy's bib on an' get her into the highchair, please.'

'I saw Grandma Bright this afternoon when I were

out playin' earlier on,' Danny informed them as he shovelled a loaded forkful of herring roes into his mouth.

'Did you? It's a wonder she didn't call in for a cuppa then,' Maggie remarked.

'She didn't have time 'cos she'd had to queue at the shop, but she said she'd be round tomorrer. She's had a letter from Uncle David.'

Maggie's stomach did a somersault as she kept her eyes fixed on her food. Opposite, she could see her husband's eyes narrow as he swallowed a mouthful of bread. Funnily enough, she got on well with her mother-in-law, which was more than could be said for Sam. He and his mother had never seen eye-to-eye because Sam always insisted that David was her favourite.

'Grandma says that Uncle David was glad to get shipped out 'cos he was fed up o' square-bashin'. But she don't know where he's gone. He weren't allowed to tell her.'

'What's square-bashin'?' Lizzie asked innocently.

'It's when they make you march up an' down the—'

'Danny, could you *please* just eat your dinner!' Maggie's nerves were stretched to the limit but her sharp tone had the desired effect because Danny became silent and bent his head across his plate.

As January 1940 progressed, the people of Coventry became more and more concerned. Hitler continued to march through Europe leaving a trail of destruction and death in his wake. Leaflets popped through their doors telling them what to do in the event of being bombed, and an air of gloom settled across the city as the war they had all prayed would soon be over raged on.

Even so, more evacuees began to drift home and slowly the classrooms filled up again.

They were almost at the end of January when the storms struck. Torrential rain and gales swept across the country, and Maggie began to feel like a prisoner in her own home, for Lucy had come down with a terrible hacking cough and she didn't dare to venture out with her.

Mrs Massey and the rest of the neighbours made sure that she had everything she needed and Maggie wondered how she could ever thank them.

'There yer go, me gel,' Mrs Massey puffed as she placed the meagre rations on the table one bitterly cold Thursday morning. 'Though how far four ounces o' butter will go between five of yer to feed I dread to think.'

'Thanks, Mrs Massey. You will stay for a cup of tea, won't you?' Maggie offered gratefully.

'Well, are yer sure as yer can spare it?' the kindly neighbour asked uncertainly.

Maggie laughed aloud. 'I hardly think one cup of tea is going to make much difference, do you? It's the least I can do for you after how good you've been to me over the last couple of weeks. I dread to think what I would have done without you. Now come on, take that wet coat off and get over by the fire.'

Mrs Massey shrugged her plump arms out of her sodden coat, and hanging it over the wooden clotheshorse, she obediently crossed to the fire and held her hands out to the comforting blaze. They were still able to get coal, which was one blessing at least.

'So how's the little 'un doin'?' She glanced at Lucy who was fast asleep under a blanket on the settee.

'Not so good, to be honest.' Maggie carefully measured two spoons of tea into the heavy brown teapot. 'I had the doctor out to her the other night and he gave me some medicine, but it doesn't seem to have done much good up to now. If anything, I think she's worse.'

When Mrs Massey placed a hand on the child's brow, she frowned. 'Poor little mite is burnin' up!' she exclaimed, and much to Maggie's horror she promptly whipped the blanket off her and rolled up her sleeves.

'Get me some cool water in a bowl,' she ordered. 'We need to bring her temperature down. The way you've got her wrapped up, she'll be cooked in no time.'

Something about the tone of her neighbour's voice made Maggie hurry away to do as she was told. Soon Mrs Massey had the child undressed down to her Liberty bodice, and as Maggie looked on with a sinking feeling in the pit of her stomach, she began to sponge the child down. Lucy whimpered and tossed her head from side to side, but Mrs Massey spoke soothingly to her until she was satisfied that she was a little cooler.

The excited chatter died on the twins' lips when they entered the room some time later to see their baby sister lying limply across the settee. They saw at a glance that their mother had been crying and looked from her to Mrs Massey in dismay. As usual in times of uncertainty, Lizzie shrank into Danny's side, her eyes huge in her small face.

'What's up wi' our Lucy then?' Danny tried to control the tremor in his voice as best he could.

'She's poorly, love, but don't worry. Mrs Massey is tryin' to bring her temperature down and we've sent for the doctor. He should be here in a minute. Now come to the table and have some of this stew I have ready for you, then I want you to both go upstairs till the doctor's been.'

'But Mam, it's cold up . . .' The words died on Danny's lips as he saw the stark terror in his mother's eyes, and in that moment he knew that Lucy must be very poorly indeed.

'Come on, Lizzie.' Suddenly the little man of the house, he began to peel his sister's coat from her thin arms and usher her towards the table. 'Let's get us tea an' then we'll have a go at that jigsaw we had for Christmas, eh?'

Maggie's heart swelled with love as she looked at him, and once more the striking difference in the twins' nature was brought home to her. Danny was like a little rock, whilst Lizzie was timid and shy. Nevertheless she loved them both equally, and as for Lucy . . . As she stared down into the flushed little face a cold hand closed around her heart. How would she cope if anything happened to her? If anything happened to any of them, if it came to that? But Lucy was special. Had always been special, from the moment she had first held her in her arms. Once again, the urge to break down and cry was on her, and Maggie wished with all her heart that she could run away and hide from the mess that her life had become.

What seemed like a lifetime ago now, she had thought that her future would be with David. They had been courting, but then they had gone to a party at his mother's house one night and Maggie had got tiddly, which hadn't taken a lot, for she had never been much of a drinker. Sam, who had never made a secret of the fact that he fancied her too, had also been at the party, and as the night wore on he had plied her with drink. She had danced with both David and Sam, and as her mind grew more and more befuddled it had got harder and harder to tell them apart. One thing had led to another until eventually she had followed who she thought was David upstairs.

The next morning, she had been appalled when she woke up lying next to Sam, and even more appalled weeks later to discover that she was pregnant. Sam had almost broken his neck to tell David what had occurred and for a time, Maggie had felt as if she would die of shame. Especially when she found out that whilst she had been lying in bed with Sam, David had been out all night, scouring the streets for her. He and her parents had been frantic with worry. Her initial reaction was to have nothing more to do with Sam after the way he had tricked her, especially when David offered to marry her anyway. But then she had looked at Sam, and decided that he had a right to bring up his own child. It wasn't as if she and David had been engaged or anything, after all. And so they had married and all had been well – until she gave birth to the twins. It was after that that Sam had begun to change, for he couldn't cope with the fact that Maggie and David remained friends. His jealousy reared its head once more, and Maggie came to realise then that, although the two men were like a matching pair from the outside, they were totally different in nature. However, as her mother was soon to point out, she had made her bed and now she must lie on it. And lie on it she had done ever since, though not a day passed when she didn't regret her choice. Still, she told herself now as she looked down on her little daughter's flushed face, it was no good crying over spilled milk. What was done was done and the time for regrets was long past.

Lucy's fever finally broke during the night. By the following morning, although still deathly pale, she was more herself and Maggie offered up a silent prayer of thanks. As long as her children were well and all together she knew that she could cope with anything that life cared to throw at her.

Chapter Five

'Thought any more about getting the little 'uns away yet, have yer?' Ellen asked.

Maggie's face became as black as the thunderclouds that were crashing overhead. 'You know I won't do that, Mam. There's no point. Mrs Massey hasn't long since brought Carol and Tony back home, as you well know. We haven't been bombed an' I have no intention of sendin' my children away just for the sake of it.'

'All right, all right, keep yer hair on. I was only askin',' her mother retorted.

Hearing the tension between the two women, the twins glanced at each other nervously. Seemed like everyone was in a bad mood nowadays, though for some reason their mam and dad didn't seem to be arguing so much lately, so that was a good thing at least. Not that their dad was there for much of the time. Most nights he would come in from work and after tea he would get ready and clear off to the Three Shuttles in Howard Street. And they did still have their Saturday matinées at the Palladium to look forward to, though even that was tinged with wartime stories on the news-reels now.

Raising their eyes, they shrugged before bending their heads across the homework that their teacher had set them to do. Grown-ups were very hard to understand at times.

At last the weather began to improve as winter gave way to spring, and the people of Coventry felt their spirits begin to lift. Rationing was still a problem, but up to now the city had not been bombed and they were beginning to feel more optimistic.

'I heard on the wireless that Vivien Leigh has won an Academy Award for her role as Scarlett O'Hara in *Gone With the Wind*,' Mrs Massey informed Maggie as they pegged the wet clothes to the washing line they shared in the back yard.

Spitting a wooden clothes peg from her mouth, Maggie grinned. 'I can't say as I've ever been a big theatre-goer but I shall definitely be goin' to see that when it comes to the Rex in June.'

'Well, I'm pleased to hear it. They reckon that new cinema is the bees-knees. You don't go out enough fer a young woman, if yer was to ask me. An' yer know you only have to ask an' I'd babysit fer yer at the drop of a hat.'

Mrs Massey couldn't have said a better thing and Maggie beamed at her kindly neighbour. Lately she was feeling a little happier, and it showed. There was something else making her smile too, though she hadn't broached what was on her mind to Sam yet. She had noticed that more and more women were going back to work, most of them in munitions factories. The government had decided to give women equal pay to the men for the duration of the war, and Maggie was toying with the idea of applying for a job herself. That is, if she could find someone to care for Lucy and the twins when they got in from school. Now here was Mrs Massey offering to babysit any time. And of course, her mother would help out too, she was sure of it. The money she earned would make all the difference to the way they lived.

Both Danny and Lizzie were desperate for new shoes. Lizzie's school skirts were well above her knees and Danny's school trousers had been patched so many times that she was ashamed to put them on him now. But if she went back to work, that wouldn't be a problem any more. She was tempted to tell her idea to Mrs Massey there and then but decided against it until she had spoken to Sam. Unfortunately, Sam was old-fashioned and believed that a woman's place was at the kitchen sink. Well, fine, let him think that. This time she was determined to get her way for once – and *damn* what Sam said.

Hands on hips, she watched the wet sheets flapping in the breeze with a broad smile on her face. It was so nice to be able to dry the washing outside again, after all the months of having it hanging around from ceiling lines and over the clotheshorse in the kitchen.

'Penny fer yer thoughts, gel?'

Maggie jumped then giggled as she snatched up the large wicker washing-basket. 'I was just thinking what a lovely day it is,' she replied, then swinging about, she went merrily back into the kitchen leaving Mrs Massey to scratch her head in bewilderment.

That night, as Sam sat at the side of the empty fireplace reading his newspaper, Maggie plucked up her courage and asked, 'How would you feel about me going back out to work?'

Had she smacked him in the mouth he couldn't have looked more shocked as he stared at her, his mouth hanging slackly open.

'*You* . . . go back to work?'

Although Maggie's heart was fluttering like a caged canary she stood tall as she stared back at him. 'Yes, *me* go back to work. What's so strange about that? Dozens of women from hereabouts have already done it. They're crying out for women workers at most of the factories at present.'

'An' what were yer thinkin' o' doin' wi' the kids?' he sneered.

'I've already thought of that,' she retorted, her head held high. 'Me mam an' Mrs Massey will have them between them. I'll slip them both a bit out of me wages each week an' then they'll feel the benefit of me workin' an' all.'

'Forget it,' he snapped, as his eyes drifted back to the newspaper. It was obvious that he thought the conversation was over, but Maggie had other ideas.

'No, Sam, I won't forget it – not this time. This is something I really want to do. I read the newspapers too and it seems that things could get a lot worse before they start to get better. I want to do me bit just like dozens of other married women are doing.'

For the first time in their married life Sam was speechless as he gazed back at her. Not once had Maggie ever defied him in anything, but on this point she seemed determined.

'Carry on then if yer so set on it,' he mumbled. 'But you'll soon see which side yer bread is buttered on, you just mark me words. I'll give yer a week in a factory an' you'll be only too pleased to come back to bein' a full-time wife an' mother.'

Maggie struggled to hide a smirk of satisfaction as a wave of excitement snaked through her. She had no doubt at all that she would earn every penny she made, but on a brighter note she would also have a measure of freedom for the first time in years. Grinning from ear to ear, she slipped out into the lane of back-to-back terraced houses and hurried over to her mother's to tell her the good news before Sam had the chance to change his mind.

The very next day, once Maggie had got the twins off to school and settled Lucy with her grandma, she set off through Swanshill and headed towards the city in her search for a job. It was a bright morning in late March and the sky was blue with fluffy white clouds. It had been a while since she'd ventured far from home, and Maggie was shocked to see the shelters that had sprung up everywhere. On the old bowling green in Bird Street a trench shelter that could house up to 642 people had appeared. Another trench shelter that would hold a further 306 people had taken the place of the tennis courts in Swanswell Park. She had heard about them from various friends and neighbours, but somehow actually seeing them brought the war ever closer.

The sight made Maggie's blood run cold, and some of the pleasure was suddenly gone from the day as she headed towards the city centre.

On 9 April, word swept through the Courtaulds factory where Maggie was now working that Hitler had invaded Denmark and Norway. The women gazed fearfully at each other before bending their heads to their work. Maggie fleetingly wondered where David might be but then pushed him firmly from her mind. From now on, Sam and the children were the only ones that she would allow herself to worry about.

When she arrived home that evening she found the twins playing in the Anderson shelter with Carol and Tony from next door. They whooped with delight when the gate swung open and they saw her before flinging themselves into her arms.

'Grandma made us some faggots an' chips fer us tea, Mam,' Danny informed her as he rubbed his stomach. 'Cor, they weren't half nice, an' she's got some ready fer you an' Dad an' all. She's in the kitchen with our Lucy.'

'Well, I'd better go an' join her then so as she can get back across the road to Grandad Bill eh?' She stroked their hair affectionately before trudging towards the back door after casting a regretful glance at the shelter. This time last year, the little garden where it now stood had been full of daffodils in tight buds about to burst into glorious life. Primroses had peeped from beneath the hedges that separated the pocket-handkerchief gardens, but now the only colour was the dark brown earth that the men had shovelled across the shiny corrugated metal roof. Still, at least it had made a good playhouse for the children, she thought, and prayed that was all it would ever be.

Ellen looked up from the sink as she entered and flashed her a smile. 'So how's it gone today then, love?'

Gratefully kicking her shoes off, Maggie sank onto the chair at the side of the table. 'Fine, but me feet feel like they're gonna drop off. I'm not used to standing on a production line all day long yet.' As she spoke she unhooked the suspenders on her stockings and rolled them down her legs then wriggled her toes and sighed with relief. 'Ah, that's better.'

'I dare say yer wouldn't say no to a cup o' tea then?'

Maggie laughed. 'Mam, at this moment in time, I reckon I could drain the pot.'

Her mother began to strain the tea into a cup and as she took it from her, Maggie asked, 'How's Her Ladyship been today?'

Following Maggie's eyes to Lucy, who was curled up in a ball on the settee fast asleep, she smiled. 'Good as gold, though I'd be a liar to say she didn't miss you. When you first leave is the worst time. She screams fit to waken the dead for a solid half an' hour. But then she settles down, an' by the time the twins get home from school she's as right as rain.'

Maggie chewed on her lip as she stared at the child over the rim of her cup. There were certain things about being a working woman again that she thoroughly enjoyed. For a start off, Lizzie and Danny were now sporting a brand new pair of shoes each, not to mention new skirts and trousers. Working also meant that she didn't have to go cap in hand to Sam for every single penny, and for the first time since she'd been married she had made a friend. Eileen was the young woman who stood next to her at the conveyor belt at work. At twenty-six, with curly dark hair and eyes that were full of fun, Eileen was only two years younger than herself, yet seemed much younger in spirits. Probably because as yet she and her husband hadn't been blessed with children, though from what Maggie could make of it, it wasn't for the lack of trying. Sadly, Eileen's husband had now been called up, and every day at work started with excerpts from the last letter he had written to her, which Eileen carried around in the breast-pocket of her overall.

Yes, to all intents and purposes, going back to work had been a good thing – and yet . . . As Maggie stared at her tiny daughter she felt a pang of resentment. Sam had been surprisingly accepting of the situation once it came about. Probably because her working had barely affected his routine at all. Each night he came home to his meal on the table just as he always had. Added to that, he now had a little more money in his pocket for trips to the local pub. It was Maggie who stayed up every night when the children were tucked up in bed catching up with the washing and ironing and housework. Only last week Sam had returned from one of his jaunts to find her polishing the front doorstep with red polish in the dark.

'You must be mad, woman,' he had muttered before lurching off unsteadily down the entry. Maggie narrowed her eyes and sent evil thoughts boring into his back but he just carried on his way. Sam's indifference and the long work hours she could cope with. It was having to leave the children that troubled her, particularly Lucy, who was becoming somewhat of a grandma's girl.

Still, at the end of the day there was a war on and everyone was making sacrifices one way or another so she supposed she shouldn't complain. And it was nice not to have to be totally reliant on Sam. A little smile played around her lips at the thought. Never in all her married life had she ever stood up to him before and it felt good, almost as if she was taking control of her own life again.

Chapter Six

"'Oranges an' lemons, say the bells of Saint Clements!'"

The happy chant floated around Maggie as she stepped past the children who were playing in the late-afternoon sunshine in Howard Street. Some of them had chalked on the pavements and were so engrossed in their game of hopscotch that they barely noticed her passing.

Up ahead, Maggie noticed a young woman who had recently started at the factory and she quickened her footsteps to catch up with her.

'Nice to be out in the fresh air again, isn't it?' she chirped conversationally when she came abreast.

The young woman glared at her. Ignoring her sullen expression, Maggie tried again. 'Live round here, do you?'

'What's it gorer do wi' you?'

Taken aback, Maggie frowned. 'Sorry I'm sure. I was only tryin' to be friendly.'

'When I want a friend, I'll ask. Till then, mind yer own bloody business.' So saying, the young woman gripped her handbag and hurried away, leaving Maggie open-mouthed to stare after her. 'Well, really,' she muttered indignantly. Only that day during their afternoon break, Eileen had commented on the girl sitting all alone in the corner of the canteen and Maggie had assumed that she was shy. Now she was inclined to think that she was just downright ignorant, and yet . . . There was something about the stoop of the girl's shoulders that told a different story. She couldn't be more than twenty at most, and yet she looked as if she had the worries of the world on her shoulders. Deciding that it was none of her business, Maggie shrugged and moved on.

The following day, as she was fitting a hairnet over her blond hair before starting work, she told Eileen what had happened the previous evening.

'I'm telling you, she almost bit my head off and I was only trying to get her into conversation,' she said.

Eileen giggled above the noise of the machines that were whirring into life in the factory. 'Told yer she looked like a sullen-faced bugger, didn't I? Happen now you'll give her a wide berth.'

The words had barely left her mouth when the topic of their conversation walked in. As Eileen and Maggie looked towards her they were shocked to see that one of her eyes was black and blue. Oblivious to the fact that she was being watched, the girl began to push her fair hair under the obligatory hairnet.

'Yer know, she wouldn't be bad-lookin' if she smiled an' used a bit o' make-up,' Eileen remarked. 'An' I wonder who gave her that shiner. It's a beauty, ain't it?'

Still smarting from the night before, Maggie shrugged. 'I neither know nor care. I'm certainly not goin' to ask an' give her the chance to snap me head off again.'

At that moment, the factory bell sounded, summoning the women to their machines and soon they were hard at work and the girl, for now, was forgotten.

* * *

'Aw, Mam. You haven't cooked the dinner *again*?' Stooping to sweep Lucy into her arms, Maggie frowned at her mother. 'I'm more than grateful to you for havin' the little 'un an' the twins when they get in from school, without you cooking dinner an' all. I don't want you overdoing it an' knocking yourself up.'

'Huh! What yer tryin' to say? That I'm past it?' Her mother glared at her as Maggie grinned. 'It'll be a cold day in hell when I ain't up to throwin' a meal together. An' don't tell me it ain't nice to come home to find that dinner's nearly ready.'

'Well, of course it is. All I'm saying is, I don't want you to make yourself bad. You do far more than enough already.' They were now into May and the warmer weather had made Ellen's ankles balloon.

'Rubbish. Now get yer coat off an' come to the table while I get across home to see to yer dad's tea.'

Maggie gratefully sank down onto a chair with Lucy still clinging to her.

'I'll tell you what,' she said, as her mother tugged her pinny straight and headed for the open kitchen door. 'When I've got the kids all settled I'll pop down to the corner shop an' treat you an' Dad to a bottle o' stout each an' ten Woodbine. How would that be?'

Ellen Sharp grinned. 'Hark at the last o' the big spenders, eh? Must be nice to have a bit o' spare cash floatin' about.'

'It is nice not to have to count every single penny,' Maggie admitted. 'Though half me wages goes across the bar of the Crown or the Lord Aylesford if I'm daft enough to leave me purse lying about. Sam can get very touchy about me being a little more independent.'

'Yes, well, there's a few men feel like that when their women first go back out to work. They suddenly feel like they ain't the breadwinner any more an' it's a blow to their pride.' Pausing to plant a kiss on her daughter's cheek, Ellen hurried away to get her husband's tea.

Luckily, Sam decided to stay in that night, so as soon as the twins and Lucy were tucked into bed, Maggie snatched up her bag and headed for the door.

'I'm just nipping out to get a few bits for me mam an' dad from the corner shop,' she told him. 'Is there anything you'd like bringing back?'

Sam, who was listening to the wireless, glanced up. 'A couple o' bottles o' bitter wouldn't go amiss. Can't give yer the money though. I'm skint till payday.'

Maggie sighed. 'Just keep your ear out for the kids, would yer? I shan't be a jiffy.'

Slipping out into the May evening, she welcomed the cool breeze that met her. She'd just washed up all the dinner pots, done a load of washing and put it through the mangle before hanging it out on the line, then got all the children ready for bed, and the night wasn't over yet. When she got home she still had the twins' uniforms to iron ready for the next day and the kitchen to clean.

It would have been pointless to ask Sam for any help. He still firmly believed that housework was a woman's duty. Still, she reasoned, she had known how he felt before she took her job so she supposed she shouldn't complain, and he *had* stayed in tonight, which made a change, though she rightly guessed that it was more to do with lack of funds than a need for her company.

She reached the corner shop only to find the shutters down and the *Closed* sign in the window.

'What's going on here then?' she enquired of a neighbour who was hurrying past.

Greta Lewis, who was known to love a good gossip, paused and shook her head sadly. 'Ain't yer heard then?

They had a telegram boy arrive on his bike earlier today. Their lad's been killed in action in France. The poor buggers are heartbroken. Mind you, who wouldn't be? This bloody war is causin' some heartache, ain't it? He was their only son. I just wonder if the missus will ever get over it. She worshipped the ground that lad walked on, so she did.' Shaking her head, she walked away as tears welled in Maggie's eyes. She'd known Ben Drew since he was in short trousers and could hardly believe that he was dead. He had been so young, with all his life before him. Her thoughts moved on to David. Would *his* mother be getting a telegram next saying that something had happened to *him*? The thought was too terrible to contemplate and she pulled herself together with an effort.

Taking a deep breath, she glanced up and down the street. The nearest shop if this one was closed was some streets away in an area of Swanshill that most people tried to avoid. It was a notorious red-light district. But what choice did she have? She had promised her mother and father a treat, not to mention Sam. Quickly making her mind up, she hurried on. The way she saw it, the sooner she got there the sooner she would be back.

After a brisk ten-minute walk, the shop came into sight. Heavily made-up girls on street corners sneered at her as she hurried past, and she saw more than one talking to men before taking their arms and leading them away. She shuddered, thinking how awful it must be to have to sell your body to make a living. Keeping her head down, she slipped into the shop and in no time at all was back out on the pavement with the things she had come for tucked in a brown paper carrier bag with string handles that cut into her hands.

She quickly retraced her steps but had only walked

the length of two streets when a girl standing on the edge of a pavement made her pause. She frowned. There was something about her that was vaguely familiar, and yet for the life of her, Maggie couldn't think what it was. Slowing her step, she came abreast of the young woman and dared to glance at her. She gasped. This was the girl who had recently started at the factory – the one she had tried unsuccessfully to befriend. The girl, unfortunately, caught sight of Maggie at the same time and colour flooded into her heavily rouged cheeks.

'So what *you* starin' at then, Miss Prim an' Proper!'

Maggie gulped deep in her throat as she took in the bright red lips and the short skirt.

'I er . . . Sorry, I didn't mean to stare,' she said hastily. 'I just didn't expect to see you round here, that's all.'

'Why, what's wrong wi' round here? Not good enough fer the likes o' your sort, ain't it?'

Maggie was momentarily lost for words. A large dark-haired man who was obviously the worse for wear, was lurching towards them and suddenly the girl was all smiles as she turned to face him.

'Lookin' fer a good time, are yer, love?' When he nodded, she quickly took his arm, before turning to glare at Maggie across her slim shoulder. 'Why don't you just piss off back to where yer came from, eh? Go on. Get back to yer cosy little hubby an' yer cosy little two-up, two-down.'

Now it was Maggie's turn to blush. She watched the odd couple stagger away, the girl almost collapsing beneath the weight of the man as she steered him along until they disappeared around the street corner. Why on earth would the girl be selling herself when she had a full-time job in the factory? It made no sense at all, but then Maggie thought back to the night the girl had snapped at her when she tried to walk with her. Whatever her reasons, she obviously didn't want Maggie to get involved so from now on she would avoid her. After all, she had enough problems of her own.

Get back to yer cosy little hubby . . . As the girl's words came back to her, Maggie nearly laughed out loud. Oh yes, she had enough problems of her own, all right. If only Miss Powder an' Paint could have known.

The following morning at work, as Eileen and Maggie chatted in the canteen during their break, the girl appeared and sank down at a nearby table. As usual she kept herself to herself, but her eyes when they caught Maggie's seemed to be sending an unspoken message.

For some reason, Maggie had chosen not to mention the incident to Eileen and now she was glad that she hadn't. After draining her mug she rose and said, 'I'm just off to the lav. I'll see yer back inside, eh?'

Inhaling deeply on her Park Drive, Eileen nodded as she glanced at the large wall clock. 'Don't be long, else you'll have old May breathin' fire down yer neck.' May was the supervisor and known to be a bit of a tyrant.

Some minutes later, as Maggie stood washing her hands at the sink in front of the long row of toilets, the door opened and the girl walked inside.

Maggie had no intention of getting her head bitten off yet again, but as she made to slip past her, the girl nervously caught at the sleeve of her overall.

''Ere, about last night – I were wonderin', could yer keep it to yerself? Seein' me on the streets, I mean? I've no need to tell yer that some o' the women who work here are hard-nuts an' they'll make me life a misery if they get to know I'm on the game.'

Maggie stared into the girl's haunted face. It was hard

to believe that this was the same woman she had caught standing on a street corner. She looked so unhappy. The bruise on her eye had now turned a deep purple colour and without her heavy make-up she looked very young.

'I'll not say a word to anyone,' Maggie murmured, and saw the girl's look of relief. 'It's no business of mine what you get up to.'

She was almost through the door when the girl muttered, 'Thanks, missus.' At a loss as to what to make of it all, Maggie picked her way back through the other women to her machine.

When she arrived home that evening, she found Sam's mother sitting at the side of the empty fire-grate.

'I sent yer mam across the road to see to yer dad's dinner,' Beryl Bright informed Maggie, flashing her a smile.

Maggie returned the smile before peeping out of the kitchen window to check on the children, who were all three happily playing in the Anderson shelter.

'I thought yer might like to know that I had a letter from our David this mornin'.'

Maggie's heart began to pound but she kept her face straight as she asked, 'Oh yes, and how is he?'

'Not so good, to be honest, but at least he's safe up to now. He's in Norway, an' the things he's seein' are breakin' his heart. You know what a big softie he is.' Beryl fiddled with the fringe of the tablecloth. 'Apparently, things ain't good out there. His friend died in his arms a while back. Seems our lads weren't properly equipped for such Arctic conditions. Let's just hope this government that Churchill is puttin' together will help 'em, eh? I tell yer, them bloody Jerries have somethin' to answer for. Though I suppose we should be grateful they're leavin' us alone. If it weren't fer the rationin', the black-outs an' the menfolk bein' called up left right an' centre, there might not be a war on fer us.'

'Let's just hope it stays that way.' Maggie thought of what David must be going through. He was such a gentle man, and she could imagine how badly seeing people die in front of his very eyes must be affecting him.

Her mother-in-law reached across to squeeze her hand as she lumbered to her feet. 'Right, well, I'd best get meself home now yer back. I just thought you'd like to hear he's safe.'

'Thank you, that was very kind of you. But aren't you going to wait and see Sam? He'll be home from work in a minute.'

Her mother-in-law shook her head. 'No, there'd be no point. You know me an' our Sam allus rub each other up the wrong way. How's he treatin' you nowadays?'

Maggie felt herself flush, and crossing to the sink she rolled up her sleeves and began to peel some potatoes. 'Oh, I can't complain.'

'Mmm. Still spendin' half his time in the pub, is he?' Seeing Maggie's embarrassment the older woman's voice softened. 'I know I shouldn't say this, Maggie, 'cos they're both me lads, but life dealt you a bad card when it tied you up to our Sam. Sometimes I can hardly believe that they're both mine 'cos they're as different as chalk from cheese. You an' our David were so right together. If only . . .'

'Mam, I know yer mean well, but don't you think it's a bit late for If Onlys now, all these years on?'

The woman's chin sank to her chest. 'Sorry, love. I've no wish to rake up old memories. It's just that . . .'

'I know.' Drying her hands, Maggie wrapped the woman in a warm embrace. 'Now get yourself home. Thanks for everything you've done.'

When the door had closed behind her visitor and Maggie was alone for a few minutes, she sank onto a chair and buried her face in her hands. *David was safe.* She'd tried so hard over the last weeks to push thoughts of him from her mind, but now she could no longer deny how much she had missed him. As the tears that she had held back flowed freely, she offered up a silent prayer of thanks.

Chapter Seven

At the beginning of June, Sam sat in the kitchen with Maggie's father, drinking beer and listening to Radio Luxembourg report that Operation Dynamo, the great evacuation of Dunkirk, was complete. Maggie hovered nervously in the background as the horrors that the British troops had been forced to endure were described. Crowds on the south-shore coasts were waving Union Jacks and shouting encouragement as the defeated troops returned aboard the huge fleets of destroyers, fishing boats, ferries and any other sea-going vessel that could carry them. All day long they had listened to shocking stories of the decaying corpses that littered the beaches of Dunkirk, and Maggie guessed that for every man who had escaped total annihilation, another poor soul had been left dead or dying. It hardly bore thinking about and her heart was heavy as she thought of all the families who would be grieving that night.

'Things certainly ain't lookin' good now.' Bill Sharp took a swig of bitter from his glass.

'Do yer reckon they'll start the call-ups again?' This from Sam.

'Wouldn't surprise me one little bit,' Maggie's father replied stoically. 'Some o' them lads won't be fit to go back after what they've bin through, an' it stands to reason they'll have to be replaced. This war is a long way from over yet, the way I see it.'

Maggie saw Sam go even paler. For all his bullying ways, she knew her husband was a coward at heart and dreaded the thought of going to war.

A silence, save for the sound of the broadcaster's voice, settled on the room as they all thought of what might happen in the not too distant future.

The following day dawned bright and sunny, but the atmosphere at the Courtaulds factory where Maggie worked was heavy. Machines stood empty and the women rightly guessed that some of their workmates were at home mourning the deaths of loved ones who hadn't returned from Dunkirk. Eileen had not turned into work either that day, and Maggie kept glancing at her friend's empty machine. What if her friend's husband had been hurt or lost? How could she find out? Somewhere tucked deep in her bag she had Eileen's address, and she decided that during her lunch-break she would pop round and see her. Eileen was a good worker and timekeeper. In fact, now that Maggie came to think about it, she couldn't recall her losing a single day since she had started at the factory, so there *must* be something very wrong.

With her mind made up, she lowered her head to her work and wished away the hours until lunchtime.

Two hours later found her hurrying down the road where Eileen lived. Number 22 Cox Street, this was it. After wiping her sweaty hand down her skirt, she knocked, but there was no answer. She knocked again, louder this time. After the third knock she began to think that no one was in. She was just about to turn and leave when she heard the sound of a door opening and someone shuffling along the hallway. When the door was opened she had to stop herself from gasping. It was Eileen, but not as Maggie had ever seen her before. Her eyes, usually so bright and sparkling, were dull and red-rimmed and she stared at Maggie as if she hardly knew her.

'Eileen, love, are you all right?' But Maggie found herself talking to thin air as Eileen turned and went back the way she had come, leaving the door wide open. Maggie stepped inside and closed the door behind her before following Eileen down the passageway and into a room at the back of the house. It was a bright sunny room that was surprisingly well furnished and decorated. A huge patterned rug covered most of the floor, and round the edges of that, the linoleum shone with polish. In the centre of the rug stood a heavy oak table and matching chairs, and pretty flowered curtains billowed softly in the breeze that blew in from the open window.

'I was worried about you,' Maggie said quietly. 'It's not like you to miss work.'

Eileen turned to her and silently handed her a telegram. As Maggie's eyes flew down the page she felt her knees go weak.

'Oh, Eileen, I don't quite know what to say.' Her eyes filled with tears as she looked into her friend's bereft face.

'Ain't much yer can say. It came just after I got in from work last night. My Graham's dead an' ain't nothin' gonner bring him back, is there?' Eileen's voice was as empty as her eyes.

'Look, you sit down an' I'll make us both a nice hot cup of tea, eh?' Maggie felt the need to do something, and for now that was all she could think of.

'Huh! Tea, yer say. I reckon I could drown in the bloody stuff I've drunk so much through the night, but go on – we may as well have another.'

Maggie stumbled into a small kitchen that was as neat and tidy as the room she had just left, and blindly filled the kettle at the sink. She found a box of Swan Vestas and struck a match then lit the gas ring and put the kettle on to boil. While she was waiting she rummaged around in the cupboards and found two pretty cups and saucers and a matching china teapot. They were so delicate compared to the heavy brown earthenware pot and mugs she used at home that they made her smile.

'You have a beautiful home, Eileen,' she called through the open door. When there was no reply she went back into the room to find the young woman standing exactly where she had left her. 'I said you—'

'I heard what you said,' Eileen snapped. 'But what is it, eh? It's nothin' more than bricks an' mortar an' fancy trinkets.' She spread her hands to encompass the room. 'This place was Graham's pride an' joy. He were forever turnin' his hand to some project or another. Wanted it right fer when the kids come along, he said. But they won't be comin' along now, will they?'

As Eileen's face crumpled, Maggie rushed to her side and wrapped her in her arms. Over Eileen's shoulder, a photo of a handsome young man in Army uniform seemed to mock her. It had pride of place on the mantelshelf. And this, she rightly guessed, was Graham. Her heart went out to her friend. She wished with all her being that she could think of something to say that would ease Eileen's pain, but words just seemed so inadequate.

Leading her to a chair she gently pressed her into it before rushing away to make the tea. Ignoring the rationing for once, she put three spoonsful of sugar into Eileen's cup. She'd heard that hot sweet tea was good for shock. Once she had pressed the cup into her friend's hands she sat down beside her.

'At least you still have your home,' she said softly.

'An' what good is this place to me now?' Eileen's eyes travelled the room. 'It don't mean nothin' without Graham here to share it with me. I think I might go back to live with me mum.'

'But your mum lives in Leicester, doesn't she?'

'Yes, she does.'

'I'll miss you, but I think I can understand how you feel.'

'Oh no, you can't! You've still got your family at home waitin' for you. I've got no one now. Graham was me whole life. I can't stay here without him. This place is too full o' memories.'

Maggie swallowed the painful lump that had formed in her throat. She would miss Eileen more than she could say, yet she understood her need to get away.

'Is there anything I can do for you before I go back to work?' she asked helplessly, and suddenly Eileen was crying again and clinging to her as if she was afraid to let her go.

'Look, I'll stay here with you for a couple of hours, eh?' Maggie offered. 'Has anyone let your mam know what's happened?'

'Yes,' Eileen sniffed between sobs. 'One o' the neighbours managed to get through to me dad at work late yesterday afternoon. Him an' me mam should be here any time now to fetch me.'

'Fine, then I'll wait with you until they come.' Maggie stroked her hair as Eileen leaned her head on her shoulder and there they sat until someone knocked on the door almost an hour later.

Once Eileen's parents were with her, Maggie shot off

up the stairs and hastily began to pack a suitcase with every item of Eileen's clothing that she could lay her hands on. The couple were kindly; they obviously loved their daughter very much and Maggie was relieved to know that she wouldn't be alone. Later, as her father loaded her bulging suitcase into the back of his shiny green Morris, Eileen clung to Maggie. 'Thanks fer stayin' wi me,' she said hoarsely. 'I hope yer don't get into trouble at work fer not goin' back in this afternoon.'

Maggie flapped her hands dismissively. 'Huh! Don't worry about that,' she urged, and then as Eileen slid into the back seat at the side of her mother, she asked, 'You will keep in touch, won't you? And take care?'

'Of course I will.'

'We'll look out for her, love. Never you fear,' Eileen's mother said, and then the car was pulling away from the kerb and Maggie waved until it turned a bend in the road and disappeared.

Standing on the pavement, she felt a great sadness settle around her like a cloak. One short telegram and her friend's life had changed forever. Suddenly, the need to be with her own family was urgent, and taking the opposite direction from the factory, she hurried away and headed for home.

She was greeted by two miserable little faces the minute she set foot through the door. Lizzie and Danny were sitting side-by-side on the settee staring off into space and she saw instantly that Lizzie had been crying.

'So what's up with you two then?' Maggie asked, trying to keep her voice light.

'Lizzie's sad 'cos she found out at school that her friend's dad got killed,' Danny informed her solemnly.

'Oh dear, I'm sorry to hear that.'

'Yes, an' now Molly will be goin' to live with her

nanny and grandad on a farm in the country, an' I won't get to see her again.' As fresh tears erupted from Lizzie's eyes, Maggie felt at a loss as to how to comfort her. It had been such a sad day.

'I don't like this war, Mam,' Danny declared. 'When will it be over?'

Pain sliced through Maggie as she answered truthfully, 'I don't know, my love.'

Major May, as she was known amongst the women, was waiting for Maggie when she arrived at work the next morning.

Arms folded across her bosom, she demanded, 'An' just where did *you* get to yesterday afternoon then, madam? I can't keep this production line goin' if you lot decide to clear off just whenever the whim takes yer, yer know.'

The young girl whom Maggie had once seen on the street corner glanced at Maggie fearfully as if it was she herself who was the victim of May's wrath. Maggie felt her colour rise as anger flooded through her veins.

'If you *must* know, Eileen's husband has been killed in action and I went to see if she was all right. Is that a good enough reason to be absent without your leave?'

May looked slightly flustered. 'Oh, I er . . . Well, obviously I could have no way o' knowin' that, could I? When will she be comin' back to work?'

'She won't.' Maggie felt a measure of satisfaction as the woman's eyes popped wider. 'Eileen's parents have taken her back to Leicester to live with them. I'll let you have their address, as I'm sure you'll want to forward any wages she has owing, won't you? And now if you'll excuse me I'd better get back to work. I don't want to upset your production line any more than I already have, do I?' And she swept past May like a battleship in full sail.

'And what are *you* standin' there gawpin' at wi' yer gob hangin' open like a goldfish's? Get back to yer machine *now* else I'll be dockin' yer pay!' May roared.

The girl scuttled past May like a frightened rabbit as the supervisor stood there with a face like a thundercloud. How dare Maggie Bright talk to her like that? And in front of half the workforce too! Huh! Well, she might have won this round but she'd just better watch out from now on. May puffed herself up to her full height and strode away to show the rest of the girls what-for. Just let one of them put a foot wrong today, and sure as eggs were eggs, she'd have them out on the pavement on their backside!

It was some time later, as Maggie sat at her machine, that the events of the last couple of days caught up with her. She blinked, trying hard to hold back the tears, but the lump in her throat was swelling and threatening to choke her, and she knew that she must get away. Almost overbalancing her chair, she got up and headed for the cloakroom with her head bent low. Once inside, she leaned heavily against the sink, and then came the tears. Hot, scalding tears that poured down her face in a torrent. She was so distressed that she didn't hear the door open behind her, and when someone put their hand on her arm she almost jumped out of her skin.

'Are yer all right then? Is there anythin' I can get yer?'

Maggie found herself looking into the face of the girl. For now, the hard front she put on was gone and her eyes were kindly and full of concern.

Maggie tried to speak but couldn't.

'I er . . . I was sorry to hear about yer mate's husband, but the way yer stood up to that tyrant an' put her in her place earlier on were brilliant. I doubt anyone has ever dared to talk to Major May like that before.'

Maggie sniffed, and despite the circumstances, found herself giving a shuddering laugh. 'I can't believe I did it now,' she hiccuped. 'I'm not usually like that. My mam always said I wouldn't say boo to a goose.'

'Well, maybe yer should try it more often. People like her will walk all over yer if yer let 'em. An' by the way, thanks fer keepin' yer mouth shut about seein' me out that night. Them lot back there,' she thumbed across her shoulder, 'would make me life a misery if they was to find out. They can be a vicious lot o' cows when they've a mind to be.' She looked at Maggie. 'My name's Josephine Matthews, by the way, but yer can call me Jo if yer like.'

When the girl tentatively held out her hand, Maggie shook it warmly.

'Thanks for coming to check on me, Jo. Perhaps we could sit together at break in the canteen? I'll be on my own now that Eileen's gone.'

Jo seemed to consider the request for a few seconds before cautiously nodding. 'Go on, then. I dare say there's no harm in that, though I don't make friends easy, as you'll discover. I prefer to keep meself to meself. That way, nobody gets to know me business.'

Maggie mopped her sore eyes. She was all cried out. The girl in front of her was almost like two different people, she thought – the Plain Jane who worked in the factory every day, and the Painted Lady who walked the streets at night. Despite herself, Maggie was intrigued.

'Right, we'd better be getting back to our machines then,' she sighed. 'I wouldn't want May breathing fire down your neck on my account.'

Jo turned without a word and left Maggie standing

there. At the door she paused to look back across her shoulder. 'I meant what I said. Me business is me own, so if we sit together in the break I don't want yer pryin' into me affairs.'

'I wouldn't dream of it.' When the door had closed behind the girl, Maggie couldn't help but grin. Perhaps Jo wasn't such a tough-nut as she liked to make out?

On the way home that night, Maggie revelled at the feel of the fresh air on her skin after the oppressive atmosphere of the factory. She would have liked to see some greenery but sadly, almost every park she passed had been ploughed up to make bomb shelters, should they ever be needed. She supposed that she was one of the lucky ones to have an Anderson shelter in her own back yard. Many people who had no room for one in their garden had resorted to making their dingy cellars into shelters. Others had cleared out their cupboard under the stairs, though how a whole family would ever fit into one of them, Maggie had no idea.

At home, the twins and Lucy were tucking into jam sandwiches. Somehow Lucy had managed to get herself covered in it, but Maggie swept the toddler into her arms and kissed her nevertheless.

'Phew, it's been hot in the factory today,' she told her mother as she bustled about the kitchen getting herself a welcome glass of lemonade.

'I can well believe it. It's been a scorcher, ain't it? Though I suppose we shouldn't complain. This pair were right hot an' bothered when they come in from school. Oh, an' while I think of it, Sam was here at lunchtime.'

Maggie raised an eyebrow. 'Sam? Are you sure?'

Her mother laughed. 'Well, I reckon you've been married to the bugger long enough for me to recognise him by now, don't you? Yes, it was Sam, an' I should warn you – he weren't in the best o' moods.'

Maggie frowned. What would Sam be doing home at that time of day? 'Do you know if he went back to work?' she enquired.

'Can't rightly say, to be honest, though I doubt it. He got changed out of his work clothes an' stamped off out with a face like a smacked arse. He was in an' out of here like a dose o' salts. Didn't even acknowledge the little 'un either.' Her mother sniffed indignantly.

The words had barely left her lips when they heard the back gate open and Sam appeared, looking more than a little sheepish.

'All right, love? Had a good day, have yer?' he asked, addressing Maggie. Her mouth dropped open. Now she *knew* that something was wrong.

Ellen hastily shuffled towards the back door. She could feel a row brewing and had no intention of being caught in the middle of it. Maggie had changed in some ways since she'd started back to work. And from where Ellen was standing, the changes were for the better. Gone were the days when Sam could treat her daughter like something he'd trodden in. Maggie would stick up for herself now instead of taking everything he threw at her.

Maggie waited until her mother had beat a hasty retreat before saying to the children, 'Have you had enough to eat for now?'

'Yes, Mam.' Lizzie's and Danny's eyes were like saucers as they sensed the tension in the air.

'Good, then take Lucy to play for half an hour until it's time to come in and get ready for bed. Tony and Carol are out the front playing marbles on the pavement, but watch Lucy on the road, won't you?'

'Yes, Mam.' Lizzie and Danny ushered their little sister

in front of them and soon Maggie heard their footsteps in the entry. When she was sure that the children were out of earshot, she rounded on Sam. 'So – what's going on then? Why were you home at dinnertime? And why are you all done up in your decent clothes?'

'Ah well, it's like this, yer see.' Sam stretched his neck and undid his shirt collar. 'I've er . . . I've gone an' got the sack.'

'You've *what*?' Maggie's voice was incredulous.

'Weren't my fault,' he mumbled, avoiding her eyes, 'That bloody foreman has had it in fer me fer ages, an' he shot his mouth off once too often so I . . .'

'You what?'

'I landed him one straight on the chin. He went down like a sack o' spuds, an' the next minute they've got me in the office an' are givin' me me marchin' orders.'

'Oh Sam, how could you?' Maggie sank onto a chair. 'The whole point of me going back to work was to bring in a bit extra, and now you've gone and put yourself out of a job.'

'There are others.' His face was surly.

'And how do you figure that out? Who's going to take you on without a reference?'

'Well, it's hardly the end o' the world, is it? We've still got your wages comin' in. It just means we'll have to tighten us belts again fer a bit till somethin' crops up.'

'Huh, *if* something crops up, you mean! How *could* you have been so stupid as to put yourself out of work?'

'Watch yer mouth, woman,' he snarled. 'You're gettin' a bit too big fer yer boots since yer went back to work.'

'And not before time, Sam Bright,' Maggie retaliated. 'I've done with being the obedient little woman. It'll serve you right if you get called-up, now you're unemployed.

78

That's what happened to Fred Smith in the next street when *he* put himself out of work.'

Sam nearly choked. 'They wouldn't do that, would they?'

Maggie's head bobbed vigorously. 'It wouldn't surprise me in the least. We'll just have to wait and see, won't we? Meantime *you* can see to the kids while I go to work an' give me mam some time off. And don't go thinkin' that I'm goin' to be handin' any of my wages to you to pass across the bar o' the pub.'

'Me – look after the kids?' The look of pure horror on his face would have been comical had she not been so angry, but as it was she turned and slammed away upstairs, leaving him with his mouth hanging open in amazement.

Once in the privacy of their room the anger fled as she sank down onto the edge of the bed. Why had this to happen now? Just when she'd thought things were looking up. For the first time in her married life she had been able to provide the children with decent clothes and a few treats, but now she would be back to scrimping and saving again. And all because Sam hadn't been able to control that temper of his.

Burying her face in her hands, she wept with frustration.

Chapter Eight

'Come on, Danny, shake a leg. We're all going to be late at this rate,' Maggie shouted up the stairs as she tied a pretty blue ribbon into the bottom of Lizzie's plait.

Seconds later, they heard the thud of his footsteps on the stairs and he erupted into the kitchen. Maggie couldn't help but smile as she looked at her son. He might have been pulled through a hedge backwards, for his hair was on end, the flies of his grey shorts were wrongly buttoned, and one of his thick grey socks had already slipped around his ankle.

'Just look at the state of you.' She grinned indulgently as she brandished the hairbrush and yanked him towards her. 'You look like nobody owns you and you haven't even stepped out of the door yet. Come on, let's see if we can't tidy you up a bit.'

'Aw, *Mam*.' Danny frowned as she started to tug the brush through his thick mop of hair, much to Lizzie's amusement. She liked to be neat and tidy, whereas her brother didn't much care what he looked like. Maggie guessed most boys of his age were much the same.

'There, that's better,' she said seconds later when she'd wiped a wet flannel round his face and tamed his springy hair. 'You look almost human now.'

Lifting a small parcel from the table, Lizzie reminded

her, 'We'll be late home tonight, Mam. It's the twenty-first and we're going straight to Sally's party from school.'

'Oh yes, of course you are,' Maggie replied absently as she quickly rubbed some Ponds cold cream onto her face. She patted on some powder and ran her lipstick over her mouth. 'It's a good job you reminded me. I've got a head like a sieve lately. I'd completely forgotten.' Snatching up her handbag and ushering the twins towards the door, she addressed Sam who was sitting with a long face at the table with Lucy. 'Don't worry about getting any dinner on the go this evening. The twins will eat at the party and I'll rustle us something up when I get in.'

'I wasn't plannin' to,' he told her sullenly. 'I've asked yer mam to have the little 'un this afternoon while I go out job-hunting.'

Maggie sighed. She knew that the sudden need to get another job was nothing at all to do with the fact that Sam wanted to be the breadwinner again. He was just fed up with having no money to pass across the bar of the local pub.

'So what time are you likely to be back then?'

'Christ, woman,' he grunted. 'You'll have me on a bloody stopwatch next. How long is a piece o' string? I'll keep lookin' till I find sommat. I could do wi' some cash fer the tram fares though.'

Maggie extracted her purse from her bag and counted a few shillings out onto the table. 'Will that be enough?'

'Huh! It'll have to be, won't it? Yer tighter wi' money than a duck's arse,' he complained.

Planting a hasty kiss on Lucy's shining hair, Maggie ignored his unpleasant remark and hurried towards the door, snatching the twins' satchels up on the way. 'Right then – we're off. I'll see you later, eh?'

At the end of the road, she parted from the twins and

hastened on towards Courtaulds. The heat had been unbearable for the last few weeks and although it was only eight-thirty in the morning, it was already becoming oppressive.

Jo was waiting at the factory gate for her as she'd taken to doing of late, and Maggie waved to her as she approached.

'Looks like it's going to be a scorcher today,' she greeted Jo as they went into the cloakroom. She was horrified to see that the girl's lip was split and a bruise showed across her eye.

As Jo fastened a hairnet across her fair curls she felt Maggie's eyes on her. 'I can see what yer thinkin' but ask no questions an' I'll tell yer no lies,' she muttered.

Maggie's kindly heart went out to her. 'Oh Jo, *why* do you do it? Was it one of your er . . . clients who hurt you like this? Surely you earn enough here without having to go out onto the streets, putting yourself at risk?'

'You know *nothin*', so why don't yer just mind yer own business, eh?'

'Because I care about you, that's why. Who did this to you? They should be bloody locked up an' someone should throw the key away.'

Maggie would have said more, but just then Gladys Harper swept past. Gladys, who worked just down the line from them, was a great Amazon of a woman. She had a big mouth to match her massive frame and loved nothing more than a good gossip, but it was well-known that she also had a kindly nature. She had even taken to bringing food in for the cats who kept the rats down in the factory.

'How's yer mam this week then, love?' she addressed Jo. 'Florrie were sayin' she's took a turn fer the worse again. Not that I'm surprised, mind. Married to that bullyin' bastard of a father o' yourn would be enough to get any woman down. I honestly don't know why either of yer stick it. Why don't yer just put him out on the pavement on his arse where he belongs, or better yet, pack up, piss off an' leave the swine to it.'

'It ain't quite as simple as that, with all the little 'uns to see to, Gladys,' Jo mumbled.

At that moment the factory hooter sounded and the women hastily put out their cigarettes and began to troop towards the clocking-in machines. Maggie's mind was working overtime as she kept a curious eye on Jo. From what she had gathered, it appeared that Jo had an invalid mother and a bullying father, plus numerous siblings. Could that be the reason why she walked the streets at night, to help keep the house going? Maggie was more than aware that it was absolutely none of her business, but she determined to find out all the same. Jo was little more than a girl, and the thought of her having to sell her body made Maggie shudder.

Glancing across at her yet again, Maggie realised that Jo could have actually been quite pretty if she did something with herself. She was slender to the point of being thin, boyish almost, but her hair was naturally blond and curly and her eyes, when they weren't shut with bruises, were a lovely sapphire blue. Maggie decided to do some detective work and try to find out a little more about her. From where Maggie was standing, Jo appeared to be a girl who was in need of a friend – whether she wanted one or not!

When Jo disappeared off into the toilets at break-time, Maggie made a beeline for Gladys, who was standing outside drawing deeply on a Woodbine. 'Gladys . . .' She faltered suddenly, wondering if this had been such a good idea after all. Then she went on: 'I know I'm going to sound like a right old nosy-parker, but I'm worried about young Jo. She's got a shiner on her again. Do you have any idea how she might have gotten it?'

'Well, that wouldn't take three guesses.' Gladys hitched her sagging bosoms up and shook her head sadly. 'A dog shouldn't have to live as her an' her brothers an' sisters do. That father o' theirs is a right old bastard to the lot of 'em. Rules 'em wi' a rod of iron, he does. The mother is bedridden, an' fer as long as I can remember, that poor little sod, bein' the eldest, has had to carry the burden o' the whole family. Yer never see any of 'em playin' out in the street wi' the other kids. The poor little sods almost shit themselves if yer so much as look at 'em. Makes yer wonder what the world's comin' to, don't it? Anyway, I'd best get back in else I won't have time fer a cuppa before we have to start again.' Grinding her cigarette out with the heel of her foot, she asked, 'Are you comin' too, love?'

'What? Oh yes, yes, I am.' Maggie followed the woman back inside with a heavy heart. It sounded as if Jo had had a terrible life. But it still didn't explain why she'd decided to become a street girl. There and then, Maggie vowed that she was going to find a way to help her, whether Jo wanted her to or not. First of all though, she would have to find out how.

'So what's up with you this mornin', then? Did yer get out of the wrong side of bed or sommat?'

Maggie ignored Sam as she hastily wrapped the children's packed lunches in greaseproof paper, and pushed them into their satchels. She could hardly bring herself to look at him, let alone speak to him, the way she felt this morning.

Picking up on her mood, the twins kept quiet as she

tugged a brush through their hair, one after the other. Normally their mam was perky in the mornings but it certainly couldn't be said of her today.

'Me mam will be over later this morning to look after Lucy. I suggest you get yourself off out job-hunting again then,' she told Sam brusquely as she ushered the twins towards the door.

'Well, what else would I be doin' wi' nothin' in me pockets?' he retaliated, but when she had disappeared through the door he scratched his head in bewilderment. Something had upset her – that was for sure.

'Is everythin' OK, Mam?' Danny gazed up at her as she marched the twins along the street.

Forcing a smile to her face, Maggie gave him a quick hug. 'Of course it is, sweetheart. I'm just a bit tired, that's all. Nothing for you to worry about though. Now off you go, the pair of you, and have a good day. I'll see you both this evening, eh? And be good for your grandma when you get in from school, won't you?'

'Yes, Mam.' The twins watched her stamp away, then shrugged simultaneously.

'Grown-ups can be hard to understand at times, can't they?'

Lizzie nodded in answer to her twin's question then hand-in-hand they hurried on their way.

Once she reached the factory gates, Maggie took a deep breath. Lately she had taken to standing outside with Jo while she had a cigarette before they started work, but this morning, the girl was nowhere in sight. Maggie headed towards the toilet block where she rinsed her face with cold water at the long row of sinks. Glancing up into the mirror, she was shocked at her reflection. There were dark circles beneath her eyes, which seemed to emphasise her pallor.

She had just dragged the compulsory hairnet out of the depths of her handbag, when the door swung open and Jo appeared.

'Thought I might find you in here when you weren't outside,' she said brightly. 'What's up then? Yer look like you've lost a bob an' found a tanner.'

Maggie concentrated all her efforts on tucking her hair beneath the hated hairnet.

The smile slid from Jo's face. 'Have I done somethin' to upset yer?' she asked.

'No, of course you haven't. But the thing is . . . well, after seeing that latest bruise I've been lying awake all night worrying about you. Don't you think it's time you told me what's going on? I want to help you, Jo.'

'Oh yes – an' just *how* do yer suppose yer can do that?' Jo faced her defiantly. 'I don't go out on the streets fer love, yer know. It's all right fer you to stand there all high an' mighty.'

The two women faced each other like opponents in a boxing ring until Jo's shoulders suddenly sagged and she leaned heavily against the sink.

'I'm so sorry, Maggie. I wouldn't upset you fer the world. Yer about the only friend I've got, or ever had if it comes to that.'

She looked so small and vulnerable that Maggie's heart went out to her before she asked softly, 'Why do you do it, Jo?'

''Cos I ain't got a lot o' choice.'

'Of course you have a choice. No one *makes* you go out onto the streets, surely?'

'Huh! That just goes to show how much you know then, don't it? If I don't go out an' tip the money up to me dad when I gets back in, me mam an' the kids cop it.'

Maggie's face mirrored her horror as she took a step towards her. 'You mean to tell me, your own father makes you prostitute yourself?'

'That's about the size of it, though to be honest when he first sent me out it was almost a relief. At least I get to choose who I go with when I'm out on the streets.'

As the implication of what she was saying sunk in, Maggie's hand flew across her mouth. 'You can't mean that your father . . .'

Jo laughed; an empty laugh that echoed around the toilets. 'Oh yes, I can. Me mam has been poorly an' confined to her bed fer almost as long as I can remember – so that left me to step into her shoes . . . in all ways.'

'Oh, my God.' Maggie could barely believe what she was hearing. She stepped towards Jo, but the girl pushed her away.

'So now yer know, don't yer? If it weren't fer the little 'uns an' me mam, I'd be long gone, but what am I supposed to do? If I don't do as he says, they suffer, it's as simple as that. An' as long as I do as I'm told, he leaves me younger sisters alone.'

'Oh Jo, I'm so sorry. I had no idea.'

'No, nor does anyone else, an' I'd prefer it to stay that way.' With that she turned on her heel and marched away as the full horror of what she had just disclosed washed over Maggie in waves.

Until their confrontation she had always felt a little sorry for herself. But now that she understood what Jo was forced to endure she felt almost lucky. Compared to Jo's father, Sam was a saint and she vowed to try harder to love him. On legs that suddenly felt like lead weights she slowly made her way to her machine and so began another monotonous day.

Chapter Nine

One balmy evening in late June, Maggie and her mother sat with their feet up in the kitchen as a cool breeze wafted through the open back door. After the intense heat of the day it was a welcome relief. The children were all fast asleep in bed, and both women were feeling relaxed, especially as Sam was out at the pub.

'I reckon I might go over home an' get meself a nice early night,' Ellen Sharp remarked.

'I think I might do the same. I have to say, this hot weather takes it out of you. It's awful in the factory. By dinnertime it's like a furnace in there.' Maggie would have said more, but suddenly a steady droning overhead broke the stillness of the early evening.

'What's that?' The words had scarcely left her lips when the air-raid siren wailed and the colour drained from her face. 'Oh, my God. Mam, what's happening?'

Seeing that her daughter was on the verge of panic, Ellen took control of the situation. 'I think this might be it, love, God help us. Now listen to me. We have to get the children into the shelter – an' quickly. Do you understand me?'

When Maggie merely stared at her blankly she crossed to her and quickly shook her arm.

'You get the twins an' I'll get Lucy. Then, when we've

got them into the shelter, we'll pop back in' an' fetch some bedding. Now come on, there's not a minute to lose.' She pushed Maggie towards the stairs door, and despite the fact that she was almost crippled with arthritis, she sprinted up them two at a time.

Seconds later, she reappeared on the landing with Lucy, who was still fast asleep, tucked warmly in a cot blanket. Maggie had hold of the twins, who were knuckling the sleep from their eyes and complaining loudly.

'Good girl,' Ellen encouraged. 'Now, get them out into the yard an' into the shelter.'

Ignoring the twins' questions, which were coming thick and fast, Maggie pushed them ahead of her, and soon they were all out in the yard. She could hear doors banging and neighbours scurrying everywhere as they too headed for their shelters.

'That's it, in you go.' Ellen pushed the children in front of her and after yanking the Anderson door open she nudged them inside. It smelled of damp earth, but there was no time to worry about that now. After depositing Lucy onto one of the makeshift bunk beds that Sam had knocked up out of any old pieces of wood he could get his hands on, she told the twins, 'Now you sit there an' keep your eyes on your sister. Me an' yer mam will be back before you know it.'

Swinging about, she dived back into the house, closely followed by Maggie, and between them they soon had two feather mattresses and a pile of pillows stacked at the top of the stairs.

'You get those into the shelter an' I'll grab some beddin',' Ellen commanded in a voice that brooked no argument. Minutes later, when she staggered back across the yard with her arms full of blankets, she dared to glance up at the sky. It seemed to be full of planes and she shuddered. It looked as if they were in for it tonight, all right.

Once inside the shelter she hastily closed the door, and for the benefit of the children, who were all wide-eyed with fright, she fixed a smile to her face.

'Now then, we're going to camp out tonight. That will be nice, won't it?'

'Don't want to camp out in here. It smells funny – an' where's me dad?' Tears were glistening on Lizzie's long lashes and she had to shout to make herself heard above the steady drone of the planes.

As if Maggie had only just thought about Sam, she glanced fearfully at her mother.

'Your dad will be fine,' Ellen assured the little girl.

Maggie was full of admiration for her mother, who was as calm as could be.

'He'll go into the pub cellar, no doubt,' she added. 'Right – let's get these beds made up for now, eh? We'll have you as snug as a bug in a rug in no time.'

For all the world as if this was an everyday occurrence, Ellen Sharp swung the mattresses onto the bedframes and in no time at all she had tucked the children in.

'There, now. You all snuggle down and try to get back to sleep. Everything will be OK, you'll see.'

Lizzie, who was lying next to Danny in the top bunk, cuddled up close to her brother, her eyes wide and fearful in the light of a candle that Maggie had lit.

'Are they goin' to drop bombs on us, Gran?' she whispered.

Her grandma smoothed her cheek. 'I don't know, sweetheart,' she answered truthfully. 'But even if they do, they can't hurt us while we're all in here.' Crossing to Maggie, who was perched on the edge of the old easy chair her mother had given to her, she pressed her hand reassuringly and whispered, 'Try an' stay calm now, love. For the sake o' the kids, eh?'

She squeezed onto the chair at the side of her daughter and wrapped her arms around her. Maggie nestled her head on her mother's shoulder as terror swept over her in waves.

'What about me dad?' she said. 'He's over at the house all on his own.'

'He'll be all right,' Ellen soothed. 'Bill is big an' ugly enough to take care of himself. He'll go into the cupboard under the stairs, an' he knows I'm here with you, so stop worrying.'

The two women fell silent as the racket overhead grew louder by the minute. And then they heard a loud whistling noise followed by the sound of a huge explosion. Maggie almost jumped out of her skin.

'Sshh.' Ellen cuddled her even closer. 'Don't get panicking. They'll be aiming for Ansty Aerodrome an' the factories. We should be safe enough. We've just got to sit it out.'

Amazingly, after a time the children drifted off back to sleep. Maggie felt as if she was trapped in a nightmare as she clung to her mother for dear life. The candle sputtered, casting an eerie glow about their tiny sanctuary, and the two women began to pray as they had never prayed before.

After what seemed an eternity, Ellen rose and approached the door. Inching it open, she peered out into the night and the sight that she saw made her mouth gape in amazement. The sky overhead was as bright as day, as thousands of tiny incendiary bombs drifted down, like tiny multi-coloured fairy-lights on parachutes. The bombs that were raining down shook the ground and she hastily elbowed the door back to.

'What's happening out there?'

When Maggie's terrified voice floated to her she shrugged. 'Can't really say. But it'll be all right. You'll see.' But despite her encouraging words, Ellen Sharp's heart was heavy. She had an awful feeling that many people would lose their lives this night.

Time seemed to stand still. They had no way of knowing how long they had been trapped in their tiny prison. All they did know was that the night seemed to last for a lifetime. Over and over again, the earth beneath them shook as an explosion ripped through the air. Apart from that, the only other sound that could be heard was the clanging bells of the fire engines and ambulances as they raced towards the fires that were springing up across the city.

At last, the drone of the planes subsided and after a time, the all clear sounded.

'Is it over?' Maggie held her breath as she stared through the gloomy light into her mother's face.

'I think so, love. At least for now. You stay there wi' the children while I go out an' see what's goin' on.' Rising painfully, she straightened and lumbered towards the door, half-afraid of what she might see when she opened it. The first thing that struck her was the overpowering smell of burning. Huge columns of smoke darkened the dawn sky, as if they were trying to blot out the sun that was just peeping over the horizon. She could hear doors opening and closing and people running up and down the street as they too emerged from their shelters and hurried away to check on their friends and neighbours.

Becoming aware of Maggie, who had come to stand at her elbow, she nodded when Maggie told her, 'I'm just going to pop over the road an' check that Dad is all right, Mam. You wait there, I'll be back in a tick.'

Yanking the yard gate open, Maggie fled down the entry, breathing a sigh of relief as she saw that all the houses opposite were still standing.

'Are you all all right, love?' Mrs Massey shouted as she emerged from her front door looking tired and bleary-eyed.

'Yes, thanks! I'm just going to check that me dad's OK.'

Maggie impatiently waited for a fire engine to speed past with its bells clanging before darting nimbly across the street. She threw her parents' front door open and shouted, 'Dad – it's me! Where are you?' After the noise and activity in the street the house felt unnaturally quiet as she waited for her father to reply. Guessing that he was probably still asleep in the cupboard under the stairs, she started towards it with a smile on her face. Her mam had always joked that Bill could sleep through anything, and it was beginning to look like he had. However, when she flung the door open, the smile slid from her face. Because the houses on the opposite side of the street to Maggie didn't have room for an Anderson shelter in the back yard, her mam had long since cleared all the rubbish out from under the stairs and made up a bed of sorts in there. At a glance it was obvious that it hadn't been slept in.

Maggie frowned. Perhaps he'd decided to go to bed and to hell with it. Fear lent speed to her legs as she thumped up the stairs, but again she was presented with a tidy – and empty – bed.

Systematically she checked every room in the house but there was no sign of her father anywhere. Unlocking the back door, she stepped into a shared yard where her mother's neighbour was staring up at the smoke-blackened sky.

'You ain't seen me dad this morning, have you?' she asked.

The woman shook her head. 'Can't say as I have, Maggie. I heard him go out last night just before the commotion started though. I thought he were coming over to you.'

'Thanks, Mrs Hughes.' Maggie locked up and returned home. Her mother was still in the shelter with the children who had just woken up.

'There's no sign of him, Mam,' she said breathlessly. 'Mrs Hughes says she heard him go out last night but she ain't seen him since.'

Ellen frowned. 'He'd probably popped up the shop for his Woodbines. But why wouldn't he have come back?' An edge of fear had crept into her voice and now it was Maggie's turn to comfort her.

'Try not to worry, Mam. He probably slipped into a shelter somewhere when everything kicked off. Let's get the children inside and give them some breakfast, shall we? I shan't be sending them to school today an' I'm certainly not turning into work. Look, by the time we've sorted the kids out, Dad will have turned up like a bad penny.'

Lifting Lucy from the bunk, she ushered the twins in front of her. Once they were all seated around the kitchen table the questions began.

'Did they drop many bombs, Mam?' The first was from Danny.

'I'm not sure, love. It certainly sounded like it.'

'Will they come back and drop some more today?' The next was from Lizzie who was trembling like a jelly.

Maggie gulped as she stirred milk into a large pan of porridge. 'I hope not, sweetheart. But let's try not to worry about it for now. We'll have some breakfast and then I'm sure we'll all feel much better.'

Her mother had wandered off into the front room and was peering up and down the street for a sign of her husband. After a few minutes she rejoined Maggie in the kitchen. 'There's no sign of yer dad, but Sam's lumberin' down the street like he's got the weight o' the world on his shoulders.'

Maggie supposed that she should feel a measure of relief, but there was nothing but resentment. Once again when she and the children had needed him, he had let them down. She listened to his heavy tread in the entry and the sound of the back gate opening, and then he was there in the doorway, looking, as her mother put it, like death warmed up.

He flung his cap onto the chair, unable to meet their eyes as the two women stared at him. After a time he muttered, 'I'm afraid I've got some bad news. Could yer both come into the front room away from little ears?'

Maggie hastily filled the children's bowls then on leaden feet she followed her mother and her husband into the immaculate little front parlour that was only used on high days and holidays.

Once out of earshot of the children, both women looked at him expectantly and, unsure of where to begin, Sam shuffled from foot to foot.

'Thing is, I were in the Three Shuttles when the air-raid siren sounded, so me an' all the other customers went down an' spent the night in the cellar there. When we come out this mornin' I bumped into Jack Morris who used to work wi' yer dad, an' it were him that told me . . .'

When his voice trailed away, Maggie shook his arm. *'Told you what?'*

He looked from one to the other before gulping deep in his throat and continuing. 'Seems they had a hit down by the Swanswell pool. Yer dad were just comin' out o' the shop nearby an' . . .'

'He's dead, ain't he?' Ellen's voice was empty of any feeling whatsoever.

Sam nodded miserably, and as his words sank in, Maggie began to quietly sob. They stood for some minutes until Ellen turned and made towards the door. 'I'd best get off then. Do you know where they've taken him?'

'Jack thinks they took the bodies to the morgue at the Coventry and Warwick Hospital. They're asking for the next-of-kin to go and identify the bodies.'

'I'll go, Mam, if you don't feel up to it,' Maggie offered tearfully.

'No, it's all right, love. It should be me that goes.'

'It er . . . might not be a very pretty sight,' Sam warned her quietly.

Ellen drew herself up to her full height. 'It would take more than a bloody bomb to stop me recognisin' *my* man. After bein' wed fer over thirty-five years I know every inch of his body like the back of me hand.'

Turning about, she quietly slipped away. Maggie knew that she should be going after her, but her feet felt as if they'd been glued to the floor and the pain in her heart was so intense that for some minutes she couldn't even speak.

It took a while for her to realise that Sam was speaking again, and a great effort to concentrate on what he was saying.

'I can't believe I've gone an' done it.' His voice seemed to be coming from a long way away.

'Done what?' Maggie asked distractedly.

His hands balled into fists of frustration. 'Ain't you heard a single bloody word I've been saying? I've been tryin' to tell yer. I went an' had a few pints yesterday dinner. I know, before yer start yer naggin', that I shouldn't have, but the thing is, I got into a bit of a barney wi' an Army chap on leave in there. Right toffee-nosed little bastard he were, an' all. Told me I should be ashamed o' meself fer doin' nothin' when there's a war on. So I . . .'

'You what?'

'I er . . . I went an' signed up.'

This shock, on top of the news about her father, was too much for Maggie to take in and her legs buckled beneath her. *'You did what?'* she gasped incredulously.

Suddenly tears spurted from his eyes as he held his hands out to her beseechingly. 'I never meant to, Maggie. Within an hour I realised what I'd done an' I went back an' told 'em I'd changed me mind – but they were havin' none of it. They told me to stop bein' so spineless an' to behave like a man. All very well fer them to say, ain't it? Sittin' there behind their neat little desks. But *I* could be on the front line. Oh Maggie, what am I goin' to do?'

His fear was so tangible that she could almost taste it, and in that moment she saw him for the coward that he really was. Drawing herself up to her full height, she faced him squarely.

'You're going to do what you should have done long ago. You're going to fight for your country. Now, if you don't mind, I'm goin' to check on me mam. As you've just told us, we've lost my dad – an' I think that makes your dilemma, as you see it, seem rather insignificant, don't you?'

As she swept past him, his mouth gaped open and he knew that there was no going back.

Chapter Ten

The morning of 3 July 1940 dawned bright and clear, but Maggie didn't notice the weather. Today she was going to bury her father and her heart felt as if it was breaking. All morning there was a continuous stream of neighbours tiptoeing in and out of her kitchen, bearing offerings of food for the tea that would take place after the service.

Across the road at her parents' home, her father was resting in his coffin in the little front parlour. All along the Lane, the curtains were drawn as a mark of respect, and everywhere was unnaturally quiet, for the mothers had kept their children in until after the funeral.

As the morning wore on, the table bearing the food began to sag beneath the weight of pastries and pies that the neighbours had donated. There were homemade pickles and cakes, and enough sausagemeat baked into little pastry cases to feed an army, as Mrs Massey declared. Maggie looked at the vast array of food. For months they had all learned to do without as the rationing grew stricter, and yet here she was confronted with a feast that she knew she couldn't touch. At the moment, everything she tried to eat seemed to lodge in her throat and threatened to choke her.

Her eyes were swollen from crying and so were Sam's, but not for the same reason. The day before, his call-up papers had dropped through the letterbox and he'd been a quivering mess ever since, not that Maggie much cared. All she could think of was saying goodbye to the father she had adored. Bill Sharp had been a kind man, greatly admired and respected by friends and family alike, as the many floral tributes that were being laid by the front door testified. Maggie had begged her mother over the last week to stay with them but Ellen had steadfastly refused whilst her father was still lying in the house.

'At least I can still talk to him at the minute, even if he don't talk back,' was her only reply, and in the end Maggie gave up asking. If truth be told she was desperately worried about her mam. Since the night of her father's death she hadn't seen her shed so much as a single tear, and to her mind that wasn't healthy.

'She's bottlin' it all up inside,' Mrs Massey said when Maggie expressed her concerns. 'An' that ain't a good thing. It'll have to find release somewhere, an' the longer it stays inside the worse it will be, you just mark my words.'

Maggie tended to agree with her. They had since learned that fifteen other souls had perished on the night of the bombings and there had been a steady stream of funerals all week.

'Word has it that they have a large amount o' cardboard coffins ready an' waitin fer the next time,' Mrs Massey had informed her, and Maggie had shuddered at the thought. It seemed so undignified somehow, to be buried in a cardboard coffin. At least her father was being laid to rest in a sturdy oak casket, which gave her some comfort. He had always paid into a small funeral insurance fund and thankfully, that would pay for most of the expense.

At twelve o'clock sharp a shiny black hearse pulled up

outside the house and the undertakers disappeared inside to screw down the coffin lid before reverently carrying it out to the hearse for its final journey.

Mrs Massey, who was staying behind to look after Lucy and get the tea ready for when the mourners got back, pushed Maggie towards the door. 'Go on, love. Go an' say yer goodbyes. The little 'un will be fine with me.'

Looking incredibly pretty in a little black hat and a smart two-piece suit that her mother had insisted she should have, Maggie pulled on her gloves, then, taking the twins by the hand, she marched towards the door with Sam close behind her.

William Sharp was laid to rest following a short, dignified service in Swanshill Evangelical Baptist Church. As Maggie threw a clod of earth down onto the coffin lid she knew that a little part of her would be buried with him. Her mother stood dry-eyed at the side of the grave, and when it was over, Maggie gently took her arm and led her away to the feast that awaited them at home. Up until now, Coventry had been subjected to only one air raid, yet that one raid had changed her life forever. She wondered briefly what the next one might bring, and shuddered involuntarily at the thought.

'Oh, come on, Mam, *please*. You've got to eat something. You've lost so much weight you'll slip down a gap in the pavement at this rate. I've made you a shepherd's pie for your dinner – look.'

Ellen Sharp continued to polish the long mahogany sideboard in her front room as she smiled at her daughter over her shoulder. 'I'll have it later, love. Just leave it in the kitchen, would yer?'

Maggie sighed. It was now over a week since they'd buried her father and it seemed that ever since, her mother had spent her hours cleaning everything in sight. It was as if something were possessing her and she couldn't sit still for more than two minutes at a time.

'Mam. I defy anyone to find so much as a single scrap of dust in this whole house. You were even outside washing the dustbin earlier on, an' don't bother to deny it 'cos Mrs Hughes saw you doing it. Now *please* come an' sit down an' talk to me, eh? The twins were askin' after you earlier on. They wonder when you'll be comin' to see them. We only live across the road, you know.'

When she snatched the duster from her mother's hand, Ellen sighed before following her into the kitchen. But even then she didn't sit down but began to smooth out an imaginary crease in the fringed chenille table-cloth.

Maggie sighed as she filled the kettle at the spotlessly clean stone sink. She'd been wondering if she should go back to work, but while her mother was behaving like this she was afraid to leave her on her own. It was as she was straining the tea into pretty china cups that an idea occurred to her. Perhaps going back to work wouldn't be such a bad idea after all.

'Mam,' she said cautiously as she placed the teapot on the table, 'I was wondering – do you think you might be able to start looking after the children again for me soon? The thing is, money's a bit tight and it'll be down to me once Sam has gone off to camp. Not that he's bringing anything in at the minute. We're getting by on a wing and a prayer at present but I can't go back until you feel up to babysitting again.'

A host of emotions flitted across Ellen's face. Since losing Bill she had barely ventured out of the house. She felt closer to him there, yet she didn't like to think of Maggie struggling.

'When were yer thinkin' o' going back?' she asked tentatively.

'Well, Sam's going next week so the sooner the better, really. If you think you're up to it, that is.'

A picture of the twins and Lucy flashed before Ellen's eyes. She knew that she'd neglected them all shamefully since the funeral. Perhaps it was time to try and get back to some sort of normality?

'All right then. But couldn't you just go part-time for a while? Just till I get properly back on me feet again?'

'I don't see why not. The way things are at the minute, they're glad of any hours people can do at the munitions factory,' Maggie replied. 'Things are getting worse, if the wireless and the newspapers are anything to go by. They reckon the Royal Navy destroyed a large part of the French fleet while it lay at anchor in Algeria this week, to stop it falling into enemy hands. Problem was, they killed a thousand French sailors in the process. Winston Churchill says he deeply regretted the action but felt he was left with no choice. I ask you – where is it all going to end?'

'It already *has* ended for me. Or it might as well have done. I just wish me an' your dad could have gone together.'

'Oh, Mam! Don't talk like that. Dad would turn in his grave if he could hear you. An' what about me an' the children? You've still got us, and what would we do without you, eh?'

Sipping at her tea, Ellen raised a sad smile. 'Go on, love, you get yerself off home now. The little 'uns will be screamin' fer their tea by now, if I know 'em.'

'Are you sure you'll be all right?' Maggie's voice was heavy with concern as she slowly drained her cup and rose from the table.

'Right as ninepence.'

After planting a kiss on her mother's pale cheek, Maggie made her way back across the road. She found Sam in the kitchen with his head in his hands, and inexplicably, she felt a pang of sympathy for him. It was more than obvious that he deeply regretted signing up, and it was also obvious that the thought of going to war terrified him. But what could she do about it? The answer came back to her: absolutely nothing! He had made his bed, and to use her mother's term, now he would have to lie on it.

Keeping her voice gentle, she asked, 'Would you like me to get you anything?'

Lucy was sitting on the hearthrug and she could hear the sounds of the twins playing with the neighbour's children in the back yard.

'What? Oh no. No, thanks. I could murder a pint though. I don't suppose you've got a few bob to spare, have yer?'

In that moment, had she had any spare cash she would have given it to him willingly, but as it was, she barely had enough to see them through the week.

'Sorry, Sam, I'm afraid I haven't, but don't look so glum. Things might turn out to be not quite as bad as you expect, once you get there.'

'Huh! It ain't the trainin' bit I'm bothered about. It's where they'll send me once the trainin's over that worries me. You've heard the horror stories on the wireless. Men are getting their heads blown off every day. It'd be just my luck if I copped it the first day out there.'

At that moment Danny exploded into the kitchen, and as Maggie turned to face him, a wave of love washed over her. With his hair tousled and his socks slipped down round his ankles, he looked adorable.

'Look at this ally, Dad! Me an Neil from up the way have been playin' marbles an' I won it off him.' He extended a grubby hand in which nestled a large glass marble for his father's inspection, but when no comment was forthcoming and his father merely gazed off into space he looked at Maggie.

'Ain't me dad very well, Mam?' he muttered falteringly.

At that minute, Lizzie, who was never more than a few steps behind her brother, also burst into the kitchen. Maggie gave Danny a reassuring smile. She knew that the twins missed their grandad dreadfully. They all did, if it came to that, but she was discovering that life had to go on and was doing her best to cope.

'Your dad's fine,' she said. 'Now come on, the pair of you. Get to the sink and wash yer hands an' I'll rustle us all up some dinner, eh?'

Danny trudged to the sink and half-heartedly twiddled his hands beneath the tap, but all the time he kept a cautious eye on his father. Dinner was a gloomy affair and Maggie was glad when it was over and she could send the children back out to play. As she stood washing up the pots she thought how much lighter the atmosphere would be when Sam finally did go, and guilt made her cheeks grow hot. What was she thinking of? As Sam had quite rightly pointed out, men were being killed every day, some of them no more than boys. He might never come home, so why then, she wondered, didn't she feel anything? She pushed the thought away and moved on to her next chore.

The following day, Maggie visited the factory and hurried inside to talk to May, who was only too happy to welcome her back with open arms.

'I was sorry to hear about yer dad, love,' she sympathised, and Maggie thought that perhaps she wasn't as bad as everyone made out, after all. It was as she was leaving the factory that Jo spotted her and hastily rose from her machine to follow Maggie outside.

'I er . . . I heard what happened to yer dad an' I just want to say I'm sorry.' She shuffled from foot to foot in the bright sunshine, avoiding Maggie's eyes as she spoke.

'Thank you. It was a shock, as you can imagine, but I've decided to come back to work next week. Sam has signed up. He leaves on Monday an' I'll be back in on Tuesday. To be honest, I'll need the money to keep the wolf from the door. But how are things with you?'

'So so.' Jo blushed beetroot red, and as she raised her head, Maggie saw that her lip was split.

'Was it yer dad or a client that did that?' she asked softly.

'It was me dad. I told him I weren't goin' out on the streets again, but he had other ideas. I tell yer, I wish it was *him* that was goin' away instead o' your Sam – an' I wish they'd blow him to smithereens. He's a bastard!' Her voice was so loaded with hatred that for a moment Maggie was speechless. Standing there, Jo looked very young without her paint and powder on, and Maggie's heart ached for her.

'Look – why don't you come round and see me one night next week?' She hadn't intended to invite Jo to her home. Somehow the words had just slipped out and there was no going back.

'Why should I do that?'

'Well, the thing is, I've just sorted Lizzie's wardrobe out an' I have a number of skirts and jumpers that might come in for one of your little sisters. The other thing is, I'll be glad of a bit of company of a night, when Sam's gone an' the children are all in bed.'

Jo stared at her suspiciously for a moment before muttering, 'Do yer *really* want a prostitute in yer home?'

'I know I was hard on you when I first found out,' Maggie told her apologetically, 'but the thing is – you're not doing it because you want to, are you? From what you've told me, you don't have much choice.'

'Yer got that right.' Jo kicked at a stone and then her face broke into a rare smile. 'If yer sure then? I'll do that. I'll pay fer the clothes though, if there's anythin' that'll fit the little 'uns.'

In that instant, Maggie realised that Jo had pride and she admired her for it.

'Well, we'll see, eh? We'll sort out what night's best for you when I get back to work next week. Meantime, I'd better go home else the children will be playing merry hell. You take care now.'

As she walked away, Jo felt a lump rise in her throat. She'd never allowed herself to have a friend before because of her circumstances. She had always been afraid of what they might think of her, if they should discover what she did at nights. And yet here was Maggie inviting her to her home regardless. With an uncharacteristic spring in her step she turned and hurried away back to her machine.

'Cor, Mam, this looks lovely!' Danny's eyes shone greedily as he looked at the lovely meal Maggie had laid out on the table. It was the day before his dad was due to leave and Maggie had pulled out all the stops to present Sam with a Sunday dinner that he wouldn't forget in a hurry. It had been no mean feat. She had begged and borrowed from different people, but now it all seemed worth it as the twins gazed down at the loaded plates approvingly. There was juicy roast beef with crispy Yorkshire puddings, and cabbage and carrots all piled on top of roast potatoes cooked just the way Sam liked them.

'Shall we sit down and have it while it's hot then?' she suggested brightly. 'And there's a big apple pie and custard for after, for those that have room for any.'

'We will,' the twins chorused, and they fell on the meal as if they hadn't eaten for a month.

Once Maggie had strapped Lucy into her wooden highchair and pulled her up to the table, she smiled at Sam. 'Come on, love. Tuck in.'

He stopped pacing up and down the room to glance at her distractedly. 'What did you say?'

'I said come and get your dinner before it goes cold. I've been standing over a hot stove all day and it would be a shame to see it go to waste.' She kept her smile fixed firmly in place, determined that the memories he had of his last day at home should be happy ones.

Reluctantly he pulled his chair up, but all he could do was push the food around the plate. 'I ain't very hungry,' he told her after a while.

'Never mind. Perhaps you'll find room for some pudding. I invited Mam to join us but she preferred to stay at home again.'

Danny paused from shovelling food into his mouth. 'Gran misses Grandad, don't she?' he asked sadly.

'Yes, she does, sweetheart. We all do, but let's not think of that today. I want this to be a happy day.'

'Huh! There's fat chance o' that, knowin' where I'm off to tomorrow.' Sam scraped his chair back from the table and stormed towards the door. 'I'm goin' out fer a bit o' fresh air. Expect me when yer see me.'

Maggie's shoulders sagged. It seemed that all her efforts had been in vain, but she didn't want to upset the children, so she said briskly: 'Right then. Who's for apple pie?'

Three little hands shot up into the air and wearily she turned away to the oven.

That evening, as darkness painted the sky above the city, a feeling of dread settled around Maggie's heart. She had wanted Sam to spend his last night at home with the children, but they had long since been tucked into bed and were all snoring softly. She paced up and down the kitchen, looking at the tin clock that stood on the mantelshelf every few minutes. Where could he be? She knew he had no money to go the pub, and as he had no other interests, she was deeply concerned. Eventually she twitched the blackout curtains tightly together and curled into a ball on the settee. Her eyes fell on the case packed ready for him at the side of the door. It was a very small case, for as the recruiting officer had told him, once he was issued with his uniform he would need very little else from home. Maggie had packed just one change of clothes and underwear, and had also slipped in a picture of the children, all happy and smiling, that she had had taken especially. She was determined to stay awake until he showed his face, but it had been a long day, and as the hand on the tin clock crept up to midnight she fell fast asleep.

In the early hours of the morning she started awake. For a moment she was disorientated, but then, as she remembered why she was there, her face creased into a frown. Sitting up slowly, she stretched her stiff arms above her head. It was then that she saw the shadow creeping across the room and her heart skipped a beat. Lunging for the light switch, she clicked it on and gasped when she saw Sam, suitcase in hand, creeping towards the back door like a thief in the night.

'Sam, where have you been? I've been so worried. And what have you got your case for? You don't have to leave until the morning.'

Unable to meet her questioning eyes, he hung his head. 'I err . . . I thought I'd head off now.'

Maggie stared at him. 'But what about saying goodbye to the children? And to me? Anyway, there are no buses or trams running at this time. Just what are you playing at?'

Hearing the suspicion in her voice, he shrugged. 'Yer might as well know now as later.'

'Know what?'

'I ain't goin'.'

'But you've *got* to go now.' Maggie could hardly believe what she was hearing. If Sam didn't turn up, he would be classed as a coward and a deserter, and would never be able to hold his head high again.

He shook his head. 'All very easy fer you to say, but I don't fancy getting me head blown off. So I've decided I ain't goin' – it's as simple as that.'

'But what will you do? They'll look for you. You won't be able to stay round here.'

'I know that.' He had the grace to look uncomfortable as he again made towards the door. Once there, he turned to look back at her. 'I'm sorry, Maggie. I know I ain't been the best husband in the world. You an' the kids will be better off wi'out me.'

'But where will you go?' she repeated.

'Better you don't know, then yer won't have to lie, will yer?'

Maggie felt as if she was caught in the grip of a terrible nightmare. 'Will we ever see you again?'

He shrugged. 'Perhaps one day, when this bloody war is all over.' Without so much as another word he silently slipped away into the night as Maggie stood there reeling from the shock.

Chapter Eleven

Pulling her coat about her, Maggie shuffled through the leaves that were whipping across the pavement beneath her feet. It was early September and there was a distinct nip in the air, which was hard to adjust to after the blazing heat of the summer.

She had been back in the factory for some weeks now. Of Sam there was no sign, and now the children had stopped asking for him, almost as if he'd never existed. Her mother was still giving her cause for concern. Ellen seemed to be slipping into a strange melancholy where no one could reach her, although she was still managing to care for the children while Maggie was at work.

Maggie was completely worn out. Gone were the days when she would go home to a house of laughter with a meal waiting for her on the table. Instead, she usually arrived home to find her mother slouched in the fireside chair, the pots piled high in the sink and the children running riot.

Today, Danny and Lizzie met her at the door, flinging themselves into her arms as if they hadn't seen her for a month. She laughed and kissed the tops of their heads as they both rushed to tell her all about their day.

'One at a time,' she smiled as she took off her coat. Her mother was in her usual position in the fireside chair.

As soon as she heard Maggie, she rose and began to shuffle towards the door.

'Won't you stay for tea, Mam?' Maggie knew what the answer would be before the question had left her lips, so her mother's reply didn't surprise her.

'No thanks, love. I'll get back off over home if you don't mind. I've peeled a few potatoes and onions for yer an' I got yer some ox liver from the butchers.'

'Thanks, Mam. I'll drop Lucy off in the morning then as usual.'

Ellen nodded and slowly left the house.

The next couple of hours passed in a blur as Maggie cooked the children a meal then prepared them for bed. When at last they were all tucked in, she began to tackle the housework. Glancing at the clock, she was shocked to see that it was almost 8 p.m. She wondered where the time had gone. Jo was calling round tonight and the house was scarcely fit to be seen. Still, she comforted herself, she's coming to see me, not the house, so she'll have to take me as she finds me. She could hear the rain that had begun to fall, lashing against the window, and briefly wondered if Jo might decide against coming out in it, but spot on eight o'clock there was a tap on the front door.

When Maggie hurried through the front room to answer it and saw Jo standing there, it was all she could do not to laugh out loud. The girl looked like a drowned rat.

'Come on in quickly. You'll catch your death standing there,' she urged.

Jo stepped inside, and as her eyes swept approvingly round the tidy room, the water began to puddle on the lino at her feet.

'Sorry. Perhaps I should have put it off till another night,' she said. 'But it weren't rainin' when I set off.'

'Stop worryin' an' don't be silly. It's only a bit of water. Now come into the kitchen by the fire and get dried off.' Maggie led the way, and once in the warmth of the little back room, she passed her a towel. 'Here, give your hair a good rub with that an' give me your coat. I'll hang it up to dry an' then I'll make yer a nice hot drink.'

Jo took the towel gratefully as Maggie filled the kettle.

'Sorry the place is in a bit of a state,' she told Jo over her shoulder. 'I only manage to keep on top through the week while I'm working, then come the weekend I give everywhere a thorough goin'-over.'

Jo could have told her that compared to the home she lived in, this was like a little palace but she remained tight-lipped until Maggie had carried two steaming mugs to the table.

'I'm afraid we're out of sugar. Our Danny used the last of it on his porridge this morning.'

'You've got this place really comfortable,' Jo told Maggie.

'I dare say it's not too bad, though it could be better if I didn't have three kids rampagin' round it. Still, I shouldn't grumble, I suppose.'

They both sipped at their drinks until Jo asked, 'Have yer heard anythin' from Sam?'

Maggie shook her head. Apart from her mother and Sam's mother, Jo was the only person she had told, about him being missing. If the neighbours had noticed that Army officials had been round to see her, they tactfully hadn't questioned her and she hadn't enlightened them as to why they had come. Their visit had turned into an ordeal, and by the time they had finished grilling her, she had been shaking like a leaf. They had even searched the house, as if they thought she might be hiding him! Finally she had been ordered to fill in endless forms, and then they had left, telling her in no uncertain terms that should she discover where he was and not tell them, then she would be considered as guilty as he was.

'Not so much as a dickie-bird,' she sighed, suppressing a shudder as she thought back to the visit. 'It's almost as if he's disappeared off the face of the earth.'

'Don't the children find it strange that he didn't say goodbye to them?'

'I think they might have for a start but they hardly mention him now.' Maggie's voice was sad. 'If I am honest, they're happier without him. He never had a lot of time for them when he was here. When he did speak to them it was usually to tell them off or to order them to be quiet.'

'Well, at least he weren't knockin' seven bells out of 'em half the time. That's where I get most of my bruises from – when I step in between my dad an' one o' the little 'uns.'

Maggie stared at her soberly. Jo was alarmingly thin, but she was wearing a very smart blue costume and had obviously made a great effort to look nice for her visit. Maggie was touched. 'That's a lovely outfit you're wearing, Jo.'

Her visitor flushed with pleasure at the compliment. 'I got it in a jumble sale over at some posh church hall in Earlsdon,' she giggled. 'I got loads o' stuff fer the little 'uns an' all, an' a nice nightie fer me mam. She were tickled pink with it when I got it home.'

'Ah, now that reminds me.' Crossing to a pile of clothes that were neatly folded over the back of a chair, Maggie carried them to the table. 'I sorted those things that Lizzie has grown out of for you. Do you think any of them might fit one of your sisters?'

As she began to hold the articles up one at a time for

inspection, Jo said, 'Cor, they're lovely, an' they'll slot on our Katie a treat. I'm goin' to pay yer fer 'em though.'

Maggie glanced at the proud jut of the girl's chin and was impressed. Jo might not have a lot but she certainly had her pride. 'I'll tell you what, let's just say you owe me a favour if ever I should need one,' she compromised.

Jo thought about it for a second and frowned. 'What sort of favour could I ever do you?'

'Well, perhaps you could babysit for me if ever I needed you?'

'What? You'd trust me to babysit fer your kids knowin' what I am?' Jo's eyes were incredulous.

'What you are is a very nice person,' Maggie replied kindly. 'And yes, of course I'd trust you with them.' She thought she saw the glimmer of tears in Jo's eyes before she hastily looked away, but then the moment was gone and their talk turned to more serious matters.

'Things are lookin' bad in London,' Jo remarked gloomily. 'The poor buggers there have copped it big time this week, accordin' to the news. They reckon the bombin' went on from early evenin', all through the night an' on into the next mornin'. They got the docks, the gas station, an' loads more places. God knows how many poor souls were left dead. Churchill ordered an attack on Berlin to retaliate, an' that got Hitler all riled up. Gawd, Maggie, he reckons he's goin' to reduce the whole of London to rubble now. It's frightenin', ain't it?' She shivered. 'I wonder how long it will be before they target Coventry again?'

Maggie trembled involuntarily at the thought. 'I don't know, but I've got the shelter all set up just in case. The last time we were bombed I went completely to pieces an' me mam had to take control of everything. This time

I know it will be down to me. Since we lost my dad, me mam barely knows what time it is. Eileen wrote to me last week. She's selling her house and told me to go round and help myself to anything that I might find useful, so I took a load of blankets and sheets. At least now if we have a raid I won't have to worry about dragging bedding across to the shelter as well as the children. I've even put a torch and some tinned food in so we should be all right.'

'You're lucky you've *got* somewhere to shelter,' Jo told her ruefully. 'If there's a raid we just have to sit it out. There ain't room in our yard fer one, an' even if there were, me mam ain't fit enough to get to it. Last time, I put the kids under the stairs an' I sat on the bed an' held me mam's hand.'

Maggie realised that Jo must love her mother very much indeed and was about to say so when Jo went on, 'How are yer managing on yer own anyway?'

Maggie shrugged. 'Not too bad, but I don't know how much longer I'll be able to keep up going to work in the factory. My mam isn't coping with things all that well since we lost Dad and I feel guilty leaving the children with her every day. Trouble is, I need the money and I can't think of a job that I could do from home.'

'Mmm . . . I can see your predicament.' Jo tapped her chin as she pondered, before suddenly declaring, 'I know what you could do.'

Maggie raised a questioning eyebrow.

'Yer could take in washin' an' ironin'. Yer know – like a laundry service? I know it ain't the most glamorous of jobs in the world but yer could deliver it back to 'em all washed and ironed.'

'The only problem with that is the weather,' Maggie pointed out. 'I'd have to have lines strung everywhere to try and get it all dry. It wouldn't dry outside if the weather was like this.'

'Mmm, there is that in it.' Jo glanced around the room as if for inspiration. When her eyes fell on a little dress of Lizzie's that was hanging on the huge wooden clotheshorse, she asked, 'Did *you* make that?'

When Maggie nodded, Jo walked across to it and fingered it admiringly. The bodice of the dress was intricately smocked and it had little puff sleeves and a broad belt in the same material that tied around the waist. The skirt was full and the pretty round collar was embroidered with tiny flowers.

'This is really beautiful,' she said admiringly. 'It must have taken you hours to make it.'

'Not really. I love sewing when I get the time,' Maggie admitted. 'I've got a Singer sewing-machine in the front room so I make most of the girls' clothes. It's much cheaper than buying them.'

'That's it!' Jo exclaimed triumphantly. 'You could set up a sewing business.'

Maggie looked doubtful, but Jo was excited now. 'Think about it,' she urged. 'Only the other day I heard one o' the women at work sayin' she'd managed to get hold of a load of parachute silk for her daughter's weddin' dress. Trouble was, she didn't know anyone who might make it up.'

Maggie rolled the idea around in her mind. It was plausible, she had to admit.

'Do you really think I'd get enough work to match my wages in the factory?' she asked dubiously.

Jo nodded. 'I ain't got a doubt about it. I bet if you put your notice in at work and we put the word around about what you intend to do, you'd have a book full of orders before you even left. You could do repairs as well.

Remember, people are havin' to make do since the war started.'

'Do you know, I think you might have hit on something there,' Maggie smiled and for the next hour they discussed the pros and cons of the idea.

By the time Jo left, taking with her the clothes Maggie had sorted out for her and a couple of sheets and blankets she had brought from Eileen's, Maggie was feeling happier than she had in weeks. It came to her with a little shock that it was the first time she'd had a girls' night with someone close to her own age for years, and she'd enjoyed it immensely. It had soon become apparent that beneath Jo's brash façade was a loving, caring girl. Somehow, Maggie felt that a friendship had been forged that night that would go from strength to strength.

As she locked up and put the guard around the fire, she thought again of the proposed new business venture. She liked the idea. She had always enjoyed sewing, and working at home would mean that she could have Lucy with her whilst the twins were at school. It would also enable her to keep more of an eye on her mother. Feeling almost light-hearted, she made her way to bed.

The very next morning she told May that she would be leaving at the end of the week. May understood her reasons, but told her that she would be missed, for she was a good worker. During the breaks in the works canteen, Maggie then began to spread the word amongst the women of what she intended to do. Just as Jo had predicted, as the week wore on they began to come to her with offers of jobs that they would like her to do.

When she told Lizzie and Danny of her intentions over dinner that night they both whooped with delight.

'So you'll be here when we come in from school then?' Danny asked delightedly.

Guilt flooded through her as she smiled and nodded. She felt that she had neglected them terribly over the last few months, but fully intended to make up for it now.

'I shall be here all the time again now,' she promised. In her mind she was already beginning to plan how she would do it. She would see the twins off to school and spend the morning doing her housework, then during the afternoon while Lucy was having her nap she would sew. She could fit in more sewing at night, once the children were in bed. There was already over a week's work in her order book, and people had begun to deliver repairs and material to her at home, including the parachute silk, which she would make into a wedding dress for her first job.

On Maggie's last day at work, Jo did something entirely uncharacteristic. As they stood at the factory gates she suddenly flung her arms about Maggie and kissed her soundly on the cheek. 'I shall miss yer,' she said. Maggie looked at her in surprise. 'Well, I don't see why you should. You can still come and see me, can't you? In fact, I shall expect you to – even more now that we won't be working together in the day.'

Jo grinned. 'I'll hold yer to that.'

'Good. I'll expect you one night next week, then. An' don't forget or I shall come lookin' for yer.'

'Tarrah then. See yer next week.' With a spring in her step, Jo set off in the opposite direction.

Maggie arrived home in a happy mood but she had barely had time to set foot through the door when it dispersed.

'That came fer yer this mornin'.' Her mother nodded towards an official-looking brown paper envelope that was propped up on the mantelpiece.

Tentatively, Maggie lifted it down and turned it over in her hand.

'Well, open it then. It can't bite,' her mother snapped. 'It might be somethin' to do with Sam.'

Turning her back on the twins who were staring at her with wide frightened eyes, Maggie slit it open and extracted the letter it contained. As her eyes flew down the carefully typed page, the colour drained from her face and she leaned heavily against the mantelpiece.

'Well, come on then – spit it out. *Is* it owt to do with Sam?' her mother demanded.

Taking her by the elbow, Maggie steered her into the front room away from the little ears in the kitchen.

'They've found him,' she told her mother.

Ellen whistled softly through her teeth. 'So where were he, then?'

Maggie gulped before answering. 'It appears that he was at his mother's. She'd been hiding him.'

Her mother's response had Maggie's eyes stretching wide with shock.

'It don't surprise me.'

'But, Mam, she *knew* that he was on the run,' Maggie gasped.

Ellen laughed softly. 'She's his mam, love. For all she declared he were a bad 'un from time to time, blood is thicker than water an' yer defend yer own. Even if yer feel at times that what they're doin' ain't right. I for one won't condemn her. If truth be told, I'd probably have done the same if it had been you. What they doin' with him now, anyway?'

Maggie looked back at the letter. 'It seems they've taken him off to the camp. He'll be punished, then he'll do his training and they'll ship him out just the same.'

'It just might make a man of him,' Ellen told her

philosophically. 'At least yer know where he is now, so you'd best put it from yer mind an' get on with things here.'

Maggie nodded slowly as she crumpled the letter in her hand. Her mother was right. Sam had committed the crime and now he must endure the punishment. After all his efforts to evade going to war, he'd still ended up being where he least wanted to be. And there wasn't a thing in the world that she could do about it. A little voice in her head whispered, 'Would you really want to?' Not wishing to answer it she hurried away to see to the children's tea.

Chapter Twelve

'There you are then, Mam. That should see you through till I get in from school.'

As Maggie looked across at Danny, who was just placing a full coal-scuttle on the hearth, her heart swelled with pride. Since his father had left, Danny had done his best to take on the role of the man of the house. He never tired of helping out or running errands, for which she was more grateful than she could say. Her small dressmaking business was doing well, and sometimes she was having to stay up until the early hours of the morning to keep up with her work. Not that she was complaining, for although she was ashamed to admit it, the house seemed lighter somehow without Sam, and the children seemed happier too.

Hurrying over to the twins, who were standing by the door, she handed them each their satchels before kissing them both affectionately.

'Put your scarves on,' she instructed them. 'It's enough to cut you in two out there and I don't want you both coming down with colds.'

Lizzie obediently did as she was told but Danny wrinkled up his nose.

'Do I have to, Mam? I feel a right cissy in that.'

Maggie stifled a giggle. The scarves that her mother

had knitted them were a little gaudy, to say the least. Ellen had used up all her odd scraps of wool and the scarves reminded Maggie of Joseph's coat of many colours. Not that Lizzie minded. In fact, she was quite taken with hers.

'Well, all right then. But turn your coat collar up instead, else you'll be getting a sore throat,' Maggie relented.

Once she had seen the twins off, she turned her attention to Lucy, who was still in her nightdress. 'Come on, sweetheart,' she crooned as she lifted the toddler into her arms. 'Let's get you dressed, eh? Then we'll pop across the road and check on Grandma before we get started on the housework.'

In no time at all, Maggie and Lucy were sitting in the warmth of Ellen's immaculate little kitchen. Maggie kept the child close at her side, for she had a habit of being able to create chaos in no time, and her mother's obsession with having everything just so had not abated.

'Mrs Massey was saying that she was going up the club tonight to have a game of housey-housey,' Maggie remarked innocently. 'Why don't you get yourself ready and go with her? It would do you the world of good to get out of the house for a while.'

'I'm quite happy in me own four walls,' her mother replied stubbornly as she flicked at an imaginary speck of dust on the gleaming sideboard that stood along one wall.

Maggie sighed. She had been trying to encourage her mother to go out for weeks, but as yet she'd had no success at all. 'Then what say you an' me go to the pictures later in the week? I could do with a night out meself, if I were to be honest.'

'Oh yes? An' what would yer do with the children while we were off gallivanting?'

'That needn't be a problem. Jo would be more than happy to babysit,' Maggie pointed out.

From the look that flitted across Ellen's face, Maggie might have suggested that she walk into a den of lions. But then she pursed her lips and firmly shook her head. 'I ain't daft, me girl. I happen to know you're snowed under with work at the moment. You're just tryin' to get me out an' about.'

'Would that be such a bad thing?' Maggie asked softly. 'Apart from crossing the road to us, you've barely set foot out of the house since Dad . . .'

'Yes, well, that's as maybe. But I'll go out in me own good time and not before, so let's leave it at that, eh?'

'I just want you to be happy again, Mam.' Maggie's voice was loaded with sadness. 'We can't bring Dad back and it would break his heart if he could see you locking yourself away like this.'

Her mother quickly turned away and began to busy herself with a pile of laundry. She longed to tell her daughter that the pain increased with every day that passed without Bill, but she knew that Maggie missed him too and didn't want to add to her hurt. Each night when she went to bed she prayed that she might die in her sleep so that they could be together again. But of course, she couldn't tell Maggie that either, so instead she said briskly, 'Haven't you got anything to do across the way then?'

Taking the hint, Maggie took Lucy's hand and walked towards the door. She knew of old that there would be no reasoning with her mother while she was in this mood and she *did* have a lot of sewing to do.

'I'll perhaps see you later then?'

Ellen's face softened as she nodded. 'Yes, perhaps you will. I'll maybe pop over to see how that wedding dress you're making is shaping up.'

Once outside in the cold September air, Maggie took a deep breath. It always upset her to see her father's chair so empty and she felt useless, for there was nothing that she could say or do to ease her mother's pain.

Quickly glancing up and down the road she hauled Lucy onto her hip and hurried across through the chilly mist that had as yet not lifted. When she reached the other side of the lane she found Mrs Massey talking to the milkman.

Lucy wriggled in her arms to be allowed down. Placing her gently on the pavement, Maggie watched her make a beeline for Dobbin, the old horse who pulled the milkcart.

'So how's yer mam doin' now then, love?' Mr Brown, the milkman, enquired kindly.

'Not so good,' Maggie admitted fretfully. 'She misses my dad something terrible.'

'Well, that's only to be expected,' he answered. 'They were like Derby and Joan, those pair – never very far away from each other. It's a crying shame from where I'm standing. But then, they reckon that the good allus go first.' As he spoke he leaned down to deposit a pint of milk onto Mrs Massey's clean doorstep, ignoring her frown of annoyance.

'Right then, I'd best get on wi' me round. This standin' about won't buy the baby a new bonnet, will it? Them as are waitin' fer their milk fer a cup o' tea will be cussin' me sommat rotten.' With a cheerful wink he set off with his crate down the row of terraced houses, whistling merrily.

Maggie smiled at Mrs Massey, then taking Lucy's tiny hand, she hauled her inside and soon she was busy at her old Singer sewing-machine again with the little girl playing at her feet.

*   *   *

Jo arrived that night to find Lizzie and Danny carefully cutting old newspapers into neat little squares that would then be threaded with string before being hung in the outside privy to be used as toilet paper. They immediately abandoned their task and ran to meet her. She was a regular visitor now, and much to Maggie's surprise, was wonderful with the children.

'How's about I read yer all a nice story then before you go to bed, eh?' Jo suggested as she threw her coat across the back of a chair.

Lizzie and Danny nodded eagerly, and soon they were engrossed in an Enid Blyton story. This was followed by hot cocoa and biscuits, which Danny devoured as if he hadn't eaten for a week.

'I really don't know where that child puts it. I'm sure he must have hollow legs,' Maggie grinned.

'Ain't nothin' much wrong wi' a child when they have a good appetite,' Jo replied. 'He's a growin' lad. Me brother is much the same. The greedy little bugger would eat us out of house an' home if I'd let him. But anyway – if you've finished, kids, I'll come an' tuck you up in bed. I might get to have a few minutes wi' yer mam then.'

Almost an hour later, when Jo and Maggie were comfortably settled at the side of the fire, a tap came to the back door.

'I wonder who that could be at this time of night?' Maggie remarked. It was almost nine o'clock and she wasn't expecting anyone. Hurrying to the door, she quickly drew back the black-out curtain and opened it to find her mother-in-law standing shamefaced on the doorstep. It was the first time she'd seen her since the night Sam left home, but she held the door wide, making the flames on the fire sputter and lick up the chimney.

'Come on in out of the cold,' she invited, and when the woman had done just that, she quickly closed the door behind her.

When Beryl Bright saw that Maggie had a visitor she flushed to the roots of her hair.

Rising rapidly, Jo flashed her a smile. 'Don't worry. I was just about to leave.'

'Oh no, please . . . not on my account,' Beryl stuttered.

'It's all right, really. I've got loads o' jobs to do at home,' Jo assured her as she dragged her coat on.

Once Maggie had seen her to the door and they'd said their goodbyes, she turned back to Beryl. The poor woman looked absolutely dreadful. She had lost a lot of weight and there were dark circles beneath her eyes that told of the sleepless nights she was experiencing.

'I'm sorry I didn't come sooner, love,' she muttered. 'It's unforgivable o' me to have left you to cope wi' the little ones all on yer own. But the thing is . . . I wasn't sure that I'd still be welcome after what I've done.' She hung her head.

Maggie led her towards the fire. 'Look, you sit yourself down and get warmed through, eh? And don't worry. You haven't done anything wrong from where I'm standing.'

'But I sheltered Sam when I knew he were shirkin' his responsibilities, even though I was so ashamed of him.'

Maggie shrugged. 'I dare say I would have done the same, if it had been my son.'

Beryl breathed a sigh of relief. 'Thanks for bein' so understandin', love. But how are you managin' all on yer own?'

'Actually, a lot better than I thought I would,' Maggie admitted. 'I've finished at the factory, but I've started to take in sewing jobs. It's long hours, but it's paying the bills and I get to be here for the children, which is worth a lot.'

Beryl's head wagged in admiration and agreement, as she slowly extracted a letter from the depths of her voluminous handbag.

'I er . . . I had this come today an' I thought yer should see it. It's from our Sam.' She watched the colour drain from Maggie's face before going on, 'I dare say he was too ashamed to write to you after what he's done.'

After passing the letter to Maggie she sat silently as the younger woman's eyes scanned the page. It was really more of a note than a letter and just said that he'd now finished his training and was about to be shipped out, though he had no idea where.

Maggie felt tears sting at the back of her eyes. He hadn't even bothered to let her know directly, which just went to show how little he thought of her and the children. As if reading her mind, Beryl reached across and squeezed her hand.

'Don't take it to heart, love. Yer know what Sam's like. He's my own flesh and blood, but he can be a thoughtless bugger at times. I've said it before an' I'll say it again: sometimes I wonder how two such different lads could have popped out o' me at the same time. I reckon all the good must have gone into our David an' left nothin' fer Sam, but all the same he's still mine an' I can't help but love him.'

'That's just as it should be,' Maggie said softly, thinking of her own children tucked upstairs fast asleep. 'Speaking of David, have you heard from him lately?'

'Not so much as a whisper fer about a month now. Last letter that came, he told me he was somewhere in France, God help him. But anyway, I ought to be going now. I'm glad that yer copin' so well. But should yer need anythin' I'm not far away, so don't hesitate to ask.'

'Thanks, I'll remember that.' Maggie trailed her to the door where they embraced.

'You take care now,' Beryl told her and then she slipped away into the cold night.

Unable to settle, Maggie went back to her sewing, and it was almost midnight before she finally climbed the stairs to bed. She'd just lifted the blankets when the sound of the air-raid siren pierced the air. For the briefest of moments she was rooted to the ground with fear. This time there was no one to help her. Even as she stood there, she heard the sound of doors opening as the street came to life and people ran to their shelters. Snatching up her dressing-gown, she yanked it on before sprinting across the landing and throwing the twins' bedroom door open. As she did so, the drone of the first aeroplanes overhead blocked out all the other noises. They were so low that she was sure they would take the roof off.

'Lizzie, Danny. Wake up!' The urgency in her voice sliced through the air like a knife. 'Come on! We have to get to the shelter. Put your dressing-gowns on and get downstairs as quickly as you can.' Racing back down the landing, she snatched Lucy from the cot at the side of her bed. By the time she got to the top of the stairs again the twins were emerging from their room, putting on their dressing-gowns and slippers, and yawning.

Forcing herself to stay calm, she ushered them in front of her. As they reached the bottom of the stairs, a huge explosion shook the house. Lizzie began to cry and shrank into Danny's side.

Running through the kitchen, Maggie battled with the bolts on the back door before finally managing to wrench it open. 'Into the shelter – *now*!'

She allowed herself to glance briefly up at the sky and was horrified by what she saw. It seemed to be full of planes. So many that they were blocking out the light of the moon. Searchlights swept back and forth, and even as she ushered her children towards the Anderson shelter, the night was filled with the sound of gunfire.

The short journey across the yard seemed to take forever, but at last she had manhandled the shelter door open and thrust them inside.

'Get into the bunks and snuggle down. You'll soon get warm again,' she told Lizzie reassuringly. The child was still softly sobbing and trembling with fear.

Once they'd all clambered into the bunks and the blankets were tucked around them, Maggie addressed Danny. 'I want you to be really brave now and look after Lizzie and Lucy for me while I run across the road to fetch your gran. As soon as we get back, I'll light the candles and make us all more comfortable.' Her teeth were chattering and Maggie had no idea if it was from the cold damp atmosphere, or fear. What she did know was that she had to get her mam to the safety of the shelter.

When Danny slowly nodded, she patted his hand. 'Good lad. I'll be back as soon as I can.' With that she slipped outside again, closing the door securely behind her.

Her mother's house was in darkness and so Maggie began to hammer on the door. 'Mam, Mam – wake up!'

Her cries were drowned out by the drone of the planes in the sky overhead, but still she continued to bang on the door until at last the bedroom window above her head was pushed open.

'Mam, there's a raid on. Get yourself down here and come over into the shelter with me an' the children,' she cried urgently.

Ellen slowly shook her head, which was covered in metal curlers. 'You get yourself back to them children. I'm stayin' put. If me time's come then I want to die in me own bed.'

'Mam, *please*!'

Ellen heard the catch in her daughter's voice, but still she called down, 'Go on, love. I'm fine where I am. Yer can stand there till the cows come home an' I won't change me mind so get back to them that need yer.' With that she banged the window shut again and Maggie could only wring her hands in frustration.

She stood there undecided for a few seconds but then raced back across the road. She had a feeling that it was going to be a very long night.

The children finally slipped into an exhausted sleep in the early hours of the morning. Maggie had no idea at all how long she had sat huddled there in the chair with a thin blanket wrapped around her. She just knew that it seemed to have been for a lifetime, and still there was no sign of the raid abating. Every now and again, as a bomb crashed nearby, the shelter seemed to shake and the sound of glass shattering was deafening. Occasionally a drop of moisture that clung to the damp metal roof would drip down onto her and she would brush it away. Maggie chewed on her lip as she thought of her mother all alone across the road. What if one of the bombs was to drop on her house? What would she find when she left the shelter? Would the houses in the Lane still be standing? Her eyes continuously went to the sleeping children. They were all so very precious to her. What if a bomb was to drop on *them*? Hotching further down into the chair, she began to pray once more.

After what seemed an eternity, the drone of the planes slowly receded and an unnatural silence settled around her. She longed to step outside to see what damage was done but until the all clear sounded she was too afraid to do so. Her eyes were gritty from lack of sleep as she kept her vigil over her children, but at last exhaustion took over and she fell into a shallow slumber.

Some time later, the sound of someone hammering on the tin door of the shelter brought her springing awake. Almost falling from the chair, Maggie winced with pain as her stiff limbs screamed a protest and then she was tugging it open and there was her mother. In a second the two women were locked in each other's arms.

'Eeh, love, yer gave me a rare fright, I don't mind tellin' yer',' Ellen sobbed. 'The all clear sounded ages ago, an' when there was no sign o' you or the children, me mind began to do overtime. Why didn't yer come out when it sounded?'

Maggie smiled sheepishly. 'I reckon I must have dropped off. Don't ask me how, 'cos the last I remember, the noise was enough to deafen you.'

Glancing across her mother's shoulder she was relieved to see that her home was still standing. As if reading her thoughts, Ellen shook her head sadly. 'They ain't been as lucky as us a few streets away. Some of the houses in Canal Street have been razed to the ground, some of 'em with people still inside 'em. Charity Cottages and Swan Road took a bashin' as well. The men are round there now, goin' through the rubble to see if they can find any survivors.'

Maggie shuddered at the thought. The air smelled of dust and soot, and for as far as she could see above the rooftops, plumes of smoke rose into the sky. Now instead of the drone of planes, the clamour of fire-engine bells hung on the air.

'Come on, let's get the children inside and put something warm inside them,' Ellen urged. 'Needless to say, they won't be going to school today.'

As the morning passed, word spread of the devastation the raid had caused. Many of the shops in Primrose Hill Street had suffered severe damage and the new Rex theatre was in ruins.

'It's ironic when you come to think about it, ain't it?' Ellen mused when the news reached them. 'They were goin' to be showing *Gone With the Wind* tomorrer.'

As yet, they had no idea how many people had died. Maggie felt as if she was living through a nightmare as they waited to hear, and all the time the sound of sirens racing from one fire to another filled the air.

Lizzie seemed to have shrunk overnight and clung to Danny who was putting a brave face on it. 'Don't worry,' he told her. 'It's all over an' done with now.'

Maggie nodded in agreement and smiled at him confidently, but deep inside she was thinking, How long for?

Another thought was growing in her mind, and no matter how she tried to push it away it wouldn't be ignored. This time they'd been lucky – but what if it happened again? And what if next time, something should happen to the children?

The only way for them to be really safe now was to let them leave with the next lot of evacuees. Just the thought of it brought hot tears stinging to her eyes. She looked across at them, drinking in every feature of their faces, and in that moment she knew that she really didn't have a choice.

Chapter Thirteen

During the week following the raid, sticky tape that looked like spiders' webs appeared across the windows in the street.

'What's that for?' Lizzie asked.

'It's to stop the glass from blowin' out if there's another raid,' Danny informed her solemnly.

Lizzie gazed back at him from eyes like saucers. Danny was so clever; he seemed to know everything. Fingering the little engraved identity disc that her mother insisted they wore around their necks, she asked, 'But they won't bomb us again, will they, Danny?'

He shrugged. 'Who knows? I heard Mr Massey tellin' a man in the street that he thinks it's far from over yet, so the chances are they *could* come again.'

At that moment a double-decker bus trundled past them and Lizzie fell silent as she thought on his words. This time she hoped that Danny was wrong. Until the bombings, the shelter had been like a playhouse to them, but now the thought of having to go inside it again filled her with dread.

In the warm little kitchen, Maggie read through the list in her hand. Gas masks, identity discs, two sets of underwear, spare shoes and socks/stockings, warm coat, sweater, handkerchiefs, pyjamas or a nightdress. Identity cards and ration books. Food for the journey, soap, toothbrush, toothpaste and a comb or a hairbrush and a towel.

When she had finished, she raised her eyes to her mother, and Ellen saw the raw pain reflected in them.

'Oh Mam, I don't think I can go through with this.'

'Yes, you can. It's for the best and well you know it. You'd never forgive yourself if you kept them here and anything happened to them. You'll still have Lucy, more's the pity. I just wish to God that she was old enough to go somewhere safe too, but they won't take pre-school children. Now try and look on the bright side – it won't be forever. No doubt they'll be home for Christmas. You've got to pull yourself together, me girl. They'll be back in a minute and you'll scare the pants off 'em if they come in an' catch you blartin'. You've to take 'em down to the doctor's after tea fer their medicals, ain't yer?'

'Yes, Mam – that's if you won't take them for me?'

A brief look of panic flitted across Ellen's features as she blurted out, 'No, no . . . it's best if you were to take 'em. I'll stay here an' mind Lucy for yer.'

Maggie blew her nose noisily. 'Well, I would appreciate you at least bein' here when I tell them they're goin' then.'

'All right, love,' Ellen told her reluctantly. 'Now come on, I'll stay an' help yer get their tea on, eh?'

Minutes later, the twins walked into the room.

'Danny's got a big piece of shrapnel he found on the way home,' Lizzie informed them excitedly.

'Has he now?' Ellen shuddered. 'And what good will that be to him?'

'There's a competition goin' on in the school playground,' Danny piped up. 'Up to now Simon Lees has got the biggest, but I reckon mine will beat it.'

Maggie shivered but managed to keep her smile in place. 'Well, if it's all the same to you, I'd rather you left it outside the back door until tomorrow. Oh, and by the way, I'll be nipping you both down to the doctor's surgery after tea.'

'What for?' Danny was frowning now as Maggie began to lay out the knives and forks so that she could avoid his eyes.

'Oh, the doctor's just going to check you both over and make sure that everything's all right.'

'Simon Lees had to go to the doctor's yesterday to be checked out because his mam's sendin' him away till the war's over.' Danny was a bright little spark for his age and was instantly suspicious. 'Are *you* goin' to send me an' Lizzie away, Mam?'

Panic gripped Maggie. This wasn't how she had intended to tell them about being evacuated. She glanced imploringly across at her mother but Ellen merely hung her head, unable to cope with the situation.

'Yes, you will be goin' away fer a time, Danny,' Maggie told him truthfully. 'You're goin' to be evacuated with lots of other children to stay somewhere safe until the war's over.'

'Where will they take us?' Danny was struggling to hold back the tears as his sister clung to his hand and began to cry softly.

'That I can't tell you,' his mother replied.

'So how will you know where we are then? How will we be able to keep in touch?'

'You'll both take a stamped addressed postcard with you an' when you get to where you're going you'll be able to send us your address. Needless to say, me an' yer gran will write to you every single week.'

Lizzie had listened in silence up till now, but suddenly

135

she launched herself at her mother and began to sob. 'Please don't send us away, Mam. I'll be so good, you won't even know I'm here, I promise.'

'Oh, sweetheart, I'm not sending you away because you've been bad.' Maggie's voice was full of anguish. 'I'm sending you both because I need to know that you're safe.'

'An' what about Lucy? Ain't she comin' too?' Danny asked.

Maggie shook her head. 'They won't let children as young as Lucy go,' she explained.

Danny thought about this for a moment. Then: 'But what happens if the bombs start again an' they get you an' Lucy?'

'I'll try very hard to make sure that that doesn't happen. But now come on. Get some tea down you. Gran has brought a pot of your favourite jam over. That will be a treat, won't it?'

Normally, Danny was like a bottomless pit when it came to food, but tonight his appetite seemed to have fled.

'Who'll get the coal in for you an' run yer errands if I ain't here?' he asked, halfway through the meal.

Maggie almost choked on the piece of bread in her mouth. It tasted like sawdust.

'I'll have to manage,' she muttered, and the rest of the meal was eaten in silence, save for the sound of Lizzie's hiccuping sobs.

Much later that night, as they huddled together in bed, Lizzie whispered, 'Where do you think they'll send us, Danny?'

Hearing the fear in his sister's voice, Danny replied bravely, 'I don't know. But we might be lucky an' get sent to the seaside somewhere. That would be good, wouldn't it? We've always wanted to see the sea.'

Lizzie shifted into a more comfortable position at the side of him. 'It would be if we were goin' with our mam. But what if they don't place us together?'

Danny's lip trembled in the darkness. 'We'll have to wait an' see. No one's said we're goin' to be split up, so why look at the worst?'

'I can't help it. Carol an' Tony weren't together when they went away last time.'

The children had been surprised earlier in the evening when they had found the majority of their classmates also waiting for medicals at the doctor's surgery.

'Well, if earlier on is anythin' to go by, almost the whole of our school is goin' to be comin' with us. In fact, I've got a feelin' there ain't goin' to be many kids left round here for a while, so at least we ain't the only ones bein' sent away. We'll try to make it into an adventure. An' look on the bright side. Mam said we might be home for Christmas.'

At that moment, Christmas seemed a very long way away, but not wishing to upset her brother or appear like a crybaby, Lizzie sniffed and smiled bravely.

'Yes, of course you're right. The time will soon pass, won't it?'

She felt his head nod on her shoulder and then they fell silent, each lost in their own thoughts.

Downstairs in the kitchen, Maggie sat at the kitchen table with her head bowed. She felt as if her whole world was falling apart. For years the children had been everything to her and the thought of being without them was terrifying, and yet the thought of what could happen to them if they stayed was even worse.

'Come on, mate. It ain't the end o' the world, yer know?' Jo smiled at her across the table and despite herself, Maggie grinned.

'You're just like my mam used to be at times, Jo. She always used to look on the bright side – till we lost me dad, that is.'

Jo's slight shoulders shrugged helplessly. She knew that Maggie was hurting but had no idea what she could do to help her.

'Will your lot be going too?' Maggie asked eventually.

Jo immediately shook her head. 'Not on your Nelly. Me dad's too tight to supply 'em with the things they'd need to take an' I couldn't kit them all out on what I get to keep o' my wages.'

'But . . . what about what you earn on your er . . . other job?' Maggie asked tentatively.

Jo dropped her eyes as a stain spread across her thin cheeks. 'I don't get to keep none o' that. The old man has it off me the minute I set foot through the door.'

'Oh Jo, why don't you stop him?'

'Huh! An' how am I supposed to do that?'

'I don't know. Report him to the Welfare or something.'

Jo laughed softly, a hollow laugh that made Maggie shudder. 'Yes, I'm really goin' to invite that lot to come hammerin' on the door, ain't I? They'd take the kids away like a flash – an' what do you think that would do to me mam?'

Maggie's heart went out to her. Jo had become a true friend over the last weeks and she wished with all her heart that there was something she could do to help her. She reached out to take her hand but Jo snatched it away.

'Look, Maggie. We agreed that we wouldn't talk about that any more, so let's just drop it, eh? Our Ruth is getting out of it, at least. She's goin' to be a Land Girl. To tell the truth, I envy her. I'd go with her like a shot but I can't leave me mam to that bullyin' bastard, can I?'

Maggie shook her head miserably. Poor Jo. She had even more worries than she herself did, and she was so young.

Crossing to a half-finished dress that was hanging over the ironing board, Jo lifted it and smiled. 'Let me guess. Yer makin' this fer Lizzie to take with her, ain't yer?'

When Maggie nodded, she laughed. 'I don't know how yer do it! Your daughter is goin' to be the best-dressed girl on the train.'

It was a pretty dress. Maggie had bought the material for a snip on the market but no one would have known it now that she had smocked the bodice. It was in a pretty shade of blue that exactly matched Lizzie's eyes. Folded across the back of a chair next to it was a smart hand-knitted jumper for Danny.

'I can't take the credit for that. My mam's been busy as well,' she said as Jo ran her hand across the soft wool. 'She's been knitting like mad. At this rate I won't be able to get all their stuff into their cases.'

Tears flooded her eyes as she looked at the two small brown suitcases that she had fetched down from the loft. She had scrubbed and polished them until the leather gleamed. Now all she had to do was pack them, which she knew would be the hardest job of all.

Still, she consoled herself, all across Coventry city other mothers were having to do exactly the same thing. The last raid had caused widespread panic and there looked set to be a mass exodus of children. She tried to imagine the streets without the sound of them playing but couldn't, no matter how hard she tried.

Sensing her friend's pain, Jo sought for words to

comfort her. 'It won't last forever,' was the best she could come up with. But inside she was thinking, Will it?

The final arrangements were made a few days later. The children would meet at the school and from there they would be taken by coach to the station. Lizzie and Danny were to be evacuated to North Wales.

'Is that by the sea?' Danny asked when Maggie told them.

'Is it very far away?' asked Lizzie.

Maggie answered their endless questions as best she could as she packed their freshly washed and ironed clothes into their little cases. They'd been issued with brown paper labels that would have their names and addresses written on. These would be tied with string to the lapels of their coats on the day they left.

'We don't need those,' Danny scoffed when he saw them. 'We ain't babies. We can remember our names and where we live.'

'I know you can, sweetheart, but everyone has to have them,' Maggie told him.

The next days passed in a blur. Maggie popped Lizzie's teddy bear into her case and Danny's marbles and his sketchpad and pencils into his, along with a black and white family photograph for each of them.

'You can put these on your bedside tables when you get where you're going so you don't forget us,' Maggie told them as brightly as she could.

'Huh! Do yer really think we'll need a photo to think of you an' Lucy?' Danny retorted in disgust.

Maggie noted that he hadn't included his father in the statement but wisely didn't comment. 'An' don't forget to fill this postcard in and post it as soon as you get there, so I'll have your address.'

Danny rolled his eyes heavenwards as Maggie snapped down the catches.

On a cold grey morning in early October, Maggie strapped Lucy into her pushchair and they set off for the school.

Grandma waved them off, her eyes overly bright and a set smile fixed to her lips. 'You both be good now, an' remember, you'll probably be home fer Christmas!' she shouted after them. Maggie had unsuccessfully tried to persuade her to come with them but she'd preferred to say her goodbyes at home.

Danny carried his own case, whilst Lizzie pushed Lucy along and Maggie carried hers.

The streets seemed to be full of mothers and fathers all trailing in the same direction, their children's brown-paper labels flapping in the buttonholes of their coats and blazers, their little gas masks slung across their shoulders.

The journey was made in silence, for Maggie could hardly trust herself to speak. When they finally reached the school playground they found a large bus waiting there and Miss Timpson ushering children aboard as she marked their names off on a large clipboard. She was going to accompany them to Wales. Most of the boys were smiling as they anticipated the adventure ahead, but many of the girls were crying and clinging to their mothers like leeches.

'Come along now. Keep it orderly, and be sure to hold on to your cases,' Miss Timpson commanded as she bustled yet another child up the steep steps into the bus. The queue slowly dwindled until at last it was time for Danny and Lizzie to say goodbye.

Maggie hugged them both, drinking in the smell of

their freshly washed hair. Danny was blinking bravely, determined not to make a cissy of himself in front of his school chums. Lizzie was openly sobbing.

'On you get then. We don't want to hold everyone up, do we?' A final kiss and Maggie was nudging them towards the steps. And then they were gone from sight for a moment until their faces reappeared, pressed up to the window.

They gazed down on their mother and Lucy below them, and just for a moment Danny's bravado slipped and his lip trembled as they waved at her frantically through the glass.

'Be good now . . . I love you,' she mouthed as the bus's engine sputtered into life. Danny saw the look of desperation in her eyes and his lip trembled even more. The bus began to move away and Maggie found herself running alongside it. The twins looked so little and vulnerable that she had to fight the urge to stop the bus and snatch them off there and then. Instead she waved and blew kisses until it disappeared through the school gates.

Suddenly, the playground was silent and deserted. Only then did she allow the tears to fall as she wondered if she would ever see her children again.

Picking up on her mother's distress, Lucy began to whimper.

'It's all right, sweetheart. Let's get you home out of the cold, eh?' Maggie turned the pushchair and with a heavy heart headed back to Swanshill.

Once back at her little terraced house, Maggie let herself in and gazed around the kitchen. The first thing she saw were the pyjamas the twins had worn the night before. It was cold, for in her haste to get the children ready, there had been no time to light the fire. Luckily,

Lucy, with her thumb jammed tight in her mouth, had dropped off into a doze, so she covered her with a blanket and then lifted the children's nightclothes and sniffed them. The scent of them still lingered, and once again tears coursed down her cheeks as she rocked to and fro.

'I hate this bloody war! I *hate* it,' she muttered to the empty room, but the only answer was the ticking of the clock, and loneliness, the like of which she had never known before, wrapped itself around her like a shroud.

Part Two

Chapter Fourteen

Once they reached the railway station, Lizzie shrank into Danny's side and gazed at the huge trains in bewilderment. The platform smelled of engine oil and smoke, and people were rushing about everywhere she looked. The grown-ups who were in charge of the children began to usher them all in different directions, until eventually only a small group was left in the care of Miss Timpson.

'Come along then, children,' she smiled encouragingly. 'Shall we get into the carriage?'

Danny had to almost haul Lizzie aboard but eventually they were seated and Miss Timpson began to lift their small cases on to the overhead luggage racks. She had barely finished when a loud whistle pierced the air. The sound of doors banging was deafening, and then the train suddenly lurched forward, causing Lizzie's eyes to nearly jump out of her head. The carriage smelled musty and that, combined with the movement of the train, made the blood drain from her pinched face.

'Danny, . . . I think I'm going to be sick.'

Seeing that her face had paled to the colour of bleached linen, the teacher quickly delved into her seemingly bottomless bag and produced a brown paper bag as if by magic.

'There you are, Lizzie. Use that if you have to. Once

147

we've got properly on the way I'll take you along to the toilet,' she told the child kindly, then she promptly produced a big tin of mints and asked, 'Anyone want one of these? They might help if any of you others are travel sick.'

Lizzie wasn't sure what travel sick meant. She had never gone further than a short tram-ride through Coventry before with her mother, but she guessed it must be this awful feeling she was experiencing now.

'Come on, Lizzie. Why don't you try one? I'm sure it will help.' As Miss Timpson offered her the sweet, Lizzie's small stomach rebelled, and bending her head she was violently sick into the bag.

'Oh dear.' Miss Timpson's black curls wagged from side to side. 'It looks like this isn't going to be the best of journeys for you, my love. We've hardly pulled out of the station yet. I tell you what, why don't we sing a song to try and take your mind off it, eh?'

She immediately launched into a version of 'Oh, we do like to be beside the seaside'. Slowly, a chorus of little voices joined in and Lizzie began to feel a bit better, until another train suddenly thundered past them on the opposite track. This, combined with the achey feeling in her tummy, was too much to bear and burying her face on Danny's shoulder, she began to wail loudly.

Halfway through the journey it started to rain, and her cries dwindled as she watched the fields flash by. Miss Timpson had come to sit beside her and she felt somehow comforted in the warmth of the kindly teacher's arms. A few of the other children, who'd been up since the early hours of the morning, dropped off to sleep, but Danny was determined not to miss a single thing. He'd never been on a train before, and although his heart was heavy at having to leave his mother, he was also excited at the prospect of seeing the sea.

'Are we almost there yet, Miss?' he asked at regular intervals.

'No, not yet, Danny,' Miss Timpson would patiently reply and then eventually she suggested, 'Why don't we have a game of I Spy? And then when we've done that, we'll unpack our lunches and eat.'

The group enthusiastically launched into the game, which passed a pleasant half-hour. During this time the train pulled into a station and lots of soldiers in smart khaki uniforms climbed aboard. They waved cheerfully at the children through the window of the carriage as they passed along the aisle that ran the whole length of the train. Some of them winked at Miss Timpson, and this, Danny was amused to note, had her blushing furiously. And then they were on their way again and Miss Timpson lifted their cases down one at a time for them and allowed them to take out the lunches that their mothers had packed for them.

By the time they'd finished eating, the fields had given way to mountains and marshland, and a bubble of excitement formed in Danny's stomach. They were almost there – he could feel it.

The journey seemed to be taking forever and he asked, 'Will we be there before it gets dark, Miss?'

The teacher smiled and nodded. 'Yes, I should think so, Danny.'

'Where will we be staying when we get there?'

'I don't know, dear,' she answered truthfully. 'There will be billeting officers waiting for us when we get to Pwllheli. They will decide who you're all going to stay with.'

'Won't *you* be staying with us?' His voice faltered for the first time.

'No, I'm afraid not. I shall be catching a train back

later this evening. But I shall make quite sure that all of you are all right first, of course.'

At that moment, another little girl, not much bigger than Lizzie, on the opposite side of the carriage, burst into noisy sobs.

'I don't want you to leave us, Miss Timpson,' she wailed. 'I want to come home with you to me mammy.'

Miss Timpson had appeared as her last link with her family, and the thought of the kindly teacher abandoning them in a strange place was the final straw.

The child's outburst silenced Danny's questions as Miss Timpson rushed across to soothe her, and for some time the carriage was silent as the other children looked on, each of them painfully reminded of the family they had left behind.

After what seemed like an eternity, the train finally began to slow and Miss Timpson told them, 'I think we're almost there, children.'

Everything was suddenly hustle and bustle as they all hurried to get into their coats and gather their meagre little pieces of luggage together. When the train came to a shuddering halt they all gazed fearfully out of the window. A large sign on the station wall said *PWLLHELI*.

Miss Timpson alighted first then handed them all down onto the platform one by one. As she was doing so, a small wizened-up woman with her grey hair pulled tightly into a bun on the back of her head descended on her.

'*Wythnos pawb*. (Greetings everybody.) And would this be the party of evacuees from Coventry then?'

Danny and Lizzie exchanged a glance at her strange accent, and for the first time since they had left home a glimmer of a smile flitted across Lizzie's face.

Turning to her, Miss Timpson nodded and held out

her hand, which the little woman pumped energetically up and down until Lizzie was sure she would shake it right off.

'Ah, it's glad I am that you've all arrived present and correct, so it is. Now follow me if you please, *blant* (children). I have a bus outside ready and waiting for all of youse.'

Another woman, who was as large as the first woman was small, came to stand beside her and they began to gabble away in a language that none of the children had ever heard before.

'They're talking in Welsh, which is their language,' Miss Timpson whispered as she saw the looks of bewilderment that flitted across the children's faces. 'But don't worry. They won't expect you to understand it.'

Danny was relieved to hear it, for he was sure he would never be able to understand a word they said. The unlikely pair herded them into a long row then began to shepherd them towards the station exit. It was a relief to find themselves in the fresh air after the smoky atmosphere of the tiny station and the musty smell of the carriage, and the children looked around with interest. Their first glimpse of Wales was disappointing, to say the least. Danny had always imagined the seaside to be a place of brilliant sunshine, but the lashing rain had slowed to a drizzle and the cobbled streets of stone cottages looked dull and uninviting. They had no time to study their surroundings, however, for the little woman was now leading them towards a bus with the precision of a Sergeant Major.

'Come along now, *blant*,' she commanded briskly. 'There is no time to be standing about now, there is still much to be done. I shall be taking you to the Sarn-Bach village hall where they will have tea ready for you, and then the people you will all be staying with will be coming to fetch you, so they will. Come along, come along now.'

The children obediently piled onto the rusty yellow bus and soon they were off yet again. The bus passed though the town and once the cottages were behind them they found themselves travelling through green fields, past mountains whose peaks were lost in the clouds. And then suddenly they rounded a bend and there it was, laid out before them. Their first glimpse of the sea. Many of the children cried out with delight, one of them Danny.

'Cor, just *look* at that.' He was unable to contain his excitement. 'It just goes on forever an' ever.'

Even Lizzie was wide-eyed with wonder now as she watched the frothy waves crashing onto the shore. She had seen pictures of the sea in books and at the cinema, but nothing could have prepared her for this vast expanse of water.

'I thought the sea were supposed to be blue!' one of the other boys exclaimed. 'That there sea is brown.'

'That's because the weather is inclement and it's late afternoon,' the little birdlike lady explained. 'As soon as the sun comes out tomorrow it will be blue, so it will, *bach*.'

The small boy had no idea what inclement meant and had no intention of showing his ignorance so he merely sniffed his disappointment as the bus trundled around yet another twist in the road. And then the sea was gone from sight as the vehicle began to wend its way up the side of a steep hill. Quaint stone cottages were dotted here and there on the hillside, with smoke spiralling into the drizzly sky from their chimneys. They passed fields full of sheep and cows that were huddled in the hedgerows as they tried to shelter from the rain, and a silence settled again as the children watched with interest.

Once the bus had reached the crest of the hill they saw a tiny village laid out in a valley below them, and even as they looked, lights began to appear in the windows of the dwellings, for the late afternoon had darkened. The old bus had laboured up the hill, but now on its downward journey it picked up speed and the village hurtled towards them. They passed a small harbour where fishing boats bobbed on the water beside a hotel that looked very grand.

'Very popular with tourists, that is,' they heard the little woman say; she had now introduced herself as Miss Williams. On they trundled, past grey cottages that all looked the same and a blacksmith's. Then they crossed a bridge and the bus drew to a halt in front of a small building with *Sarn-Bach Village Hall* painted above the door.

The hall was built in the same grey stone as the cottages, and lights burned brightly from its bare windows.

'Don't they have to use black-out curtains here?' Lizzie whispered to Danny.

He pursed his lips. 'Don't look like it,' he whispered back, but there was no time for further comment, for as soon as the driver turned off the bus engine, Miss Williams leaped to her feet and clapped her hands.

'Now then, children, I want you all to collect your luggage together and follow me in an orderly line.'

Once more the children found themselves lined up on the car park as Miss Williams ticked their names off on her clipboard. When she was content that they were all present and correct, she marched them towards the hall with Miss Timpson following behind. Just once, Lizzie dared to glance back at her and Miss Timpson gave her a reassuring wink. By now the children looked a sorry sight, not at all like the smart little individuals their mothers had waved off only that morning. Many of them had come from the heart of the city and were pale and thin. Added to this, they were all tired from the long journey, so they made a pitiful sight as they trooped into the hall with their gas masks slung across their shoulders, clutching their rucksacks and suitcases.

The babble of foreign-sounding voices died away as the children trailed into the hall. They blinked as their eyes adjusted to the harsh, bare electric light bulbs strung at intervals along the ceiling. A trestle table was set with dishes and cutlery.

'Leave your luggage by the door now,' Miss Williams ordered. 'And then kindly take a seat at the table, children.'

At the end of the table was a huge tureen that was emitting delicious odours, and as Danny and Lizzie sat down they realised that they were very hungry. Three women, who the children later learned came from the village, were rushing back and forth, filling glasses with milk and ladling a thick stew onto plates as the newcomers were seated.

After tasting hers, Lizzie whispered to Danny, 'What *is* this?' It was certainly like no other stew she had ever tasted.

Before Danny could answer her, one of the women, who had overheard her question, grinned at her and replied, 'Why, it's a good old Welsh rabbit stew, *bach*.'

Lizzie almost dropped her spoon as her stomach rebelled at the thought. She and Danny had once owned a pet rabbit called Flopsy, who had lived in a hutch in their back yard, and the thought of eating one of his cousins was more than she could cope with.

Danny felt much the same way but he was hungry so

he ate his anyway. As the meal continued, the sound of motors pulling onto the little gravel car park outside filtered into the hall.

Seeing Danny look towards the sound, Miss Timpson leaned over and whispered, 'That will be the people you are all going to be staying with.'

Newcomers began to filter into the room and the children watched them curiously. Men, women and children of all shapes and sizes were soon crowded down the opposite wall.

At last the meal was over and Miss Williams, who they were later to discover was the billeting officer for that area, again took up her clipboard and approached the different families, pointing to children on their table as she did so.

By now, Lizzie's eyes were almost starting out of her head and she was clinging on to Danny's hand beneath the table as if she would never let it go. They saw Miss Williams pointing to different children, and people shuffled forward to introduce themselves to their new charges until there was only them and another two children left seated at the table.

And then suddenly there was a large woman in a voluminous coat with a red-faced man at the side of her lumbering towards them. Lizzie knew instinctively that they were heading for her and Danny, and she choked back the sob of fear that was lodged in her throat.

'Right then, it's Lizziebright, is it now?' The woman was towering over her and holding out her hand, and Lizzie tentatively shook it as her head bobbed up and down in agreement.

'Good, good. This is Mr Evans, my husband. You'll be coming to stay with us for a while. You collect your things then now, *bach*, and come along with us.'

Lizzie was pleased to note that the woman looked kindly, so she plucked up the courage to ask, 'What about my brother Danny. Isn't he comin' too?'

'Ah, sadly we only have the room for one evacuee, *bach*. My husband is the local blacksmith and our cottage only has two bedrooms, so you'll get to have a room all to yourself, so you will. Won't that be nice now, eh?'

Lizzie stopped and shook her head as panic engulfed her. 'I ain't goin' without Danny,' she stated stubbornly.

Fearing a tantrum, the woman looked at her husband, who scratched his head, bemused.

'Now, now, don't take on, so. You'll get to see your brother every single day at the village school, so you will. And then of course you'll be able to play together after school too, when the weather permits. So come along now. Show the others what a big brave girl you are.'

Lizzie flashed Danny a look of pure desperation, but all he could do was shrug his shoulders as the large fair-haired woman led her away. He was so intent on watching the plight of his sister that when a man's voice addressed him in an English accent he almost jumped out of his skin.

Glancing up, he found himself looking into the frowning features of a giant. The man had jet-black hair, which was slicked away from his forehead. A large black eye-patch covered one eye, and below that Danny saw that one side of his face was horrifically disfigured with livid red scars. His brain immediately began to work overtime. Perhaps the man was a hero who'd been injured in the war? He had no time to think on it, for suddenly Lizzie's voice pierced through the babble of voices in the hall.

'Danny. *Dannnnnnnny!*'

His face crumpled as he saw the big woman dragging Lizzie towards the door. His sister was looking across her shoulder imploringly at him, as tears rained down her face, but he was powerless to do anything about it. Even as he watched, she disappeared through the door into the darkening evening, and his heart did a somersault in his chest.

The man standing beside him said not a single word until Danny finally dragged his eyes away from the door and looked back up at him.

'Danny Bright, is it?' the man snapped. 'I'm Mr Sinclair and you're coming to stay with me.'

Danny nodded fearfully. The man wasn't the nicest to look at and he didn't seem to be any too friendly either.

'Good. Get your bags and follow me then. I haven't got all night to waste.'

Too afraid not to obey, Danny scooted away from the table, almost overturning his chair in the process, and snatched up his small suitcase. He noticed that all the other villagers were chatting and standing about in little groups, but no one spoke to the man as he headed purposefully towards the door.

Once outside, he nodded towards a small car that was parked against the hall. 'Get in there.'

Obediently, Danny clambered in as the man slid into the driving seat. 'Wh . . . where are we going?' he dared to ask in a very small voice.

'To my home on the hillside, of course. You'll find it basic but comfortable. Let's just hope that you don't have to stay too long.' As he spoke he was reversing the car onto the road and for a time Danny was silent as he enjoyed his first ride in a motorcar. He kept watch for a sight of his sister as they drove through the village but there was no sign of her, so when they hit the unlit roads Danny leaned back in his seat and studied the man from the corner of his eye.

'Do you live very far away?' he ventured eventually.

The man sighed as if it was too much trouble to have to reply. 'Not really. You'll be well within walking distance of the village school.'

Danny gazed at the window but it was dark now and the drizzle had caused a mist, which made it difficult to see beyond the car headlights. Leaning his head against the back of the seat he rested his eyes and before he knew it, he had fallen fast asleep.

The man shaking his arm brought him springing awake. He blinked, and as the man climbed out of the car he scrambled out and snatched his suitcase before following him up a path that led to what looked like a large house, surrounded by trees nestling in the hillside.

There were no lights on in the windows, which looked like dark hungry eyes blinking out into the night. The place looked cold and uninviting, and when Danny involuntarily shuddered he wasn't sure if it was through cold or his circumstances. A picture of the cosy little kitchen back at home flashed into his mind and he had to blink away the tears.

He stood silently in the misty drizzle as the man took a key from his pocket and unlocked the front door. He went in ahead of Danny then motioned with his hand for the boy to follow him. As he snapped on the light, Danny blinked and looked around at what was to be his home for the unforeseeable future. He found himself in a spacious hallway with various doors leading off it. An ornately carved banister curved upwards to the first floor. He followed the man to a doorway right at the end of the long hall and found himself in what was obviously the kitchen. The room was reasonably clean and tidy, though there were no knick-knacks of any description to make it homely. A large scrubbed table took up the centre of the room, surrounded by four matching hard-backed chairs. A dresser in the same wood stood against the far wall, holding various plates, dishes and bowls. In a corner was a deep stone sink with a window above it, and on each side of the fireplace was an armchair. A large cooking range, in dire need of blackleading, stood apart from the sink but other than that, the room was bare. There were three more doors leading from the room, which the boy would later discover led to the stairs, the outside yard and a deep walk-in pantry.

A huge tabby cat was curled up fast asleep on one of the chairs, and when Mr Sinclair saw Danny looking at her, he told him, 'That's Hemily. I bought her to catch the mice round here but she tends to eat and sleep for most of the time. And that's Samson.' Even as he spoke, a huge black Labrador with a furiously wagging tail lumbered towards them. Danny would have loved to stroke him but was too afraid to in Mr Sinclair's presence, so he just stood mutely as the man bent to fondle the huge dog's ears.

The man seemed as ill-at-ease as Danny felt, and when he straightened he told him brusquely, 'You can hang your coat there. There are some hooks on the back of the door. Then, if you follow me, I'll show you where you'll be sleeping. I've no doubt you'll be tired after your journey.'

Clutching his case, Danny trod across the dull red tiled floor, followed the man back the way they had come and up the staircase. He glanced curiously at the doors leading off the hallway as they passed through it, but was too afraid to ask where they led. At the top of the stairs, the man marched along to a door which he pushed open. Danny stepped past him into a sizeable room that again was scantily furnished.

'You'll be sleeping here,' Mr Sinclair said. 'If you need to . . . you know, there's a chamber pot under the bed. You can empty it into the outside lavatory in the morning.'

He was about to close the door when Danny plucked up his courage and asked him, 'Sir, what am I to call you?'

The man paused. 'My name is Eric – Eric Sinclair. You can call me Mr Sinclair.'

'Yes, sir,' Danny replied, remembering his manners, and then the man closed the door and he was finally alone.

His eyes scanned the room. A large brass bed was placed against one wall with a big wardrobe one side of it and a chest of drawers the other. On the opposite wall, a pretty china jug and bowl stood on an elaborately carved washstand, which he noted was full of cold water. This, he guessed, was where he would be expected to wash in the morning.

On the other wall was a huge window with plain dark curtains drawn tightly across it. Crossing to it, Danny swished them aside and peered out into the night. Below him he could vaguely make out the shape of what appeared to be a number of outbuildings, but beyond that he couldn't see for the swirling mist.

Sighing, he hoisted his case onto the bed and began to unpack the contents into the chest of drawers. Then, pulling on his pyjamas, he snapped off the light and clambered into the big brass bed. He shuddered as he snuggled down into the cold sheets and instantly his thoughts turned to his sister. He hoped that she was having a better reception than he was, for without saying a word, Mr Sinclair had made it more than obvious that Danny wasn't welcome there. If that was the case, Danny wondered, why had he agreed to take him?

He started as the lonely sound of an owl hooting in a nearby tree pierced the unnatural silence. He could hear the wind whistling through the trees and snuggled further down the bed. And only then did he allow himself to be a little boy who was far away from home as he cried himself to sleep.

Chapter Fifteen

Down in the village, Lizzie was having a much more cheerful welcome to her new home. Mr and Mrs Evans showed her into a little stone cottage next to the village smithy that seemed to be bulging with ornaments on every available surface. Compared to the house that Danny was to stay in, the cottage was tiny, but it was also warm and welcoming. Mrs Evans, who was the mother of two grown-up sons, was looking forward to having a little girl to fuss over, and it showed.

Mr Evans looked on indulgently as she cooed over their new arrival.

'Now, *bach*,' she told the child in that curious, lilting voice that Lizzie was struggling to understand, 'if there's anything you need, anything at all, you just ask me or Mr Evans now.'

Lizzie, whose eyes were red-rimmed from crying, nodded as she looked around the bright little room. Everything shone like a new pin and it was warm and cosy, with a great fire roaring up the chimney.

'Come along, *cariad*. I'll show you to your room. Give me that case and let me carry it for you. And Father, while we're gone, you put the kettle on now.'

Like a child with a new toy, she took Lizzie's hand and led her upstairs. When she threw open the bedroom door where Lizzie was to be staying, the little girl's eyes opened wide with amazement. A little bed covered in a pretty pink satin bedspread stood against one wall, and bright flowered curtains hung at the window which, Lizzie was later to discover, overlooked the village green and the duckpond. The gaily-painted walls were covered in pictures of fairies, and on the windowseat sat dolls and teddy bears of various shapes and sizes. A soft rug covered the shining linoleum on the floor, and the huge wooden wardrobe and matching chest of drawers had been polished until Lizzie could see her face in them. Even as Lizzie gazed around her, Mrs Evans was unpacking her case, keeping up a continuous stream of cheerful chatter as she did so.

'Have you ever been to the seaside before then, *bach*?'

Lizzie had no idea why Mrs Evans kept calling her *bach* and *carry* something. She could only surmise from the way it was said that it was some form of endearment. She shook her head, setting her fair curls dancing, and the big woman's heart melted with sympathy for the child. It must be hard for her to travel so far away from her mother at such a young age. And then to be parted from her brother only added insult to injury.

At the thought of the boy, a frown flitted across the woman's face. God help the poor little mite, being sent off to that dreadful man up in the hills. None of the villagers liked him, from what she could make of it, and was it any wonder? In the years since he'd moved there he had never shown the slightest inclination to become one of the community. Indeed, he was bordering on becoming a recluse, venturing down into the village only once a week to the post office and to buy groceries. He had snubbed everyone's efforts to include him in village life, and the locals had long since given up trying, herself included, though that didn't stop him from being something of a mystery. Miss Tibbs, who ran the village post office, had once confided to her that each week he posted off a huge envelope to an address in London, and this had added to his air of mystery. Who could he be writing to? And why did he never have any visitors?

Despite herself, she found him intriguing. Had it not been for the terrible scarring to his face, he could have been a handsome man, if not the friendliest person in the world. She recalled the night they'd all been summoned to the village hall to discuss the expected evacuees, and the terrible fight Miss Williams had waged with him to get him to agree to take one.

'You have no choice in the matter,' she had informed him coldly in that lisping Welsh voice of hers, and he had stormed out of the building with murder in his eyes.

'Anyone would think we were asking him to take Jack the Ripper into his home instead of an innocent child,' Miss Williams had sniffed, incensed, causing a murmur of amusement to ripple through the rest of those present.

Her thoughts were pulled back to the present when she came to a stamped addressed postcard tucked into the bottom of Lizzie's bag. 'Well, look at that now, *bach*. Your mammy must love you very much. We'll make sure that we put your address down and post this back to her first thing tomorrow, shall we?'

The mention of her mother was too much for Lizzie, and suddenly the tears that she'd held back for the last few minutes spurted from her eyes again. With an agility that was surprising in a woman of her size, Mrs Evans sprinted across the room and snatched her to her ample bosom.

'There, there now, *bach*,' she soothed. 'You'll be seeing your mammy again soon enough, never you fear.'

It was obvious that the child was loved and cared for, from the pretty clothes that she had taken out of her case. The little dresses had all been handmade and folded with care. Blodwyn Evans's sympathy extended to the mother, who must be missing the girl as much as she was missing her. And so there they stood until the child had cried herself out.

'That's better now.' The woman gently dried the wet cheeks and led her back towards the door. 'Come away down now. From what I saw at the village hall you'd hardly eaten enough to keep a sparrow alive. And you're so thin and pale. Some good country fresh air will soon put roses in your cheeks. Let's get some supper inside you, eh? Then I'm sure you'll start to feel better.'

Once back in the warmth of the kitchen the woman bustled about getting some supper ready for Lizzie. Only a matter of minutes later, she placed two lightly boiled eggs and some bread and butter that she had cut into soldiers in front of her, and Lizzie's mouth gaped open in pleasant surprise.

'Hard to get, were they, back at home?' Mrs Evans chuckled. 'Well, don't forget you're in the country now, and eggs are ten a penny here. Now come on, get them down you, *bach.*'

Lizzie's appetite suddenly returned and in record time she had cleared her plate, much to the delight of the kindly woman. 'That's better,' she crooned as she poured some thick creamy milk from a jug into a glass. 'Now, try that. That will soon put some flesh on your bones.'

Lizzie sipped at it then quickly drained the glass. She had never tasted such wonderful milk in her whole life.

'It's buttermilk,' Mrs Evans explained and the child finally offered her a weak smile. Perhaps it wasn't going to be so bad living here after all.

From his place behind the newspaper, Mr Evans frowned. His wife was clearly taken with the child. He just hoped that she would cope with the loss when young Lizzie returned to her family. Blodwyn had spent days getting the little bedroom ready for her evacuee, and many tears had been shed in the process as he had carried down from the loft under the eaves all the things that had once belonged to the little daughter whom they had lost at the age of six. Oh, they had been blessed, and had then gone on to have two fine sons, but even so he knew that his wife had never got over the loss of their little Megan.

Lowering his head he turned his attention to his paper as the painful memories flooded back.

A pale grey light flooding through the gap in the curtains woke Danny the next morning. He yawned and stretched, then when he remembered where he was, a frown settled across his face. He was just wondering if he should get up or stay where he was when the smell of bacon floated tantalisingly up the stairs to him. His stomach groaned, so hastily throwing back the bedclothes he washed and pulled on his clothes.

Crossing to the door, he cautiously opened it, and after sticking his head out, glanced up and down the landing. It was deserted, so making his way to the top of the stairs, he stared down into the hallway below. That too was deserted, but here the smell of bacon cooking was much stronger, and he allowed his stomach to rule his head and descended the stairs.

'Your breakfast is ready, boy,' a deep voice boomed as he turned into the hallway. Danny bravely walked towards the kitchen door, which was slightly ajar.

He was surprised to see Mr Sinclair standing at the

range expertly flipping bacon over in a large pan. He'd assumed the night before, when Mr Sinclair had collected him from the village hall, that Mrs Sinclair must have been unable to come, but still there was no sign of her when he peered around the room.

'Sit yourself down at the table and have this while it's hot,' Mr Sinclair ordered, scowling as he looked towards the child.

Danny, suddenly remembering that he hadn't combed his hair, quickly licked his fingers and tried to flatten his unruly curls. Just for a second he thought he saw a flicker of amusement flit across Mr Sinclair's face, but when he blinked and looked again, the man's expression was as straight as ever. In the harsh light of day, he saw that one side of the man's face was even more disfigured than he'd realised, and he had to try his best to stop himself from staring at him. As he seated himself sedately at the table, Samson rose from his place in front of the fire and ambled across to him. Danny risked giving him a very quick stroke before folding his hands neatly in his lap.

If up to now his host and his accommodation had proved to be somewhat of a disappointment, his breakfast certainly wasn't. Mr Sinclair piled his plate with rashers of crispy bacon and fluffy scrambled eggs that made Danny's mouth water. This was washed down with copious amounts of freshly brewed tea and finished off with slices of toast dripping in butter.

When he had finished Danny leaned back in his chair and smiled appreciatively. 'That was delicious, Mr Sinclair. Thank you very much.'

His host looked vaguely embarrassed as he snatched up the child's empty plate and carried it to the sink. An uncomfortable silence settled on the room until Danny eventually asked, 'Is there anythin' that you'd like me to do?'

Mr Sinclair shook his head. 'No, and seeing as it's Saturday you might as well go out and amuse yourself as best you can. Be sure to be back in for your dinner, though.'

'What if I er . . . get lost?' Danny questioned nervously.

'Just ask for *Tremarfon* – that's the name of the house. The villagers all know where I live. You can't get lost though, if you keep to the road. It will take you straight down to the village and back again.'

Danny slid from his chair and edged towards the door, afraid that the man might suddenly change his mind and decide to make him stay in. Lizzie was somewhere down in the village and he was desperate to find out how she was. He cast a regretful glance at the dog, who was watching him expectantly. He would have liked to take him for a walk, but was too afraid to ask Mr Sinclair if he was allowed to.

'I'll see you at dinnertime then?' the little boy said timidly. A curt nod was the only response. As he stepped through the door, the view that met him took his breath away. As he'd thought, the house was surrounded by trees that dropped down to the village, but above the treetops was a stunning view of the sea. He hesitated, longing to make his way down to the strip of beach he could see shining in the sun. But then he turned towards the village, passing a huge outbuilding as he went. There would be time to explore when he had found out where Lizzie was and made sure that she was all right.

He could see the village nestling in the valley below him as he followed the road that wound its way down the hill. Unlike yesterday, it looked set to be a fine day and he stared about him with interest. There were other houses and cottages set into the hillside, and it was as he was passing one that a small head suddenly popped up over a hedge.

'Y'awight then, mate?' a cheerful little voice piped up. The next second, a wooden gate flew open and a boy about the same age as himself appeared. He was dressed in short grey trousers and a blazer that had long since seen better days. His socks had slipped down to around his ankles and his shoes were badly scuffed, but his smile was as bright as the sunshine and almost as bright as the shock of ginger-red hair that sprouted in unruly tufts from his head.

'You one o' the new kids what arrived yesterday then, are yer?' he asked cheekily, in a broad cockney accent.

'Yes. My name's Danny Bright and I'm staying up at *Tremarfon* with Mr Sinclair.'

'Cor blimey! Rather you than me, mate,' the boy declared. 'That bloke gives me the shivers wiv his eye-patch an' his scars.'

'He's all right actually,' Danny told him, though he had no idea why he was defending the man.

'Goin' down into the village, are yer?' the boy asked.

When Danny nodded, he fell into step beside him. 'They call me Soho Gus,' he introduced himself. 'I've been 'ere fer a couple o' months now. I'm stayin' wiv the Thomas family at *Derwen Deg* back there. They're all right an' all, though the old woman 'as got a gob on 'er like a parish oven when she lets rip. It's a wonder me old gel don't 'ear 'er back in the East End when she starts. *Derwen Deg* is a farm, see, so that's 'ow I know your Mr Sinclair. He comes down every mornin' fer his milk.'

Danny found himself really smiling for the first time since he'd left home, and hoped that he had found a friend. He was about to answer when something in the top pocket of the boy's blazer caught his eye. He could have sworn he'd seen a movement, but thought he must have imagined it. He stared again, and sure enough, seconds later a small black nose appeared and he gasped in amazement. Following his eyes, Soho Gus laughed.

'Meet Albert, me mate,' and reaching into his pocket, he brought out a large white rat whose whiskers twitched and shone in the sun.

Danny could hardly believe what he was seeing and was rendered temporarily speechless.

'I brought 'im wiv me. After all, I could 'ardly leave 'im at 'ome an' expect the old gel to look after 'im, could I?' Gus chuckled. 'Mrs Thomas ain't too keen, to tell the truth, but it's like I told 'er – me an' Albert come as a pair.'

He held the rat out to Danny, and after he had dutifully stroked him, Gus popped him back into his pocket.

'So what yer goin' down into the village for then?'

'I'm hoping to find my twin sister. She arrived yesterday with me but we were split up. I think the lady that took her said that her husband was the village blacksmith?'

'Ah, she'll be at *Ty-Du* wiv the Evanses then. I know where it is. I'll take yer there, if yer like.'

Danny nodded eagerly. 'Oh, yes, please. Lizzie was really upset last night and I just want to make sure that she's all right.'

Gus wrinkled his nose in disgust. 'I can't say as I like girls,' he admitted. 'But then if she's yer twin, I suppose it's awight. Come on, we'll be there in a jiffy.'

Danny stayed close to his side as they made their way into the village, looking this way and that as he went. It looked much prettier in the sunshine, though after living in a city, Danny was shocked at how small it was. There was a little village shop that seemed to sell everything from pots and pans to groceries, and next to that was a tiny post office. Slightly further on was what Danny rightly assumed was the village school. It had painted railings all around it and a small concrete playground where the children were allowed to play outside when it was fine. Next to that was the village church, a picture postcard affair with beautiful stained-glass windows that sparkled in the sunlight, surrounded by a beautifully kept churchyard.

Turning a corner, Soho Gus pointed beyond a village green that was surrounded by cottages. 'That's the smithy. Yer should find yer sister in that cottage stood next to it. Old man Evans is awight. He let me 'ave a go wiv 'is bellows one day when 'e were shoein' a horse.'

Danny was suddenly nervous as he slewed to a stop. What if the people who had taken Lizzie in wouldn't let him see her?

Sensing his new friend's indecision, Soho Gus nudged him sharply in the ribs with his bony elbow. 'Well, go on then, man. What yer waitin' for? She ain't gonna bite yer 'ead off, yer know.'

'Will yer wait for me?' Danny asked.

Gus nodded vigorously. 'Course I will, mate. I'll take Albert to wait over by the duckpond.' He strolled away as Danny tentatively approached the cottage door. He could hear banging and hammering coming from the smithy next door and wiped his suddenly sweaty hands down his trousers before knocking.

Almost immediately, he heard someone approaching, and the next second the door swung open and he was gazing into the face of the big woman he had seen at the village hall the night before.

'I . . . I've come to see me sister,' he stuttered as hot colour burned into his cheeks.

The woman's face broke into a friendly smile. 'Ah, so I see, *bach*. Come away in now. It's right glad she'll be to see you, so she will.'

He stepped past her into a room that was neat and tidy and very homely. Nothing at all like the house where he was staying. The ceilings were low and beamed, and everywhere he looked were brasses, polished until they shone like mirrors.

The woman crossed to a door and shouted up the stairs, 'Come down now, Lizziebright, *bach*. You have a visitor.'

He heard the sound of footsteps overhead and someone clatter down the stairs, and then Lizzie was launching herself across the kitchen at him as if she hadn't seen him for months.

Her kindly host felt a stab of envy sharp as a knife. It was more than obvious where the small girl's affections lay. It was the first time she had seen her really smile since she arrived. She clearly adored her family, which forced Blodwyn to think on her husband's warning. *'Don't go getting too attached to the child now,* bach. *Remember she has a family that she will be returning to one day, and that's just as it should be.'*

Fixing a cheery smile to her face, the woman told Danny, 'It's good to see you, Dannybright. Will you be staying awhile? You're more than welcome to.'

Disentangling Lizzie's thin arms from his waist, Danny glanced wistfully towards the sun that was streaming through the cottage window, casting a pool of golden light onto the carpet.

'I was wondering if perhaps Lizzie and I could go out to play for a while? I made a new friend on my way here who knows his way about, so I promise we wouldn't get lost.'

'Oh, and who would that be then?' Blodwyn smiled.

'Soho Gus. He lives up the hill near me.'

'Ah, I think I know the laddie you're talking of. Doesn't he have a pet mouse that he carries about with him?'

'It's a rat actually,' Danny informed her gleefully. 'His name is Albert and Soho Gus carries him everywhere in his pocket. He said he'd take Lizzie an' me down to the beach if you'd allow it.'

That was a pleasure that Blodwyn herself had been hoping to share with Lizzie later in the afternoon, but seeing the expectant look in the children's eyes she didn't have the heart to refuse them.

'Very well then,' she said. 'But only for a couple of hours, mind. And don't get going into the sea. There are currents out there that could sweep you away in no time.'

'We won't,' the twins chorused, and Lizzie ran to fetch her shoes as Blodwyn turned her attention to Danny.

'So, how is your stay with Mr Sinclair going then, *bach*?'

Danny shrugged. 'All right, I suppose. Mr Sinclair is very quiet but he cooked me a lovely breakfast.'

'That's good then.' The conversation was stopped from going any further when Lizzie shot back to stand next to Danny's side.

'You be sure to have her back for dinner now, laddie. You can stay for some yourself if you've a mind to.'

Danny shook his head. 'Thank you, Mrs Evans, but I'd best get back to Mr Sinclair's. I promised I'd be home for dinner.'

Blodwyn nodded understandingly. 'That's fine, *bach*. I have no wish to get you into trouble on your very first day here. Now off you go, the pair of you, and have a good time. Oh . . . and Lizziebright, pop this postcard to your mother in the postbox as you pass, *bach*.'

Lizzie took the proffered card and they walked sedately to the door, but the second they were outside they broke into a run and hurried across to Soho Gus, who was lying on the deep green grass at the side of the duckpond.

He leaned up onto his elbow, almost squashing Albert in the process as he heard them approach, and then the strangest thing happened. Less than an hour ago, he had confided in Danny that he didn't like girls, but the second he laid eyes on Lizzie, who was looking very pretty with her blond hair tied up in a red ribbon, Gus blushed to the roots of his hair.

'This is me sister, Lizzie,' Danny informed him, as Lizzie glanced shyly at his new friend.

Gus was totally tongue-tied, and for now all he could do was nod. Lizzie was like no other girl he'd ever set eyes on before. The girls back in the East End where he had come from tended to be skinny, grubby little things, and the Welsh girls he'd met since coming here just ignored him. But Lizzie . . . She was beautiful in Gus's eyes and he was sure that she must be a princess in disguise. Thankfully she was so intent on studying Albert that she didn't notice his reaction to her, and by the time she turned to say hello he had managed to compose himself.

'Hello, Soho Gus,' she smiled, and even the sound of her voice was wonderful to him.

''Ow'd'ya do,' he managed to mutter as his heart fluttered in his small chest. Hauling himself to his feet he began to lead the twins through the village, trying his best to pull his socks up and tidy himself as best he could as he went.

'There's loads to see,' he informed them, hoping that Lizzie would be impressed. 'There's the sea an' the beach. Oh, an' there's some crackin' caves an' all. Then on a clear day yer can see Snowdon from 'ere. But be careful if yer go fer a jaunt over the fields though. There's disused mineshafts everywhere, an' should yer fall down one o' them, you'd be a bleedin' gonner.'

The twins' eyes stretched wide when he swore, but as they were soon to discover, swearing came as naturally to Gus as saying their prayers each night did to them.

'So, do yer still wanna see the beach first then?' he asked, and when they nodded excitedly he grinned and led them on, pointing out the shiny red postbox on the way. Lizzie kissed her card before she posted it. Danny on the other hand was acutely aware of Gus watching him so he popped his in with the minimum of fuss.

On the way they told each other of the places they were staying.

'Mrs Evans seems nice,' Danny remarked as they strolled along.

'She is – and so is Mr Evans,' Lizzie said. 'But they call me Lizziebright an' sometimes they gabble away in a language that I can't understand. But what about you, Danny? That horrible man who came for you frightens me. He's all scarred and ugly, and he didn't seem very kind either.'

'He's all right really,' Danny told her. 'A bit on the quiet side, but his cat an' dog are lovely. The cat is called Hemily and the dog's called Samson. He's a Labrador an' he's enormous. I was goin' to ask Mr Sinclair if I could bring him out with me for a walk but I daren't just yet.'

'Perhaps he'll let you when he gets to know you a bit better?' Lizzie suggested wisely. Danny nodded in agreement but then the conversation dried up as they reached the top of a cliff and the sea came into sight.

Their first walk on the beach was something that Lizzie and Danny would never forget. Lizzie squealed with delight at the feel of the soft sand between her toes, and despite Mrs Evans's warning, she couldn't resist a paddle in the sea. Throwing her shoes and socks into a heap she splashed in the frothy waves that were crashing onto the shore with gay abandon. For a while, Danny and Gus stood back and watched her, but her laughter was so infectious that soon their shoes and socks had joined hers and they ran into the shallows. They searched for shells on the beach and then spent a pleasant hour looking for crabs in the little rock pools that the sea had left behind.

Eventually, Gus told them, 'I reckon we ought to be 'eading back now. We've gorra bloody good way to go an' we don't wanna get into trouble, do we?'

Once they'd brushed the sand from their feet and put their shoes and socks back on, they began the climb up the side of the cliff that would lead them to the village. As they neared the blacksmith's, Lizzie became quiet again and asked fretfully, 'You *will* come to see me again, won't you, Danny?'

'Course I will,' he assured her, sad that the morning had come to an end. At Mrs Evans's door he gave her a very brief hug, conscious of the fact that Gus was watching his every move.

'See yer later,' he said, and as he moved away he saw fresh tears well in her eyes.

Lizzie watched until Danny and Gus were gone from sight then slowly turned and tapped at the door of *Ty-Du*. Mrs Evans had told her to walk straight in, since this was her home for the time being, but somehow she didn't feel that she could. It *wasn't* her home, no matter how cosy it was. Home was with her mother in Coventry.

Chapter Sixteen

As Maggie lifted an envelope from the doormat, she frowned. Who would be writing to her?

'What's that letter you've got there?' her mother asked from the doorway.

Maggie shrugged, then withdrew a crumpled sheet of paper. As she read down the page, the colour drained from her cheeks and her hand flew to her throat.

'Lord love us. Whatever's happened now?' Ellen asked apprehensively.

'It's from David,' Maggie managed to tell her. 'He's stationed in France and it sounds like the troops there are living in hell. The poor souls are dropping like flies, according to this. But there's worse than that. It seems that Sam is out there too.'

'Good God.' Ellen could understand Maggie's distress. There was no love lost at all between the two brothers. It seemed ironic that, after avoiding each other at home for years, they now found themselves fighting side-by-side on a bloody battlefield.

'Ah well, happen this might be just what's needed to bring them closer,' she said optimistically.

Maggie looked at her as if she had taken leave of her senses. Both of them knew it would take a lot more than that. Maggie had no time to dwell on it though, for just then Lucy tottered up to her with her potty clutched in her tiny hand.

'Wee-wee, Mammy.'

Maggie had been trying to potty train her for weeks, with very little success up to now. Lucy tended to tell her she needed the toilet when the deed had already been done. Not that Maggie minded. Now that the twins were gone, Lucy was all she had left and Maggie worshipped the very ground she walked on.

'All right, darling. Who's Mammy's good girl then?'

Lucy flashed her a toothy grin and for now Maggie tried not to think of anything else but this precious child in front of her.

As David crawled through a sea of stinking mud he tried to keep a picture of Maggie and Lucy in the forefront of his mind. His stomach was growling with hunger and he felt sick and cold. Of course, he knew that he was one of the lucky ones. Only yesterday, young Jimmy Harris had died in his arms on the battlefield. Jimmy had been just nineteen years old and the joker of the bunch. David knew that he would never forget the sight of the young man dying for as long as he lived. He had promised Jimmy that when he got home, he would go and see his parents for him. *If* he got home, that was. All around him, soldiers were dying in their hundreds, yet still they were told to push on. It was no easy task, loaded down as they were with their gas masks, and rifles slung across their aching shoulders. Earlier in the day he had finished the last of the water in the bottle that was also slung across his shoulder, and right now he would have given anything for a drink. It didn't help to know that somewhere on this very same field was his twin brother, Sam. When they had first run into each other,

David had offered his hand and told Sam that it was time to put the past aside. But Sam had slapped it away and David knew then that he had more of an enemy in his own brother than any German he might be forced to confront on the battlefield. It was a chilling thought. The smell of diarrhoea and death was putrid in his nostrils and he kept his lips clenched tight shut.

Above him, the sky lit up as bright as day as another barrage of gunfire rattled into the night. Just then, he felt himself come up against something that smelled worse than anything he had ever smelled in his life, and he realised with a shudder that it was a corpse. Swallowing the vomit that rose in his throat, he wriggled his way around it in the cloying mud. Poor bastard must have been lying there for ages to stink like that, he thought. His mind slipped back to his training days. He had thought *they* were hard, but nothing could have prepared him for this. The nightmare had begun when they were shipped out, packed like sardines in a troopship. His biggest fear then had been that he would die on the battlefield. Sometimes now he thought it would be a relief. A bullet whistled past his head and slightly in front of him he heard the grunt of yet another comrade as they dropped to the ground. Many of his comrades' bodies had never been recovered, for the mud had sucked them down. He shuddered as he thought of them lying there and prayed that if he should die he would at least be buried in a proper coffin in his homeland.

Up ahead he could vaguely see the edge of the foxhole that the soldiers had dug. If he could only get to that, he could rest for a while at least. With the last of his strength he dragged himself on as a picture of Maggie and Lucy floated before his eyes.

*   *   *

Maggie was bathing Lucy in front of the fire when the dreaded sound of the air-raid siren filled the air. Snatching the child from the tin bath she wrapped her in a towel and sprinted out of the house with her in her arms. In her haste, she almost collided with Mrs Massey in the shared yard, and the older woman steadied her before gently urging her towards the shelter.

'I reckon I'll come into your shelter wi' you, love, if yer don't mind?' she panted. 'The old man's on fire-watch an' I don't much fancy sittin' in our shelter on me own. Would yer mind?'

'Not at all,' Maggie told her, pushing Lucy into her arms. 'Will you take her in, Mrs Massey, while I go an' try to persuade me mam to join us?'

'Course I will, love.' With her head bent, Mrs Massey did a dash to the door of the shelter, which she wrenched open. 'Don't think much o' yer chances of persuading her out o' her house though,' she shouted above the wail of the siren as Maggie disappeared off down the entry.

Minutes later, she was back. Mrs Massey had already lit the candles, put Lucy into her vest and nightdress, and tucked her into the bunk with her teddy. One glance at Maggie's crestfallen face told her that she had been right.

'Havin' none of it then, is she?' she whispered into the flickering light.

Maggie shook her head regretfully before heading for the door again.

'Where you off to *now*?' Mrs Massey asked in exasperation.

'To make us a flask of tea,' Maggie flung back. 'If these bloody Germans are goin' to keep us holed up in here all night again then I want me cuppa at least.'

A glimmer of a smile played around Mrs Massey's

lips as she watched the young woman's retreating figure. Since first taking the job in the factory, Maggie had changed almost beyond recognition. She had grown up and become stronger, and since Sam had left and the twins had been evacuated, she'd become stronger still. Mrs Massey admired her; it hadn't been easy for the girl, yet here she was caring for her child and sewing every hour that God sent to make a living. Maggie had somehow come out of her shell and shown that she had guts.

The raid went on well into the early hours of the morning as the women cowered in the shelter listening to the devastation going on all around them. Every now and again, they would hear a loud whistle as a bomb plummeted towards them, and then the walls of the shelter would shake as it found its target.

'They sound a bit too close fer comfort,' Mrs Massey breathed as she made the sign of the cross on her chest. The sound of shattering glass drowned out anything else she might have said, and the smell of burning grew over-powering. Only the fear of what she might see stopped Maggie from throwing open the shelter door, for she was beginning to feel claustrophobic. And so they sat on in silence, listening to the boom of the guns and the drone of the planes overhead, broken only by the clanging bells of the fire engines as they raced from fire to fire. More than once the sound of a wall crashing down reached them too and they glanced at each other fearfully in the flickering light of the candle.

'Do yer reckon the houses are still goin' to be standin' if we get out of here?' Mrs Massey whispered.

Maggie noticed that the older woman had said 'if' and reached across the enclosed space to gently squeeze her hand. She would have liked to offer words of reassurance, but truthfully as the night wore on she was beginning to fear that they would never leave the shelter alive.

When at last the all clear sounded, Maggie offered up a silent prayer of thanks as she pushed the shelter door open. The first thing she saw was that her home was still there. The second was Mr Massey, who had spent a long night on fire-watch, just emerging from the entry. The tiny man looked unbelievably weary and his shoulders were stooped as if they had the weight of the world on them. He was so filthy that only the whites of his eyes showed in his soot-black face, but still he asked, 'Are yer all right then, love?'

Maggie nodded as tears sprang to her eyes. 'Mrs Massey has been in here all night with me,' she told him as he headed for his back door. He stopped and turned back to her.

'Thanks, love. I'm afraid some o' yer windows have blown in – look.' He pointed to the glass that was strewn across the yard. Maggie hadn't noticed it before but now fear flashed into her eyes.

'What about the houses on the other side of the road?'

He rightly guessed that she was afraid for her mother. 'Some o' them were hit,' he said, 'but don't worry. It was the ones farther down that took it. Yer mam's is all right.'

Seeing that the elderly man was fit to drop, Maggie once again pulled herself together as Mrs Massey crept out of the shelter behind her. 'Come on into my house,' she urged as she turned back to fetch Lucy, who had slept through it all. 'I'll make us all a nice hot drink, eh?'

'Now that sounds about the best thing I've heard all night.'

After picking their way through the glass they trooped wearily into the kitchen, but when Maggie went to light the gas on the cooker nothing happened.

'They've probably hit a gas main down the street,' Mr Massey suggested.

'Not to worry. The fire's still in so I can boil a pan on there. At least our houses are still standing, which is more than can be said for some of the poor souls in the street.'

Maggie turned on the tap and sighed with relief when water trickled out of it. 'Well, we still have some water,' she said as brightly as she could. Once she'd filled a pan and placed it onto the glowing coals to boil, she made for the front door, wishing to give her neighbours a moment alone.

The sight that met her eyes when she stepped into the Lane made her gasp. Much further down, two houses had had their entire fronts blown off. A dressing-table with a brush and a mirror still on it was teetering half on and half off the edge of what had once been someone's bedroom. Maggie thought it was one of the saddest sights she had ever seen and went back inside with tears in her eyes.

'Did they get out of the houses?' she asked as she poured boiling water over the tea leaves in the pot.

Mr Massey sighed. 'Some of 'em did. They've set up places for some of the homeless in the church, an' the Salvation Army have shelters they can go to for a while an' all. But not everybody was lucky. I don't mind tellin' yer, I've seen sights this night that will stay with me fer the rest o' me days. Those bloody Jerries have a lot to answer for, an' that's a fact.'

At that moment, the kitchen door swung open and Maggie's mother waltzed in as if it had been just another night. Maggie was getting the bottle of milk out of the cool pantry. She glared at her.

'Have you *seen* what's happened to the houses further

183

down the lane?' she snapped. 'It could have been *your* house that took a hit, and you would have been a sitting duck, lying there in your bed being so stubborn.'

'Well, as luck would have it, it wasn't my house,' Ellen told her smartly. 'The way I see it, when yer card's marked you'll go wherever you are, an' as I've told yer before, I intend to be in me own bed when that day comes, God willin'.'

Maggie was so light-headed with relief that she slopped the tea all over the tablecloth as she poured it into the mugs. Not that it really mattered. Everything seemed to be covered in a fine layer of soot anyway. The biscuit barrel was too, but the ginger nuts went down a treat with the tea.

Once Mr Massey had gratefully drained his mug he rose, yawning. 'I'll just go an' get me head down for an hour, love, then I'll come round an' board yer windows up for yer.'

'Thanks, Mr Massey, I'd appreciate that. But are you sure you wouldn't like another drink before you go?'

He limped towards the door, closely followed by his wife. 'No, thanks all the same, love. I'm about dead on me feet. It's been the longest bloody night o' me life an' I'll be good fer nothin' now till I've had a bit o' shut-eye.'

Minutes later, Ellen rose too. 'I'll be getting back across the road now, if yer sure you're all right, love.'

'I'm fine, Mam,' her daughter assured her. 'I'll see you later, eh?'

Once the door had closed behind her, Maggie looked across at Lucy, who was sucking at the bottle of warm milk she had given her. They'd survived yet another night of bombing, but how much longer would their luck hold?

After she had washed and dressed Lucy, and coaxed

her to eat her breakfast of toast made with a toasting-fork on the fire and a scraping of Bovril, Maggie set about trying to clean the soot-covered room. Lucy was happily settled at the table looking at the pictures in a storybook when the back door suddenly flew open and Jo walked in unannounced.

'Why, Jo, whatever's the matter?' One glance at her friend told Maggie that something was seriously amiss.

Jo swayed, and if Maggie hadn't hurried across and caught her, she would have fallen in a heap. Leading her to the table she sat her down and fetched a damp cloth to wipe the smoke from her face.

'There now, that's better, isn't it? Now – can you tell me what's wrong?'

For a moment Jo's mouth worked but no words came out so Maggie stood patiently waiting.

'They've all gone,' she said eventually.

Maggie frowned in confusion. 'What do you mean? Who's gone?'

'All of 'em. Every last one. Me mam, all the little 'uns . . . an' me dad. The house took a direct hit, an' by the time I got home the fire engine was there trying to put the flames out. There ain't nothin' left but a pile o' burnin' rubble. An' my family's all under it somewhere.'

'*Oh, my dear God.*' Maggie's hand flew to her mouth in horror as Jo stared off into space, dry-eyed. She was obviously deeply in shock. Maggie wrapped her arms tightly around her. 'Where were you when all this happened?' she gasped, thankful that her friend had escaped.

'Where do yer think?' Jo's voice held a wealth of shame and regret. 'I'd gone to stand on a street corner to earn the old man an extra few bob.' She laughed bitterly and the sound made the hairs on the back of Maggie's neck stand to attention.

'But then the air-raid siren went off an' this bloke grabbed hold of me arm an' dragged me into the nearest shelter wi' him an' his missus. By the time we come out this mornin', the house were gone. Nothin' but a heap o' steamin' rubble, an' the whole o' me family buried somewhere beneath it. It's funny when yer come to think of it, ain't it? I won't have to stand on any more corners. I *prayed* fer somethin' to happen so that I wouldn't have to go out toutin' fer business any more, so in a way *I've* caused it haven't I? Me prayers were answered. Trouble is, I've lost me mam an' the kids an' all.' And finally Jo's tears exploded from her as if a dam had broken.

'Oh Maggie. What am I goin' to do?' she sobbed breathlessly.

Maggie rocked her to and fro. 'I'll tell you what you're going to do. You're going to stay here with me and we're going to get through this together.'

Chapter Seventeen

Fearful of being late for his dinner, Danny sprinted the last few yards up the hill to Mr Sinclair's house. He needn't have worried, for as he rounded the corner he saw the man just emerging from the long outhouse that ran below his bedroom window.

The man stared at him coldly for a moment before locking the door and dropping the key into his pocket.

'I'm not late, sir, am I?' Danny asked breathlessly.

'No, you're not,' Eric replied curtly before briskly striding across the yard. Danny cast a curious glance at the building he'd just emerged from as he followed him. He wondered what Mr Sinclair had been doing in there, but there was no way to find out, for the windows were covered in heavy blinds so that no one could peep through them.

'Is that a shed?' he blurted out as his curiosity got the better of him.

'No, it is *not* a shed, and *no one* goes in there except me. Do you understand?'

'Yes, sir.' Suitably chastened, Danny stayed silent for the rest of the short walk to the house. Samson's greeting was far more amicable as he waddled over to him with his tail wagging furiously. Danny fondled his silky ears as his host crossed to the cooker to check on the meal that was cooking. A delicious smell of roast beef was issuing from it, and Danny's stomach rumbled in anticipation. He knew that if the dinner was as good as the breakfast he had eaten earlier that day, he wouldn't be disappointed. He was soon proved to be right when Mr Sinclair carried a loaded plate to the table and slapped it down in front of him. There were crispy roast potatoes and slices of thick roast beef on a bed of cabbage, all covered with thick juicy gravy. After the huge breakfast Danny had eaten he was sure that he wouldn't be hungry for the rest of the day but now he fell on his food as if he were ravenous, and in double-quick time had cleared his plate. Forgetting his fear of the man for a moment, he flashed him a smile.

'That was one o' the best dinners I've ever had,' he told him appreciatively. 'Do you always do the cookin'?' he went on. 'Or does Mrs Sinclair do it when she's here?'

The man's face might have been set in stone as he snapped back, 'There *is* no Mrs Sinclair.'

Danny flushed. He felt as if he was walking on eggshells, for he just couldn't seem to say the right thing. 'Sorry,' he mumbled, but the man merely gathered up the dirty plates and carried them to the sink as if Danny wasn't there.

Hoping to make amends, the boy asked, 'Would you like me to wash them up for you? I used to wash up fer me mam sometimes back at home. An' I used to get the coal in for her after me dad went.'

Curious despite himself, the man asked, 'Went where?'

'To war.' Danny's small face creased into a worried frown as the man dried his hands on a tea-towel and watched him from the corner of his good eye.

Eric Sinclair had made no secret of the fact that he didn't want an evacuee staying with him, and he and

Miss Williams had had a right old battle, until eventually he was forced to agree to take one. Even now, he was still smarting from the way she had manipulated him into agreeing. And yet, already he felt himself warming towards the child. He was a polite lad and obviously eager to please, despite the cold welcome Eric had extended to him. He determined to try a little harder. After all, the child hadn't asked to be here.

He forced himself to enquire, 'What did you get up to this morning then?'

Danny's face immediately lit up with a smile. 'I started off fer the village to look fer me sister, an' on the way I made a new friend. He lives in the house just down the way. He's an evacuee too an' his name is Soho Gus – he lives in London. He took me into the village an' showed me where Lizzie is stayin', then we all went down to the beach. It was really grand. Lizzie an' I ain't never been to the seaside before,' he finished breathlessly.

Eric was amazed but politely refrained from saying so. Instead, he walked to the window and stared out beyond the huge outbuilding to the sea. He was standing with the unscarred side of his face to Danny and the child found himself feeling sorry for the man. When he stood like that he was actually quite handsome – until he turned around, that was. It was no wonder that there was no Mrs Sinclair when he came to think of it, for who would want to marry a man who was so horribly disfigured?

When Eric turned back to him, Danny flushed, hoping that he hadn't read his thoughts.

'I have to go out now. Do you think you'll be able to keep yourself entertained for a few hours?'

Danny nodded numbly as the man headed towards the door. Once there he paused to look back. 'If you should need me I'll be in the big outbuilding. Knock on the door, but don't try to come in because you'll find it locked.'

As soon as the door had closed behind him, Danny slid off his seat and scuttled across the room to watch his progress across the yard. He was consumed with curiosity. What could the man be doing in there that warranted him keeping the door locked, he wondered.

Bored now, he began to wander around the room with Samson close at his heels. Eventually he went into the large entrance hall and, after plucking up his courage, he began to open the various doors that led off it to peek into the rooms beyond.

One was a spacious lounge with a large three-piece suite and a sideboard in it. The next was a dining room with a table and chairs the like of which Danny had never seen, set out in the centre of it. Danny wished that his mam could see it. It made the table and chairs in their kitchen back at home look like something that had come out of a doll's house. Although, there seemed to be something missing . . . He suddenly realised what it was. There was not a single ornament anywhere. Apart from the furniture, the rooms were bare and looked unlived-in. The third room had him gawping in surprise, for it proved to be a library that was packed full of books on three walls from floor to ceiling. In the middle of the room was a large, dark wood desk; a great leather chair was pushed up to it. However, it wasn't this that caught Danny's attention but the pictures that were hanging on the fourth wall. Completely forgetting that he shouldn't even be there, Danny gazed up at them enraptured.

One of them was a picture of the sea, and was so lifelike that Danny could almost feel the spray from the waves as they crashed onto the shore. The second was a country scene of a village that looked vaguely familiar. Squinting up at it, he tried to think where he'd seen it before. And then it came to him: it was Sarn-Bach itself. He could even see the blacksmith's where Lizzie was staying with Mrs Evans, and the duckpond over the road from it. He studied it for a long time before moving on. The next was another sea scene, but this time with a fisherman's small boat riding the waves. Again, it was so realistic that he could almost believe he was being tossed and turned on the choppy grey waves.

The last and final painting was a portrait of a woman. Danny could hardly take his eyes from it, for the woman was so beautiful. About the same age as his mother, she had blond hair and twinkling blue eyes that exactly matched the colour of the pretty blouse she was wearing. He was so engrossed in studying it that when Samson nuzzled up to him, he almost jumped out of his skin.

'Crikey, boy. Yer give me a rare old turn then,' he grinned as he bent to stroke the dog's silky back. 'Come on, we'd best get out of here. There'll be hell to pay if yer master catches us creepin' about where we shouldn't be.' Grabbing the dog's collar, he hauled him out of the room, casting one last look at the magnificent paintings. Danny had always loved art at school and was forever scribbling or drawing something. But those paintings made him feel inadequate and he wondered if he would ever be able to turn out anything half as good. The thought sent his mind racing to his pens and pads tucked in the bottom of his case upstairs.

'Come on, boy.' He took the stairs two at a time with Samson close on his heels. 'Let's go an' get me pad an' pencils an' do a few pictures of our own, eh?'

In no time at all he had left the house and was standing

at the side of the outbuilding, beyond which was a magnificent view of the sea. Settling himself onto a handy boulder, he began to sketch, and the time slipped away as he lost himself in the pleasure of trying to bring his picture to life. He was shocked when he looked up to see that the afternoon was beginning to darken.

'Blimey, we'd better get back inside,' he told Samson, who rose and stretched lazily. 'I hope Mr Sinclair ain't missed us.'

Gathering together his paraphernalia, he raced towards the house. There was a light burning in the kitchen window and his heart jumped into his throat. Would Mr Sinclair be angry with him for not telling him where he was going?

Forgetting to knock, he spilled into the room and blurted out, 'I'm sorry if I'm late. I decided to do some sketchin', an' the time sort of slipped away. I didn't go far though, I was only at the side of—'

'I know exactly where you were. I saw you when I came back across to the house,' Eric informed him. 'Now go and wash your hands or do whatever it is children are supposed to do before a meal and come and get your tea.'

Dropping his pads onto the settee, Danny hurried across to the deep stone sink and dutifully ran his hands beneath the tap. The water was icy cold and made his fingers tingle.

When he turned back, Mr Sinclair was once more standing at the door. 'Help yourself to whatever you want on the table. There should be more than enough there for you. I shall be in the outbuilding. If I'm not back by the time it gets dark, get yourself washed and up to bed.'

'Yes, sir.' Danny's stomach sank as the man closed the door behind him and silence settled on the room.

Even the sight of the crusty loaf and the dish full of jam and real homemade butter on the table did nothing to cheer him. He wondered what his mam and Lucy would be doing back at home as a wave of homesickness swept over him. Ever since they had arrived in Wales, Danny had had to be strong for Lizzie, but now he did what any nine-year-old boy in his circumstances would have done. He lowered his head into his hands and cried for his mam.

Down in the village, Lizzie was having her tea too but the atmosphere in the little cottage was much lighter than up at *Tremarfon*.

'Come along now, *bach*,' Mrs Evans encouraged. 'Just try it. I'm sure you'll like it.'

Lizzie eyed the dish full of bread and warm buttermilk liberally sprinkled with sugar uncertainly but lifted her spoon and tried it all the same. To her surprise she found it was delicious, and in no time at all she had eaten every bit.

'Now *there's* a good girl.' Mrs Evans beamed her approval as she scuttled away to fetch a homemade sponge cake oozing jam and cream to the table. 'Keep this up and we'll soon have some fat on those skinny little bones of yours, won't we, Father?'

Daffyd Evans smiled at his wife as she fussed over the little one. Blodwyn was obviously loving having a child in the house again, particularly a little girl. As memories of their beloved little Megan popped into his head he pushed them away. Even now, after all these years, it was still too painful to think of her.

Lizzie meanwhile was tucking into her cake with a vengeance. She had never had a great appetite, but the morning spent in the fresh air had heightened it. Blodwyn thought she could detect the first bloom of a few roses in her cheeks too. But she was *so* quiet. Blodwyn had watched her come back down the village street that lunchtime with Danny and his little friend, and her face had been wreathed in smiles. But the second she'd walked back through the cottage door, it was as if shutters had come down across her eyes and she hadn't so much as grinned since. Mentally, she scolded herself. The child had only been with them for one night up to now. Everything was bound to seem strange to her. She just needed a little more time, that was all. And then she would surely come out of her shell.

On Sunday morning, Danny stood at his bedroom window gazing at the mountains in the distance. With their snow-capped peaks reaching into the clouds they made a spectacular sight. The vast expanse of open space was almost more than he could comprehend, after being used to living in a city. And the food – it was as if the war hadn't touched Wales at all.

Downstairs he could hear Mr Sinclair pottering about the kitchen preparing breakfast so he dragged himself away from the view. He hastily cleaned his teeth then threw on his clothes before tugging a comb through his hair and venturing downstairs. The wireless was on, and the first thing he heard as he entered the kitchen was the broadcaster telling of the air raid on Coventry that had lasted throughout the whole of the night. He froze in his tracks as he listened to the tale of devastation the bombs had caused. There were houses flattened and people dead, and he felt his knees begin to buckle. What if anything had happened to his mam and Lucy? Would that mean that he would have to stay here with someone who obviously didn't like him forever? The thought was too much to bear and he suddenly felt guilty. He'd been out enjoying himself yesterday, splashing in the sea with Gus and Lizzie, while his mam must have been locked away in the damp Anderson shelter with no one to look out for her and Lucy.

Glancing around, Eric saw the boy standing there. He was as white as a ghost, and he cursed himself for not switching the report off before the child came down. Swiftly crossing to the wireless, he turned it off.

'Look, Danny, try not to worry,' he said awkwardly. 'If anything had happened to your family back home, we would have heard. We would have had a telegram, or the police down in the village would have received a call.' Even to his own ears the words sounded inadequate, but for now he could think of nothing else to say. He'd never had a lot to do with children before and felt totally out of his depth.

Danny grasped at this straw nevertheless. 'Do yer really think we would have?' he asked in a scared voice.

Eric nodded. 'Absolutely. No doubt about it, so try to forget what you heard. Come on, I've cooked the breakfast. We might as well eat it while it's still hot, eh?'

They were the first kind words he'd uttered to Danny since the child had arrived, and they brought tears stinging to Danny's eyes. Perhaps Mr Sinclair wasn't quite as hard as he tried to make out.

Even so, he struggled to swallow the food on his plate. It seemed to lodge in his throat and more than once he was afraid that he was going to be sick.

After a time, Mr Sinclair picked up his plate and carried it away. Danny expected to be scolded for wasting food, but he merely told him, 'Don't worry about it. No doubt you'll have an appetite like a horse's by dinnertime. You can always make up for it then.'

'Thank you, sir,' he muttered miserably.

Eric turned to face him, not knowing quite how to

begin. 'Look, Danny,' he managed eventually, 'if you're going to be staying here for a while, which it looks as though you are, "sir" is a bit formal. Why don't you call me Eric?'

Danny had been taught to always call adults by their surnames, and to go from calling his host sir to Eric in one great step seemed strange. However, he had no wish to offend the man, so he replied, 'Yes, sir . . . I mean, Eric.'

He was surprised when the man's face broke into a smile, a *real* smile for the very first time. Once again he found himself thinking how sad it was that Eric was disfigured down one side of his face. He could have been really handsome, were it not for the eye-patch and the scars beneath it. As if reading his mind, Eric's face suddenly became impassive again.

'Right, seeing as it's Sunday and there's no school again, why don't you go out and amuse yourself. Lunch will be at about two o'clock. Make sure that you're back for then. Oh, and be sure to put your coat on. It looks cold out there.'

Danny silently nodded before skittering away to his bedroom where he shrugged his skinny arms into the sleeves of his coat. He really didn't know what to make of Eric, as he was now supposed to call him. For just a while this morning he had seen a gentler, kinder side to his nature, but now he was back to being a cold fish again. Danny shrugged. As long as his mam and baby sister were safe and sound, and Lizzie was happy at the blacksmith's, he felt he could cope with anything. Of course, there was still the ordeal of a new school to cope with, but that didn't scare him half as much as the news report had, about the bombs raining down on his home town.

Chapter Eighteen

As Danny dawdled down the lane that would take him to the village, his shoulders were stooped and his thoughts far away with his mother in Coventry, and so it was a shock when Soho Gus suddenly appeared from behind a hedge as if by magic.

'Cor blimey, whassa matter wiv you, mate?' he asked. 'You've got a face on yer like a wet weekend.'

Danny tried to explain 'Mr Sinclair . . . I mean Eric . . . had the wireless on this morning and it were saying that Coventry got bombed again last night.'

'Ah, I see – an' you're worried about yer family back there, is that it?'

Danny nodded miserably as Gus came to stand beside him. At the sound of voices, Albert promptly popped his head out of Gus's pocket before turning tail and snuggling back down again. Normally, Danny would have found this highly amusing, but at present he couldn't have raised a smile if he had wanted to.

'Look, try not to worry, mate. If anyfink had happened to 'em they'd 'ave let yer know by now,' Gus told him kindly.

'That's what Mr . . . Eric said,' Danny confessed.

'Well, there yer go then. An' he ain't lyin'. There were a girl down in the village until a couple o' weeks back an' her family copped it in London. She got a telegram to say the whole lot of 'em was dead.'

Danny squinted across at him. 'What happened to her?'

'She got sent to some orphanage somewhere. Poor little sod.'

Danny shuddered at the thought, but even so he started to feel slightly better. Surely Eric and Gus wouldn't *both* lie to him?

'Where yer headin' anyway?' Gus asked, glad of a chance to change the subject.

'I thought I'd nip down into the village and see Lizzie fer a couple of hours.'

'It's a good job I bumped into yer then, 'cos I can save yer a wasted journey,' Gus told him. 'Mr an' Mrs Evans will be at church till lunchtime. They go regular as clockwork every Sunday, come rain, hail or shine. No doubt they'll have dragged your Lizzie along wiv 'em.'

'Oh.' Disappointment clouded Danny's face until Gus suggested brightly, 'Why don't yer come an' take a look around the farm wiv me? Mr Thomas has gorra tractor. He gave me a ride on it once an' they've got loads of animals.'

Danny perked up immediately. 'That would be smashin'. But are yer sure they wouldn't mind?'

'Nah, they won't mind,' Gus assured him as he led him towards the gate. They walked on side-by-side, and when they rounded the farmhouse Danny found himself in a large yard. His eyes nearly popped out of his head as a chicken came noisily clucking up to him. On the other side of the yard was a large barn, and through the open door he could see the tractor Gus had told him about and massive bales of hay stacked one on top of another.

'That's fer the animals in the winter,' Gus informed him, and again they moved on to what Danny was soon to discover were two enormous pigsties.

As the huge pink animals came snuffling up to them he watched in fascination, and was deeply impressed when Gus reached across the wall to scratch one of them on the nose. In a far corner, another one was lying on her side in the dust whilst what appeared to be dozens of tiny piglets squealed and suckled at her, climbing over one another in their haste to feed.

'What do they eat?' Danny asked.

Gus chuckled. 'Just about anyfin' that stands still fer long enough,' he told him. 'Every night Mrs Thomas lumps all the leftover food into a huge pan an' boils it down to make swill fer 'em. Yer should see 'em go at it when she tips it into the trough. You'd fink they hadn't been fed fer bleedin' months. I reckon they'd eat till they burst if you'd let 'em. Still, at least we're sure they'll be nice an' fat fer Christmas.'

'I should be back home wi' me mam by then,' Danny said wistfully, trying desperately hard not to think of the fate mapped out for the unfortunate animals.

Gus opened his mouth to tell him he didn't think there'd be much chance of that, but then closed it abruptly. Danny was down in the dumps enough already without him adding to his worries. He eventually managed to persuade Danny to move on, and took him to see the cows, which were lined up in the milking shed ready to be milked.

'Mrs Thomas will be out in a minute to see to 'em,' Gus informed him. '*Derwen Deg* supplies most o' the village wiv milk, an' wiv what's left over Mrs Thomas makes her own butter an' cheese in the dairy over there. It's good stuff, I don't mind tellin' yer.' He rubbed his stomach and Danny found himself smiling. Soho Gus was certainly a character, there was no denying that. Next they came to an enormous orchard.

'These trees were bowed down wiv the weight of apples an' pears not so long ago.' Gus stared up at the leafless trees and remembered. 'I'm bloody glad they've all bin picked now, I don't mind tellin' yer. Mrs Thomas had me out here every single day fillin' baskets full o' the bleedin' things. Most of 'em are wrapped in paper an' stored in the farmhouse cellar now to see us through the winter.'

Back at home, with the strict food rationing, fruit had been a rare treat for Danny. He would have been only too glad of the chance to go fruit-picking but he didn't want to offend his newfound friend by telling him so, so he merely nodded. Next, Danny showed him the chicken-houses.

'That's another o' me jobs,' he complained. 'Every mornin' I 'ave to crawl inside 'em an' collect all the eggs. I sometimes fink that's why the Thomases decided to take a lad instead of a girl, so as I could help out wiv all the jobs around the farm. Most o' the farmers here-abouts do the same fing. Perhaps it's just as well Sinclair got bullied into takin' you on. Otherwise yer might have found yerself on a farm like me, bein' used as a bleedin' labourer.' Despite what he was saying, there was a huge grin spread all across his face so Danny guessed that it probably wasn't as bad here as Gus was making out. They walked on until they came to a large duckpond and there they sank down onto the damp grass.

For a while, a silence settled between them as they watched the ducks swimming around, and then Danny asked, 'Do you miss your mam an' dad, Gus?'

Gus shrugged. He could have told his friend that living

here was like living in heaven compared to where he'd come from, but was too proud to do so. Instead he reluctantly admitted, 'I miss me mam sometimes, but I never knew me dad. He pissed off when I was just a baby.'

'Don't you have any brothers or sisters?'

'I do, but they're both much older than me an' they left 'ome years ago. I don't rightly fink me mam even knows where they are now. Mind you, she don't know where she is 'erself half the time. She's usually too pissed.'

Danny's eyes grew sympathetic. It didn't sound as if Gus had been too happy at home, one way or another, but before he could comment on it, the other boy suddenly leaped up, anxious to change the topic of conversation.

'Right then. That's yer guided tour just about over fer now. What do yer wanna do next?'

Not knowing the district, Danny had absolutely no idea what to suggest. 'You think of something,' he urged Gus.

Scratching his head again, Gus stared thoughtfully off into the distance. 'We'll go for a walk up into the hills. 'Ow do yer fancy that? There's a crackin' good view from the top o' that one there, though I'll warn yer, yer'll know you've climbed it by the time yer get to the top.'

'Sounds good to me,' Danny agreed equably and so they set off to explore.

The view from the top of the hill, when they finally reached it, was every bit as good as Gus had promised it would be, and Danny was open-mouthed as he looked around him.

'You could think yer were on the top o' the world here,' he said in awe, for never in his life had he known that such wide-open spaces existed. To one side of them the sea stretched away into the distance, and on the other side lay the village nestled deep in the valley below, surrounded by mountains. It was a sight that Danny would never forget.

Far out at sea they could just see a huge ship on the horizon.

'I bet that's a warship headin' fer somewhere,' Gus muttered. 'It's too big to be a fishin' boat, that's a fact. An' that's something else we can do another day, come to think of it. I'll take yer down to the harbour so yer can see the fishin' boats. I dare say Lizzie might like to see 'em too.' He kept his face turned away from his friend so that he wouldn't see the flush that had risen in his cheeks at the mention of her name.

'Not half she wouldn't,' Danny told him enthusiastically. 'Trouble is, we start at the village school tomorrow an' it will be dark by the time we've got home an' had our teas.'

'So, we'll plan it fer next Saturday then, shall we?'

Again Danny nodded, before reluctantly following his friend back down the way they'd come. By then it was time to part and make their separate ways home for their dinner.

'See yer later,' Gus called cheerily across his shoulder, and feeling somewhat brighter than he had earlier in the day, Danny turned towards the path that would lead him to *Tremarfon*.

Once again Eric surprised him with a delicious meal. Today he'd cooked roast pork, and at first Danny's stomach revolted as he thought about the fat pink pigs he had seen shuffling about in their sty. Back at home, meat had simply been something that you found in a butcher's shop window, and he had never really given much thought as to where it actually came from. But then hunger took over, and with the help of Samson, to whom he managed to slip bits under the table when Eric wasn't looking, he cleared his plate. An enormous apple pie followed the main course.

'Did you cook this too?' Danny asked admiringly as he shovelled it into his mouth.

'No, I didn't, actually,' Eric admitted. 'I'm fine at simple plain food but I couldn't turn out anything like this. I bought it from Mrs Thomas, with whom your friend is staying, when I went to collect the milk this morning. What did you get up to?'

While they had a cup of tea, Danny launched into a description of the things he had seen and the walk up the hill.

'I couldn't see Lizzie though, 'cos Soho Gus told me that Mr and Mrs Evans would have taken her to church,' he finished breathlessly, then as an afterthought he asked, 'Do *you* ever go to church?'

'No, I don't,' Eric said abruptly, and again Danny saw him stiffen and somehow he knew that their conversation was at an end.

Hastily scraping his chair back from the table, he asked, 'Would yer like me to help wi' the washin'-up?' He was eager to make amends for whatever it was he'd said that had upset Eric, but the man shook his head.

'No, I'll leave them in soak until later. I have things to do now so I'll get across to the outbuilding. I'm sure you can find something to do to amuse yourself until teatime.'

Danny's heart sank into his boots. It looked like he was going to spend an afternoon alone, unless he called round for Soho Gus. He abandoned that idea almost immediately. The mood Eric was in, he didn't really want to ask if he was allowed back out.

Eric snatched up some keys from the dresser and without so much as a backward glance, strode out of the kitchen.

Left to his own devices once more, Danny sighed and sank down into one of the fireside chairs. Samson immediately pottered up to him and placed his enormous head in Danny's lap.

Danny absently fondled his ears as he stared into the flickering flames. He wondered what his mother would be doing and hoped that she was all right. Then his thoughts turned to Lizzie and a large lump formed in his throat. Until they'd come to Wales the twins had never been parted, and he missed her more than he could say. From the time when they had both taken their first faltering steps, within minutes of each other, Danny had assumed the role of Lizzie's protector. Now suddenly he felt powerless, as if a part of him had been amputated. She would be back at the Evanses now. The urge came on him to go and see her, but then a picture of Eric's stern face flashed before his eyes and he changed his mind. Slowly tears welled in his eyes and because there was no one there to see, but the cat and the dog, he let them roll down his cheeks unchecked.

'I don't half miss her, Samson,' he muttered miserably. The dog nuzzled his hand and gazed up at him from sympathetic eyes as if he could understand the child's loneliness.

'Will you *please* come away from that window, Lizziebright, and stop scratching your head now. Whatever is the matter with you, *bach*?'

Lizzie started guiltily and edged towards the table in the centre of the room. They had just had a delicious Sunday roast and Mrs Evans was none too pleased with her for leaving most of it.

Mr Evans hadn't done too good a job of clearing his plate either, Lizzie had noticed. He had the most terrible cough, and after a while of sitting at the table he had excused himself and buried his head in the Sunday newspaper.

Crossing to Lizzie, Mrs Evans untied the pretty red bow from the child's hair and let it tumble in all its glory across her shoulders. 'Let's be looking at what's making you scratch,' she said as she parted the hair into sections. After a few seconds she let out a whoop of dismay. 'It's just as I thought, Father!' she exclaimed. 'The little one has headlice, and it doesn't take two guesses as to where she got *them* from. I bet she picked them up from that lad from London that her brother has been knocking around with. By all the saints, the lad looks as if a dip in the bath would do him the world of good, so it does. That Gwyneth Thomas should be ashamed of herself.'

'Now then, Mother,' her husband said softly. 'There's no saying that that's where the child picked them up. She could have had them when she arrived.'

'*I did not!*' Lizzie spat indignantly. 'My mam used to go through mine an' Danny's hair with a nit-comb every Friday after our baths.'

It was the most that the little girl had said all in one go since her arrival, and the couple gaped at her, until Blodwyn pulled herself together and exclaimed, 'Then I must have been right, mustn't I now! Anyway, wherever they came from, they most certainly *are* there now and so we will have to get rid of them. At the moment there only seem to be the odd one or two, but they hatch out very quickly so we have to act quickly.'

Lizzie recalled a schoolfriend who had caught nits as they called them, back in Coventry. After the shame of being singled out by the 'nit nurse', who was a regular visitor to the school, she had been sent home, only to return the very next day looking like a shorn lamb. Her mother had placed a pudding basin on her head and then cut all the way around it to make her infestation easier to deal with. The other children had mocked her and called her 'Nitty', which had reduced the poor child to tears every playtime and dinnertime until her hair began to grow again. Lizzie wondered if the same fate was about to befall her.

'Me mam won't like it if you chop all me hair off,' she declared as she began to edge towards the door. As comprehension dawned on Blodwyn's face she smiled broadly. 'Why, *bach* – whatever gave you the idea that was my intention? It would be a crime to chop off your crowning glory, so it would. No, no. What I have in mind is much less dramatic, though no doubt you'll end up with a sore scalp by the time I'm done. We're going to wash it in carbolic soap and then comb every single one of the little menaces out with a nit-comb.'

Deciding that this sounded like the lesser of two evils, Lizzie relaxed a little and watched as Mrs Evans placed two large pans and a kettle full of water to boil on the hob.

Almost two hours later, Blodwyn beamed with satisfaction. 'That should do it,' she declared. 'I doubt there's anything left living in there now.'

Lizzie didn't doubt her for a second. Her scalp felt as if it was on fire, and the smell of the carbolic was making her eyes sting. She was amazed that *she* had survived – let alone any of her unwelcome visitors.

Throwing the last bowl of water down the sink, Mrs Evans told her, 'Sit by the fire, *bach*. You hair will dry in no time, so it will, and then we'll put it into plaits and it will be a picture come morning.'

Lizzie obediently sank down onto the hearthrug. Mr Evans winked at her from behind his paper and once again her eyes turned to the little leaded window. Why hadn't Danny come to see her today, she wondered. And what was he doing now?

As if reading her thoughts, Mrs Evans filled a glass with buttermilk and called her to the table. 'Get that down you now, *bach*. I'm determined to put a bit of meat on your bones. I can't have the children at school calling my Megan Skinny Ribs, now can . . .'

To Lizzie's amazement, Mrs Evans suddenly clapped her hand across her mouth and hurried from the room, her eyes brimming with tears.

'Who's Megan?' Lizzie asked innocently.

Mr Evans wondered what he should tell her. Seeing no reason to lie, he eventually told her, 'Megan was our daughter, *bach*.'

Lizzie was puzzled. 'What do you mean, *was* your daughter? Why isn't she now? Where is she?'

Another fit of coughing brought Mr Evans leaning forward in his chair, but after a while he managed to tell her, 'Megan died when she was just a little girl.'

Lizzie's heart was sad as she thought of the little girl she had never met.

'That's probably why Mother called you Megan back there,' the kindly man went on. 'She hasn't had a little girl to fuss over since Megan died. But you mustn't mind her. She means no harm.'

Lizzie nodded solemnly. Poor Mrs Evans. She must still miss Megan dreadfully to have called her by her late little girl's name. Her thoughts were interrupted by Mr Evans hauling himself out of the chair. 'I'll just go and see that she's all right,' he said. 'You'll be fine on your own for a while, will you, *bach*?'

When Lizzie nodded he pottered away, and once more Lizzie crossed to the window. Her eyes flew up and down the lane outside, and when she saw no sign of Danny, her heart sank. She felt overwhelmingly sorry for Mrs Evans, and Mr Evans too, if it came to that. But she wasn't their little girl and never would be. *Her* mother was back in Coventry, and Danny was somewhere up on that bleak hillside, though he might have been a million miles away. As homesickness washed over her she lowered her head and wept. Somewhere, Danny was crying too, she could feel it. Right since they had been babies, they had seemed to be linked by some unseen bond that always told one how the other was feeling, even when they were apart, which was rarely up until now.

She thought of the horribly scarred man that Danny was being forced to stay with, and shuddered with revulsion. What if he was being cruel to Danny? What if he'd locked him in a cellar with rats and no food? Perhaps that was why Danny hadn't been able to come and see her. Her imagination began to run riot and suddenly she knew that she *must* see him. Glancing at the door through which Mr Evans had recently disappeared, she satisfied herself that he wasn't on the way back to the kitchen, then creeping towards the door she opened it as quietly as she could and let herself out into the fast-darkening afternoon.

She had no doubt at all that she would be in serious trouble when she got back for not asking if she could go out alone. But for now her need to see her twin was stronger than her fear of risking the Evanses' wrath.

Chapter Nineteen

As the cold October air wrapped itself around her, Lizzie faltered and her courage momentarily failed her. It was already cold as darkness crept across the village, and she wished that she'd thought to put her coat on. But it was too late to worry about it now. If she were to go back inside to get it, the Evanses might realise her intentions and then she wouldn't get to see Danny.

Throwing her damp hair across her shoulders, she raced down the village street in the direction of the road that led up the hill to where he had told her he was staying. Once out of the village, the dim street-lights stopped and Lizzie felt scared as she began the long climb. Occasionally, she passed a cottage or a house nestling in the hillside, but she didn't see a single soul. The only sounds were the wind whistling in the trees and the distant crash of the waves. When a fox suddenly shot across the road in front of her, Lizzie's heart almost leaped out of her chest with fright. It was getting darker by the minute and for the first time she began to wonder if this had been such a good idea. After all, she wasn't even sure that she was going in the right direction. Forcing herself to stay calm, she tried to remember the name of the house that Danny had told her he was staying at. It began with a T, she was sure of it. It was *T . . . Tr . . . Tremarfon*. That was it!

She stumbled along the bumpy road. When shortly after, she saw the lights of a house twinkling in the gloom, she breathed a sigh of relief, but when she came level with the gate, her heart sank. The name of this house was *Derwen Deg*. Something about it sounded familiar . . . and then she remembered. This was where Soho Gus had said he was staying. She couldn't be that far away now, for Danny had told her that Soho Gus lived just down the road from him. With a renewed effort she hurried on, her breath hanging on the air in front of her, and sure enough, she soon saw the lights of another house up ahead. It was a huge house, surrounded by trees that seemed to be standing guard over it, but there were no lights shining from the front windows. Cautiously, she crept around the side of it past a huge outbuilding. There were lights on in there but when she sneaked up to the window and tried to peep through, she was prevented from doing so by the heavy blinds that had been lowered across it.

Picking her way across the gravel, she approached the back of the house, and as a dog began to bark somewhere, she was rewarded with a light shining from what she supposed to be the kitchen window. On tiptoe she peeped inside. Her heart almost exploded with joy when she saw Danny curled up in a chair at the side of a roaring log fire. Not caring now who might hear her, she began to hammer on the door and when it was opened seconds later by Danny himself, with Samson at his side, she flung herself into his arms, laughing and crying all at the same time.

'Lizzie! What are *you* doing here?' he gasped, drawing her inside. 'You're freezing!' As the warmth of the room hit her like a slap in the face, her cold cheeks began to glow.

'I . . . I had to come,' she gabbled breathlessly. 'I just got this feeling that you were sad an' you needed me.'

Danny shook his head in amazement as he glanced back across her shoulder. 'How did you get here? Did Mr and Mrs Evans bring you?'

'No. I came on my own. I dare say I'll be in terrible trouble when I get back, but I don't care. I just *had* to see you.'

'Oh, Lizzie, I—' When a large shadow suddenly fell across the bare floor, both children looked towards it with terror burning in their eyes.

'What's this then?' Eric demanded as he looked across at the two guilty faces.

Lizzie pressed so close to Danny that she nearly melted into his side as she stared in horror at the black eye-patch on the man's scarred face.

Danny immediately drew himself up to his full height as he shielded Lizzie defensively. 'This is Lizzie. She's me twin an' she's staying down in the village with the Evanses.'

'I'm well aware of that,' Eric told him coolly as he closed the door behind him. 'What I want to know is, what is she doing here?'

Lizzie opened her mouth to reply but no sound came out. Eric was staring at her and she felt herself shrivel to half her size beneath his scrutiny.

'She was feeling a bit homesick so she came to see me on the spur of the minute,' Danny told him.

'Does that mean Mrs Evans doesn't know where you are?' Eric asked, and Danny was relieved to hear that his voice was not unkind. It would have been very hard to be under the circumstances, for Lizzie was a sorry sight. Her hair was hanging in damp rats' tails and she was dressed in a little dress and cardigan that were nowhere near warm enough for this weather, and she was shivering uncontrollably.

When she whispered, 'No,' Eric walked towards her

and, drawing her gently away from Danny's side, he led her to the seat that her brother had recently vacated at the side of the fireplace.

'I think we'd better get you wrapped up and something warm inside you, otherwise you're going to catch your death. Danny, put some milk into a saucepan to warm, would you? I'll only be a minute.'

Danny breathed a sigh of relief as he scurried away to do as he was told, and seconds later, Eric reappeared with a warm blanket that he laid loosely around Lizzie's heaving shoulders. He then carefully poured the warm milk into a mug, keeping a watchful eye on his uninvited visitor all the while.

By the time Lizzie had swallowed the drink, a little colour had returned to her face but she still looked mortally afraid. Eric was not offended. He knew the effect his scarred face had on people, which was why he preferred to shut himself away on the hillside.

'Look, I think we ought to get you back to Mrs Evans now,' he told her gently. 'She'll no doubt have a search-party out for you by now, and I don't want to be accused of harbouring you. If you just wait there with Danny for a minute I'll go and get the car out.'

'Mr Sinclair – I mean Eric – couldn't she stay here just for tonight?' Danny pleaded.

Feeling totally out of his depth, Eric said irritably, 'I just explained to you why we should get her back. Now please let me go and get the car and let that be an end to the matter.' So saying he turned about and strode away, slamming the door behind him.

Lizzie instantly began to cry again. 'I don't want to go back to the Evanses', Danny,' she sobbed.

'Why? Are they cruel to you?'

'No, no, it's not that. It's just that I miss you . . . and

Mam and Lucy. Why won't they let us go home? I wouldn't cry if the bombs fell again and we had to go into the shelter, really I wouldn't.'

Danny bent to wrap his skinny arms around her. 'I know you wouldn't,' he soothed. 'But it ain't as simple as that. You've got to try an' look at it from our mam's point of view. She didn't send us here because she wanted rid of us. She loves us, but while we're here she knows we're safe. While we're at home she's worried all the time that something's goin' to happen to us. We've got to stick it out for her, Lizzie. Try an' cheer up. It won't be forever. This war can't go on fer much longer, can it?' The words sounded empty even to his own ears but for now they were all he could think of to say. 'An' another thing – tomorrow we're startin' at the village school. We'll be together all day from Monday to Friday then, so it won't be so bad, will it?'

'I . . . I suppose not.' Lizzie sniffed doubtfully as the sound of Eric's car pulling up outside the door reached them. Taking her hand, Danny hauled her to her feet.

'Come on. Let's go an' face the music. An' try to remember what I said. We could even be home fer Christmas.' He led her outside and bundled her into the car, and soon they were on their way down the steep hillside. Lizzie sat silently. She had always longed to have a ride in a car but tonight the experience held no pleasure for her. She was mortally afraid of what Mrs Evans was going to say when Eric delivered her back to the cottage, and terrified that Danny would be in trouble because of her misdemeanour.

Her worst fears were realised as they drove along the village street towards the blacksmith's. It seemed that half the villagers were out looking for her, and torches blazed into the darkness. The door to the Evanses' cottage swung open in the biting wind and Mrs Evans was running up and down the road like someone demented as she searched every nook and cranny.

'Uh, oh!' Eric murmured as he drew the car to a halt.

Instantly, Mrs Evans ran towards it and peered through the window, and when she saw Lizzie she wrenched the door open.

'Why, Eric Sinclair. *Shame* on you, man!' she screeched. 'To take a defenceless child off like that without telling us your intentions. I've been half out of my mind with worry, so I have.'

Hearing the commotion she was making, the villagers began to approach the car, and when they saw the missing child safe and sound they melted away back to their homes. Meanwhile, Mrs Evans yanked Lizzie unceremoniously out of the back seat as she wagged a furious finger at Eric.

'It wasn't *his* fault,' Danny declared indignantly as Mrs Evans ranted on at the innocent party. 'Lizzie was feelin' lonely so she took it on herself to come an' see me. There ain't no harm done, is there?'

His words fell on deaf ears as Mrs Evans ushered Lizzie towards the cottage.

'Leave it, Danny,' Eric told him wearily. 'She's in too much of a lather to listen to reason tonight.'

He was just about to reverse the car when Daffyd Evans appeared at the window.

'All's well that ends well, man,' he said by way of an apology. 'You mustn't take too much notice of the wife. She was terrified that something had happened to the child. No doubt she'll give you an apology tomorrow when she's had time to calm down.'

Eric nodded, his lips set in a hard line, then without a word he turned the car and roared out of the village.

'I'm sorry, Eric.'

When the small voice sounded from the back seat, Eric shook his head. 'It's not your fault, Danny. Nor Lizzie's either, if it comes to that. And don't worry about the tongue-lashing I just got. The villagers make no secret of the fact that I'm not welcome here, which is why I tend to keep myself to myself. I am to blame for this as much as anybody. I should have realised that, being twins, you and Lizzie would want to see each other. If I'd thought to invite her to the house all open and above board, none of this would have happened. But er . . . thanks for trying to stick up for me.'

Danny felt his cheeks flame in the darkness. Eric could be really nice when he wanted to be.

Once they were all safely back inside the cottage, Mrs Evans hugged Lizzie fiercely. 'Eeh, Megan, you gave me a rare turn then, so you did,' she almost wept.

Her husband, who was looking on, said firmly, 'Mother, the child's name is *Lizzie*.'

'Oh yes, so it is,' she flustered.

From the second that the girl had stepped through the door he had feared that this would happen. Blodwyn seemed to think that Lizzie could take the place of the child they had lost. But somewhere was Lizzie's mother, and one day, God willing, Lizzie would return to her. Perhaps it would be best for all concerned if that day was to come sooner rather than later, for Daffyd Evans was beginning to think it might all end in tears.

Once his wife had shepherded the little girl upstairs, he sank into the fireside chair as yet another coughing fit overtook him. Hastily snatching a handkerchief from his trouser pocket he held it to his mouth until the spasm had passed. Then, holding it away from him, he gazed at the stain on it in the light from the fire. More blood. Hearing

Blodwyn's step on the stairs, he flung it into the roaring fire where the flames quickly consumed it. Stifling a wry smile he wondered how long it would be before he completely ran out of handkerchiefs. But then it didn't really matter. What Blodwyn didn't see wouldn't hurt her.

When they'd moved to the blacksmith's cottage less than five years ago, Daffyd had hoped that it would be a new start for both of them. It certainly had been for him. After years of living in a tiny, tied miner's cottage up in the hills, this new home had seemed luxurious, and not to have to go down into the bowels of the earth each day to earn a living was an added bonus. He had learned the trade of blacksmith from his father many years ago as a boy, but then he had married Blodwyn and gone into mining as so many of the Welsh menfolk did.

He'd thought he had finally escaped the mines and all they represented, but he hadn't allowed for the legacy that his years down the pit had left him: the blood on his handkerchief each time he coughed. And the cough was getting worse, though he would never have admitted it to his wife.

His worried eyes strayed to the stairs door. From above, the sound of Blodwyn fussing over the child like a mother hen floated down to him.

He shook his head in bewilderment. Blodwyn had changed already in the short time since the child's arrival, and if he were any judge, not for the better.

On Sunday, for the first time in more years than he cared to remember, she had failed to make her ritual trip to the churchyard with flowers for Megan's grave. It was just as if she saw the child reincarnated in Lizzie. Burying his face in his hands, the sick man shook his head from side to side. Why did things always have to be so difficult?

* * *

Back at *Tremarfon* the mood was not much lighter. Danny hurried away upstairs and slipped into his pyjamas, then quietly made his way back downstairs to say goodnight. He found the kitchen empty except for Samson and Hemily, who was curled up in a ball fast asleep in the fire-side chair.

Stepping back into the hall, he noticed that the library door was slightly ajar so he tiptoed towards it and inched it open. The room was in darkness save for the light of the moon that was flooding through the window. Eric was standing with his back to him, staring up at the painting of the woman Danny had admired the day before. Something about the stoop of his shoulders told of a great sadness, and Danny suddenly felt as if he were imposing on something that he shouldn't see. Quiet as a mouse, he crept back up the stairs and slipped into bed, shuddering at the cold sheets. It had been a funny old night, one way and another, and he for one would be glad to see the back of it.

Like Lizzie in the blacksmith's cottage down in the village, he wondered what his mother would be doing now. In his mind's eye he could see her, sitting at her sewing-machine with the firelight playing on her hair, turning it to the colour of wheaten gold. If he closed his eyes tight and really concentrated, he could almost smell the sweet, clean scent of her.

We could be home for Christmas, he had told Lizzie, and he clung to the thought, for he didn't know what to make of Eric at all. One minute he felt as if he was in the way, and the next minute the man would be kind to him. It was all very confusing and once again he wondered at the complexity of adults.

Sneaking out of bed, he crept towards the window and stared out into the starry night. A silver moon was sailing high in the sky and the sea in the distance looked as if it had been sprinkled with fairy dust. The wind was bending the trees, making them appear as if they were trying to pull themselves free of their roots, as they swayed erratically to and fro. The vast spaces made the small terraced house in Coventry where he had come from appear even tinier and cramped than it was. And yet, he would have given all this up there and then to be tucked up back in his own little bed at home with Lizzie curled up beside him.

His troubled eyes returned to the moon as a thought suddenly occurred to him. That very same moon was shining down on his mother. 'Will you tell her I miss her?' he whispered to the bright shiny orb, then he climbed back into bed where he tossed and turned until sleep finally claimed him.

Chapter Twenty

Early the following morning, as Maggie snatched up the cards from the doormat, she almost sobbed with relief. At least now she knew that the children had arrived safely at their destination. It was a crying shame that they had been split up. She had prayed that Lizzie and Danny would be placed together, but those prayers had gone unanswered.

'Any news?' her mother shouted from the kitchen.

'Yes, the cards with the addresses have turned up, but Mam, they've been split up. How do you think Lizzie will cope with that?'

Ellen sighed. 'You'd be surprised, love. Children are a lot more resilient than folks give 'em credit for. Just so long as they can see each other from time to time, I've no doubt she'll manage just fine.'

Maggie wished that she could believe her, but somehow she didn't. In the short time since the twins had gone, her mother had been venturing over to see her a little more, and the last thing Maggie wanted to do was upset her, so she wisely said nothing.

Ellen tried to cheer her up. 'You did the right thing letting them go, love. Look what's been happening in London this last few days. The poor sods there barely know what's hit 'em, an' who's to say it won't be our

219

turn again next? They've hit the Woolwich Arsenal, a gas station an' the docks, an' that's not to mention the devastation they've caused in the city itself. They reckon three hundred bombers and six hundred fighters were flyin' over the Thames at one time. Nearly a thousand enemy planes! Anyway, that's enough o' that. At least the twins are out of it now.'

Deep down, Maggie knew that her mother was right, but still she felt their absence.

Minutes after the children's postcards had arrived in Coventry, Eric was shaking Danny's arm, to wake him. The child stirred and looked up at him sleepily. The bed was warm and he was reluctant to be disturbed.

'Come on,' Eric told him. 'It's your first day at school today so you don't want to be late, do you? I have your breakfast ready downstairs when you've washed and dressed.' Without another word he turned and left the room.

Danny stretched and yawned lazily as he looked towards the window. Great fat raindrops were lashing against the glass and the sky was leaden and grey. Swinging his legs out of bed he shuddered as his feet came into contact with the cold lino. The water that he dipped the flannel in was even colder, and by the time he'd struggled into his clothes he was shivering. Dragging a comb through his hair he lifted his shoes and headed for the kitchen. At least it would be warm in there.

Eric had a huge pan of creamy porridge bubbling on the stove, and when Danny appeared he nodded towards the table. 'Sit yourself down. This will soon warm you up.' Ladling a generous portion into Danny's bowl he then picked up the sketches that Danny had left lying about and began to thumb through them.

'You know, these are actually very good. Have you ever thought of trying your hand at painting?'

Danny nodded eagerly through a mouthful of porridge. 'Oh yes, I got to do paintin' at me old school sometimes. Not at home though. Me mam couldn't afford all the brushes an' paint an' such so I just used to sketch at home.'

'Mmm. Then how would you feel if I were able to supply you with some?'

Danny stared at him as if he could hardly believe what he had just heard. Was Eric playing some sort of practical joke on him? When their eyes met he nodded cautiously. 'I'd love to have some paints,' he admitted, 'but they're very expensive, yer know.'

Eric waved aside his concerns. 'Don't you get worrying about that. I think you have a flair for art that should be encouraged.'

Danny's chest puffed out to almost twice its size in delight, and seeing his reaction, Eric nodded. 'Right, that's settled then. I'll have some ready for you when you get home from school. I'll be able to give you a few pointers in the right direction if you'd like me to.'

'Why, do yer know how to paint, then?'

A flicker of amusement played around Eric's lips. 'You could say that. But never mind that for now. You've got your first day at school to get behind you first. I've done you a packed lunch over there on the dresser. You know where the village school is, don't you?'

Danny nodded as he spooned the last of his porridge into his mouth then slid smoothly from his chair. Picking up his lunchbox, he eyed a huge brown envelope that was lying beside it. The sight of it made him think of the postcards he and Lizzie had posted off to their mother on Saturday.

'Eric,' he asked tentatively, 'how long do yer think it would take fer a postcard to reach me mam from here?'

'Oh, not more than a couple of days if the post is getting through all right, I shouldn't think,' Eric told him.

Danny smiled. If Eric was right, then his mam might be reading them right now. The thought made him feel closer to her somehow.

'Thanks fer this.' He waved his lunchbox at Eric, then moving towards the door, he told him, 'I'll see yer later then. Ta-ra.'

Again he thought he detected a flicker of amusement as Eric raised his hand. 'Ta-ra.'

Once outside, Danny pulled the collar of his blazer up, and with his head bent against the rain, began the steep descent down the hillside. He'd gone no more than a few yards when he heard something and paused.

'Pssst . . .' There it was again. Glancing into the trees that bordered the road, he smiled with relief as Soho Gus appeared, sporting a brand new haircut.

'Thought yer might like a bit o' company walking to school, seein' as it's yer first day,' Gus told him cheerfully.

Danny dragged his eyes away from his friend's hair and grinned as Albert's little white head appeared from the top pocket of Gus's blazer. The pocket had now stretched to at least three times its original size, which was hardly surprising when Danny came to think of how much time Albert spent in there.

'Don't the teachers mind yer takin' Albert to school?' he asked with a broad grin on his face.

'They ain't gorra a whole lot o' choice in the matter, 'ave they?' Gus sniffed. 'Where I go he goes, an' that's the end of it, though I admit I do pop him in me desk during the day.' He fell into step beside Danny and soon the village came into sight far below them as they splashed through the puddles.

'So how's it goin' back there then?' Gus asked inquisitively. 'An' have yer found out why Eric locks himself away in that big outbuildin' yet?'

'No,' Danny admitted regretfully. 'But he ain't half bad when yer get to know him a bit. In fact, he's offered to set me up with some paints an' brushes when I get home from school this afternoon.'

Gus's eyebrows disappeared into his short fringe, which up to now, Danny had tactfully refrained from mentioning. 'I wouldn't have taken you for one o' those arty-farty types,' he teased.

Danny shrugged defensively. 'I like to sketch *an'* paint if it comes to that. Always have done. There's nowt wrong with that, is there?'

Not wishing to offend his newfound friend, Gus hastily shook his head. 'No, 'course there ain't. I were only teasin'.'

As he spoke, he noticed Danny looking at him and his hand self-consciously flew to his freshly shorn hair. 'Yer can blame that sister o' yourn fer this haircut. All hell were let loose at *Derwen Deg* last night, I'm tellin' yer. That nutty Mrs Evans come chargin' in sayin' as your Lizzie had got nits off me an' somethin' about Lizzie goin' missin'. She reckons as Eric had her up at *Tremarfon*.'

'Lizzie *did* come to see me without telling Mrs Evans she was going,' Danny said, 'but it weren't Eric's fault. In fact, he got the car out an' took her back.'

'Well, I got the blame fer the nits. Mad old cow, that Blodwyn is,' grumbled Gus. 'The second she'd gone the old woman were snippin' at me hair like she were shearin' a bleedin' sheep. *An'* she made me wash it in carbolic soap,' he added, deeply aggrieved.

'Did she find any nits?' Danny asked with a twinkle in his eye.

Gus wiped his nose along the length of his blazer sleeve, leaving a slimy trail. 'As it 'appens she did,' he said with dignity. 'But that don't mean to say your Lizzie got 'em off me, does it? I might've got 'em off *her*, beggin' yer pardon, that is.'

Seeing as how Lizzie and he had mixed with no one else since arriving in the village, Danny thought it highly unlikely that she could have caught them from anyone else. But he cleverly changed the subject by asking. 'What did you mean just now when you called Mrs Evans a mad old cow?'

'Exactly what I said. Everyone knows that she's barmy. Apparently she lost a kid some years ago, an' accordin' to the villagers she went a bit funny in the 'ead like. She had two lads an' all, but they scarpered as soon as they were old enough to leave 'ome. She's got a lot o' nerve though, to come up to *Derwen Deg* like that.'

By now they were on the road that led into the village. Other children had appeared from nowhere and were heading in a steady stream towards the village school. Not one of them so much as looked in their direction, which Danny found rather strange. Back at school in Coventry, a newcomer was eyed with curiosity, but he and Gus might have been invisible.

'As yer can see, the Welsh kids ain't too fond of us foreigners,' Gus commented. 'It ain't too bad though. We evacuees get to go in a separate class, so the only time we really see 'em is durin' break and lunch-hour.'

At that moment, they saw the cottage door next to the blacksmith's open and Mrs Evans appeared, clutching Lizzie's hand. Lizzie spotted the boys almost immediately and would have waited for them, but when she paused, the huge woman bent to whisper something in her ear and then hauled her on.

'Didn't I tell yer she weren't all the ticket?' Gus snorted. 'Their cottage ain't a stone's throw from the school, so why is she walkin' her there?'

Having no answer to Gus's question, Danny merely shrugged as they hurried to try and catch Lizzie up.

It was as they were passing the village hall that Gus told him, 'They're havin' a dance there on Sat'day night. I dare say the Thomases will be goin'. They reckon they have a rare good time, jitterbuggin' an' everyfink. Problem is, they won't let kids go so I'll probably get left at home on me own.'

'I've never been to a dance,' Danny said, 'but I did used to go to the pictures back home most Saturday mornings. We saw some crackin' good films. Don't they have a picture-house here?'

'Nah. Yer have to go into Pwllheli. Mrs Thomas goes sometimes, 'specially if there's a Humphrey Bogart film on, but there's nuffin' like that here in Sarn-Bach. Nothin' excitin' *ever* happens here – we're stuck in the back o' beyond.'

Danny thought that Sarn-Bach was the most beautiful place he had ever seen but decided against saying it.

The school playground was teeming with children of all shapes and sizes. It was surrounded by tall metal railings that made it look a bit like a prison. Danny was looking around with interest when Lizzie spotted him. Pulling her hand away from Mrs Evans's larger one, she hurtled towards him.

'Danny!' Her face lit up at the sight of her twin. 'Are you all right?'

'Course I am. Why wouldn't I be?' Danny blushed with

embarrassment as some of the children looked towards him. Thankfully, just then a bell sounded and the Welsh children instantly began to form straight lines. His embarrassment faded away to shock when the same wizened-up little woman who'd met them off the train appeared in the school doorway.

'That's Miss Williams,' Gus hissed in his ear. 'She teaches the evacuees 'cos she can talk English. The other teachers gabble away in Welsh all the bleedin' time, an' yer can't understand a word they're sayin'.'

Danny nodded as Miss Williams began to herd the evacuees into a separate line. She glared at Mrs Evans, who was once again clutching Lizzie's hand, and the woman turned the colour of a beetroot as she reluctantly loosened her grip.

'Now then, children. Follow me,' the teacher commanded, and so began one of the strangest days Danny and Lizzie could ever remember as she marched them into the school. The Welsh children were herded into classrooms whilst the rest of them, children ranging from five to fourteen years old, were left standing in the hall.

'Ain't we going into separate classes?' Danny managed to whisper to Gus.

Gus answered him from behind the back of his hand. 'Gerroff wi' yer. This is as good as it gets.'

Danny thought it was very strange. Back at school in Coventry, all the children in his class had been roughly the same age, but here it seemed that age was irrelevant. Still, he decided, with a shrug of his shoulders, they were all in the same boat so he might as well just get on with it.

They were led into a room with three lines of desks and chairs set out in regimental rows. It was a small room compared to the rest of the classrooms, but because of its high ceiling it still managed to be cold.

'Crikey, yer could freeze in here,' Danny commented quietly to Gus.

'Right,' Miss Williams rapped with authority. 'Less talking now, boy. You are not here to talk – you're here to learn. Little ones to the front, older ones to the back.'

The children quickly slid behind their desks as Miss Williams began to hand out paper and pencils, and soon they were busily doing arithmetic.

It was playtime before Danny and Lizzie got to meet their classmates properly, but the second they were outside in the playground, Gus began to introduce them.

'That's Nick over there.' He pointed to a boy who was rampaging around the play area like a mad thing. 'An' her over there is Audrey, an' that's . . .' He rambled on as Lizzie and Danny looked on. They were sure that they would never remember everyone's name but didn't want to offend Gus by stopping him.

'An' this,' Gus told them finally, 'is Sparky, me mate. He's from the East End an' all.'

The twins nodded at a solemn-faced, dark-haired little boy with startling blue eyes. He was considerably smaller than Danny and looked just as untidy. But there was something about him that didn't seem quite right, and this was borne out when Gus whispered behind his hand, 'Sparky is a bit slow, like. Yer know? A bit doo-lally.' He tapped his forehead to add emphasis to his words. 'On top o' that, he was what they call a blue baby when he were born so he gets out o' breath real quick. But he's harmless enough really. He tends to get picked on, so I stick up fer 'im.'

When Lizzie smiled at Gus admiringly, the small boy felt as if he would burst with joy. She looked absolutely beautiful today. Her long fair hair was tied into plaits with shiny blue ribbons, and she was wearing one of the dresses her mother had painstakingly stitched for her. Gus knew for sure that she was the prettiest girl in the whole of the playground. In the whole of the world, if it came to that, but of course he didn't tell her so. He didn't want Sparky and Danny to think that he was going soft.

'What's a blue baby?' Danny asked inquisitively.

'It means he were born wiv a hole in his heart,' Gus informed them knowingly. He was about to go on when someone called Lizzie's name. They looked towards the sound to see Mrs Evans waving at them over the railings.

'Oh no.' Lizzie felt embarrassment flood through her as she reluctantly walked towards her.

'Tut tut.' Mrs Evans frowned as she approached. 'Whatever are you doing out here without your coat on, Lizziebright? You'll catch your death of cold, so you will. But never mind that for now. See? I've brought you a nice apple to eat in your break. I don't want you getting hungry and it's a long time until dinnertime.'

Lizzie awkwardly reached through the railings and took the proffered fruit, wishing that Mrs Evans would just leave. None of the other mothers or carers had come and she could hear children sniggering behind her.

'Thank you,' she muttered, and to her relief, Mrs Evans turned and began to stride away. 'I'll be here to meet you at lunchtime,' she called over her shoulder.

'Oh no, really. There's no need. I know the way—' Lizzie began, but it was no use. Mrs Evans was already out of earshot. Mortified, she pushed the apple into the pocket of her dress and crossed to join the others.

'What was all that about?' Danny asked as she drew abreast.

'Oh Danny, I don't like living with Mrs Evans.' Lizzie's voice faltered.

'Why not?'

'She's . . . well, she fusses over me all the time.'

'That's hardly a bad thing,' Danny sensibly pointed out. 'It just means that she likes you, that's all.'

'No, no, it's more than that. It's like . . .' Lizzie struggled to find the right words to describe how she felt. 'Last night I woke up an' she was standin' over me bed stroking my hair.'

Danny sighed. 'What's so terrible about that? She was probably just checking that you were all right.'

'But she kept calling me Megan. She does it all the time, especially when Mr Evans ain't there.'

Danny scratched his head. It did sound strange, he had to admit. However, the conversation was stopped from going any further when a teacher appeared and began to ring a bell, heralding the end of break.

'We'll talk more about it later,' Danny assured her, then taking her firmly by the hand he led her back to the classroom.

Chapter Twenty-One

Closing the stairs door softly behind her, Maggie looked across at Jo, who was sitting at the kitchen table, listening to the radio.

Maggie had a mountain of sewing to do now that she'd put Lucy to bed, but first she was going to treat herself to a well-earned snack.

'Do you fancy a sandwich, Jo?' She went towards the pantry.

'Sshh,' Jo said immediately as she hung on the broadcaster's every word.

Maggie shrugged as she took the loaf from the bread bin and lifted two plates down from the dresser. She had just smeared a meagre amount of butter onto two slices and begun to spread them with fishpaste when the broadcast finally ended and the haunting strains of Joe Loss's Orchestra playing 'I'll Never Smile Again' echoed around the small room. Sighing deeply, Jo joined her at the kitchen table.

'Things are goin' from bad to worse,' the girl said gloomily. 'Apparently the Italians attacked Greece today. Some of our warships are on their way out there right now to give Greece some back-up. The King an' the Prime Minister have both pledged to give full aid to the Greeks. It seems the whole world is gettin' drawn in. Ugh, it don't bear thinkin' about really, does it?'

'No, it doesn't.' Maggie's thoughts went to Sam and David. Were they on their way to Greece right now, in some great battleship? There had been no news from either of them and she was beginning to worry. She hadn't really expected Sam to get in touch, but she thought it strange that David hadn't written to his mother again at least. She said as much now to Jo, who listened soberly.

'Well, whether they are still alive or whether they ain't, there's not much you can do about it, is there?'

Maggie was forced to agree. In the short time that Jo had been lodging with her, the two young women had become very close. Courtaulds factory had been bombed, and Jo now worked in a small but select dress shop on Primrose Hill, which was just as well, for she had moved in with Maggie with nothing but the clothes she had stood up in. Working at the shop had enabled her to buy herself a few new clothes each week from her meagre wages, plus Maggie had made her some smart skirts from offcuts of material that she had got from Coventry market for a snip. Initially, Jo had borrowed some of Maggie's clothes, which had hung off her, for she had lost an enormous amount of weight.

The new outfits she'd selected had come as a surprise to Maggie. They were nothing at all like the gaudy concoctions she had worn to walk the streets in, nor yet again anything like the loose baggy affairs she had worn to work in the munitions factory.

At the moment she was wearing a tasteful knitted twin-set in a soft shade of blue, and a straight navy skirt that fell sedately below the knees. Her hair had grown a little and was inclined to be naturally wavy, and devoid of the heavy make-up she had worn to attract clients, she looked totally different, apart from the dark shadows

231

beneath her eyes and her gaunt cheeks, which told of her inner pain.

Maggie knew that Jo still missed her family dreadfully. Some nights she cried out in the grip of a nightmare and Maggie would race across the landing and wrap her in her arms as Jo sobbed her heart out. Personally, Maggie was inclined to think that Jo had gone back to work far too soon. But as she had soon rediscovered, Jo could be stubbornly independent.

'I'm not goin' to sit here on me arse all day an' sponge off you,' the girl had declared indignantly when Maggie suggested she should give herself a little more time to grieve. 'If you're good enough to let me stay here fer a while, the least I can do is pay me way. Besides, if I'm working an' keeping meself busy I'll have less time to think, won't I?'

Maggie had reluctantly agreed, although the trauma Jo had been through had deeply affected her too. Following the night of the raid, Jo had returned to the ruins of her home to watch her family being dug from the wreckage one by one. It had been a heartbreaking sight, and even the men who were digging had been reduced to tears as they passed out the broken little bodies of Jo's siblings. Then they'd had the funerals to endure and Maggie had been impressed at Jo's resilience, wondering how she would have coped in the same situation.

Maggie's mother had taken to Jo straight away, and so had all the neighbours when they learned of the poor girl's plight. The only one who was giving cause for concern was Mr Massey, who had eyed Jo suspiciously.

'Ain't I seen you somewhere before, gel?' he'd asked as he rubbed thoughtfully at his chin.

'I err . . . I don't think so.' Panic had flared in Jo's eyes as she blinked rapidly.

Once alone with Maggie, she'd been almost beside herself with fear. 'He's seen me out on the game,' she had told her fretfully.

'You don't know that, so don't jump to conclusions,' Maggie had soothed, but even so, Jo was on edge every time she saw him now, and she avoided him like the plague.

It was of him that Jo now spoke as Maggie placed her supper in front of her. 'I passed Mr Massey in the entry tonight as I was comin' back in from work.'

'Did you?' Maggie asked absently, her thoughts far away with Sam and David. 'Did he speak to you?'

'Yes, he did. But it's the way he looks at me that's unnervin'. It's as if he's rackin' his brain to think where he's seen me before.'

Hearing the fear in her friend's voice, Maggie pulled her thoughts back to the conversation they were having. 'Oh Jo, I really do think you're fussing over nothing. Even if he *has* seen you before, it doesn't mean to say that you were standing on a street corner. Swanshill isn't that big a place. He could have seen you outside the factory gates or anywhere, if it comes to that.'

'I suppose you're right,' Jo admitted reluctantly, 'but wouldn't it be awful if it all comes out – just when I've got the chance to put the past behind me.'

Seeing that Maggie's mind wasn't 100 per cent on what she was saying, she suddenly felt guilty. Maggie was going through her own private hell at the minute, worrying about the twins. Not a day went by when she didn't talk about them or stand on the doorstep looking for the postman, who she prayed would deliver news of them.

'Did the postman bring anythin' interesting this morning?' she asked.

Maggie shook her head as her eyes strayed to the two rather bedraggled postcards propped up on the mantelshelf.

'No, nothing since those postcards came with the twins' addresses on them, although I have written back to them. But then the post is all over the place at the minute. So I suppose I'm expecting too much too soon. I would love to hear from them though.'

'Of course you would, and you will,' Jo told her softly as she heard the longing in her friend's voice. 'Look at it this way: at the minute, no news is good news. I've no doubt there's many a poor sod out there tonight who would do anything not to have had a telegram today. And at least you know they're safe.'

Maggie nodded more cheerfully as she thought on her words. Jo was quite right, of course, but it didn't stop her missing them.

As David looked around him he felt as if he were caught in the grip of some ongoing nightmare. A carpet of corpses spread before him, and although it was still night the sky above was alight with tracers. His eyes darted from side to side. All day he had been looking out for his twin brother, but up to now he had seen no sign of him, although he knew that Sam was there somewhere. There was a need in him to speak to Sam. To tell him that he loved him despite the fact that they had never been close. Perhaps it was because as time passed he had the uncanny feeling that his days were numbered.

Hearing someone behind him, he turned and opened fire. The bullet got the German by chance in the centre of his forehead and the soldier, who David now saw was no more than a boy, looked mildly surprised as he sank to his knees before dropping face down.

David felt nothing. Just a few short months ago he would never have believed that he could kill someone, but now it was kill or be killed. He paused to rest his aching feet. The skin had long since peeled off them through a combination of the rigid Army boots he was forced to wear and the wet, sodden fields he had traipsed across. It was as he was standing there that he became aware of another figure stumbling towards him through a haze of gunsmoke. He had just raised his rifle to fire again when a familiar voice floated to him on the cloying air.

'David . . .'

His finger hovered on the trigger as Sam's soot-blackened face appeared out of the mist. Relief washed over him as he lowered his rifle.

'I've been looking for you. I was worried that you didn't make it.' He had to shout to make himself heard above the bedlam that was going on all around them.

As they silently faced each other, David was shocked to see the hatred burning in his brother's eyes.

'Don't yer mean yer were hopin' that I *hadn't* fuckin' made it?' Sam grated. 'It would have left the way clear fer yer to head fer home an' take me family with a clear conscience then, wouldn't it?'

'Don't talk such rubbish!' David snapped. 'This is hardly the time for talkin' about ridiculous things like that. They are *your* family. Maggie made her choice many years ago. You'd do more good to concentrate on stayin' alive at the minute. Chances are, neither of us will get home the way things are goin' here.' He ducked as a bullet whistled past his head but Sam stood his ground with his rifle aimed at his brother. As David became aware of his brother's intentions, his eyes stretched wide with alarm.

'Don't be such a bloody fool, man.'

The words had scarcely left his lips when the sound of another bullet, briefly illuminated by a Verey light, whizzed past him. Sam jerked like a puppet on a string. One of his hands clutched at his stomach and David watched in horror as blood began to seep through his brother's fingers to stain the mud that was caked on his uniform.

'Oh, my God.' For a second he was rooted to the spot, but then as Sam's knees began to buckle he sprang towards him with tears streaming down his face. It was then that Sam fired with the last of his remaining strength and a burning pain ripped through David's arm, causing him to drop his rifle into the putrid mud. The blast lifted him from his feet and knocked him flat on his back, but then somehow, he managed to roll over and crawl across to Sam. The short distance between them seemed to take forever as sweat stood out on his brow, but at last he reached Sam, and dragging himself up onto his one good arm he gazed down into his twin's face. Sightless eyes stared up at him and he knew instantly that his brother was dead.

'Sam . . .' His voice was no more than a whisper as he felt his life's blood seeping out of him. It shouldn't have been like this. They had grown in the same womb side by side and should have been friends; should have loved each other. Instead, Sam had tried to kill him.

He had always imagined that he would die in his own comfortable bed, or perhaps in an easy chair at the side of a roaring fire, an old, old man with a loving family gathered around him. Not on some godforsaken field miles away from home. Suddenly he didn't want to fight any more. Sam was out of his pain and David wanted to join him. Delicious warmth stole over him as a picture of Maggie and Lucy flashed in front of his eyes. Laying his head on his brother's still chest he waited for death to claim him. They had come into the world within minutes of each other. It was only right that they should leave the same way.

Mrs Massey was washing the front windows with vinegar and water when the sound of a bicycle trundling down the street distracted her. Dropping the cloth back into the bucket, she looked up and the sight she saw made her heart skip a beat. A young man on a bicycle was bearing down on her. Instantly she knew that he was bringing a telegram, for his eyes were scanning the door numbers of Clay Lane as his feet pumped at the pedals. She prayed that he would go straight past, but her prayers went unanswered, for when he was only a couple of doors away he slammed on his brakes and slewed the bicycle to a halt. Her heart was thumping so loudly now that she was sure he would hear it as she thought of her two boys.

Propping his bike against the wall of the house he asked, 'Mrs Bright?'

Relief made her knees go weak as she shook her head. It appeared her boys had been spared for now, though the telegram he was clutching in his hand didn't bode well for Maggie.

'This door here,' she told him, and nodding, he stepped past her and rapped on it loudly.

Mrs Massey wanted to disappear and leave Maggie in privacy for the ordeal ahead, but her legs seemed to have developed a will of their own and she stood there as if she had been rooted to the spot.

The whir of Maggie's sewing-machine, which could vaguely be heard out on the pavement, stopped abruptly, and the next second she heard the bolts being drawn back and Maggie appeared with a mouthful of pins and a length of parachute silk slung across her shoulder.

The colour drained from her face as her eyes became riveted on the paper in the boy's hand.

'Mrs Bright?'

She nodded numbly, unable to speak through the mouthful of pins.

He handed her the telegram. 'There you go then, ma'am. I'm sorry.'

Turning away, he clambered back onto his bicycle and rode off as Maggie stared in disbelief at the piece of paper in her hand. Her mind was in turmoil. Had something happened to the twins – or was it Sam?

Seeing her bewilderment, Mrs Massey suddenly leaped towards her and, taking her elbow, drew her back into the privacy of her front room. Up and down the street, net curtains were twitching as women thanked God that the dreaded telegram hadn't come for one of them.

'Shall I make yer a nice strong brew, love?' she offered for want of something to say.

Maggie seemed not to hear her and stood there as if she had been cast in stone. Pressing her down onto the nearest chair, Mrs Massey ruffled Lucy's curls before hurrying away to put the kettle on. When she returned, Maggie was sitting exactly where she had left her with the telegram, still unopened, clutched in her hand. She raised her eyes and looked beseechingly at Mrs Massey, who gently took it from her.

'Shall I open it for yer?'

Maggie nodded, so placing her thumb beneath the edge of the envelope Mrs Massey slit it open and withdrew the telegram within. Time stood still as the older woman's eyes scanned the page, then she turned towards

Maggie. At that moment the door burst open and Ellen appeared. The neighbours had wasted no time in telling her that Maggie had received a telegram and she had run across the Lane.

'What's happened?' she asked breathlessly as she put a protective arm about Maggie's shoulders.

'It's Sam.' There was a catch in Mrs Massey's voice. She had never professed to be a lover of Maggie's husband. In fact, there had been times when she had thought him to be a right bastard – but she wouldn't have wished anyone to die like this. 'I'm afraid he's been killed in action, love.'

A wealth of emotions flitted across Maggie's face as she leaned heavily against her mother. Sam was dead. The words whirled round and around in her head yet somehow they wouldn't sink in. Sam *couldn't* be dead. He hadn't even wanted to go to war in the first place. There must be some mistake.

'He . . . he can't be,' she stuttered. 'They must have got it wrong.'

Mrs Massey shook her head sadly. 'I'm afraid there's no mistake, love. Here – read it fer yerself.'

As Maggie's eyes flew across the page, tears started to spill down her cheeks. *It is with great regret that we write to inform you that your husband, Corporal Samuel Bright, was killed in action whilst . . .*

The rest of the page became a blur as tears gushed from her eyes.

'There, there, love,' Ellen comforted her, tears standing in her own eyes. 'It's a wicked shame that a man so young should be cut down in the prime of his life, but at least you have the comfort of knowing that he died for King and country.'

Maggie's tears suddenly turned to hysterical laughter.

'That's a joke. They almost had to *drag* him there, kicking and screaming!'

Mrs Massey and Ellen exchanged a worried glance above Maggie's head. It was common knowledge that Maggie and Sam's marriage had never been a bed of roses. But all the same he had been her husband, for better or for worse, and this was not going to be easy for her.

'What am I going to tell the children?' Maggie exclaimed in a high-pitched voice that sounded nothing like her own.

'Don't get frettin' about that fer now,' Ellen advised. 'Let's just cross each bridge as we come to it, eh? You have to get used to what's happened yourself, before you even think about what we're going to tell the little 'uns. They're safe an' sound an' well out of it, thank God.'

Maggie prayed that her mother was right. Somehow, she would get over this. She knew she would, but if anything were to happen to the children, she didn't know how she would cope. The initial feeling of shock began to ebb away and guilt quickly took its place. She and Sam had never even said a proper goodbye. In truth, she had known that she'd lost him on the night he left the house to hide at his mother's, but at least he had still been alive out there somewhere. Her thoughts turned to David. Was *he* still alive?

She sprang out of the chair with tears still wet on her cheeks. 'I have to go and tell Sam's mother,' she gasped. 'I don't want her hearing the news from someone else.'

Ellen agreed in principle with Maggie's comment, but all the same she didn't want Maggie to go alone after the shock she had just received. The thought of going with her struck terror into her heart. Since the death of Maggie's father she had never ventured farther than over the road to Maggie's house, and even though Beryl Sharp lived only a few streets away, to her mind it appeared like a mammoth journey.

Forcing herself to stay calm she said, 'I'll come with you,' but thankfully, Maggie shook her head.

'No, Mam. I appreciate the offer but this is something I have to do on my own. It's not going to be easy for her and she might not like to have anyone else around. It knocked her for six when she lost Sam's father seven years ago, but this is going to be even worse for her to cope with. You somehow don't expect your children to die before you, do you?'

Ellen guiltily swallowed the relief that had risen in her throat as she nodded understandingly. 'If that's what you want, love. You get off and take as long as you like. Lucy will be fine here with me, won't you, sweetheart?'

Thankfully, Lucy was oblivious to everything that was going on and smiled disarmingly up at her gran as Maggie walked from the room to get ready. Whilst she was upstairs she heard the back door open and Jo, who was on her lunch-break, appeared, closely followed by Mr Massey, who was looking for his wife.

Maggie heard the whispers as her mother solemnly told them what had happened and Jo's gasp of dismay. When she re-entered the room, Jo flew across to her and wrapped her in a friendly embrace. 'I'm so sorry, Maggie.'

She shrugged. 'It's one of those things, isn't it? No doubt I'll not be the only one to get a telegram today.' Her eyes came to rest on Mr Massey. He was about to leave to do his stint for the ARP, and was standing turning his tin cap in his hand near the door, his eyes fixed firmly on Jo.

Suddenly his eyes almost started from his head as it finally came to him where he had seen Jo before.

Ever since she had moved in with Maggie, it had been preying on his mind but now it finally came to him.

'*Good God above*. You were the one that used to stand on the end of Beagle Street of a night!' he exclaimed tactlessly. 'An' don't bother to deny it, 'cos I used to work wi' a young bloke that were one o' yer regular customers. Many a time I told him, "Mind what yer doin', son. Yer never know what yer might pick up from these street girls." Maggie – were you aware that you had a prostitute livin' in yer house?'

A stunned silence settled on the room. Jo shrivelled with dismay. She'd hoped that she had managed to put her past behind her, but now here it was, ready to smack her in the face again.

It was Mrs Massey who, after her initial shock, managed to take control of the situation. Grasping Maggie firmly by the elbow, she steered her towards the door.

'You get off now, love,' she told her kindly, and then turning her attention back to her husband she snapped, 'As for *you*, this is neither the time nor the place so shut yer trap, will yer? Even if what you're sayin' is true, happen there was a reason for it – but now is not the time to be delvin' into it. It's none of our business, and I reckon as how you should apologise to young Jo here. Poor Maggie has more than enough on her plate to be dealing with at present wi'out you adding to her troubles. The lass has just found out that her husband is dead, an' it's the twins' tenth birthday soon, an' she's breakin' her heart over that an' all because she won't be able to spend it with 'em.'

Mr Massey had the good grace to hang his head in shame as Maggie stepped past him and closed the door behind her. Once outside in the chilly air she breathed deeply, attempting to calm herself down. What a day this was turning out to be; she wondered if it could get any worse. As she forced herself towards her mother-in-law's home she prayed that there wouldn't be yet more bad news waiting for her there. Had anything happened to David, his mother would have received a telegram too. This thought, on top of everything else, was almost more than she could bear.

Chapter Twenty-Two

As Mrs Evans waddled past the smithy she paused. A large horse that was waiting to be shod was impatiently pawing at the ground outside. Poking her head round the door, she was just in time to catch her husband leaning heavily against the anvil. Seeing her, he quickly swiped an oily rag across his mouth.

'What's to do then, Father!' she exclaimed.

Thrusting the rag into the depths of his leather apron pocket, Daffyd gave her a weak smile. Behind him, a wide stone shelf bearing various tools stood above a roaring fire and the atmosphere was sooty and heavy with smoke.

'Oh, I just thought I'd stop for a breather,' he told her, none too convincingly.

Stepping into the hot gloom over the square-headed nails that were scattered across the natural rock floor, she asked, 'Are you not feeling well, Daffyd?' Her voice was laden with concern.

'Never felt better,' he lied. 'But what are you doing out and about at this time of the morning?'

She grinned. 'I popped up to the school to take Lizziebright some fruit for her break. It was a pleasure to see her face, so it was. Bright by name and bright by nature, that little one is.'

'Just so long as you remember that her name *is* Bright.'

'Why, Father, I can't think what you could mean,' she said indignantly, and flouncing about, she stormed from the smithy, leaving him to shake his head with concern.

Just as she had promised, at lunchtime she was waiting at the school gates. Lizzie's heart sank into her boots when she saw the big woman standing there. She had begged to be allowed a packed lunch so that she could spend her lunch-hour with Danny, but Mrs Evans had almost had a fit when she had first suggested it.

'Eeh, what are you thinking of, *bach*?' she had gasped in horror. 'Why make do with bread and cheese when you can have a good hot substantial meal inside of you? Didn't I tell you when you arrived that I was going to fatten you up? No, *cariad*, you'll come home with me where you belong.'

And so Lizzie was marched back though the village and presented with a huge plate of faggots and peas. But worse was still to come. She had barely finished her meal when Mrs Evans threw her hands in the air as if the end of the world had come.

'Why, *bach*. You've got gravy all down your dress, so you have. But never mind. I have just the thing for you to slip into.'

Crossing to a large box that Lizzie had noticed when they first entered the room, she rummaged around in it for a few seconds and then produced a little woollen skirt and a Fairisle cardigan. Holding them against Lizzie, she sighed with satisfaction. They had once belonged to Megan and had languished in the loft for years, but now she could put them to good use again. Luckily, they were an almost perfect fit, for although Megan had been younger than Lizzie when she died, she had been a tall leggy girl, whereas Lizzie was much shorter.

In no time at all, Mrs Evans had whipped the dress over the child's head and slipped the other clothes onto her. Lizzie shuffled from foot to foot uncomfortably as she looked across at the dress Mrs Evans had discarded. Her mother had made it with love, and somehow when she was wearing it, Lizzie felt closer to her. The cardigan felt itchy on her arms, though luckily her Liberty bodice stopped it from scratching her chest. Too afraid to voice her opinions, she remained silent as Mrs Evans stood back to admire her with tears in her eyes.

'Ah, my sweet Megan. You look beautiful, so you do,' she whispered softly.

At that moment, the door opened and Mr Evans stepped into the room, ready for his own lunch. As his gaze settled on Lizzie, the colour drained from his face and he looked as if he had seen a ghost.

'For the love of God, *whatever* do you think you're doing, Mother?' he gasped disbelievingly.

Realising that there was something going on here that she didn't understand, Lizzie looked from one to the other of them with interest.

Drawing herself up to her full height, Mrs Evans stared back at him defiantly. 'They were lying in the loft doing no good to man nor beast, as well you know,' she shot back at him. 'But I cannot discuss it with you now, Father. I have to get Lizzie back to school. We'll talk about it when I return. In the meantime, you'll find your dinner in the oven.'

Once the door had closed behind them, Mr Evans dropped onto the nearest chair, his appetite gone. It was beginning to look as if his worst nightmare was starting, all over again.

*   *   *

246

Accompanied by Gus and Sparky, Danny had found a quiet corner of the playground where he unpacked his lunch. Gus's eyes sparkled greedily at the sight of it. Today, Eric had packed him great doorstop sandwiches oozing with butter and fresh-made cheese. A rosy red apple and a little bottle full to the top with thick creamy milk were jammed in next to them but Davey barely noticed.

'I could give yer a hand wiv 'em if yer not hungry,' Gus offered. 'What's up wiv yer, anyway? Yer seem to be miles away.'

'It's Lizzie,' the boy confessed. 'I just get this funny feelin' in the pit of me stomach whenever something's not right with her. She's the same if something's not right with me. We've been like it since we were babies, accordin' to me mam.'

Helping himself to a sandwich, Gus grinned. 'Well, there can't be that much wrong wiv 'er. She ain't bin gone that long an' she'll be back in a minute.'

Danny supposed that Gus was right. Hesitantly, he picked up the other sandwich. In no time at all they had polished off the remainder of the lunch between them and they crossed to the railings to wait for Lizzie. Sure enough, she soon appeared with Mrs Evans tightly gripping her hand, looking none too pleased at all. At the school gates the woman bent to place an affectionate kiss on her cheek, but the second she released her hand, Lizzie shot across to join Danny.

Hastily unbuttoning her coat, she pointed to the offending outfit. 'Look what she's made me wear,' she complained.

Danny scratched his head in bewilderment. 'That ain't one of the dresses our mam packed, is it?'

Lizzie's head wagged indignantly from side to side.

247

'No, it's not. Mrs Evans made me take my dress off because she said I'd got gravy down it, but I hadn't. Then she put these on me an' I don't like them. They belonged to her little girl who died.'

'Gerroff!' Gus exclaimed in horror. 'That's really spooky, innit? Why would she do that?'

'I've no idea,' Lizzie said, looking thoroughly miserable. 'I know me mam wouldn't be pleased though. An' neither was Mr Evans, especially when she called me Megan. I've got a funny feelin' they'll have a row when she gets back home.'

Danny draped a comforting arm around her shoulder. 'Never mind,' he told his twin. 'They don't look *that* bad.'

Gus thought that Lizzie would have looked beautiful dressed in a paper bag, but refrained from saying so as the bell heralded the end of the lunch-hour.

'Come on, we'd better get in,' he urged as he ushered them towards the school. Lizzie and Danny exchanged a glance before obediently trooping in after him.

By the end of the day, Lizzie was in better spirits. The next day was hers and Danny's birthday and she knew that her mam would never forget that.

'Do yer reckon we'll get a card each through the post?' she asked Danny excitedly as they shrugged into their coats in the cloakroom.

'No doubt about it,' he assured her with a grin. 'Our mam would *never* forget our birthday. Does Mrs Evans know about it?'

Lizzie shook her head. 'No, I didn't tell her.'

'Why not?' Soho Gus gasped incredulously. The way he saw it, the more people you told about your birthday, the more presents you got. 'Did you tell Eric it were *your* birthday, Dan?'

When Danny shook his head too, Gus sighed. 'Yer a right pair, you are. Fancy not tellin' anyone.'

Danny regarded him sadly. 'No doubt we'll hear from our mam, an' our grans will probably send us a card too. We don't need nothin' off nobody else. It won't be the same anyway wi'out our mam to share it with.'

Gus stared at him as if he'd lost his marbles but refrained from saying any more until they were walking up the hillside. The air was alive with the sound of birdsong and Danny was enjoying it, until Gus suddenly blurted out, 'I reckon you ought to at least tell Eric it's yer birthday tomorrer. Think how he'll feel when yer cards arrive if you ain't even told him.'

Danny pondered on Gus's words. After a while he had to grudgingly admit that he might have a point. As things worked out he didn't have to tell him, for when he arrived home, Eric pointed to three envelopes propped up on the mantelpiece.

'They came for you this morning,' he informed him. 'And they look suspiciously like cards to me. You haven't had a birthday and not told me, have you?'

Danny felt himself blushing. 'It's tomorrow actually. I was going to tell you tonight – honest I was.'

Eric stifled a smile. 'That's all right then. Now come and get your dinner while it's hot.'

The birthday was momentarily forgotten as Danny sat down at the table and eyed the oven with anticipation. Lamb chops, baked potatoes and carrots, with plenty of gravy and a Bakewell tart to follow. Cor!

The next morning, he opened his cards propped up against his pillows in bed. It had been a great temptation all night to see them sitting there on his little chest of drawers but somehow he felt that it wouldn't be quite the same if he opened them on the wrong day. Just as he'd thought, there was one from his mam and Lucy, and one from each of his grans. As he stared down at the familiar writing he felt a big lump forming in his throat. In his mam's card was a ten-shilling note, which was just for him alone. He felt rich and immediately wondered what he should spend it on. Clambering out of bed, he shuddered as his feet connected with the cold floorboards then padded over to his wardrobe and tucked it away in the pocket of his Sunday-best blazer.

Once he'd dragged his clothes on, he hurried down to the kitchen to find Eric standing at the stove stirring a pan of fried bread and mushrooms.

'Happy Birthday,' he greeted him, then nodding towards a large parcel wrapped crudely in brown paper he told him, 'There's a bit of something over there for you off me. I'm afraid I didn't get you a card though.'

'S'all right,' Danny grinned as he fell on the parcel and started to tear it open. When the gift was finally revealed, Danny became silent as he stared at it in awe.

Taking the child's silence as disappointment, Eric apologised. 'I know it's not much, but I thought it would be a lot easier for you to cart about than a full-size one.'

'But it's lovely! In fact, it's the best present I've ever had,' Danny gasped. Eric had made him a small easel that Danny could use for the canvases Eric had supplied him with.

A smile of pleasure and embarrassment spread across Eric's face as he ushered Danny to the table, and once again, the little boy found himself thinking, He's all right really. An' he'd be quite handsome if it weren't for all them scars. This was turning out to be not such a bad birthday after all.

His happiness proved to be shortlived, however, for when Mrs Evans dropped Lizzie off at the school gates, his twin ran across to him with her eyes red-rimmed from crying.

'Did you get a card from our mam?' she demanded. When Danny nodded, fresh tears started to flow. 'Well . . . I never did!'

Danny stared at her aghast. Why would his mam, and his grans for that matter, send cards to him and not to Lizzie? It didn't make any sense.

'Perhaps yours will come today while yer at school?' he suggested hopefully.

Lizzie shook her head, setting her fair hair bobbing on her shoulders. 'I said that to Mrs Evans but she reckons out of sight out of mind. She says our mam is probably too busy to bother about me now.'

'Rubbish!' Danny exclaimed. 'Our mam loves us both an' she would *never* send one of us cards an' not the other.'

Gus was watching the proceedings with a thoughtful look in his eye. 'I reckon there's somethin' fishy goin' on 'ere,' he said. 'Yer don't think Old Lady Evans would keep the post from gettin' to Lizzie, do yer?'

Now that Gus had mentioned it, Danny could see that it might make sense. 'How could we find out?'

Gus mulled it over for a moment. 'We could look out for the postman on Saturday when we ain't at school an' ask 'im if he's delivered any mail fer Lizzie to *Ty-Du*. There ain't *that* many houses in the village so he'd be sure to remember.'

'You're right,' Danny agreed. 'We'll do that.' Taking a small handmade card from the inside of his blazer pocket, he handed it to Lizzie. He had sketched a lovely picture of the blacksmith's cottage on the front and written inside it the night before for her, after taking a bath in Eric's enormous bathroom.

'Here, I know it ain't the same as havin' one from Mam, but at least you've got somethin'.'

She nodded and gave him a weak smile before moving off into their classroom.

'I'm gonna get to the bottom o' this,' Gus declared angrily as he followed her. Seeing the look in his friend's eyes, Danny had no doubt at all that he would do just that.

Chapter Twenty-Three

'So, do you think I should tell the children that their father has been killed?' Maggie asked as she chewed on the end of her pen. She was writing a letter to each of the twins and wasn't sure what she should tell them. Of course, she knew that they would have to be told about their father's death eventually, but wondered if it might not be best to wait until she could tell them face to face?

Jo confirmed her feelings. 'Might be best to wait till you get to see 'em,' she said. 'I mean, it ain't goin' to be easy for 'em, but at least if you're there they'll have someone to turn to.'

'You're right,' Maggie agreed relieved. 'I won't tell them what's happened to your family either just yet.' With her mind made up she bent to the letters in front of her with a heavy heart.

On 13 October the children were herded into the village hall to listen to Princess Elizabeth make her debut radio broadcast; she was helped along by her younger sister, Princess Margaret Rose, and the children listened in awe to her melodic voice as she addressed the evacuated children everywhere.

Gus and Sparky had come alone, as had Danny, but as usual, Mrs Evans stayed close to Lizzie's side, ready to whip her away the second the broadcast was over.

Lizzie was totally enchanted as she listened to a real live princess address them all, but Danny had far more exciting news and could hardly wait to tell it to her as he waited for the broadcast to end.

At last the radio was switched off and Danny produced a letter from his pocket and waved it in her face. 'Look, it's a letter from Mam. Did you get one?' he asked excitedly. When Lizzie slowly shook her head he frowned but was stopped from saying anything further when for some reason, Mrs Evans suddenly pounced on Lizzie, brandishing her coat at her.

'Come along now, *cariad*,' she breathed. 'We want to get home before it starts to rain, so we do. It's been threatening all day and I don't want you getting wet and catching a cold now.'

For once, Lizzie chose to ignore her as she stared at the envelope in Danny's hand. Why had her brother received a letter and not her? Mrs Evans flushed with guilt as she read the child's mind. A letter *had* arrived for Lizzie that very morning – but she had flung it into the fire, just as she had done with her birthday cards. Of course, she excused herself, she had only done it to prevent Lizzie from getting upset. She didn't want a letter from home to unsettle her. When she grasped Lizzie's arm and tried to force it into the sleeve of her coat, the girl pulled away from her.

'Never mind,' Danny said as he looked at her downcast face. 'Yer can have a read o' mine. Perhaps yours will come tomorrow? Please may I show it to her, Mrs Evans?'

An angry flush stained the big woman's cheeks as she saw that they were attracting curious glances. Grudgingly she nodded as Danny led Lizzie to a chair at the side of the hall.

Once he'd finished reading the letter aloud to her, Lizzie smiled. 'Fancy Jo stayin' with Mam at our house. I hope she's still there when we go home. Jo was nice, wasn't she?'

'Yes, she was.' Danny nodded in agreement. 'It's funny Mam ain't said why she's stayin' there, though. Jo was always harpin' on about her little brothers an' sisters, so I wonder who's lookin' after them now?'

Lizzie shrugged her slight shoulders. 'I've no idea. I'm just glad Mam ain't all on her own with Lucy. With Jo there she'll have someone to keep her company, 'specially as Gran don't get out an' about so much any more.'

Soho Gus and Sparky looked on enviously. They'd already been in Wales for months but so far hadn't had so much as a single letter between them; not that they expected one. Gus also looked slightly guilty, for up to now he'd had no luck at all in getting hold of the postman as he had promised to.

'Right, if that's all done I'm afraid I shall have to get her away home now,' Mrs Evans said bossily. 'And if the rest of you have got any sense, you'll get yourselves away home too. There's a rare storm brewing, you just mark my words, and sorry you will be if you get caught out in it.'

Lizzie reluctantly allowed her to do up her coat, and as she was marched towards the door she turned and waved to her brother.

Once they'd gone, Soho Gus sighed. 'Word 'as it that Mr Evans is on 'is last legs,' he confided in a whisper to his captive audience. 'He ain't opened the smithy fer three whole days now, an' I heard the Thomases sayin' as how they'd heard he'd got the dust on his chest.'

'What's the dust?' Danny asked.

'It's a disease o' the lungs that miners get when they've

spent a long time underground,' he replied. 'Mr Evans spent years down the pit till they bought the smiffy an' moved to the village. I'm surprised as Lizzie ain't told yer.'

'She ain't had the chance to,' Danny grunted. 'Mrs Evans don't give her a minute to herself so I've hardly had time to talk to her on her own fer days.'

'Mmm, I know what yer mean.' Gus nodded understandingly. 'She lays it on a bit thick wiv her, don't she?'

Dragging themselves to their feet, the three small boys made their way to the door where they stood surveying the wet cobblestoned street. Just as Mrs Evans had predicted the rain had begun to fall in a slow drizzle that soaked them to the skin within minutes.

Lifting Albert from his top pocket, Soho Gus tucked him down the front of his threadbare blazer.

'Suppose we might as well 'ead fer home,' he said mournfully. 'Ain't much point stayin' out in this, an' I've got me jobs to do at *Derwen Deg*.'

At the end of the street they said goodnight to Sparky before beginning the long trek up the hill towards their billets.

'So 'ow are yer gettin' on wiv Eric nowadays then?' Soho Gus asked breathlessly.

Danny swiped a big raindrop from the end of his nose and grinned into the fast-darkening afternoon. 'Just the job, to tell yer the truth, though he still tends to tuck himself away in that outhouse every chance he gets. I don't mind though, 'cos he's sorted me some oilpaints an' watercolours an' brushes out, an' most nights I paint pictures now. Eric reckons I have a flair fer it.'

Danny glanced at him curiously. 'What sort o' paintin' do yer do then?'

'Anythin' that comes to mind,' Danny told him. 'Last

night I did a picture of Samson, an' when Eric came across he said it was really good. He's shown me how to mix the paints to make different colours an' everythin'.'

Soho Gus was impressed but still intrigued as to why Eric should lock himself away so often in the huge barn-like building. As a thought suddenly occurred to him, his voice rose with excitement. 'I reckon we should try to find the key to the outbuildin' some time when he's down in the village an' let ourselves in to see what he gets up to in there.'

Danny was horrified at the very suggestion. 'We couldn't do that!' he said.

'Why not? We wouldn't be doin' any harm, an' he ain't never gonna be none the wiser if we put the key back before he gets home, is he?'

'I suppose not,' Danny admitted, ashamed that he found the idea appealing. By now the rain was coming down in torrents and they put all their efforts into staying upright as they laboured up the hillside.

At *Derwen Deg* they parted and Danny began the last leg of his journey as Gus's suggestion rolled around in his mind. His curiosity was further fuelled when he arrived home to see the lights from the outbuilding shining through the heavy blinds into the darkness. Eric was obviously locked away in there again. Splashing through the muddy puddles as quietly as he could, Danny once again stood on tiptoe and tried to peer through the windows, but it was useless. He could see absolutely nothing. Shrugging, he entered the kitchen and began to peel off his wet clothes as Samson washed him with his great wet tongue. Minutes later, Eric appeared in the doorway, eyeing his bedraggled charge with amusement.

'Get yourself upstairs and change into something dry,'

he said, 'then come back down here and we'll get something warm inside you. After that we could do some more work on your painting if you like? And then tonight, you really must have a bath.'

Danny placed his dripping shoes on the hearth to dry, then squelched across the room in his soaking socks and hurried away upstairs. He returned in his pyjamas, dressing-gown and slippers minutes later, with an armful of wet clothes which Eric hung across the wooden clotheshorse in the corner.

A large dish of rabbit stew and dumplings was steaming on the table and Danny's stomach rumbled with anticipation. Once he had sated his appetite, and polished off a piece of bread pudding and cream, he rubbed his small bloated stomach and sighed with contentment. Eric might not always be the most friendly of hosts but he certainly couldn't fault the meals he provided. Nor for that matter, the painting lessons he was providing him with. Already in just a few short hours, he had taught Danny the art of making skin textures look real and so much more, and Danny was becoming justifiably proud of his efforts. He had never used oils before, and there was so much to learn about painting on canvas.

Soon they were both seated in front of a big easel that Eric had erected at the side of the fireplace and yet another lesson began. But this one was due to be short-lived, for Eric suddenly remembered, 'I've got to nip down to the village to post a letter while there's still time. You'll be all right here on your own till I get back, won't you?'

Danny nodded as Eric thrust his long arms into a mackintosh. The firelight was playing on the black patch that covered one eye, and in this light the burns that ran down his face from beneath it looked even more vivid. Danny suppressed a shudder of revulsion as he turned his attention back to the painting in front of him. It was then that he saw Eric drop a bunch of keys onto the end of the draining board. They were the keys to the outbuilding, he was sure of it after seeing Eric use them so often. Temptation beckoned as he remembered what Soho Gus had suggested. He could nip across and take a look inside whilst he was gone and Eric need never be any the wiser.

Terrified that Eric might be able to read his mind, he fixed his eyes firmly on the painting in front of him and held his breath as the man strode towards the door.

'Will you be going in the car?'

Eric shook his head. 'No, not tonight with the roads as they are. With all this rain they'll be treacherous but I shouldn't be more than an hour. If you get tired, take yourself up to bed. You can have a bath tomorrow instead.'

Danny nodded, and once the door had closed behind Eric, his eyes strayed to the keys. It was the first time that he'd ever known Eric to leave them lying about and he wrestled with his conscience as his mind began to work overtime. What if he were to discover something terrible in the outbuilding? Perhaps Eric was a smuggler? After all, he did live very close to the sea. Or worse still, he might be a murderer and have dead bodies locked away in there. He gulped deep in his throat as his imagination ran riot. Perhaps things were better left as they were. What he didn't know couldn't hurt him, and yet . . .

Crossing to the sink, he lifted the keys from the draining board, and of their own volition, his feet began to move towards the kitchen door. And then it was open and he was looking towards the outbuilding, whose windows were still alight. It was like a magnet and he found himself splashing across the yard once more, oblivious to the rain that was lashing down. When he reached the door he fumbled with one key after another until one suddenly slid smoothly into the lock and he heard it click open. There was no stopping now as slowly he inched the door open. He had intended to do no more than peep inside before scuttling back to the warmth of the kitchen, but the sight that met his eyes made him walk to the centre of the room and stare around him in open-mouthed amazement.

He was in an artist's studio, and everywhere he looked were canvases in various states. Some were finished, some had barely been started on and others were half-done. The one thing that they all had in common was that each and every one of them, even to a child's untrained eye, was magnificent.

Now that Danny was actually inside the building he could see the attraction of the room for an artist. One wall on the other side of the room was taken up by a huge plate-glass window, through which he guessed the sun would stream during the day. It also overlooked the sea, although at the moment all he could see was rain lashing against it. Against another wall was a long trestle-like table and when Danny approached it he saw that it was covered in illustrations, each and every one beautifully done. Forgetting all about the fact that he shouldn't even be there, he lifted them one at a time, marvelling at the detail and the colours. He was so absorbed that when a sudden sound made him turn round, he almost jumped out of his skin to see a stern-faced Eric glaring at him.

'Just *what the hell* do you think you're doing?' The words came out on a growl and instantly Danny began to quake.

'I . . . I'm so sorry,' he stuttered, deeply ashamed of himself. 'I was just so curious about what yer did in here that I thought I'd just take a little peep. But I didn't mean no harm – honest I didn't – an' I ain't hurt anythin'.'

The rain that was dripping from his mackintosh began to puddle on the floor about his feet as Eric stared coldly at the child. Danny could see that he was absolutely furious, and he trembled with fear.

'I trusted you and now you've *totally* abused that trust,' Eric stormed. 'I told you quite clearly that this room was *out of bounds*, didn't I? How *dare* you come in here! I *knew* I should never have agreed to take you in.'

Again Danny told him, 'I'm s . . . sorry, sir. Really I am.'

They faced each other for some seconds until Eric's shoulders suddenly stooped. 'I'm deeply disappointed in you, though I dare say there's no harm done,' he finally muttered. 'But I would ask you to keep quiet about what you've seen in here tonight. I don't like all and sundry knowing my business.'

Danny's head wagged furiously in agreement. 'I won't say a word to no one, honest I won't. But did you *really* do all these?'

As he spread his hands to encompass the beautiful paintings that surrounded him, Eric reluctantly nodded. 'Yes I did.'

Danny turned his attention to a picture of a ship in full sail on a choppy sea and sighed with admiration. Lifting his hand, he stroked it reverently. It was so life-like that he could almost imagine he was on board; could feel the waves tossing him this way and that.

'I'd do anythin' to be able to paint like this,' he breathed.

Eric came to stand beside him. 'You could, one day,

if you listen to what I tell you. You have a natural gift. I saw it in the first sketch you left lying about.'

'They must be worth a small fortune,' Danny said quietly. 'Ain't you ever thought of sellin' any of 'em?'

Instantly, Eric's face was hard again as he turned away. 'I think it's high time you were in bed now, don't you?'

Danny scooted nervously past him but at the door he paused to look back. 'I'm sorry,' he apologised contritely again, then he scuttled across the yard and up to his room where he lay in bed with the wonderful scenes Eric had created once again before his eyes.

Down in the village, Lizzie huddled in the outside privy, or the *ty-bach* as Mrs Evans called it, and listened to the furious row that was taking place in the cottage kitchen.

Earlier that evening, despite her protestations, Mrs Evans had cut Lizzie's hair to shoulder-length. It would be easier to brush and to manage now, she had explained to the child as her curls fell to the floor in great long lengths. But Lizzie had an idea that it was more to do with the fact that she now looked more like the little girl in the picture that stood in pride of place on Mrs Evans's mantelpiece.

Mr Evans had borne out her theory when he emerged from his sickbed to get a glass of water and stretch his legs. 'Ah, Mother!' he exclaimed in horror as he gazed at the shining tresses strewn about the floor. 'Whatever possessed you to do this? The child's mother will not be pleased that you've done this without her permission.'

Mrs Evans stuck her chin out defiantly. 'Whilst she is in my care, *I* shall decide what's best for her,' she declared.

Lizzie shot past her, glad of a chance to escape, and sat with her knickers round her ankles as the row raged on. Strangely, she liked the *ty-bach*, for it was one of the few places that Mrs Evans didn't follow her to. Set at the bottom of the garden, at the end of a twisting path, it was surrounded by trees that tapped at the roof in the wind. Lizzie supposed that it was a fairly crude building, with its corrugated roof and thick stone walls, but she loved the earthy smell of it and the little sheets of newspaper cut into neat squares that hung on a string from a nail in the wall. The toilet itself was nothing more than a plank of wood with a hole cut in it, beneath which Mr Evans regularly laid a fresh bed of cinders. Lizzie escaped to it as often as she could, and there she would think of her mother and home. Now in the comforting darkness her hand explored her freshly shorn hair and she wondered what Maggie would say when she saw it. She had an awful feeling that she would be very angry, as she remembered back to how Maggie would painstakingly twist rags into it on bath nights to tease it into ringlets. A great fat tear trembled on her lashes as homesickness swept over her. She had no doubt that Mrs Evans meant to be kind, but sometimes Lizzie felt as if she was suffocating her, especially when she insisted on calling her Megan. Only today during her lunch-hour, Mrs Evans had whispered to her that from now on, whenever they were alone, she must answer to the name of Megan. 'But,' she had said, 'it must be our secret.'

Too afraid to argue, Lizzie had nodded her agreement but something didn't feel right. After all, her name was Lizzie, so why should she have to answer to another name?

Becoming aware that the arguing had stopped, she climbed down from the seat and inched the privy door open. Even bedtime was becoming a nightmare now, for Mrs Evans would creep into her room and whisper endearments into her ear. Hoisting her thick cotton knickers up, Lizzie tucked her Liberty bodice into them and straightened her cotton petticoat, before running through the rain back to the warmth of the kitchen.

'Have you heard anything from the children yet?' Jo asked as she threw her coat off and held her hands, which were blue with cold, out to the comforting warmth of the fire. She was late and Maggie had just begun to get worried about her.

Maggie shook her head as she slipped Lucy's nightdress over her head. 'No, not yet, but with the way the post is I'm not sure when they would have got their letters, so I'm not overly concerned yet.'

Crossing to the table, Jo sat down. 'When are you going to go and see them and tell them about their dad?' she asked tentatively.

Maggie shuddered at the thought of it. 'I shall go to see them as soon as I can,' she told her, not relishing the thought of breaking the news to them. 'But how has your day been? I was just beginning to get a little worried about you.'

'I er . . . I had an appointment,' Jo hedged.

She seemed preoccupied as she stared down into her mug, and Maggie frowned. Now that she came to think about it, Jo hadn't seemed herself for some days. She was just about to ask Jo if there was anything she could help her with, when the back door suddenly swung open and her mother-in-law appeared, closely resembling a drowned rat.

Lucy ran to her in delight, throwing her arms about her grandma's thick waist, but instead of lifting her as she normally would, the woman just smiled at her vaguely. Something was wrong; Maggie could tell from the woman's pale face.

'Get that wet coat off and come and sit by the fire,' she said, desperately trying to postpone what would surely be yet more bad news. Jo tactfully disappeared upstairs, her own news untold.

Beryl Bright wrung her hands together as she looked across at her daughter-in-law. Maggie had had so very much to put up with lately, and here she was about to deliver another blow. Her own heart felt as if it was about to break and she just wanted to get this over with as soon as possible, but Maggie wasn't making it easy for her.

'Maggie, I have to tell you that—'

'Isn't it cold for the time of year?' Maggie interrupted, intent on putting off whatever it was Beryl had come to tell her. 'Why, when Jo got in, her poor hands were blue with—'

'*Maggie*! For God's sake, stop rabbiting on! Don't make this harder for me than it already is,' Beryl pleaded. 'I have to say it and then I'll be gone.'

Maggie's shoulders suddenly sagged and she became silent as she gazed at her mother-in-law. 'Something's happened to David, hasn't it?'

When Beryl slowly nodded she screwed her eyes tight shut as pain, sharp as a knife, stabbed at her heart.

'I had a telegram today,' Beryl muttered. 'David is missing.'

Relief flooded through Maggie as her eyes snapped open. '*Missing*? But that means that he might still be alive then! He could have been taken prisoner, or even be in a military hospital somewhere.'

'He could be,' Beryl said heavily, 'but I don't think we should raise our hopes up.'

Maggie's chin jutted with annoyance. 'All right then – you think the worst if you like, but *I* certainly shan't,' she said rudely. 'As far as I'm concerned, David is still alive somewhere and I refuse to believe anything other until we're told differently.'

Beryl wiped her hand wearily across her eyes. One of her sons was dead and now the other was missing, and yet she supposed there just *might* be something in what Maggie had said. She would certainly try to hold on to that thought, for at the moment she felt as if her life was falling apart. Seeing the dejection in the woman's face, Maggie swiftly crossed to her and wrapped her in her arms.

'I'm so sorry but we'll get through this,' she whispered softly. 'We're family.' But inside she was thinking, What is left of us.

Chapter Twenty-Four

Two days after her mother-in-law's visit, Maggie got up to find Jo slouched in the chair at the side of the dying fire.

'What's wrong with you then? Not feeling so chipper today?' She watched Jo curiously as she bent to rake out the ashes before throwing some coal onto the glowing embers.

Jo shook her head and pulled Maggie's old dressing-gown more tightly about her. She had already decided that she wasn't going into work today, even if it meant risking the wrath of Miss Hutchinson, who ran the shop where she worked with a rod of iron.

'How about I make you a nice bit of breakfast then, eh? Everything always looks better on a full stomach,' Maggie offered, but Jo merely shook her head and continued to gaze off into space. In no time at all the fire was burning brightly and they were sitting opposite each other. Maggie was determined to find out what was wrong with Jo, for she seemed pre-occupied and edgy. Her mother had mentioned it too, so Maggie felt that now was as good a time as any to try and get to the bottom of what was troubling her.

'So, how about you tell me what's wrong then? I know something's been on your mind. You haven't been . . .

oh, I don't know. You just haven't been yourself for the last few days.'

When Jo dragged her eyes away from the flickering flames, Maggie was shocked to see the misery in them. Deciding that she might as well get it over with, Jo plucked up her courage and said, 'Maggie, you've been as good as gold to me. In fact, I don't know how I would have got through the last few weeks without you. But the thing is . . .' she swallowed and forced herself to go on. 'The thing is, I shall be moving out soon.'

'You'll be what?' Maggie was shocked to her core. She and Jo had become close during the time that Jo had been living with her in Clay Lane, and the thought of losing her was a shock. 'But why, Jo? I thought you liked living here. Is it something I've done?'

'Of course it isn't. I love living here, but I . . . Well, let's just say I have to go.'

'Are you in some sort of trouble, Jo?' Maggie asked slowly. 'If you are, I'm sure we could sort it. You know what they say – a trouble shared is a trouble halved.'

Jo laughed then – a hard, cynical laugh that tore at Maggie's heart. 'You couldn't halve this one,' she said bitterly.

'Right, so you are in some sort of trouble then,' Maggie declared triumphantly. 'Come on, spit it out. This is me, Maggie . . . remember?'

Tears suddenly spilled over Jo's lashes and trickled down her cheeks. 'All right then, but I warn yer – you ain't goin' to be pleased. Yer see, the thing is . . . I'm in the family way.'

Maggie was filled with dismay. 'But how? I mean – who?'

Jo shrugged. 'Your guess is as good as mine. Just when I have the chance to put the past behind me, this has to go an' happen. It's sod's law really, ain't it? I was always so careful in that department, or at least I thought I was, but obviously I slipped up, didn't I? So I suppose yer could say it serves me right.'

Maggie sat in stunned silence as she tried to digest what Jo had just told her, but eventually she asked, 'Are you quite sure? What I mean is, you've gone through a lot lately an' sometimes that can make your monthlies stop.'

'Oh, I'm sure all right,' Jo told her. 'That's why I was late home the night Beryl came around. I'd been to the doctor's and I was goin' to tell yer then but I didn't have the heart to when I knew yer were worryin' about David.'

'How far gone are you?' Maggie asked.

'About three months, accordin' to the doctor. The way I see it, I've got three alternatives. One, I could pay a visit to Old Lady Moon in Beagle Street. Trouble is, I've heard horror stories about the damage she's done to some young women who've gone to her for help. She uses a knitting needle to rid them of their problem apparently.' She shuddered at the thought of it and went on, 'Two, I could disappear fer a few months an' give the little 'un up fer adoption when it puts in an appearance. Or three, I could settle somewhere away from here an' make out that I was a widow an' keep it.'

Maggie stared at her thoughtfully for a few moments before suggesting, 'Or four, you could stay here with me and brazen it out.'

'I could hardly do that, could I, what with Old Man Massey next door knowin' how I used to make a livin'?' Jo scoffed. 'He'd never let me live it down. I'd be the talk of the street, if I ain't already, an' so would you be fer puttin' me up.'

'So?' Maggie was indignant. 'Let them talk. You and

I both know that you didn't do what you did from choice. What other people choose to think is up to them. And please don't worry about me. This is *my* house and I'll have in it who I choose. But the thing is, Jo, what do *you* want to do? Would you like to keep the baby?'

Jo shook her head miserably as her hand settled on her stomach. 'No, I don't,' she admitted. 'Every mornin', I get up an' hope that I'll be bleedin', that it will just go away – but I ain't that lucky. I reckon I'll have it an' then give it up fer adoption.'

'Well, the choice is yours,' Maggie said, as she reached out to squeeze her hand. 'But I'll stand by you, whatever you decide.'

Jo looked thoroughly wretched. 'I can't let you do that. You know how strict Miss Hutchinson is. She'll get rid o' me like a shot when I start to show, an' how am I goin' to live then? I certainly ain't stayin' here to be a burden on you. You sew all the hours God sends as it is to keep yer head above water, wi'out havin' me to worry about.'

'Nonsense,' Maggie declared. 'We'll work something out. Once you finish work, you could perhaps do the housework and look after Lucy while I take on a bit more sewing. We'd get by one way or another, so let's not hear any more silly talk about you leaving. We're friends and I'm not going to let you down.'

When Jo saw that Maggie meant every word she said, she could have wept with relief. In Maggie Bright she had found a true friend indeed.

Throughout the day, Maggie kept up a constant stream of cheerful chatter to try and raise Jo's spirits. It seemed to do the trick, for when Jo eventually went off to bed that evening to have an early night, she seemed a little brighter.

Once the stairs door had closed behind her Maggie

breathed a sigh of relief and took her foot off the treadle of her sewing-machine. Until recently she'd always done her sewing in the rarely-used front parlour, but now that the weather had turned chilly it made economic sense to work in the kitchen. That way she need light only one fire, which saved on the coal bill.

Standing, she stretched her stiff limbs, then crossing to the door she slipped out into the yard and gazed up at the sky. This had always been her favourite time of day. High in the sky, a silver moon sat proudly above black velvet clouds like a queen on her throne; surrounded by twinkling stars that seemed to be paying homage. For a few moments Maggie lost herself in the beauty of it as she shivered in the cold evening air. Her mother had remarked earlier that there was snow in the air, and Maggie could well believe it. Over the yard, the sound from the Masseys' wireless faintly reached her, but not a chink of light showed from the heavy black-out curtains that covered the windows.

It had been a huge effort to put on a cheerful face all day for Jo, and now that she no longer had to keep up the pretence, she sagged against the brick wall. Ever since Beryl's visit she had pushed thoughts of what might be happening to David to the back of her mind, but now they surfaced like unwelcome visitors.

And Sam. Poor Sam. She was well aware that she had never truly done right by him, and now he was dead and it was too late to try and make amends. Her thoughts moved back to David as tears welled in her eyes. The very best that she could hope for was that he was lying in a military hospital somewhere or that he had been taken a prisoner of war. Neither options were very nice but were infinitely preferable to thinking of him lying dead somewhere.

And now she was faced with this latest crisis. Never for a second had it occurred to Maggie to abandon her friend in her hour of need, but Maggie was sensible enough to know that the months ahead were not going to be easy. Money was tight as it was, and soon she would have to support Jo and a new baby too – if Jo chose to keep the child, that was.

The wind swirled some russet and gold leaves that had been snatched from the oak tree at the bottom of the garden around her feet, and shuddering she headed to the back door.

Once back inside the cosy kitchen she carefully pulled the blackout curtain across the door and crossed to a black and white picture of the twins that took pride of place on the mantelshelf. Lovingly she traced their faces with her finger as she ached for them. Soon she would have to go and see them, to tell them the news about their father. Apart from the fact that she missed them more than she could say, the idea of it brought her no pleasure. He had been their father, after all.

Her eyes came to rest on the fine parachute silk that she was presently transforming into yet another bridal gown. She was so tired that she could barely keep her eyes open, but if it was to be done in time for the wedding a week on Saturday, she would have to work into the early hours of tomorrow morning to finish it.

With nothing but the ticking of the clock to keep her company, she squeezed back behind her machine and in no time at all, even that sound was drowned out by the whir of the needle as it flew back and forth across the material.

Within weeks, Danny's skinny legs were beginning to fill out and his cheeks became rosy, due no doubt to the fresh air and the healthy food that Eric supplied him with.

Danny refrained from mentioning the night he had sneaked into the studio, and much to his delight, the painting lessons continued.

'Eric showed me how to hold a palette properly last night,' he bragged to Soho Gus as they walked to school one morning. His life was beginning to fall into a pattern now. Each day he would meet Gus outside *Derwen Deg*, then when they reached the village they would call for Sparky who lived in the flat above the bakery with the baker, his wife and their own three children.

Eric was still cool towards him – apart from the times they spent in front of the easel, that was, and then he would become a different person as he patiently showed Danny all the tricks of the trade. Already, under Eric's guidance, Danny had turned out a fairly presentable portrait of Samson and a seascape, of which he was inordinately proud.

Gus, however, still had grave reservations about the man. 'If yer ask me he's weird,' he stated in his own forthright manner. ''E fair gives me the creeps wiv that eye-patch an' all them scars. Ain't he never told yer 'ow he got 'em?'

Danny shook his head.

''Ave yer ever seen him wivout his eye-patch?' Gus probed, with all the morbid curiosity of a child. ''As he got an eye under it?'

The thought that he might not had never occurred to Danny, and he shuddered. 'I wouldn't have a clue,' he admitted, 'but I do know that the scars ain't just on his face. I came down early the other mornin' and he was havin' a wash at the sink, an' the scars are all across his chest too. Soon as I walked in he pulled his shirt on like a shot.'

'Perhaps he's a war hero,' Gus suggested as his imagination took a hold. Again Danny could only shrug and for a while they walked on in silence. The weather had turned bitterly cold and Danny was glad now of the mittens and scarf his mother had packed for him. The landscape had changed in the short time he had been there, and now the last remaining leaves clung to the branches of the trees before being whipped away by the wind that whistled down the hillside. They swirled about the boys as they walked along before settling on the ground to form a carpet of autumn colours. Danny was sure that he'd never seen anything so lovely, but then he knew that he could never tire of the feeling of space here after the confinement of being brought up in a city.

All in all, he was as happy as he could be, apart from the fact that he missed his mam and Lucy, and he was concerned about Lizzie. Mrs Evans was like her shadow now, and apart from the odd minutes that they managed to snatch in the school playground during break-time, he rarely got to see her on his own. He had been appalled when Mrs Evans cut her hair off, but now that he was getting used to it shorter he quite liked it, for it had sprung up into tight little curls that bobbed about her chin when she moved.

Lizzie had confided to them that she was worried about Mr Evans, who had now taken to his bed for most of the time. The smithy was still closed and Lizzie would often come home from school to find the village doctor's bicycle propped against the wall. Mr Evans would sometimes be sitting in the fireside chair – his huge callused hands spread across the armrests – and he always raised a smile for her, even though he was struggling to breathe. Lizzie had decided that she liked Mr Evans far more than his wife, which was strange really, because it was always Blodwyn who fussed over her. She noticed that Daffyd always smelled of iron and smoke – no doubt caused by the long hours he had spent in the smithy, but it wasn't a nasty smell; in fact, Lizzie had grown to quite like it.

Today, after meeting Sparky, the boys noticed that the bicycle was there again but they had no time to comment, for as they drew abreast of *Ty-Du*, Lizzie appeared in the doorway with a big grin on her face. After hastily closing the door behind her she skipped across to the boys.

'I'm allowed to walk to school on me own today, 'cos the doctor is in there with Mr Evans again,' she told them gleefully.

At the sight of her, Gus's heart began to beat so loudly that Albert popped his head out of his top pocket to see what was going on. Luckily, Lizzie was too intent on answering Danny's questions to see the flush that rose in his cheeks.

'I think Mr Evans must be really poorly,' she told them on a more sober note. 'I could hear him coughing all night, an' then early this mornin' Mrs Evans ran for the doctor. She's flappin' about like yer wouldn't believe.'

'What does the doctor think is wrong with him?' Danny asked as they moved along the cobbled street.

Lizzie shrugged. 'I couldn't tell you. They always jabber away in Welsh for most of the time.' Leaning towards Danny she whispered, 'I reckon it's something really bad because when he coughs I've seen blood on his handkerchief.'

'Gerrout!' Gus exclaimed, who had overheard what she'd said.

She nodded her head in confirmation. 'It's true . . . honest.'

The children's attention was distracted from what Lizzie was telling them when they became aware of Sparky's laboured breathing as he hurried along trying to keep up with them. They all slowed their steps and Sparky smiled at them gratefully.

'Ah well, at least it means we get to walk together fer a change,' Danny grinned, and nodding, Lizzie slipped her hand into his as they went on their way.

That evening, the walk home from school was hard for Gus and Danny, for an early frost had already begun to form and the fallen leaves made the uphill trudge very slippery. There was a cold wind whipping through the barren branches of the trees overhead, so by the time they reached *Derwen Deg*, their legs were aching and they were breathless and tired. On top of that, Danny was concerned because Lizzie hadn't returned to school after their dinner-break.

'Do yer reckon she's ill?' he asked Gus.

'Nah, she were bright as a button this mornin',' the other lad assured him. 'Mrs Evans probably hadn't had time to get her dinner done wiv the old bloke bein' ill. If anythin' were seriously wrong you'd 'ave heard. The least bit o' bleedin' gossip goes through the village like wildfire. She'll be at school tomorrow, you just mark my words.'

Danny hoped he was right, but all the same he was subdued when he arrived back at *Tremarfon*, as Eric was quick to note.

Slinging his gas mask onto the settee, Danny slipped despondently onto the nearest chair.

'Everything all right at school, is it?' Eric enquired as he laid the table for tea.

Danny nodded. 'Yes, everything's fine there. It's Lizzie I'm worried about. She didn't come into school this afternoon.'

Eric could see that Danny wasn't himself but felt powerless to help him. He had never been that good with children, possibly because he'd never had a lot of contact with any before. Taking Danny in had been like doing a crash course in childcare, and he had been totally against the idea, yet strangely as time passed he was finding the child to be good company.

Unsure of what to say, he carried a large plateful of shepherd's pie to the table and instantly Danny looked a little happier. The main course was washed down with a brimming jug of buttermilk. Eric found himself grinning, which gave his face a lopsided appearance, as Danny looked across at him sporting a white moustache. His grin was returned when he next fetched a big dish of rice pudding from the oven. The top was golden brown and crispy with sprinkled nutmeg, just the way that Danny liked it, and despite the fact that he had only just eaten his dinner he managed to down two helpings as Eric looked on with an amused smile on his face.

'Cor, that were the business,' Danny declared admiringly as he swiped the back of his hand across his mouth. 'Who learned yer to cook like that?'

Eric shrugged as he rose to carry the dirty pots to the sink. 'I just taught myself. It was either that or you starve if you live alone.'

Danny cocked his head to one side as he observed Eric pottering about the kitchen. Crossing to the fireside chair, the boy lifted Hemily onto his lap and suddenly asked, 'Did you always live alone?'

Instantly the shutters came down over Eric's face and Danny could have bitten his tongue out. Why did he always have to go and put his foot in it just when Eric seemed to be warming to him a little?

'Have you got any homework to do?' Eric asked coldly, completing ignoring Danny's question.

The boy nodded. 'Yes, I've got to do some sums an' hand 'em in tomorrow.'

'Right – then I suggest you get them done. I've got things to do over in the studio. Oh, and by the way, you'll find a letter on the mantelpiece. It came for you this morning.'

A radiant smile illuminated the little boy's face, and he rose from the chair so quickly that poor Hemily dropped in a heap onto the hearthrug. In no time at all he was once again sitting at the kitchen table with a letter from his mother spread out in front of him. As he greedily read the words, he had to blink to stop his tears from falling. Suddenly it was harder to picture her face when he closed his eyes, and this frightened him, although he could still imagine the lovely smell of her – Pond's cold cream and cooking and babies all rolled into one. In the letter she told him that she was now sewing to earn some money and that she, Lucy and the two grandmas were all well. She told him that Jo was still living with her too, which pleased him, for he liked to think of his mother having someone to keep her company. One part of the letter that did trouble him was the part where his mam asked why Lizzie hadn't written to her. Danny knew that Lizzie had, she'd told him so, and Mrs Evans had promised to post her letter in the shiny red postbox in the village for her once she had bought a stamp for it from the little post office. Stranger still, why hadn't his mam written to Lizzie? This was his *second* letter and Lizzie was really upset because she hadn't received even one. Perhaps it was the post, he decided. There was a war on, after all, not that you would have known it here in Wales. Here the bombs and the sound of guns seemed a million miles away. And the space . . . his mam would have loved it here, he knew.

He wondered when she would manage to get to see them, and whether Eric might let her stay overnight when she did finally manage it. He dismissed that idea almost immediately. He would never have the courage to ask, but perhaps Mrs Evans might let her stay there with Lizzie? He abandoned that idea too as he remembered how poorly Mr Evans was. Then his face brightened. Perhaps she would fit in just a short visit before Christmas? Even if they only saw her for a few hours it would be better than nothing, although she hadn't mentioned that she had any plans to come. But then even if she didn't, it was almost November already and his mam had told them before they left that they might be home for Christmas.

Home for Christmas! The thought brought a grin stretching from ear to ear. Eric was all right, and Soho Gus and Sparky were great friends, but there was nowhere like home and never would be.

Chapter Twenty-Five

As Bonfire Night approached, the village children began to prepare a huge bonfire on the green opposite the smithy where Lizzie lived. Every day as they passed it on their way to school, the boys would wonder at the way it had grown overnight.

'I ain't never seen a bonfire as big as that,' Gus marvelled. 'Come to fink of it, I ain't never seen a bonfire at all. There weren't room to light one round where I came from. Not wivout settin' light to the houses, anyway.'

Danny chuckled as he stroked Albert. Gus had allowed him to carry him some of the way to school and his whiskers were twitching, making Sparky giggle.

'Did you ever 'ave a bonfire, Danny?' Gus enquired.

Danny nodded as his mind went back in time. 'Yes, we did, as a matter o' fact. Before they built the Anderson shelters we used to 'ave one on the gardens at the back. Eeh, it were grand. Me mam used to buy us rockets that went as high as the stars. She'd stand 'em in empty milk bottles an' then me dad or Mr Massey, that's our neighbour, used to light 'em an' off they'd go. The neighbours all used to give us their old clothes so as we could make a Guy Fawkes, an' fer a few nights before we lit the fire we'd stand on the street corner with him an' ask passersby fer a penny fer the guy. With the money we made we'd buy sparklers. They were me favourites, 'cos once they were lit yer could wave 'em about an' write yer name in the dark wi' 'em. An' then me mam an' Mrs Massey would push spuds into the side o' the fire an' we'd split 'em open when they were cooked and put butter in 'em.'

Gus and Sparky listened with envy, thinking Danny's family must have been quite well off. Where they came from, every spare penny was spent on food, and even then there was never enough of it, which was why they were both so taken with Wales. By now they were almost at the school gates and were just about to enter them when someone running across the cobbles made them look back across their shoulders.

Mrs Roberts, who Sparky was staying with in the village, was running towards them, her huge breasts jiggling up and down as she ran. She was brandishing something in her hand, and as she drew closer, the boys were alarmed to see it was a piece of yellow paper.

'Bleedin' 'ell,' Gus muttered under his breath. 'It looks like a telegram.'

They stood silently as Mrs Roberts wheezed up to them. 'Tell . . .' she struggled to get her breath as she draped a chubby arm about Sparky's slight shoulders. 'Tell the teacher that Sparky won't be in this morning, boys, would you? I have something to tell him that would be best told back at home.'

Sparky was staring up at her uncomprehendingly as the two boys solemnly nodded. Then she gently turned the little lad about and led him back the way she had come.

'What the bloody 'ell were all *that* about?' Gus mumbled.

Danny handed Albert back to his owner. 'I've no idea, but we'd best get in else we'll be late, an' then we'll 'ave Miss Williams breathin' down us necks.'

Gus popped Albert back into his top pocket and then the two boys silently entered the school.

Sparky didn't come into class at all that day, but during the afternoon there was a tap at the classroom door and the children all turned in their seats to see Mrs Roberts beckoning to Miss Williams.

'*Blant, pawb i gyfrif.*' Realising that she had resorted to her native tongue in her consternation, Miss Williams immediately corrected herself. 'Children, everyone to count,' she barked as she sharply rapped on the blackboard with a lethal-looking cane. 'I shan't be a moment. Whilst I'm gone, you are to get on with your arithmetic, do you all hear me?'

'Yes, Miss Williams,' the class chorused as she barged past them. They all bent their heads to the books in front of them, but many of them were watching the window that ran all along the side of the classroom where they could see Miss Williams and Mrs Roberts talking. At one point during the conversation, Miss Williams' hand flew to her mouth and she looked distressed, but when she re-entered the classroom some minutes later she was once again in control of herself.

'Children, your attention, please.' She rapped on her desk with the dreaded cane as the children's heads slowly rose to look at her curiously. 'I'm afraid I have some very sad news for you all,' she began. 'As you are all aware, John – or Sparky as he is known to you all – is staying with Mr and Mrs Roberts in the village. Sadly, she has just informed me that he has received some very bad news. During an air raid on London last night, Sparky's family were all killed. The time ahead is going to be very difficult for him, so I want you all to promise me that when he returns to school, you will all be kind to him.'

'Bu . . . but what will happen to him now then, miss?' Gus asked tentatively. 'Will he stay on wiv Mrs Roberts?'

'I have no idea what will happen to him long-term, Gus,' she replied truthfully, 'but yes, I would think he will certainly be staying with the Roberts family – until the war is over, at least. I should imagine he will then be transferred to an orphanage somewhere.'

Lizzie, who was sitting in the front row, promptly burst into tears as she thought of poor Sparky's plight. How awful it must be for him to have lost every single one of his family all in one go.

To everyone's amazement, Miss Williams then revealed a side of her that none of them had ever seen before when she went to Lizzie and stroked her hair soothingly. 'There, there, *cariad*, 'tis a dreadful thing that has happened, to be sure, but we can all help him through it. War is a terrible thing all round, but then we must always look on the bright side. It can't go on forever, now can it?'

As Danny stared miserably down at his grubby hands he wasn't so sure, and he felt Sparky's pain. How would he and Lizzie feel if anything were to happen to their mam and Lucy? Lizzie glanced across at him and he knew that she was thinking exactly the same thing.

Bonfire Night came and went, but the huge bonfire on the village green was dismantled and never lit. Word had spread that no bonfires should be lit anywhere in the country. London was being heavily bombed and the villagers agreed that although Wales was a long way away, they could not risk drawing attention to themselves.

Sparky eventually returned to school, his eyes sunk deep into their sockets and red-rimmed from crying. His lips had taken on a bluish tinge. Both Danny and Gus desperately wanted to tell him how sorry they were for what had happened, but somehow they couldn't seem to find the right words so they remained silent and life went on as before, for them at least.

As the middle of November approached the mountain-tops were covered in snow and the inhabitants of Sarn-Bach woke one morning to find the landscape coated in a thick frost. Both Danny and Lizzie were enchanted with the sparkling trees and the rooftops of the cottages that looked like something out of a fairytale, but Gus did nothing but complain about it.

'Bleedin' weather,' he was constantly heard to say. 'Trust us to get stuck in the middle o' nowhere. It's enough to freeze the 'airs off a brass monkey 'ere.'

Lizzie giggled, a rare occurrence nowadays, for the mood was sombre in the smithy cottage.

'Mr Evans has been poorly all night,' she told the boys on the way to school one day. 'The smithy hasn't been open fer ages now an' he doesn't even get up to sit in the chair any more.'

'Don't sound like he's gonner be 'ere fer much longer,' Gus commented. 'Sounds to me like he's about ready to kick the bucket.' He had the good grace to look ashamed when Lizzie glared at him.

'That's an awful thing to say, Gus,' she admonished him. 'Mr Evans is really nice.'

'Well, I dare say 'e is, but that don't mean that 'e can't snuff it, does it?'

Lizzie tossed her head and flounced away in front of him as Gus chewed on his lip. 'I reckon yer could say I put me big bleedin' foot in it there, eh?'

Danny nodded grimly. 'You said it. I wonder what will happen to Lizzie though? If Mr Evans dies, I mean.'

'I dare say she'd stay on wiv the old dear – though I don't think she'd much like that. Old Blodwyn probably means well, but I reckon Lizzie feels a bit suffocated by her sometimes, don't you?'

Danny nodded in reply. Lizzie was unhappy and it showed, and on more than one count. He knew that she found Mrs Evans overbearing, but she was also fretting because as yet, she still hadn't received a single letter from their mam, though he'd had two so far. He had mentioned the fact to his mother in his last letter to her, and when her reply came she had assured them that she had written to them both, so why had Lizzie not received any of hers?

'Yer don't reckon that Mrs Evans *could* be keepin' 'em from her, do yer?' Gus asked when Danny mentioned it to him.

'But why would she do that?'

'Perhaps she wants to keep Lizzie all to 'erself,' Gus suggested sagely. 'I mean, fink about it. She don't barely let 'er out of 'er sight, an' you 'ardly ever see Lizzie dressed in any o' the clothes she came wiv now. She always seems to be wearin' somefin' that belonged to Mrs Evans's daughter . . . what were 'er name now? Megan. If yer were to ask me, I'd say it ain't 'ealthy.'

Danny was inclined to agree with him, as that little worm of unease wriggled its way around his stomach. But what could he do about it? He couldn't talk to Eric about it. If he did, the man would think he was mad. And if he wrote his concerns to his mother, she would worry herself sick. After giving it a lot of thought he decided that the best thing he could do would be to keep quiet, but to watch the situation closely, or at least, as closely as he could.

* * *

As they were walking home from school one day, Soho Gus had a brainwave.

'Why don't we go down to the beach?' he suggested. 'The rockpools will likely all be frozen over an' we could skate on 'em.'

Danny was sorely tempted. He could never have enough of the beach but was concerned about what Eric would say. Only two days ago, he had been severely scolded by Eric for being late home from school when he and Gus had gone off on one of their adventures.

'Shouldn't we go home first an' tell the folks where we're goin'?'

'Nah. If we do that, they'll only say we're to wait till the weekend,' Gus replied scornfully. 'It's gettin' dusk already an' yer know what they're like. They still treat us like babbies whenever they get the chance.'

They'd come to the opening that led down the steep hillside to the beach below, and Danny eyed it longingly. Seeing his hesitation, Soho Gus told him persuasively, 'I could show yer some o' the caves down there, while the tides out. I guarantee yer ain't never seen nothin' like it. The villagers reckon they were used by pirates years ago to store fings in. Just imagine, we might get to find some treasure, then we could buy our families a house here an' they could all come to stay out the way o' the war.'

'Well . . . I suppose just half an hour wouldn't hurt,' Danny said doubtfully, and before he knew it he was scrambling down the cliff in hot pursuit of his friend. Once they reached the deserted beach, Danny stared at the sea in awe. Just as Soho Gus had told him, the tide was some way out and the waves were thundering onto the sand in great frothy clouds of spray before being snatched back out to sea, as if by some unseen gigantic hand. The sky overhead was the curious colour that lingers between day and night, a mixture of purples and soft mauves, and he wished that he had his paints there so that he could try and catch it on canvas.

In no time at all, their gas masks and satchels were discarded and they were racing along the beach with all the energy of youth, enjoying the feel of the wind in their hair. They skidded across icy rockpools giggling in gay abandon as they went. When they came to the caves that were sunk deep into the side of the cliff, Danny peered inside the shadowy interior.

'It's a bit dark in there, ain't it?' he ventured, concerned that Gus would think he was a scaredy-cat.

Gus ignored him and plunged fearlessly inside. 'Come on, it's great,' he called, his voice echoing hollowly off the dripping stone walls.

Danny tentatively followed him, his eyes stretching wide as he stared into the gloom. The caves were enormous and went so far back into the cliff that he was amazed.

'Let's see if we can't find some treasure then,' Gus shouted, and soon they were in their element as they scurried here and there. The only treasure they unearthed, however, were shells, which Danny crammed into his pockets with the intention of passing them on to Lizzie the next day.

They were so absorbed in their treasure-hunt that they soon lost track of time, but eventually it became so dark that they could scarcely see the entrance to the cave. 'Do yer think we've been here fer more than half an hour?' Danny asked as he upended an old crate that stood against the wall of the cave.

Gus shrugged as he straightened and stepped over an indignant crab as it scuttled out of his way.

'I ain't sure, but I dare say we'd better get back, else they'll be sendin' a search-party out fer us.'

Turning as one, they fumbled their way to the entrance of the cave and were shocked to see that the tide was sweeping in and was only yards away from them.

'Bleedin' 'ell!' Gus gasped in alarm as he looked along the beach. The sea was already lapping against the cliff in places, effectively stopping them from going back the way they had come.

'We'll have to shin up the cliff,' he told Danny, but the other boy shook his head.

'You can if yer like, but I'm goin' back the way I come. If I don't get me gas mask an' me satchel, I'll get a right ear-waggin' off Eric, not to mention Miss Williams. All our homework is in our bags, don't forget.'

Soho Gus nodded in agreement. 'Yer right. An' I forgot I left Albert in me bag so he wouldn't get wet. I tell yer what – let's take our shoes an' socks off an' make a run fer it.'

In no time at all, both boys had their shoes dangling from their hands as they watched the fast-approaching tide.

'Right, now when I say, make a run fer it,' Gus commanded. A wave rolled in across their bare toes and they both shuddered as they waited for it to ebb.

'Right – *now*!'

As one, they gambolled across the beach, keeping as close to the cliff-face as they could. By the time they managed to reach their discarded schoolbags they were both breathless and their trousers were soaked right up to the knees. Gus sat down on a large rock and began to wipe the wet sand from in between his toes before tugging his damp shoes and socks back on, then waited while Danny did the same.

As they surveyed each other, they began to giggle. The wind and the spray from the sea had whipped their hair into a tangle and with their soaking trousers and grubby hands they looked a right sorry sight.

'Do yer reckon we're gonna get it in the neck?' Gus asked.

'Probably, but it was that good it will be worth it,' Danny replied, then with a last look at the sea they began the long ascent up the cliffside.

Danny's worst fears were confirmed when, as he neared *Tremarfon*, he saw Eric standing at the window looking out for him.

'Where the hell have you been?' he demanded, the second Danny put his foot through the door.

'I er . . . Well, the thing is, Soho Gus wanted to show me the caves down on the beach an' we just sort o' lost track o' time,' Danny admitted sheepishly.

Eric lifted a plate out of the oven and slammed it down onto the table. Danny eyed it with distaste. Whatever it was, it was all shrivelled up and looked very unappetising.

'I'm just about sick of you two clearing off willy-nilly. Wouldn't it have been courteous to come and tell me you were planning to go out first?' Not waiting for an answer, Eric went on, 'There's your dinner, young man. Or at least what's left of it. Don't blame me if it's inedible.'

Obviously deeply annoyed, he snatched up his coat and slammed out of the house without so much as another word.

Shame-faced, Danny eyed the ruined dinner. He supposed now that he *had* been rather thoughtless. Eric had obviously been very worried when he didn't arrive home on time. A smile spread across his face at the thought. If Eric was worried then it must mean that he cared for him . . . at least a little bit?

Lifting a piece of the now unidentifiable meat from his plate, he offered it to Samson who, after giving it a sniff, pushed his nose in the air in disgust and walked away to collapse in front of the fire. Hemily did the same when Danny offered her some so he scraped the meal into the bin and put his plate in the sink before crossing to stand at the kitchen window. The lights of the outhouse were shining into the darkness outside, which meant that Eric must be in there painting.

Crossing to his own small easel, Danny pulled it into the light, and while the memory was fresh in his mind, he began to try and capture the picture of the windswept beach on canvas.

Down in the village, Lizzie was cowering at the side of the fire as she listened to Mr and Mrs Evans having a blazing row. They were upstairs in their bedroom, but even so, Lizzie could hear every single word they said.

'Mother, you *have* to give the child some freedom,' she heard Mr Evans say. His voice was wheezy and weak, but nonetheless it carried down the stairs.

'I have no idea what you're talking about,' his wife retaliated. 'Now come along and drink this soup whilst it's hot. You know what the doctor said. You have to keep your strength up.'

The sound of a spoon clattering onto the bare wooden floorboards above told Lizzie that Mr Evans was not prepared to do as he was told, even if he was poorly.

'Daffyd, *shame* on you, after I've gone to all the trouble of making it for you too!'

'*Bugger* the soup and *listen* to me, will you, woman?'

There was an outraged cry from Mrs Evans and then

a softening in his voice as her husband addressed her again. 'This obsession with the little one is unhealthy, Blodwyn. Surely you can see it? She's a grand little girl, there's no denying it, but she's not yours! Stop and think what you're doing, love; you drove our boys away with your obsession.'

'And do you really think I don't know that, Father?' The woman's voice was full of sorrow.

'Then why are you dressing her in Megan's clothes? And why did you get all of our daughter's dollies down out of the loft for her?'

'Because they were lying up there doing nothing. It was her birthday and her mother didn't send her anything, did she? So how could I see the child with nothing? You're letting your imagination run away with you, so you are.'

A coughing fit stopped Mr Evans from arguing further and Lizzie listened with dread as she heard Blodwyn's footsteps on the stairs. When the woman appeared in the doorway balancing a tray, she nodded at Lizzie affectionately.

'Now then, *bach*. I'll just set these dishes in the sink and then we'll do your homework, shall we?'

Lizzie sighed resignedly, longing for the time when she could escape to her room, and wishing with all her heart that she was back at home in Coventry, with her mother.

Chapter Twenty-Six

Heaving herself up from her knees in the outside privy, Jo swiped her hand across the back of her mouth. For the last week she seemed to have done nothing but vomit and she felt like death on legs. Up until now she had managed to be on time for her job every single day, but she wondered how much longer she could manage it. Apart from herself, Maggie and Ellen, no one else knew of her condition as yet, but in a few weeks' time she would no longer be able to conceal the fact, and then there'd be hell to pay. Especially when that nasty little man, Fred Massey, got to hear of it. It was a day she dreaded, for ever since recognition had dawned in his eyes, the man had regarded her with contempt as if she were something that the cat had brought in. Luckily she was still as thin as a matchstick and, apart from the tenderness in her breasts and a tiny swelling in her stomach, as yet there was no sign of the pregnancy.

Sighing, she pushed the door open and, pulling her cardigan more tightly about her, she hurried through the bitterly cold air to the back door. Maggie was in the kitchen singing to Lucy as she tried to tempt her to eat some breakfast. The little girl had come down with a heavy cold and was far from well, which was giving Maggie cause for grave concern. Never the most robust of children, Lucy seemed to fall prey to every cough and cold that was going around, and at this time of year there were plenty of them.

'How is she this morning?' Jo asked as she shut the back door behind her.

'Not too bad. But how are *you* feelin'?' Maggie glanced across her shoulder at Jo's peaky face. 'You look absolutely ghastly.'

'Thanks a lot,' Jo chuckled as she wound a scarf around her neck and picked up her coat. 'You certainly know how to make a girl feel good.'

'Well, I'm only speaking the truth,' Maggie told her. 'But if it's any consolation, I know exactly how you're feeling. I was as sick as a dog every single morning, all the way through when I was carrying the twins. Why don't you have a day off an' put yer feet up by the fire?'

'Huh! I'll be havin' enough o' them soon enough. No, I'm all right really – and I'd sooner work while I can. I just wish the sickness was only in the mornin's. As it is I seem to be runnin' to the lav every half-hour. Miss Hutchinson commented on it the other day an' I had to tell her it was how the cold weather affected me. I don't know how long she'll swallow that excuse for, though.'

'Try not to worry about it,' Maggie replied kindly. 'We'll cross each bridge as we come to it, eh?'

As Jo looked across at her, the girl wondered how she would have coped without Maggie over the last few months. She had never had a true friend before, and to her Maggie was worth her weight in gold.

'Right, I'd better get off, else I'll be out of a job sooner than I thought,' she said briskly. 'Is there anything you'd like me to do before I go?'

'No, but there is something you could help me with tonight. I have to get this wedding dress and veil over to

293

Godiva Lane and I wondered if you'd come with me, to help me with the box. It's not going to be that heavy, just awkward really. I thought perhaps me mam could pop over an' have Lucy fer an hour while we delivered it. That is, if you don't mind?'

'Course I don't mind,' Jo assured her. She looked at the dress on the tailor's dummy that Maggie had picked up for a snip from a rummage sale.

'I just hope they're happy with it,' Maggie said worriedly. 'She gets married this Saturday and I stayed up until two o'clock this morning getting it finished.'

'Happy with it? Why, I should think she'll be bloody ecstatic!' Jo declared. 'You've really excelled yerself this time. Royalty could walk down the aisle in that. No one would ever believe that it were made o' parachute silk. Anyway, I'm off. See yer later.'

With a last cheeky grin she disappeared out of the door as Maggie gazed at the wedding dress. It was one of the most complicated patterns she had ever under-taken, but she had to admit to being quietly pleased with it. She'd spent numerous hours sitting covering with silk the row of tiny buttons that ran from the long train at the back to the neckline, not to mention the hours and hours she had spent hand-stitching the lace onto the sweetheart neckline and the sleeves. She had two reasons for wishing to deliver it that night. One was obviously to make sure that the fit was just right. But secondly, she was hoping that she would be paid, for the coal was running dangerously low and she was trying to keep a constant temperature in the kitchen at least because of Lucy's cold.

Her mother walked in just as Maggie was tying the ribbons on Lucy's Liberty bodice. Ellen immediately spotted the beautiful dress in the corner of the room, and she exclaimed, 'I have to say it, our Maggie, you've really excelled yerself this time! That dress is fit fer a princess!'

Her daughter grinned. 'I'm glad you think so. Actually, I was hoping to deliver it tonight with Jo, and I was just saying to her that I wondered if you'd mind having Lucy for an hour while we did so?'

'No problem at all,' her mother assured her as she bent to place a kiss on her granddaughter's head. 'It ain't as if I've got what you could call a hectic social calendar, is it?'

'You could have, Mam,' Maggie pointed out. 'Why you choose to stay in, night after night, is beyond me. Mrs Massey is always askin' you to go to Housey-Housey with her. You never even bother goin' to the pictures any more.'

'That's because I have no wish to,' her mother informed her shortly. 'But anyway, let's not start all that again. We've already been down that road. What did Danny have to say in the letter you got from him yesterday? Is he all right? An' have you still not had one off Lizzie yet?'

'No, I haven't.' Maggie's voice was laced with concern. 'Danny sounds all right, but says in his letter that Lizzie has never received any of mine, yet I always post them together. I can't understand it. I think this time when I reply, I'm going to put Lizzie's in with Danny's. That way, he can pass it on to her, because he seems to be getting his all right.'

'Sounds a bit fishy if yer were to ask me,' Ellen commented. 'It can't be nothin' to do wi' the post not gettin' through, otherwise Danny wouldn't be receiving his either, would he? You don't think the people Lizzie is stayin' with are keepin' yer letters from her, do you?'

'The thought had occurred to me,' Maggie admitted,

'but why would they do that? According to Danny they adore Lizzie, though the man of the house is really poorly at the moment.'

'What's up wi' him?'

Maggie shrugged as she coaxed Lucy to drink some of the warm milk she had just made her. 'Danny didn't say. I feel as if I'm being torn in two at the minute. I'd hoped to get to Wales to see them both soon. I can't put off telling them about their dad forever. But then Lucy came down with this cold and I don't feel right going while she's not well. On top of that, I have a pile of sewing to catch up on once I've delivered this wedding dress, and I can't afford the train fare till I've done that and been paid for them.'

'I could lend yer a bit,' Ellen offered.

Maggie shook her head. 'Thanks, Mam. I appreciate the offer but I can manage,' she told her proudly.

As Ellen looked across at her daughter, it struck her just how much she had changed in the past months. Maggie had always been a quiet, subservient sort of girl, but now the stronger side of her personality had emerged, which was just as well, from where Ellen was standing. She certainly had enough on her plate at the moment, there was no denying it, and although Ellen was happy to help out wherever she could, she didn't want to look as if she was interfering, so she remained a quiet presence in the background, ready to step forward, when and if she was needed.

Placing her ration books on the table, she said, 'Will you be wantin' me to have Lucy while you pop up the shops later on?' When Maggie nodded she pushed the books towards her. 'Good, then would yer mind pickin' my shoppin' up while yer about it? Ain't no sense in us both venturin' out in this weather, is there?'

It was on the tip of Maggie's tongue to tell her mother that it would do her good to get out for a while. But mindful that it could cause yet another argument if she did, she simply nodded and stayed tight-lipped.

As Maggie prepared to go to the shops later that afternoon she was shocked to see the date on the ration books. It was 14 November already, which meant that Christmas was racing towards them all. Her brow furrowed at the thought. Things had been quiet in Coventry recently; there had been no air raids for weeks, for which Maggie was grateful. The thought of having to drag Lucy out to a freezing cold shelter in the dead of night didn't bear thinking about. Even so she was quite aware that the city might have been lulled into a false sense of security. Every day the newspapers were full of the latest atrocities of war and she knew that it was a long way from being over. Her hopes of having the twins home for Christmas were dashed as the days passed with no sign of the war abating. The thought of spending it apart from them brought tears stinging to her eyes. It felt like years since she'd seen her children. It didn't matter that she was merely one of many parents in the country who were in exactly the same boat; the knowledge brought her no comfort and she missed Danny and Lizzie more with every day that passed.

Pulling herself together with an enormous effort, she began to put her coat on. Her mother would be over at any minute to look after Lucy, and Maggie had no intention of letting Ellen find her crying. She still had Lucy to worry about and she must make her a priority until such time as it was safe to have the twins home again. As she had discovered, life went on – even with a war raging all around them.

* * *

As evening descended on the city, a thick mist began to form across the pavements, turning the icy paving slabs into a skating rink.

'You'll be lucky to get there and back without goin' yer length,' Ellen told Maggie and Jo as she settled herself into the fireside chair.

Maggie laughed. 'You're about right there, Mam, especially as we've to jiggle this box between us.'

Crossing to an enormous cardboard box that she'd managed to scrounge from the corner shop, she opened the lid and she and Jo began to carefully fold the wedding dress into it.

'Christ, do yer reckon it's big enough?' Jo remarked. 'An' fancy deliverin' such a lovely dress in a box that were used fer packin' soap powder.'

Maggie eyed the OMO logo with amusement. 'Well, this was the only one I could get that were big enough,' she explained. 'The other boxes were all too small, an' the dress would have been creased to high heaven by the time we got it there.'

Once the train had been carefully folded in to Maggie's satisfaction, she closed the lid. 'Right, that's it. I dare say we'd better get off. There's a rare frost settling already so the sooner this is done the better. Are you quite sure you'll be all right with Lucy, Mam?'

'Huh! Why wouldn't I be? We're always all right, ain't we, me darlin'?'

Lucy snuggled down into her gran's lap, clutching her dolly and smiling up at her adoringly; as Maggie looked at them in the glow from the fire, love for them both made her heart sing. She and Jo grabbed the box between them and started towards the door. It was almost six o'clock.

'We should be back fer half seven at the latest, Mam.

See yer later.' Suddenly dropping her side of the box, she hurried back to kiss them both soundly. 'I know I may not say it often, but I do love you both,' she whispered.

Ellen blinked away tears at the unexpected show of emotion. 'Get off wi' yer, yer daft ha'porth,' she said shakily. 'You'll have me blartin' in a minute.'

Maggie hurried back to where Jo was waiting for her, and in no time at all they were on their way. The box was as light as a feather but awkward to manoeuvre round corners, which had Jo cursing in no time as they struggled along the almost-deserted streets. High above the city, the barrage balloons bobbed on their strings like enormous grey elephants and the spire of the Cathedral stood proud.

It took them nearly half an hour to reach Godiva Lane, by which time their hands were so cold that they'd turned blue.

'It would be just our bloody luck if we got there an' they weren't in,' Jo grumbled.

'They'll be in,' Maggie assured her as she peered at the house numbers. Stopping outside one, she rapped at the front door and was rewarded by the sound of footsteps.

The mother of the bride-to-be answered the door and beamed when she saw Maggie standing there. 'Why, is it all done?' she asked excitedly, and when Maggie nodded, she ushered her and Jo inside. 'You couldn't have come at a better time,' the woman assured her. 'Betty is just in from work so she'll be able to have a final try-on before the big day.'

When Maggie and Jo left the house later, Maggie was beaming from ear to ear. The bride had looked truly breathtaking in the dress and it had fitted her like a glove, which was a huge relief. Better still was the fact that Maggie's wages were tucked deep in her coat pocket, with a couple of pounds extra as a bonus.

'I can afford to buy the twins a little present now,' she confided to Jo.

'Why don't yer treat yerself fer a change?' Jo suggested. 'Every spare penny yer get goes on either the kids or the house, from what I can see of it.'

Now that they no longer had to balance the box between them, Jo had sunk her hands as far down in her coat pockets as they would go, but she was still shivering with cold.

'There's nothin' I need,' Maggie told her. Jo was just about to come back with a caustic reply when the sound of sirens suddenly pierced the air.

'Oh no,' Maggie groaned. 'We're still a good half an hour away from home an' me mam's there all alone with Lucy.'

'She'll be all right,' Jo assured her. 'I bet even now she'll be bundlin' her up an' headin' fer the shelter. Yer mam ain't daft.'

'I'm well aware of that,' Maggie snapped, far more sharply then she'd meant to. Instantly contrite, she reached across to squeeze Jo's arm. 'Sorry,' she said. 'I just want to get home, that's all.'

They quickened their footsteps, but they had gone no more than two streets on when the sound of the ack-ack and Bofors guns burst into life as the first planes droned overhead in the moonlit sky. All around them, doors were opening and banging shut as people scurried past them to seek the safety of the shelters, and in no time at all the previously deserted streets were echoing with the sounds of children crying as distraught parents tried to soothe them.

'We need to get to a shelter,' Jo gasped as she pressed her hand into her side to ease the stitch there. 'I don't think I can run much further.'

Maggie felt as if she were being torn in two. She longed to get home to her mother and Lucy, yet didn't want to leave Jo all alone. Even as she struggled with her dilemma, the sky suddenly lit up with parachute flares that the planes had dropped to highlight the city below. They hung above them like great white iridescent chandeliers. Maggie gazed up in wonder, which quickly turned to horror as the first phosphorus exploding incendiary bombs came hurtling towards them. They looked like falling stars but Maggie knew that once they hit the ground they would burst into flames, which would act as targets for the planes overhead to drop the more deadly bombs on.

''Ere, you two. Don't get standin' there like lumps o' lard. Do yer want to get yer 'eads blown off? Me an' the missus are goin' to the shelter at the end o' the street. Yer can tag along with us.'

The speaker was an elderly man with his braces dangling round his waist, accompanied by an old woman whose head was covered in a brightly coloured head-square.

Without waiting for a reply, he grasped her elbow and she felt herself being tugged along behind him. By the time they reached the end of the street she was breathless. He shoved her into the communal shelter in front of him before turning to usher his wife and Jo in after her. The shelter seemed to be teeming with people, as Maggie tried to adjust her eyes to the gloom. The air smelled damp and the children's cries echoed off the cold stone walls as the old man struggled to pull the shelter door shut. The sound of it clanging to sounded like the closing of a prison cell door and Maggie began to sob as she thought of her mam and Lucy all alone back at home.

Jo placed her arm around her as the second wave of planes sounded in the sky overhead. Then suddenly the children's cries were drowned out and the shelter seemed to shake as the first bomb exploded nearby. The Coventry blitz had begun, and for most of the people huddling there that night, life would never be the same again.

Chapter Twenty-Seven

As Maggie and Jo huddled together, a continuous stream of bombers passed overhead and they felt their city shake with the force of the raid. They had assumed that the main targets would be the industrial factories, so were shocked to hear the bombs falling so close to them. Some minutes later they heard a hammering on the door and the same old man who had led them to the shelter struggled to open it. A young man almost fell into the shelter before the door clanged shut behind him.

'They're targetin' the city,' he gasped. 'Saint Michael's Cathedral has taken a hit already. The fire-fighters are there but the roof's on fire an' they reckon it's useless. The centre is like an inferno; some o' the fire-fighters are dead already.'

A horrified silence settled on the people in the shelter as they tried to absorb what the young man was telling them. To everyone there, the Cathedral was the heart of the city and they couldn't envisage the fall of such a fine building.

'It's mad out there,' he went on with a catch in his voice. 'There's houses goin' down like nine-pins. Whole streets wiped out just like that, as if they'd never been.' A particularly close explosion silenced him as the shelter shuddered again. But once it had settled the young man gabbled on, 'They're usin' landmines now an' all. At this rate there'll be nothin' left standin' by the time we get out o' here.'

'*Shut up!*' The old man saw that the young man was becoming hysterical. Somewhere at the back of the shelter, a woman began to pray, and for Maggie the whole event took on an air of unreality. She knew only too well the devastation landmines could cause. They took the form of a large metal box that would slowly and silently float down on a parachute to explode above ground level with a deafening roar, flattening anything and everything that happened to be beneath it. What if one of them was to fall on her house? Would the shelter be enough to protect Lizzie and her mam?

Suddenly she knew that she couldn't just sit there. She had to get home to them. Pulling herself away from the wall, she began to wade through a sea of people towards the door as ear-shattering explosions sounded in her ears. But when she reached the door and attempted to open it, hands reached out to stop her.

'What yer tryin' to do – get us all killed?' a man barked at her accusingly. 'Move back there an' try to stay calm, can't yer?'

Maggie sagged against the damp wall as tears slipped down her cheeks, and in that moment she felt totally useless. All she could do now was add her prayers to those of the woman at the back of the shelter.

The raid went on and on, and as the hours passed, the spirits of the people in the shelter sank lower and lower.

'What time do yer think it is?' Jo whispered in her ear after what seemed like a lifetime.

Maggie shrugged. It was too dark in the shelter to see the face of the cheap watch on her wrist, even with the flickering candles that someone had managed to light.

As the night wore on, there was little resistance from the ground, for many of the defence stations had run out of ammunition, but still the raid continued with no let-up.

By now a silence had settled in the shelter. Outside, the only sounds were the fire engines' sirens mixed with the crash of explosions.

At last, at around five o'clock in the morning, the first bombardment began to abate and at six fifteen, the all clear finally sounded.

Slowly, the people in the shelter began to emerge into the streets, or what was left of them. Shocked and tired they stood silently in the drizzle as they tried to take in the aftermath of the attack. What was left of their once fine city lay in ruins beneath a great black cloud of smoke. The city centre was ablaze, and many of the factories had been burned to the ground. In parts, flames as high as a hundred feet licked into the sky, and all around, the suburban streets were littered with rubble that only hours before had been people's homes.

As they stood there gazing about them in stunned disbelief, an Army truck rumbled towards them and troops began to pour out of the back of it armed with picks and shovels.

On legs that felt as if they had turned to jelly, Maggie staggered towards a weary-looking soldier and grasped his arm. 'Please – can you tell me, is Clay Lane still standing?'

Hearing the urgency in her voice he sadly shook his head. 'I couldn't tell you, love. We've just come from trying to put out the fire at Saint Nicholas's Church, or I should say what's left of it, in Radford. I ain't never seen nothing like it in me life. There were people shelterin' in the crypt there, for Christ's sake. Huh! Some sanctuary that turned out to be, didn't it? Even the House of God ain't safe from this bloody war. They were still diggin' out the dead when they ordered us to come here.' He shrugged Maggie's hand from his arm and staggered away, leaving her to stare after him in open-mouthed horror.

The houses on one side of the street were completely flattened, and injured people sat on the kerbs in a daze waiting for the ambulances to arrive. Others were wailing and digging at the rubble with their bare hands as they frantically searched for loved ones.

'Come on, love.' Jo's voice brought Maggie out of her trance-like state. 'Let's try an' get back home. Happen everything will be fine there. There's nothing we can do here.'

'Don't get goin' near the centre,' a man who was standing nearby warned. 'The whole place is like an inferno an' the trams are destroyed. If you've far to go you'd be best to wait here for help.'

Maggie shook her head. 'Thanks, but I have to go. Me mam an' me little girl will be worried sick about us.' So saying she set off at such a pace that Jo had to almost run to keep up with her. As they turned from one street into another, Maggie tried to close her eyes to the horrific sights. Bodies were being carried from the ruins of homes and laid on the pavement. The clamour of ambulance bells, fire engines and children crying were ringing in her ears, but she dared not stop to offer help. She *had* to get home to her mam and Lucy – to some sort of normality.

The journey took almost twice as long as it should have, for the pavements were strewn with bricks and rubble. More than once she stumbled, and soon her hands and knees were cut and bruised, but Maggie didn't feel a thing. The overpowering need to see her family safe and sound seemed to somehow block out all other sensations.

Jo stumbled along behind her as a feeling of foreboding settled around her heart. The nearer they got to their destination, the more the feeling grew, for there seemed to be no let-up in the devastation anywhere along the way. Whole streets had fallen prey to the air raid. Only a day before they had been neat rows of terraced houses, now they resembled nothing more than a demolition site.

At last they turned the corner into Clay Lane and only then did Maggie stop as her hand flew to her mouth. The houses on the side of the street where her mother lived were still standing, though the glass had been blown from the windows. But on her side of the street there was nothing but smouldering piles of bricks and rubbish.

'Noooooooooo!' The sound that issued from her mouth was so heart-wrenching that Jo would hear it in her worst nightmares for the rest of her life. She reached out to try and touch Maggie, but her friend was running like the wind in the direction of where her house had stood.

Troops were frantically digging through the rubble as she approached, and one of them stepped forward and tried to prevent her from going any further. She fought him off like a wildcat, her eyes standing out from her strained face.

'This is *my* house,' she gasped as she struggled in his arms. 'My baby an' me mam . . . they're in the shelter out the back. I've got to get to them.'

The soldier hastily barked an order at a young lad, who immediately began to scramble across the bricks towards the place where the yard would have been. Maggie could just make out the roof of the shelter and she began to pray as she had never prayed before as she watched him slipping and sliding across the bricks. Eventually he disappeared behind the pile of rubble that was all that was left of her home and time stood still as she waited for him to reappear.

After what seemed an eternity she saw him clambering towards them again and she held her breath. As he slid down the slope in front of them he called out: 'The shelter's still intact – but there's no one in there.'

'Oh, my dear God.' Maggie's eyes began to sweep back and forwards across the rubble. 'I told her to use the shelter. I *told* her!'

Jo, traumatised by the scene, and by all the raw memories of her own tragedy, had begun to cry as she realised what had happened. Ellen had refused to use the shelter since the night Maggie's father had died, and it appeared that last night had been no exception. Which meant . . . Ellen and Lucy were somewhere beneath that wicked-looking pile of bricks.

Like someone possessed, Maggie sprang forward and began to dig amongst the rubble with her bare hands. Seeing that there would be no stopping her, the soldier joined his efforts to hers as Jo looked on in horrified fascination.

Twenty minutes later, Mrs Massey appeared from one of the houses that was still standing across the street and hurried over to them.

'Maggie, for the love of God come away,' she implored the young woman, as tears ran down her cheeks. 'Come on over to Gwen's with me. There's no gas or electric but she's set the kettle on the fire so you can get somethin' warm inside yer.'

Oblivious to everything but the need to find her family, Maggie worked on as Mrs Massey eyed her with consternation. Stepping closer, she tried again. '*Please*, love. There's nothing you can do here. Leave it to the troops. They'll come and tell you if they find anything.' She placed her hand on Maggie's arm and tried to draw her away but Maggie rounded on her so furiously that it was all Mrs Massey could do to stay on her feet.

'*Get off me – do yer hear?*'

Jo steadied the woman as she stared at Maggie in shock.

'She doesn't mean it,' Jo defended her.

'I know that, love, an' me heart is breakin' for her,' Mrs Massey replied as she took a step back. 'May God help her through the trials that lie ahead.' Seeing that Jo looked dead on her feet, she gently placed an arm around her waist.

'Come on pet. You look like *you* could do with a good strong cuppa.'

Jo looked towards Maggie and opened her mouth to refuse, but Mrs Massey was having none of it. 'There's nothin' you can do to help her by stayin' here. This is somethin' she has to go through alone, more's the pity.'

With dragging steps, Jo followed the kindly woman across the street.

Within no time at all, the unrelenting drizzle had soaked Maggie to the skin and her hands were raw and bleeding, but still she worked on side-by-side with the troops.

Later in the morning, Ministry of Information vans began to slowly tour the city telling the people who had become homeless where to obtain food and shelter. Canteens sprang up, and slowly the dispirited souls who had nothing but the clothes they stood up in could be seen trooping towards them.

Maggie ignored the loudspeakers as she worked

diligently on. She would find them; she had to. Perhaps her mam had had the sense to shelter under a table or something? In her mind's eye she could see Lucy leaping towards her unhurt when they finally freed her from her prison; could feel her little arms about her neck, and smell that sweet baby scent that was hers and hers alone. Maggie would scold her mother for not using the shelter then embrace her and promise to never, ever leave her alone again.

The picture in her mind drove her relentlessly on, even when the troops stopped occasionally for a well-earned cup of tea supplied by one of the neighbours who was still fortunate enough to have a home.

Just before lunchtime, she found the photograph of the twins that had stood in pride of place on the mantelpiece. The frame and the glass were broken but their smiling faces spurred her on as she tucked the photo into the pocket of her ruined coat. Just a few more feet to go and they would reach the solid oak table that had stood in the centre of the room.

The force of the blast that had rocked the house had sent the bedroom furniture crashing into the kitchen below. The men had thrown what remained of it into the street and now they were unearthing kitchenware. It was at this point that Mr Massey appeared. He was still wearing his tin hat and looked drained and tired, but nevertheless he set to with a will and added his efforts to theirs.

Maggie flashed him a brief grateful smile before turning her attention back to the task at hand.

Suddenly a shout went up and a silence settled as the men all looked towards it. Mrs Massey and Jo had just appeared with yet more trays of tea in their hands and they hurried across the road just in time to see one of the troops stand with a little doll in his hand.

'Over here!'

Time seemed to stand still as Maggie felt the world sway. On hands and knees, she crawled across the debris towards him but once she was close he looked away from her with tears streaming down his soot-blackened cheeks.

With a feeling of dread she looked down and there they were. Lucy wrapped tight in her grandma's arms on what had once been the floor of her kitchen.

Lucy had learned to crawl on that floor. She had taken her first steps across it. She had played with her dollies on it for countless hours – but she would never play on it again, for at a glance Maggie knew that both Lucy and her mother were dead.

She could feel a scream building in her throat, but somehow it seemed to lodge there though it echoed in her head, far louder than any of the bombs she had heard during the night before.

Somehow she managed to gently disentangle her child from her mother's arms and as the men looked soundlessly on she sank onto the debris and began to tenderly rock her to and fro as she crooned her favourite lullaby.

> *Rockabye, baby, on the tree-top.*
> *When the wind blows, the cradle will rock.*
> *When the bough breaks, the cradle will fall.*
> *And down will come baby, cradle and all . . .*

A hush fell on the people assembled there, and then they all bent their heads and openly wept as the sweet strains of the lullaby floated on the air.

Part Three

Part 3 here

Chapter Twenty-Eight

Eric rapped sharply on the door and was rewarded seconds later when it inched open and Mrs Evans's face appeared.

'Why, Mr Sinclair. Come away in.' It was impossible to keep the surprise from her voice as she stood aside for him to pass her.

Once in the immaculate little kitchen he removed his cap, acutely aware of her eyes on the scars on his face. Irritation laced his voice as he explained, 'I thought I ought to come and see you. Have you had the wireless on this morning?'

She shook her head. 'Indeed, I haven't had a moment to listen to it. Should I have?' As she spoke she ushered him towards the table and uncomfortably he sank down onto one of the chairs.

'It seems that Coventry, where the twins come from, was heavily blitzed last night. According to the papers, the raid caused utter devastation. There are hundreds dead and injured, by all accounts, and the city centre is in ruins, including the Cathedral. Three-quarters of the city's factories were destroyed and thousands have been made homeless.'

When she stared at him uncomprehendingly, he went on, 'It seems that Swanshill, which is where the twins lived, was badly bombed too.'

'It's right sorry I am to hear it,' Blodwyn told him. 'But what can *we* do about it?'

He ran a hand distractedly through his hair. 'I was hoping you would tell me. You see, until I had Danny come to live with me, I hadn't had an awful lot of contact with children. Do you think we should tell them, or perhaps try to find out if their mother and sister are all right?'

'Oh, no,' Blodwyn declared, just a little too quickly for his liking. 'Lizziebright is well settled and I don't want her upset. Think about it – what could they do, apart from worry, even if we did tell them? No – I think the least said the better on this matter.'

Eric frowned uncertainly. 'But what if they hear it from someone else? Won't that be worse than if they'd heard it from us? The newspapers are full of it, and children do talk, you know. King George is visiting the city tomorrow to offer condolences, then everyone will be talking about it.'

Pursing her lips, Mrs Evans rose from the seat she had taken opposite him. 'As I said, Mr Sinclair, I think we would be wise to leave well alone. Now, if you'll excuse me, the doctor will be here to see my husband at any minute.'

Eric rose and edged towards the door, wishing that he had never bothered to come. She followed him and opened the door without a word. Once he had stepped outside she gave him a curt nod.

'Good day, Mr Sinclair.'

The door closed in his face as Eric stood there. He glanced up and down the cobbled street, then, with his head bent against the bitingly cold wind, he hurried away.

For Lizzie and Danny, the day passed uneventfully. After school, Danny said his goodbyes to Lizzie outside *Ty-Du*

and went on his way with Soho Gus and Sparky as Lizzie
gazed at the cottage windows. The doctor's bicycle was
propped against the wall, but as this was becoming a
regular occurrence she wasn't overly concerned until she
stepped inside. Almost at once she sensed that something
was wrong. The fire had burned low in the grate and
there was no welcoming smell of dinner cooking for the
first time since she had come to stay there.

After slinging her gas mask and satchel onto the
nearest chair, she went to the stairs door and peered up
to the dim landing above. She could faintly hear the
sound of Mrs Evans and the doctor talking, and she
hovered there uncertainly, wondering if she should call
up to them. It was then that she heard the doctor say,
'I'm afraid it's not looking good, Blodwyn. I could have
him transferred to the hospital if you'd rather he be
there?'

'You'll do no such thing,' was Blodwyn's reply. 'This
is his home and this is where he will stay. Until they
take him out of here in a box, that is.'

Lizzie knew then that Mr Evans must be very ill
indeed, and a frown settled across her small face. He had
always been the one to stick up for her when Mrs Evans
was fussing over her, and she wondered what it would
be like to have to live here alone, if anything should
happen to him.

She didn't have long to ponder, for at that moment
she heard the doctor snap his bag shut and he and Mrs
Evans appeared at the top of the stairs.

'Aw, Lizziebright!' the woman exclaimed. 'I didn't
know you were home so soon – and me with no dinner
on the table for you. What am I thinking of, eh?'

The doctor gave her a curious look but saying nothing
he quickly descended the stairs.

'I shall call back in a couple of hours after I've done my surgery,' he informed her from the doorway. 'Until then, just try to keep him as comfortable as you can.' He smiled kindly at Lizzie and then he was gone. Mrs Evans bore down on Lizzie to wrap her in a warm embrace. The girl felt like telling her that she had only seen her at lunchtime, not a year ago, but seeing that the woman was upset she held her tongue.

'Now then, *bach*, what sort of a day have you had then, eh?'

Looking very solemn, Lizzie looked her straight in the eye and asked bluntly, 'What's wrong with Mr Evans?'

The woman started as if she had been doused with a bucket of cold water before replying, 'Come and sit with me, *bach*. There is something I need to tell you.'

Lizzie obediently slid onto the settee and Blodwyn sat next to her, fiddling with her handkerchief as she sought for the right words. Eventually she said, 'Mr Evans is very ill, Lizziebright . . . very ill indeed. In fact, the doctor thinks . . . Well, he thinks that Mr Evans may be leaving us soon.'

'What! You mean he might *die*?' Lizzie's eyes were fearful as she remembered the blood on his handkerchief and the terrible hacking cough.

The big woman swallowed. 'Yes, *bach*, he has the dust disease. You see, before we lived here, we lived up in the hills in a tiny miner's cottage, and Mr Evans worked down the pit. He never liked it, but his grandfather was a miner as was his grandfather before him, and so it was expected that Daffyd would be the same. The only man of the family who *never* worked down the pits was Daffyd's father, who was a blacksmith. Daffyd decided to go down the pit because we got a small cottage to live in that came with the job when we married. He never liked it, so when the opportunity arose to buy the smithy here in Sarn-Bach, he seized the opportunity with both hands and here we've been ever since. The pit closed down not long after we left and the cottages are all empty now – but we had some happy years there. Our two boys and Megan were born there, as it happens.'

Her eyes had become dreamy as Lizzie asked quietly, 'Where are your sons now?'

'Moved away,' Mrs Evans sighed. 'They were good lads, but after we lost Megan they accused me of loving her more than I loved them. As soon as they were old enough, they flew the nest. I don't know where they are now.'

'And did you?' Lizzie questioned in the forthright way that only a child could.

The woman looked shocked, and as if she were fighting some inner battle, but after some seconds she slowly nodded.

'I suppose I did, but I couldn't help it. Megan was my whole life. I had always wanted a little girl, which is why I was so thrilled when you arrived. You are so like her. When my poor Daffyd is gone, at least we'll still have each other.'

Lizzie shuffled uncomfortably in her seat. 'Not for too long we won't,' she whispered. 'Don't forget – as soon as the war is over, me an' Danny will be goin' home to our mam and dad.'

A strange look flared in the woman's eyes as she stroked the child's hair. 'We'll see,' she said softly. 'But now I had better get you fed. I don't want it said that I neglect you. Not when you are the most important person in my life.'

Lizzie found this a very strange thing for her to say when her husband was lying upstairs so ill, but she kept her lips clamped tight shut. She wished that Danny were there or that her mam would just walk in through the door to take her home. Home . . . just the thought of it made the lump in her throat swell again.

'I . . . I have to go to the privy,' she blurted out, and without waiting for an answer she fled to the back door, yanked it open and escaped into the cold, early evening air. Already a thick frost had made the grass stand to attention, but Lizzie was oblivious to the chill as she sped down the twisting garden path. Once she had slammed the toilet door she dropped her knickers around her ankles and clambered up onto the cold wooden seat. And then at last she let the tears of home-sickness and confusion fall. Mrs Evans had never shown her anything but kindness, so why then did her flesh crawl every time the woman so much as touched her, she asked herself?

And her mam: why had she written to Danny and not to her? It was all beyond her understanding, but in that moment she yearned to have her brother beside her.

They were almost halfway up the steep hill that led to their temporary homes when Danny stopped dead in his tracks.

'What's the matter wiv you, then?' Gus enquired.

Danny shuddered as if someone had stepped on his grave, and his brows raced together in a frown. 'I ain't sure, but sommat tells me that Lizzie ain't happy.'

'Oh, give over, will yer?' Gus scoffed. 'We left her not 'alf an 'our since, an' she were all right then, weren't she?'

'She's not now. I can feel it – I tell yer. It's always been the same ever since we were little. Lizzie got measles once an' though I didn't get 'em I had all the same symptoms,

320

right down to the itchin'. I remember the doctor tellin' our mam he couldn't understand it.'

'Now that is *right* bleedin' weird,' Gus said as he scratched at his wild mop of ginger hair. 'Do yer think we should go back down to the village then?'

Danny paused. He desperately wanted to, yet he was afraid of upsetting Eric again so soon after their last escapade.

'I hadn't better,' he said finally. 'I don't want to get on the wrong side of Eric again. I dare say whatever it is will wait till mornin'.'

Gus nodded in silent agreement as he lifted Albert from his pocket and set him on his shoulder. And so they went on their way, each lost in their own thoughts.

By the time Danny got home he was frozen to the bone and glad of the welcoming warmth as he walked into the kitchen. Eric was sitting in a chair at the side of the fire reading a newspaper, but he instantly shoved it behind a cushion and rose. Crossing to the kettle he filled it at the sink, setting the old pipes clanking.

'There's another letter come for you. On the shelf there – look.'

Danny's mood instantly improved as he recognised his mother's handwriting. Settling himself into the chair, he ripped the envelope open as Eric set about preparing his meal. His face lit up when he found two letters inside: one for him and one for Lizzie. That should cheer his sister up when he gave it to her tomorrow at least. His eyes hungrily scanned the neatly written pages, feeling his family close to him as he read of what was going on back at home. Then, when he had finished, he started back at the beginning and read it all over again.

'Everythin' is fine back at home,' he told Eric brightly,

and the man was glad that he had his back to him so that Danny wouldn't see the concern on his face. The letter had obviously been written some days ago – but were things still fine back there in Clay Lane now?

He wrestled with his conscience. Half of him wanted to tell Danny what had happened in Coventry the night before, yet the other half of him was happy to take the coward's way out and say nothing, as Mrs Evans had advised.

Turning about, he began, 'Danny, there's some . . .'

When Danny looked up at him with an expectant smile on his face, the words died on Eric's lips.

'Yes? What were yer about to say?'

'Oh, er . . . it was nothing really. Why don't you nip out and get some logs in for the fire, eh? The meal should be ready in a jiffy.'

Danny obligingly hopped off the chair, and when he returned some minutes later, clutching an armful of logs, he sniffed at the air appreciatively as the smell of cabbage and pork chops met him at the door.

'Cor, that smells nice. I'm that hungry I could eat a scabby horse,' he declared.

Eric found himself smiling. When he'd first been forced to take Danny in he had resented the child's presence, but now he found himself enjoying his company. It suddenly occurred to him how quiet it was going to be when the child returned to his mother – *if* his mother had survived the Blitz, that was. A cold shiver ran up his spine and far more curtly than he had intended to, he told Danny, 'Get to the table. Your dinner's ready.'

Some commotion on the landing and the sound of hushed voices woke Lizzie in the dead of night. She yawned and stretched as she peered towards the door of her pretty little bedroom. She thought that it sounded like the doctor's voice but couldn't be sure. Snuggling back down beneath the soft blankets, she struggled to stay awake but soon her eyes grew heavy again and in no time at all she was fast asleep.

The next morning, she woke and lay for a moment enjoying that special time that comes between waking and being fully awake. Eventually she struggled out of the bed and realised that, for once, Mrs Evans hadn't hung the clothes she wanted her to wear that day on the door of the wardrobe. A smile broke out on Lizzie's face as she quickly selected some of the clothes she had brought from home and put them on. It felt nice to be wearing her own things again and not those of dead Megan Evans. She brushed her hair, which was now just beginning to grow again, and cleaned her teeth, then crossing to the window she drew the curtains aside and gasped with delight. Overnight it had started to snow and the village of Sarn-Bach had become a glistening white wonderland. Almost beside herself with excitement, she pounded down the stairs and burst into the kitchen.

'Mrs Evans – it's been sno . . .' her voice trailed away as she saw Mrs Evans huddled in the depths of an armchair and Mrs Wigley the vicar's wife pottering about the room.

Mrs Wigley smiled at her kindly. 'Good morning, Lizzie. I'm afraid we have some very sad news for you. During the night, Mr Evans passed away, God rest his soul. So I shall be getting you off to school today as Mrs Evans isn't feeling quite herself.'

Lizzie looked across at Blodwyn. Her eyes were puffed from crying and she looked very pale and old. But the biggest surprise for Lizzie was that she didn't even attempt to acknowledge her. It was as if she wasn't even there. Unsure of what she should say, she cast a glance at the vicar's wife, who smiled at her reassuringly before leading her to the table.

'Sit yourself down, *bach*, and have your breakfast. Then we'll get you off to school. There's no point in keeping you out of your routine. No doubt Mrs Evans will be feeling better later on when the shock has worn off a little bit.'

'I don't *want* her to go to school! I need her here with me!'

The vicar's wife stared at Mrs Evans in astonishment, for these were the first words she had uttered since she had arrived there.

'Now, now, Blodwyn. I understand that you have had a nasty shock, but there's nothing to be gained from upsetting the child now, is there?'

Mrs Evans turned red in the face as she rounded on the poor woman in a fury, but Lizzie luckily couldn't understand a word she said, for she had reverted to talking in her native Welsh.

Like a spectator at a tennis match, Lizzie's eyes flew from one to the other as the two women batted angry words back and forth. Then suddenly it was all over when Mrs Evans broke into a torrent of tears and buried her face in her apron.

Mrs Wigley hovered uncertainly before turning her attention back to Lizzie. There would be time to deal with Blodwyn when she had seen to the child.

'Come along to the table now, *cariad*,' she urged as she ladled some thick porridge into a bowl and sprinkled it liberally with brown sugar. 'You'll need something warm inside you today. And have you got any Wellington boots? I'm thinking you'll be needing some. The snow is coming down thick and fast and we don't want your feet to get wet, now do we?'

Lizzie shook her head, her eyes never leaving Mrs Evans's face as she sidled onto a chair by the table. She gulped her breakfast down as quickly as she could then pounded away back up the stairs to rummage for her boots in the bottom of the wardrobe.

She returned to the kitchen minutes later, wrapped up as if she was going to the North Pole. She had on her warm coat and Wellington boots, and had also put on a hat, scarf and mittens that Grandma Bright had knitted for her, last Christmas.

The vicar's wife looked at her approvingly as she ushered her towards the door. 'Now there's a sensible girl. Off you go then, and try to have a good day, and don't worry too much about what is going on here. Things will work out, I'm sure.'

Lizzie nodded numbly as she stepped out into the winter landscape. Within seconds she was coated in thick white flakes that settled on her clothes and clung to her eyelashes. The milk cart, pulled along by a great brown horse, was labouring down the street towards her, and she waved gaily at Mr Todds, the milkman, momentarily forgetting the sadness that she had just left behind. She had gone no more than a few steps when Danny's voice pierced the air.

'Here, Lizzie, hold up!'

Giggling, she waited for him, along with Soho Gus and Sparky, to catch up with her, and then they began to troop through the snow together.

'I've got something really good to tell you,' Danny informed her breathlessly.

'Really? Well, I've got something really *sad* to tell you – but you go first.'

Barely able to contain his excitement, Danny did better than that as, delving into the coat of his pocket, he produced the letter their mother had written to her.

'Mam sent this for you, in wi' mine. She was concerned 'cos you hadn't got any of the others she'd written. But there's even better news than that! Go on – read it, an' you'll see. She's goin' to try an' come to see us soon.'

Lizzie's whole face lit up, causing Gus's young heart to skip a beat. She really did look very pretty when she smiled, and he knew in that moment that Lizzie would always be the only girl he could ever love.

'When? When is she coming?'

'Read the letter an' you'll see, won't yer?' Danny grinned. 'Though she ain't said what day or anythin'. Just that she'll be comin' as soon as she can. I dare say she's got to sort out who to leave Lucy with. It would be too far for her to come, so I dare say she'll leave her with either Gran or Jo.'

From the shelter of the post-office doorway, which she'd stepped into to read her letter, Lizzie nodded as her eyes slowly slipped down the page. It said much the same as Danny's and her heart lifted at the thought of seeing her mother. Folding the precious letter carefully, she tucked it deep into her pocket before once again joining the boys in the snow.

'Right, so what's your news then?'

Lizzie solemnly looked back at Danny. 'It's Mr Evans. He passed away in the night.'

'Cor blimey!' Gus exclaimed. 'Yer mean he like . . . *snuffed* it?'

When Lizzie nodded, the three boys shook their heads in disbelief.

'Poor old sod. So what will 'appen to yer now, then? Will yer still stay on wi' Mrs Evans?'

'I suppose so.'

The tone of her voice told Gus that Lizzie wasn't exactly enamoured of the idea, and he asked, 'Incha happy there?'

'Not really,' Lizzie said guiltily, 'though Mrs Evans *is* very kind to me. In fact, she's *too* kind.'

Gus stared at her as if she'd taken leave of her senses. ''Ow the 'ell can anybody be *too* kind?'

Lizzie tried to think how to explain the way she felt.

'Is she still callin' you Megan?' Danny asked softly.

Lizzie's head bobbed. 'Yes, she is. She didn't used to do it so much in front of Mr Evans, but now he's gone . . .'

By now they were approaching the school gates and Danny gave her hand a squeeze as they headed across the playground. 'Perhaps Eric would let yer come an' stay wi' us?' he suggested.

Lizzie looked at him hopefully. 'Do you really think he might?'

'Ain't no way of knowing till I ask him, is there? But the worst he can say is no, ain't it? So it's worth a try.'

The sound of the bell ringing stopped the conversation from going any further, but as Lizzie trailed into the cloakroom she was smiling.

A teacher who had never taken their class before was waiting for them when they all piled into the classroom. He did speak English, but his Welsh accent was so strong that the children could barely understand a word he said.

'Stone the bleedin' crows,' Gus muttered as he slipped Albert into his satchel.

'This should be a laugh. I wonder where Old Lady Williams is?'

Miss Williams was at that very moment tapping on the door of the blacksmith's cottage. The vicar's wife opened it and ushered her inside, and then she stood to one side as Miss Williams approached the grieving widow.

'I'm so sorry to hear your sad news, *bach*,' she told Blodwyn sincerely. 'Daffyd was a lovely man and will be sorely missed by all who knew him. But I'm not just here to offer my condolences. I have to speak to you about what will be happening to Lizzie Bright now. As you know, I'm the one responsible for arranging the evacuees' billets and it's plain as the nose on your face that you'll not want the child here now after what's happened. You have enough on your plate without having to worry about her.'

Mrs Evans struggled out of her trance-like state to stare up at her visitor. 'And *why* wouldn't I want Lizziebright here now?' she asked angrily.

Miss Williams took a hasty step back as she looked towards Mrs Wigley for support. 'Well, I was just thinking that with a funeral to arrange and such, you'd be too busy,' she stammered.

'Then you thought wrong,' Mrs Evans snapped. 'The girl stays here with me and that's an end to the matter.'

'But—'

'I don't want to discuss it!'

Miss Williams felt the colour flare in her cheeks.

Mrs Wigley clumsily attempted to help. 'Blodwyn, Miss Williams is right,' she said. 'You have a lot to deal with right now and I'm not sure that this is the right place for the child at present. Death is a frightening thing to a little one. Would it not be wiser to let Miss Williams move her on, just until you've got over the worst of the shock?'

'*No!* How many times do I have to tell you? Now please, if this is all you've come to discuss, I'd like you both to leave.'

The two women looked at each other aghast as they moved towards the door. Blodwyn seemed more concerned about Lizzie than the loss of her husband at present, but then they supposed she was still in shock.

'Perhaps it would be best if we came back when you've had time to think it over?' Miss Williams suggested tentatively as they hovered by the door.

A surly nod was their only answer as they let themselves out into the fast-deepening snow.

Chapter Twenty-Nine

'Mr Bright, can you hear me?'

David struggled to open his eyes, blinking in the harsh light of the hospital tent. A young nurse swam into focus and he heard someone groaning. After a few moments, he realised it was himself.

'Wh . . . where am I?' His voice was weak.

'You're safe,' the nurse assured him kindly. 'And that's all you need to know for now. In a few days' time you'll be shipped back to a military hospital in England.'

He tried to lift his head but a searing pain shot up his arm, making him gasp, and she gently pressed him back into his pillows. 'Try not to move. The doctor will be around to see you again in a minute. I don't mind telling you, you had us worried there for a while. We didn't think you were going to make it.'

'Wha . . . what's wrong with my arm?'

Lifting the chart that was hooked across the bottom of his bed, she wrote something on it before answering him, 'You were shot in the arm, but try not to worry. The doctor will do everything he can to save it.'

He screwed his eyes tight shut. What did she mean, the doctor would try to save it? And how had he got shot? Try as he would to remember, his mind was a blank. He could recall creeping across the field with guns going off all around him. He could see the rotting corpses and smell the blood and fear, but when he tried to remember past that, it was as if he had hit a brick wall.

Seeing his distress, the nurse patted his good hand. The other appeared to be swathed in bandages up to the armpit and felt incredibly heavy and painful.

Someone calling distracted her and she looked along the row of beds. 'Try to get some rest,' she said, and he watched her walking away before sleep claimed him once again.

The next time he woke, the same young nurse was carefully unwinding the bandages on his arm. Behind her stood a young man in a doctor's coat who looked incredibly tired.

'Hello, I thought you were going to sleep the clock round again,' the nurse joked. Once the bloodied bandages were removed, a terrible rotting smell filled his nostrils and he flinched as the doctor stepped forward to peer at his wounds.

'Mmm, it's gangrene I'm afraid,' he heard him say through a haze of pain. 'You'd better prepare him for surgery. We stand a chance of saving him if we take it off just below the elbow.'

David wondered what the doctor was talking about but it was too much of an effort to ask somehow. It sounded as though some poor bugger was about to lose a limb. Closing his eyes, he waited for sleep to rescue him again.

Ellen Sharp was buried in the little cemetery where, only a few short months before, the elderly woman had laid her husband to rest. The body of her little granddaughter Lucy was buried in the same coffin, which somehow made Maggie feel fractionally better. At least Lucy was not alone.

The day was raw, with a thick frost coating the ground. In the London Road Cemetery another funeral was taking place on a much larger scale, for a mass grave had been dug for all the unidentifiable victims of the Coventry Blitz. The whole city was in mourning as it struggled to come to terms with the terrible event. Today, however, Maggie could think of nothing but her own great loss, and as Mrs Massey stood at her side the young woman's pain was so tangible that her neighbour could almost reach out and touch it.

'*Earth to earth, ashes to ashes . . .*' The vicar's voice droned on until Maggie felt as if she would scream. Every morning since the night of the Blitz she had awoken, praying that all this was just some horrible nightmare. But now, as she stared down on the cheap coffin, there was no denying it. Her mother and Lucy were gone from her forever, and all she could do was pray that they had moved on to a better place.

When the vicar threw a few clods of frozen earth down onto the brass nameplate, Maggie kissed Lucy's dolly and threw it down into the grave. It landed with a small thud, its bright plastic eyes staring up at the leaden sky. It hit Maggie with a small shock that Lucy would never see the sky again, and suddenly the tears that she had held back spurted from her eyes in such a gush that she was momentarily blinded.

Mrs Massey sprang forward and caught her in her arms as Maggie swayed precariously on the edge of the grave. And then at last it was over and she was being led away, Jo and Grandma Bright following closely behind. They passed through the lych-gate as yet another coffin was carried through it, and the harassed vicar hurried back into the church to begin the next funeral service.

Beryl Bright wrapped Maggie in a loving embrace. 'You know as soon as yer up to it, you an' Jo can move in wi' me, don't yer, love? There'll always be a home for you there.'

Maggie nodded but her eyes were empty, and she didn't really hear what Beryl was saying.

'I'll get her back to Doris's fer now, love. Don't get worryin' about her,' Mrs Massey said. 'No doubt when she's over the shock she'll be glad to take you up on yer offer.' Turning to Maggie, she took her elbow and led her towards the waiting car. 'Come on, love,' she urged. 'What you need now is a good stiff drink inside yer.'

She helped her into the car and Jo squeezed in next to her as Maggie fought the urge to laugh. Here she was, burying her child and her mother, and Mrs Massey was telling her that what she needed was a good stiff drink. It sounded so ludicrous somehow under the circumstances, yet she knew the woman meant well. In fact, she shuddered to think what she would have done without her over the last few days – or the other neighbours, for that matter.

Doris Keen had put both her and Jo up without a word of complaint, despite the fact that her house was filled to overflowing with two teenage sons and three daughters. Two of the girls had been sleeping downstairs to accommodate them, but of course, it couldn't go on, though Maggie couldn't bring herself to think ahead as yet. Perhaps tomorrow, she promised herself as the car slowly drove through the icy streets.

Troops that had been drafted in from as far away as Manchester were working everywhere they looked, tirelessly digging for human remains in the piles of rubble

333

that still covered the streets. The spirits of the people of Coventry had been somewhat lifted by the visit from King George a few days before, and already the gas and electricity had been restored to most of the homes that were still standing. The sight of the King tramping through streets in deep mud and climbing over piles of rubble had restored the people's determination to survive. His visit had ended with him standing in the ruins of the once-beautiful Cathedral, his head bowed in sorrow.

But his sorrow could be nothing to the pain that Maggie was feeling now as they moved on to Doris's home. There would be no funeral tea, nothing to mark the passing of her mother and child, for it was all the people could do at the moment to feed themselves. In the pocket of the black coat, loaned to her by one of the kindly neighbours, was the picture of the twins that she had unearthed from the pile of rubble that had once been her home. She had kept it beside her, for the twins were all she had left in the world now and she clung to the photo as if it were a lifeline.

Doris leaped on her the second she stepped through the door with tears streaming down her haggard face. She was a tall thin woman with hair that always reminded Maggie of cotton wool from the numerous times she had bleached it, but she had a heart as big as a bucket.

'Come on, sweetheart. Get yourself over by the fire. You too, Jo. You both look perished. While yer thawin' out I'll rustle us up a bite to eat, eh?'

Sinking down into the fireside chair, Maggie stared into the flames, and as Doris saw the emptiness in her eyes she broke into a fresh torrent of weeping. 'God love us, when is all this heartbreak going to end, I ask meself?'

Jo began to fill the kettle as Doris tried to compose

herself, wrinkling her nose in distaste as she stared at the sink full of dirty pots. Doris was a lovely woman but she would certainly never win any awards for house-keeping, and that was a fact.

Following Jo's eyes, Mrs Massey rolled her sleeves up and began to lift the dirty crockery onto the draining board. 'Right, let's get some o' this lot washed and dried, shall we? Then we'll take the mats out an' give 'em a good beatin'. No offence meant to you, Doris, but wi' all these extra bodies in the house I dare say a bit of a hand won't come amiss.'

Doris sniffed before nodding. From where she was standing the house was perfectly all right as it was, but if Mrs Massey wanted to work herself into the grave then let her.

David lay in bed listening to the sounds going on all around him. Men were moaning with pain. Others were delirious and calling for their loved ones. Less than an hour ago he'd watched the little nurse respectfully place a sheet across the face of the poor bloke in the bed next to his, and minutes later they had wheeled him away. The bed had come back empty, but it hadn't stayed that way for long. Now a young man who looked to be little more than a boy was lying there, pitifully crying for his mother. There was a cage beneath the blankets on his bed, and he had heard the doctor tell the nurse in hushed tones that the poor lad had lost both his legs. David could barely comprehend how the young man must be feeling. He himself had been to theatre earlier in the day and was still feeling groggy from the anaesthetic, but thankfully the pain in his arm had eased from a raging fire to a dull ache now.

Glancing at the cage that covered it beneath the sheets

he briefly thought about feeling along the length of it, but then decided against it. He didn't want to set the pain off again.

Staring up at the roof of the tent, he tried again to remember how he had come to be here but it was too much of an effort. And then suddenly he thought of Maggie and Lucy, and for the first time in days a smile danced across his lips. As soon as he was feeling a little better he'd write to them and let them know he was all right. The doctor had informed him that, as soon as he was well enough to travel, they would be sending him home, which he thought was strange. He'd assumed that, as soon as he was mended, they'd send him back to camp – not that he was complaining.

'Nurse.'

She hurried across to him with a smile on her face though he knew she must be feeling exhausted.

'Is there any chance of you getting hold of some paper and a pen for me, please?'

'Of course there is – but not tonight, eh? Let's wait until tomorrow when you've properly recovered from your operation. I can help you to write a letter then if you like?'

He grinned. 'I don't think that will be necessary, thanks. I can write, you know.'

'But . . .' Her voice trailed away as she stared at him sadly.

'But what? What were you about to say?'

'Oh, nothing. Let's leave it until tomorrow when the doctor's been to see you. Now, is there anything else you'd like me to get you?'

'A pint of bitter wouldn't go amiss,' he told her with a twinkle in his eye.

She laughed as she straightened the cover on his bed.

'I'm afraid bitter isn't on the menu here. But I *could* get you a nice cold glass of water.'

'I dare say that'll have to do then,' he sighed, and she pottered away as he sank back into the pillows.

During the night he found himself caught in the grip of a terrible nightmare and he tossed and turned until his blankets were in a tangle all about him. He was on the battlefield again and Sam was there pointing a gun at him. But Sam was his *brother* – why would he want to shoot him?

'Private Bright . . . David, wake up. You're having a nightmare.' The voice made his eyes blink open. Slowly he looked around him, and as he realised where he was, he tried to raise his arm to swipe the sweat from his brow. A bandaged stump that finished just below the elbow confronted him and for a moment he stared at it in stark disbelief.

'Wh . . . where's my arm?' he gasped incredulously. The young nurse scurried away, only to return seconds later with a weary-faced doctor in a white coat that was spotted with blood.

'Private Bright.' His voice held all the weight of the world. 'I was going to come and see you in the morning, but seeing as you're awake I may as well tell you now. I'm afraid the injury you received to your arm had turned gangrenous by the time they brought you in. I had no choice but to amputate – but in fact you've been very lucky. Had it been left any longer, it could have killed you.'

David tried to take in what he was saying. '*Lucky*? Are you mad, man? You're standing there telling me you've chopped my arm off and you're telling me I'm *lucky*? How am I going to manage? I'll be a bloody cripple. No good to neither man nor beast!'

Hearing the panic in his voice, the doctor tried to soothe him. He had been through this exact same thing more times than he cared to remember, and was heartsick of it. 'It won't be as bad as you think, once you get used to it,' he assured him, but David wasn't listening, for suddenly in his mind's eye he could see Sam staring at him, his finger poised on the trigger of his rifle, ready to fire. It was *Sam* who had shot him. He closed his eyes as it all came flooding back and tears crept from beneath his lids to roll down his cheeks. It hadn't been a nightmare at all. It had been true; it had really happened. Turning on his side, he began to sob.

In the neat parlour of the vicarage, Miss Williams sipped at her tea from a dainty cup and saucer.

'I have to say I'm very concerned about Blodwyn,' she confided to Mrs Wigley, who was sitting opposite her. 'I know she's going through a trying time, what with losing Daffyd an' all, but I wonder if it's wise to leave young Lizzie Bright there. The poor woman seems to be a little . . . unhinged?'

'I know exactly what you mean,' Myfanwy Wigley replied. 'But shock does funny things to people and everyone reacts differently. She seems very attached to the child, and my fear is that if we move her, Blodwyn might feel she has no one at all. Perhaps it would be wise to delay the decision about the child's future until after the funeral?'

'Well . . .' Miss William's voice was filled with uncertainty. 'The trouble is, young Lizzie seems so unhappy. She could barely concentrate at school today and she looked as if she were ready to burst into tears at any minute. Of course, I feel desperately sorry for Blodwyn too, but as the billeting officer for the evacuees, my main concern is for the children.'

Both women lapsed into silence as they pondered on the dilemma, until eventually, Miss Williams said, 'Very well then. We'll wait until the funeral is over. But I have to warn you, if Lizzie is still unhappy then, I shall have no choice but to find her alternative accommodation.'

As the day of the funeral approached, the little village of Sarn-Bach went into mourning.

Eric noticed that Danny was unusually quiet, and on the eve of the funeral he finally asked him, 'Is something troubling you, lad?' The child had barely touched his meal, which was unusual for him.

Danny's chin drooped onto his chest as he nodded miserably. 'It's Lizzie. She ain't very happy living with Mrs Evans any more.'

'Why's that then?'

The boy shrugged. 'Ever since Mr Evans died, Lizzie reckons Mrs Evans has been actin' a bit strange.'

'In what way?'

'Well, she calls Lizzie "Megan" all the time now – that's the name of her little girl who died – an' she makes Lizzie wear the clothes that belonged to her. She's even cut her hair. She told Lizzie it was to tidy it up, but Lizzie reckons she did it to try an' make her look even *more* like Megan.'

Eric's brow creased with concern. 'Has this been happening just since she lost Mr Evans?'

Danny's head wagged from side-to-side. 'No, it were happenin' before, but since he died it's got worse. She won't let Lizzie out of her sight an' even followed her to the toilet last night.'

'I see.' Eric stood staring thoughtfully out of the window for a few minutes before asking tentatively, 'How do you think Lizzie would feel about coming to stay with us for a while?'

'What? Do yer *really* mean it?' Danny asked incredulously, and before stopping to think, he launched himself at Eric and threw his arms around his waist.

Eric felt his cheeks flame; it felt nice to have someone show him some affection. 'I wouldn't have said it if I didn't mean it,' he told Danny gruffly, as unfamiliar feelings fluttered to life inside him. 'What say we wrap up and go and ask her? Mrs Evans might be glad of the break, with the funeral so close. We'll have to walk down into the village though. There's no way we'd get the car through the drifts.'

Danny was struggling into his Wellington boots before Eric had even finished speaking, terrified that he might change his mind.

By the time they reached the bottom of the hill, they were breathless, and their cheeks were glowing from the cold snow that was blowing into their faces. As Danny began to tire he reached out to grasp Eric's hand and the man looked down at him in embarrassment. His first instinct was to shake Danny off, and yet the small hand nestled in his own felt so comforting that he walked on in silence. As he suddenly thought of the newspaper hidden behind the cushions back at home, guilt flooded through him. What if the twins' mother had been killed during the Blitz? What would happen to them then?

Pushing the thought away, he bent his head and they proceeded through the village in silence. When they finally reached the blacksmith's cottage, Eric rapped sharply on the door and seconds later he heard the sound of the bolts being drawn. Mrs Evans peered through a gap in the door at them and it was all Danny could do not to gasp aloud.

Her hair was standing out around her head in lank unruly wisps, and she looked as if she hadn't washed for days. Her eyes had a wild look about them that sent shudders up Danny's spine, and he was reminded of the witch in the picture books his mother had used to read to him and Lizzie when they were little.

'Yes!'

Danny shrank into Eric's side at the curt tone of her voice.

Nonplussed, Eric stared back at her. 'I know this is a difficult time for you, Mrs Evans, but there's something I'd like to discuss with you.'

'Can't it wait?'

'Not really.'

Tutting with annoyance, she said, 'Then you'd better get on with it.'

'May we come in? I have Danny with me and it is rather cold out here.'

A refusal hovered on her lips, but then she became aware of Lizzie, who had come to stand at her side. The girl was gazing past Eric to Danny with a look of yearning on her face, and having no wish to upset her, Blodwyn opened the door and allowed them to step inside.

'What is it you want to discuss then?' she asked shortly. 'I'm burying my husband tomorrow and am in no mood to stand here making small talk, I can assure you.'

Eric decided to get straight to the point. 'I was wondering if it would be a help to you if I took Lizzie to stay with Danny and myself for a few days?'

Her eyes almost started from her head. 'And why would I want you to do that?' She glared at him indignantly. 'Sure, Lizzie is fine company for me at the minute.'

Eric glanced at Danny just in time to see his face fall and decided to try again. 'I thought you might need some time to yourself. And besides that, I think Danny and Lizzie would enjoy being under the same roof again, if only for a short time.'

'Then you thought *wrong*, Mr Sinclair. I can assure you that Lizzie and I are fine as we are, and certainly don't need your interference. So if that is all you've come to say, I'll thank you to leave now.'

Eric looked helplessly from Lizzie to Danny, but seeing no option other than to do what the woman asked, he turned around and opened the door.

'I'm sorry if I've upset you,' he apologised. 'It was certainly not my intention. Now I'll wish you good night.'

The door slammed so quickly behind him that he felt the wind of it as he grinned wryly at Danny. 'I think that's what you call being sent away with a flea in your ear,' he told him, then hand-in-hand they began the long journey home.

On the morning of the funeral there was no let-up in the weather and the snow continued to fall in a great white sheet that obliterated the landscape. Curtains were kept tightly drawn as the gravediggers began the unenviable task of digging the grave. It took two of them the whole morning, for the ground was frozen solid. As quickly as they threw the earth out of the grave, it filled up with snow again and their patience began to ebb. But at last it was done and they threw a tarpaulin across the gaping hole and hurried away to warm themselves at their firesides.

The road to Pwllheli had been blocked for days so it was decided that four of the village men would carry Daffyd Evans's body from the small chapel that nestled in the hillside at the side of the church, to his final resting-place. There was little choice, for the hearse and the undertakers from Pwllheli couldn't have gotten through the snowdrifts even if they had wanted to.

The village school was closed for the day as a mark of respect, and as the solemn procession through the little village began, Lizzie found her small hand gripped tight in Mrs Evans's larger one.

She was thrilled to see Danny and Eric standing at the gate of the church, and she flashed Eric a tremulous smile. Lizzie's small heart had pounded with anticipation at the thought of being with Danny again. Perhaps after the funeral was over Mrs Evans might change her mind and decide that she *did* need some time to herself after all. The girl clung to this hope as Danny gazed at her sympathetically.

Eric placed his hand on the boy's shoulder and squeezed it reassuringly, and Danny smiled up at him as the congregation trooped silently into the small picturesque church. The time had come to lay Daffyd Evans to rest.

Chapter Thirty

A furious hammering on the front door early on a cold and frosty morning brought Doris bustling down the stairs, cursing as she went.

'Keep yer bloody 'air on!' she shouted peevishly as she struggled with the bolts. Tightening the belt of her old candlewick dressing-gown, she patted the metal curlers on her head and yanked the door open to find Beryl Bright smiling from ear to ear on the doorstep.

'Let me in, love,' Beryl pleaded. 'It's enough to freeze yer socks off out 'ere.' Before Doris had a chance to reply, Beryl had shot past her into the kitchen and demanded, 'Where's our Maggie?'

'Upstairs in bed, where all god-fearin' folks should be at this time o' the mornin',' Doris snapped back at her. Suddenly, to her amazement, Beryl caught her around the waist and began to dance her around the room.

'I've just had the most *wonderful* news!' Her delight was so infectious that Doris found herself grinning despite the fact that she was none too pleased at being dragged out of bed.

'Well, if it's that good, I'd better go an' fetch her then. God knows it's about time we had some good news fer a change. Stick the kettle on, Beryl. I'll be back in a jiffy.'

She shuffled away back up the stairs as Beryl sighed

344

at the mountain of washing up, stacked on the wooden draining board. But then she grinned again. What did it matter? Nothing mattered today, after the wonderful telegram that she had just received. Upstairs, she could faintly hear voices, and minutes later, Maggie and Jo emerged from the stairs door. Jo was rubbing the sleep from her eyes and was as pale as a ghost, and Maggie didn't look much better.

'Christ, what a pair!' Beryl exclaimed. 'Still, never mind. If the news I've brought yer don't put a smile on yer faces, then nothin' will.'

Maggie eyed her curiously but Jo suddenly pressed her hand across her mouth and made a bolt for the back door. Beryl watched her go but Maggie, in no mood for niceties, demanded sharply, 'Spit it out then, this good news, whatever it is.'

Fumbling in her bag, Beryl produced a telegram with a flourish and began to wave it in the air. 'This came this mornin'. It's about David. They've found him an' he's alive.'

Maggie felt the room sway as shock coursed through her.

'See – it ain't all doom an' gloom after all, is it?' Beryl chuckled. 'I tell yer, it were the last thing I were expectin'. Yer could have knocked me down with a feather when it arrived. But it's wonderful, ain't it? At least one o' me boys will be coming home.'

A smile of relief spread across Maggie's face as she hugged Beryl. 'Yes, it is wonderful news,' she agreed. 'But doesn't it say where he is?'

'Just that he's in some military hospital somewhere, an' that as soon as he's well enough they'll be shippin' him back home. Apparently, he was found on the same night as Sam was killed an' he's been there ever since.

345

Why they ain't let us know sooner, God only knows, but still, all's well that ends well, eh?'

'If he's in a hospital he must have been injured then,' Maggie said cautiously.

'Injured or not, at least he's alive,' Beryl told her sensibly. 'An' once we get him home we'll soon have him ship-shape again between us, which leads me to the next thing I've come to see you about.' She glanced at Doris apologetically before going on, 'Ain't it about time yer came to live with me now, love? I know Doris has done yer proud an' I'll never be able to thank her enough, but let's face it: yer all jammed in here like sardines in a can. It can't be easy fer Doris wi' two extra mouths to feed, an' I feel as if it's my turn to do a bit now, so won't you consider it? There's me rattlin' round like a pea in a pod back there, an' the thing is, you'd be doin' me a favour if you did but know it, 'cos once our David gets home I shall need a hand to take care of him if he's been hurt, an' I ain't as young as I used to be.'

Maggie stood in an agony of indecision but she needn't have worried, for Doris suddenly pottered across to her and hugged her affectionately.

'You go, love, if you want to. I were just a port in a storm to get yer through the worst. But Beryl has a point. Families should stick together at a time like this. Not that I want rid of yer, of course. Yer know yer welcome to stay fer as long as yer want, but I certainly won't be offended if yer decide to go with yer mother-in-law.'

Maggie gave her a grateful smile. This rough diamond of a woman had stood by her through the worst time of her life, and she would never, ever forget it, but that left just one more problem, the way she saw it. Looking towards Beryl, she now voiced it. 'What about Jo? She hasn't got anyone but me now an' I wouldn't want to leave her. You see, the thing is, Jo is going to have a baby.'

When both women burst into laughter, Maggie looked at them in astonishment.

'Do yer really think we hadn't guessed that?' Doris snorted. 'Why, it's been as plain as the nose on her face fer weeks. Yer can't hide things like that from women who've been through it, love.'

'Too right,' Beryl agreed. 'And as to your question – well, Jo would come with you, of course. I wouldn't expect you to abandon her.'

'The tongues will be wagging when word gets out, though,' Maggie warned.

'Huh! Because she ain't got a ring on her finger, do yer mean? With a war goin' on, I think I can safely say she won't be the only one. An' anyway, it ain't nobody else's business, so let 'em gossip if they've a mind to. Me back's broad an' I can take it if you pair can. There's a sewin'-machine sittin' idle back at my place. Yer could take up sewin' again an' get a bit behind yer fer when this bloody war is over. Meantime, I could lend you a bit so yer could pay the twins a visit, once David is safely home. I reckon that would perk you an' them up no end at the minute.'

Maggie nodded. 'It would be lovely to see them,' she admitted as tears started to her eyes. 'Though I don't know how I'm going to tell them about what's happened to their dad and their grandma and our Lucy.'

'Now then, don't get blartin',' Beryl ordered gently. 'Just go an' get yer things together. Yer know what they say – there ain't no time like the present.'

Maggie climbed the stairs in a daze, but for the first time since the dreadful night when she'd lost Lucy and her mam, she felt as if she were focused again. She still had the twins to think of, and although she knew she would never get over the loss of their baby sister, she had to think of them now.

In no time at all, she and Jo had packed their few belongings into brown paper carrier bags. The neighbours had all whipped round and supplied them both with the barest essentials of clothes. They were neither grand nor particularly well-fitting, but Maggie and Jo were more grateful than they could say, for the raid had left them with nothing but the clothes they had stood up in.

Once at the door, Maggie clung to Doris tearfully. 'I shall never be able to thank you enough for what you've done for us both,' she told her, narrowly missing being stabbed in the eye by one of Doris's fearsome metal curlers, that rarely came out apart from when she was going anywhere.

'Get off wi' yer,' Doris told her. 'It were a pleasure. Just make sure yer come an' see me from time to time, eh? An' remember, you're a young woman an' a lovely one at that. You may think yer life is over at the minute but you've still got a lot o' livin' to do. Every cloud has a silver linin' an' you'll come through this. Now go on, get off wi' yer before you have me blartin' too.'

The three women set off across the frosty pavement, but at the end of the street Maggie paused to look back at the ruins that had once been her home. It was hard to imagine it as it had been, now.

Beryl took her arm. 'Come on, love. No lookin' back, eh? We have to put this behind us now an' look to the future. Let's get you home an' settled in.'

Maggie nodded solemnly as Jo slipped her arm into hers and hauled her on her way.

*   *   *

'Bleedin' 'ell. We ain't never gonna get home at this rate,' Gus complained as he and Danny laboured up the hill. 'Poor old Albert will 'ave frostbite if I don't get 'im in out o' the cold soon.'

Danny chuckled despite the fact that snow had come in over the top of his Wellies and his feet were frozen. 'Never mind. At least we don't have to go to school tomorrow.'

'We might never go back to school again if it keeps comin' down at this rate,' Gus grumbled. 'It's all right, them shuttin' the school till further notice 'cos o' the weather conditions, but the trouble is, yer can 'ave too much of a good thing. Knowin' my luck, I'll get roped in helpin' around the farm again. They had me herdin' all the cows into the barn last night till God knows what time. I don't mind tellin' yer, by the time I got to bed I was frozen through.'

They ploughed on, often wandering off the path, for the snow was so deep that everywhere looked the same. Every now and again, Albert's head would peep out of Gus's top pocket, but then with a tweak of his whiskers and a shudder he would burrow back down again out of sight.

Danny began to get concerned as his imagination started to work overtime. They seemed to have been walking forever and he wondered if they were going in the right direction. He was just about to say as much to Gus when he thought he saw a shape lumbering towards them through the snow. Swiping the snow out of his eyes, he peered ahead – and sure enough, the shape of a man slowly drew closer. All the tales he had ever heard of Abominable Snowmen suddenly flashed into his mind and his heart began to race until a voice he recognised called, 'Hello there! Is that you, Danny?'

He sighed with relief. It was Eric. In no time at all he'd come abreast of them.

'I was a bit concerned you might stray off the path and get lost so I thought I'd come down to meet you,' the man explained.

Danny felt himself flush with pleasure. Perhaps Eric did care about him after all, if he'd taken the trouble to do that?

Seeing that the small boys looked totally exhausted, Eric stood them either side of him, then taking one of their hands in each of his own he began to haul them through the drifts.

Soon after, *Derwen Deg* came into sight and he nudged Gus towards the gate that led to the farmhouse. 'Go on, I'll just watch till you're safely inside then we're going to push on,' he told him.

Gus smiled at him gratefully. 'Thanks a lot. Tarra then, both.'

They watched him go in through the door, then Eric turned his attention back to Danny. Up here, high on the hill, the storm had turned into a blizzard and they could barely see a hand in front of them.

'I tell you what, how about I give you a piggy-back?' Eric suggested. Danny stared at him uncertainly but then before he could stop him, Eric had squatted down in front of him. 'Hop on,' he urged. 'And once you have, wrap your arms around my neck and your legs around my waist, then bury your face in my shoulder. I'll have you home before you know it now.'

Danny self-consciously did as he was told and was amazed when Eric began to stride surefootedly through the drifts. Just as he'd promised, the lights of *Tremarfon* soon appeared ahead of them and he breathed a sigh of relief. Once Eric had kicked the kitchen door open, he placed Danny down onto the red tiled floor and began to peel his wet outer clothes off him. There was a welcoming fire roaring up the chimney, and after hoisting Hemily out of the fireside chair, he plonked Danny down into it. Samson immediately pottered over to him and put his head in his lap as Hemily sauntered indignantly away with her tail swishing angrily in the air.

Eric chuckled as he hung up Danny's wet clothes, and the boy held his chilled hands out to the warmth of the fire. For the first time since he'd been there, he felt as if he had come home. But more importantly, he felt wanted. It was a nice feeling, and he basked in it as he watched Eric from the corner of his eye. He suddenly realised with a little shock that for some reason, Eric didn't appear quite so daunting now. Admittedly, the eye-patch and the scars were still there for all to see, but somehow they weren't quite so scary any more. Perhaps it's 'cos I've got used to them, he mused. Or could it be that, underneath, Eric ain't quite as hard as he likes to make out? Whatever it was, it made Danny happy, and he settled back contentedly into the chair until his dinner was ready.

Down in the village, Lizzie was having her dinner too, but the atmosphere was nowhere near as easy as it was up at *Tremarfon*.

'Come along now, Megan,' Mrs Evans urged her. 'How are you going to grow into a big strong girl if you don't eat your soup? Look, I've done you chicken, your favourite.'

'M-m-my name isn't Megan, it's Lizzie,' the child stuttered for at least the tenth time that night.

The woman seemed not to have heard her. She prattled on, 'I was thinking, now that they've had to close the school down, I could be teaching you for a while.

We could start after dinner, if you like. After all, if I want my girl to be top of the class, we can't be shirking now, can we?'

Lizzie gazed miserably down at the dish in front of her. Mrs Evans had forgotten to warm it and a layer of grease floated on the surface, making her stomach revolt. Blodwyn seemed to be forgetting a lot of things these last few days. Only yesterday she had sprinkled salt instead of sugar onto her porridge and then forced her to eat it, insisting that it was good for her. Lizzie had somehow managed to do as she was told, but the second she got to school she'd had to run to the little toilet block where she had been violently sick. Another strange thing that Mrs Evans had started to do was talk to someone whom Lizzie couldn't see, which was very unnerving to say the least. But worst of all was the fact that she made Lizzie sleep in her big double bed with her. Lizzie hated it and would balance precariously right on the edge of the big feather mattress as far away from the big smelly woman as she could get.

Seeing the child's hesitation now, a note of irritation crept into Mrs Evans's voice. 'Can you see her, Father? Turning her nose up at good food, indeed. Why, there's many a child would be grateful of such a feast, is there not?'

Lizzie followed her eyes to the chair at the side of the fireplace but there was no one there and she began to get frightened. Why did Mrs Evans keep talking to Mr Evans when they'd recently buried him in the little churchyard in the village? Perhaps he'd come back as a ghost that only Mrs Evans could see? The thought of it made her tremble as the hairs on the back of her neck stood to attention. She wished Danny were there with her, or better still, her mother. She had promised to come and see them in her last letter, so why hadn't she done so?

'*Megan*, stop daydreaming, child, and eat your soup.'

Lifting her spoon, Lizzie valiantly tackled the greasy mess in front of her. Her mother would be bound to come soon – she had to.

When Danny came down to breakfast the next morning, Eric had a surprise waiting for him.

'Look, I got to thinking,' the man told him. 'I don't want you getting bored while the school is closed so I knocked that up for you. I don't profess to be the best carpenter in the world, but I thought it might do you and your mates good to have a bit of fun.'

Danny gasped with delight. Propped up against the back door was a sledge that Eric had made from bits of wood that he had found knocking about. Just as he'd said, it wasn't the best-looking sledge Danny had ever seen, but even so it looked sturdy and the lad could just see himself whizzing down the hillside on it.

'Why, it's wonderful,' he exclaimed with a smile on his face that lit the whole room up. 'Soho Gus will be dead jealous when he sees it. Can I try it out now?'

'Well, it might be a good idea to get some breakfast inside you first,' Eric smiled. 'And then if you wrap up warmly I can't see any reason why you shouldn't take it out for an hour or so. I have to go down into the village to the post office, and while I'm there I'll see if there's any mail for us. There's no way the postman will try to battle his way up the hillside in this weather.'

Danny nodded as he curiously eyed the huge envelope on the dresser. Every single week Eric went down into the village to post one off, but Danny still had no idea at all what was inside them. All he did know was that they were all posted to the same address in London. However, this morning he had far more pressing things on his mind as he thought of all the fun he and Gus were going to have on his new toy, so he attacked the lightly boiled eggs Eric had made for him and then flew up the stairs to get dressed for outdoors.

When he came back, Eric had dragged the sledge outside for him. Proudly, Danny grabbed the string handle and started to haul it through the snow. Once they came to the end of the drive, he eyed the downhill slope doubtfully. It looked very steep.

Seeing his hesitation, Eric chuckled. 'Well, get on then. Even if you fall off you're hardly going to hurt yourself, are you? The snow is so thick it will act like a cushion.'

Clambering aboard, Danny lifted his feet as Eric stood behind him.

'Ready?'

Danny nodded. Eric leaned down to give him a push, and the next minute he was moving, slowly picking up speed as he went. In no time at all he was hurtling down the slope and he whooped with delight. This must be what it feels like to fly, he thought to himself as he gave himself up to the sensation.

The snow had stopped falling for now and everywhere looked breathtakingly beautiful. Even the leafless trees looked pretty, for their barren branches were heavy with snow that sparkled like diamonds in the watery sun.

Seeing *Derwen Deg* ahead of him, Danny decided to call for Soho Gus. The only problem was, he didn't know how to stop the sledge. His problem was solved when it suddenly came up against a large stone that was buried beneath the snow, and he was catapulted forward to land in an undignified heap at the side of the gatepost.

Eric's laughter echoed on the air as Danny emerged

from a snowdrift looking like a snowman. The only thing that was hurt was his pride, however, for just as Eric had promised him, the snow had cushioned his fall.

Danny realised that he had never heard Eric laugh before and a grin split his face as he shook himself off.

'I don't think I've quite got the hang of it yet,' he shouted up at Eric unnecessarily, and the man laughed even louder as Danny shook himself like a dog and snow flew in all directions.

Gus, who had been playing snowballs, popped his head over the hedge as he heard the commotion. When he saw the sledge, he raced through the gate and gazed at it enviously.

'Cor blimey, that's a beauty. Where did yer get that from?'

Danny cocked his head up at Eric, who was walking down the slope towards them. '*He* made it fer me out o' some wood he found lyin' about. Do yer fancy havin' a go on it?'

'Not *'arf.*' Needing no second invitation, Gus handed Albert to Danny and sat astride the broad wooden seat. 'Give us a push then,' he ordered, and Danny was happy to oblige.

Gus almost took off as the sledge hurtled down the hill, and Eric, who had joined them, felt a lump form in his throat. Danny was gazing with such pride at his new toy, as if he had handed him the Crown Jewels. And yet it was just a few bits of wood that Eric had knocked together.

Danny's small hand found its way into his as he watched his friend's antics with glee. 'Thanks, Eric. It's one o' the best presents I've ever had. Me dad never made me nothin' like that.'

'Perhaps he never had time?' Eric suggested generously.

'Huh! More like it would have wasted time he could spend in the pub.' There was such a wealth of sadness in the child's voice that Eric was rendered temporarily speechless. Not wishing to lose the light-hearted atmosphere of only minutes before, however, he said, 'Come on, else the speed your mate is going, he'll be over the clifftop and straight into the sea.'

Smiling again, Danny loosed his hand and they both started down the hill after Gus, lifting their feet high in the deep snow. By the time they reached the village, all three were breathless but in fine spirits. Eric hadn't had so much fun for ages.

'How's about we call round for Lizzie?' Danny suggested to Gus.

The other boy shrugged. 'We could try, but I doubt the old witch will let her out of her sight.'

Danny secretly agreed with him but decided to try all the same, so they dragged the sledge along between them until *Ty-Du* came into sight. At that point Eric left them to go and do some shopping.

'Right, here goes,' Danny said eventually, when he'd plucked up enough courage. 'Nothin' ventured, nothin' gained – an' the worst she can say is no, ain't it?'

Leaving Gus in charge of the sledge, he approached the shiny red cottage door and, lifting the brass knocker, rapped loudly.

After a while he began to think that there was no one in, but then Lizzie's pale face suddenly appeared at the little leaded window and a broad smile spread across her face when she saw who it was. Danny turned his attention to the door as he heard the bolts being drawn and the next instant he was looking into Mrs Evans's distracted face.

'Good morning,' he said politely. 'I was wondering if

Lizzie could come out and play with us for a while. Eric has made me a sledge and—'

'*Absolutely not!*' Mrs Evans cut him short mid-flow. 'Do you really think I want to risk her catching cold? Why, it's enough to cut you in two out there.'

Lizzie suddenly appeared at her side and gazed up at her. 'I could wrap up really warm,' she pleaded.

As Mrs Evans glanced at the girl's expectant face she seemed to hesitate for a second, but then her face hardened again. 'I said no for your own sake. No one should be out in this weather unless it's absolutely unavoidable, so get yourself home, Danny. I can't think what Mr Sinclair was thinking of, to let you out in this in the first place.'

Lizzie's face fell as Danny opened his mouth to try once more, but before he had a chance the door was closed in his face.

'What did I tell yer?' Gus muttered scathingly. 'I reckon that woman's gone a bit barmy. It's Lizzie I feel sorry for though. She's got a lot to put up wiv, havin' to live there.'

Suddenly the day didn't seem quite so bright as Danny thought of his twin's dejected face. 'Shall we head back home?' he said to Gus.

'Might as well. There ain't no point hangin' around the village if Lizzie can't come out wiv us. I ought to be gettin' back anyway. I promised I'd 'elp round up the sheep this afternoon.'

Dragging the sledge about, they began to haul it back the way they had come.

'Never mind, mate,' Gus said eventually, hoping to raise his friend's spirits. 'We'll be back at school as soon as the wevver improves a bit then you'll get to see your Lizzie again.'

Danny nodded, but an uneasy feeling was growing inside him. Lizzie had looked so unhappy and . . . he struggled to think of the word he was looking for . . . *desperate* – that was it. He determined to talk to Eric about his concerns again the second he got home. Not that he really thought there was much the man could do to help after the last visit to the cottage, when Mrs Evans had almost bitten his head off.

'Why don't yer write to yer mum if yer that worried about Lizzie?' Gus suggested, as if he could read Danny's mind.

Danny tossed the idea over in his mind before slowly nodding. 'I reckon I might just do that,' he replied. Up until now he hadn't wanted to worry Maggie, but now he had the distinct feeling that he should. With a new purpose he quickened his pace as Gus struggled through the snow behind him.

Chapter Thirty-One

'Now, are yer *quite* sure that there's nothin' we've forgotten?' Beryl fussed as she plumped the pillows on the settee for the countless time.

Her eyes kept straying to the window as Maggie and Jo exchanged an amused glance. If truth were to be told, Maggie was feeling almost as nervous as her mother-in-law, for David was coming home today. But she couldn't tell her that, of course.

The kitchen was sparkling and the appetising smell of a beef stew and dumplings, which just happened to be one of his favourite meals, was floating around the room. A huge fire was roaring in the grate and Beryl was almost beside herself with excitement, mingled with apprehension, for as yet they were unaware of his injuries.

At one point she had almost carried his bed downstairs, but Maggie had managed to talk her out of it. As she'd pointed out, David would want things to be as normal as possible, and if the need for the bed to come down arose they could always do it once he had arrived.

Beryl glanced at the clock again as she had every two minutes since 6 a.m. She'd intended to start her cleaning last night, but yet another raid had prevented it and they'd all spent the night cowering under the stairs, for there was no room in the garden for an Anderson shelter.

Thankfully, the raid had lasted nowhere near as long as the one that had changed Maggie's life, though of course it had left yet more death and devastation in its wake. Maggie was restless, for as soon as David was home she knew that she could then go to see the twins. It would not be an easy visit, with the sad news she would have to tell them, but even so the need was on her now to hold them in her arms again, even more so since she had lost Lucy.

Dinnertime came and went, and Beryl lifted the stew from the cooker, fearful of it being spoiled. But then at last an ambulance pulled up outside and Beryl shot from her seat, almost tripping in her haste to yank the front door open.

All along the street, net curtains were twitching but she was oblivious as she kept her eyes trained on the back doors of the ambulance. The driver climbed down and opened them, then carefully pulled down the steps while Beryl prayed as she had never prayed before.

And then there he was, and a little sob caught in her throat, for her son looked nothing at all like the healthy young man she had waved away a few months back. He seemed to have shrunk to half his size, and his clothes hung off him. His eyes were sunk deep into sockets that were surrounded with deep shadows. A coat was slung loosely around his shoulders, but he did manage to walk down the steps unaided and she clung to him as she openly sobbed with relief. It was as she was hugging him that she became aware that one of his sleeves was partially empty, and her eyes stretched with horror.

'Can we just get in, Mam?' he asked impatiently, deeply aware of the neighbours who were trickling out onto their doorsteps.

'Oh, son, I'm so sorry. Of course we can. It's just that

I'm so pleased to see you.' She nodded her thanks at the ambulancemen who were busily closing the doors, then hurried him inside to where Maggie was standing waiting to greet him.

'Hello, David,' she said softly. There was so much she wanted to say, but nothing she could think of sounded right.

'Come on. Let's have that coat off you an' get you over by the fire,' Beryl gushed. As she slipped it from his shoulders and saw the empty sleeve tucked up just below his elbow she felt her heart would break, but she kept her voice light. 'I've done you yer favourite stew an' dumplins, and don't say no to it 'cos you look like yer need feedin' up, me lad. A few weeks o' good home cookin' an' we'll have you fit as a fiddle again,' she declared.

Deciding to get it over with, David raised his arm, or what was left of it. 'I hardly think I'll ever be that again, Mam, not with this.'

She shook her head in denial. 'It could have been a lot worse,' she told him. 'It could have been both yer legs, like poor Bill Stretton over in Beagle Street. At least you can still get about, an' once you get used to it, you'll be surprised what you can do wi' one arm.'

Glancing at Jo self-consciously, he allowed his mother to ease him into the chair, and stepping forward, Maggie introduced them. 'David, this is my friend, Jo. She was staying with me before . . .' Glancing at Beryl helplessly she wondered if she should tell him of the tragic events that had led to Jo and herself staying with Beryl. But then she decided that as he was sure to find out anyway, she might as well get her bad news over with.

As Beryl fussed with the dinner, Maggie hesitantly began, 'The thing is, a lot has happened since the last time we saw you. The twins were evacuated to Wales, and a couple of weeks ago . . .'

Jo squeezed her arm reassuringly, and somehow she managed to go on. Slowly she told him of the night of the Blitz and, as he listened intently, his face crumpled and tears began to trickle down his cheeks.

'You're telling me that Lucy is *dead*?' he said hoarsely. An unspoken message that neither Beryl nor Jo could understand seemed to pass between them, and a silence settled on the room as he tried to digest the tragic news.

'Sam is dead too,' she finished lamely, but even as she said it a shutter seemed to come down over his eyes, though he said not a word.

'Oh.' David gazed back at her pain-filled eyes and in that moment he knew that he would have to take the secret of what had happened between Sam and himself to his grave.

Turning his head, he stared into the back of the fire as pictures of Lucy flashed in front of his eyes. Through the long, long hours spent on the battlefield he had imagined coming home to her; had imagined her squealing with delight when she delved into his pocket, or when he tossed her high into the air. Now he would never see her again, never hold her or smell the sweet baby scent of her.

'I'm so sorry, Maggie.' The words sounded so inadequate but he knew that there was nothing he could say that would ease her loss. Ever since the dreadful day when he had woken in the hospital tent to discover that they had amputated his arm, he had been racked with pain, but it was as nothing to the pain he was feeling now.

'That's enough o' that fer now then,' Beryl stated firmly. 'This is a day fer rejoicin', not sorrow. There have been times when I thought we'd never see you again – but here you are so we should give thanks fer that, if nothing else. Now, Maggie an' Jo, you get the table laid. You'll all have a dish o' this stew if I have to tip it down yer throats. That beef cost me two weeks o' coupons so I don't want it going to waste.'

The meal was nothing at all like the joyful occasion Beryl had imagined it to be, but then, as she was slowly realising, David was nothing like the man he had been when he left to go to war. And it was nothing at all to do with his missing limb. There was a stoop to his shoulders now and lines on his face that hadn't been there before – a look of unspeakable sorrow in his eyes, as if he had seen things that no human being should ever see.

But then, she tried to console herself, should she really expect anything else? The war had changed all of them, but it was even worse for the men like David who had seen it first-hand. Could she *really* expect him to come back and go on as if nothing had ever happened, after the atrocities he must have witnessed?

She determined to go gently with him. It was going to be a long slow job to restore him to the man he had once been, but she would do it; she *had* to, for he was all she had left now.

That night, Maggie tossed and turned as sleep evaded her. Jo had been softly snoring for hours in the single brass bed only feet away from hers. She was aware that, just across the landing, David was spending his first night for months on a soft mattress, and hoped that he was sleeping peacefully. After pummelling the pillow she tried another position, as she willed herself to sleep, but it was useless so eventually she crept out of bed and down to the kitchen. Perhaps a nice hot drink would help her to sleep?

Crossing to the sink, she filled the kettle, lit the gas ring and set it on the stove to boil. As she turned to get the teapot she became aware of someone sitting in the shadows at the side of the fire, and her heart leapt into her throat.

'Couldn't you sleep either, Maggie?'

Recognising David's voice, she sighed with relief before answering, 'No. I thought a cup of tea might help. Would you like one?'

He nodded and watched silently as she pottered about getting the mugs ready and spooning the tea leaves into the pot.

Once it was poured she placed his mug in his good hand and took a seat opposite. He stared at her in the flickering firelight, thinking how beautiful she looked before saying, 'We need to talk, don't we?'

'Yes,' she whispered. This was the moment she had been dreading, but now that it had come it would be almost a relief to get it over with.

'I think you know what I'm going to ask you, don't you?'

She nodded, as tears pricked at her eyes.

'Maggie, I can ask it now that Sam is dead. I have nothing to gain by knowing the answer but I'd still appreciate the truth . . . *Was Lucy my child?*'

Gazing down into her mug, Maggie's mind flashed back across the years to the one and only time in her married life when she and David had allowed their feelings for each other to get the better of them. She'd had a particularly awful row with Sam that night before he had slammed off out to the pub, and so it had seemed natural to pour her feelings out to David when he visited later that evening.

The twins had been in bed and she was sitting there

feeling more than a little sorry for herself when David had appeared. He had listened to her and sympathised, and for the first time since Sam had tricked her into sleeping with him, she'd felt warm inside and loved. She had always loved David, and Sam had always known it, but until that night she had never been unfaithful to her husband and had always tried to be a good wife. That night, however, she and David had both succumbed to their desire, and there, in front of the fire, he had loved her with a tenderness that she had never known with Sam. After it was over they had both been full of remorse and swore to each other that it would never happen again. It never had, but the following month, when Maggie discovered that she was pregnant, she knew that she would always have a part of David in the child he could never claim as his own.

Now, as she looked across at him with pain bright in her eyes, he had his answer, and he buried his face in his hand and wept – for hadn't he always known deep down that Lucy was the product of their love? The little girl had lived and died never knowing how much he had loved her, and now she never would. The realisation was tearing him apart as Maggie put her arms around him and held him close.

'I'm so sorry, David,' she whispered brokenly into his ear as his body shook with sobs, but he couldn't answer. Once again, life had dealt him a bitter blow.

The very next morning, a letter from Danny, poked though the letter box by Mr Massey on his way to work, plopped onto the doormat and Maggie swooped on it with a cry of delight. However, her joy was shortlived as her eyes scanned the page, and her brow creased in a frown.

'What's up now?' Beryl asked fearfully as she cut up David's sausages for him.

'Danny says that Lizzie isn't very happy,' Maggie informed her. 'Mr Evans, who she was staying with, has passed away and Danny reckons that ever since then, Mrs Evans has gone a bit funny in the head.'

'What do yer mean, *funny*?'

Maggie's shoulders trembled. 'He says that the woman won't let her out of her sight an' that she keeps calling her Megan.'

'An' just who the hell is Megan?' Beryl asked, bewildered.

'According to Danny, it was her little girl who died.' Real concern laced Maggie's voice now as a shiver ran up her spine. 'He says she's cut Lizzie's hair and makes her sleep in the same bed with her.'

'I don't like the sound o' that,' Jo piped up as she buttered some toast for David.

'Neither do I.' Maggie chewed on her lip as she reread the letter. It sounded no better at all for a second reading. 'What do you think I should do?'

'Well, from where I'm standing it don't sound too healthy,' Beryl stated. 'Now I come to think about it, a few things don't seem quite right. For a start-off, this might explain why Lizzie never got any of your letters. Perhaps this Mrs Evans never passed them on to her? Danny got his, didn't he, and if it were the post, his would have gone astray too, surely?'

A cold hand squeezed Maggie's heart as she considered the possibility. It was David who finally said, 'Do you think you should go and see her?'

'O' course she should. The poor little mites don't know about what's happened here yet. As far as they know, they still have a dad, a sister an' a gran waitin' at home fer 'em, plus they've no idea that that home has been flattened, an' all. I know you've been puttin' off tellin' 'em fer all the right reasons, Maggie, but surely now you *need* to go – if only to put yer mind at rest. The way children get things muddled up, you'll probably find Lizzie happy as Larry, but will yer be able to rest now until yer know fer sure?'

Maggie had been dreading having to tell the twins of all that had happened at home, but now she couldn't put it off any longer.

'I can let you have the train fare,' David offered, although he hated the thought of her leaving so soon after his return.

She smiled at him gratefully. 'That's really kind of you, but I've managed to save a little. Your mam has been letting me use her sewing-machine and so I've been able to get a bit of work done. But how will you all manage here if I go?'

'No trouble,' Jo assured her. 'I can help Beryl and David with anythin' that needs doin'. That is, if yer don't need me to come with yer?'

'No, you stay here,' Maggie told her. 'It might be better if I'm on my own to break the news to the twins. Besides, I'll feel easier knowing that you're here to help out till I get back. Now that you're only working part-time you should manage between you.'

Since the night of the Blitz, Jo had reduced her hours to afternoons only, for the constant sickness was beginning to wear her down. Also, her stomach was finally beginning to swell. Only the day before, she'd noticed Miss Hutchinson watching her curiously as she dressed the shop window. So far, she had managed to disguise the bump by wearing slightly larger skirts that Maggie had run up for her on the sewing-machine, but she wasn't sure how much longer she would be able to hide her pregnancy.

As Maggie was speaking, she noticed the way David's eyes were straying to the small lump that was just beginning to show on Jo's stomach. Jo noticed at almost the same time and Maggie saw colour rush into her cheeks.

Feeling that she needed to explain, she said casually, 'Did I mention that Jo was going to have a baby, David?'

The colour in Jo's cheeks turned from a faint pink to beetroot red as Maggie went on, 'Jo's husband was killed in service, which was why she ended up staying with me.' She hated having to lie to him, yet desperately wanted to save Jo's feelings.

However, she needn't have bothered, for Jo suddenly blurted out, 'You don't have to lie for me, Maggie.'

Shamefaced, Maggie hung her head as David stared at them both in bewilderment.

Holding her head high, Jo looked him straight in the face. 'I never had a husband, or a friend for that matter – till Maggie took me under her wing, that is. I was a . . . a prostitute. I ain't proud of the fact an' I know you'll probably despise me now that you know. But the way I see it, your mam was good enough to take me in, an' there shouldn't be lies between us.'

Both Maggie and Beryl stared at her in open-mouthed admiration, realising just how much courage it must have taken to come out with the truth. David meanwhile looked totally amazed as he stared back at her.

'I ain't askin' fer sympathy if that's what yer thinking,' Jo told him coldly. 'I've done the crime an' now I have to take the punishment. I'm fully aware that no decent man will ever touch me with a bargepole, but I don't care. I've got hands, an' once the baby comes, I'll work to keep us both. If I decide to keep it, that is, an' I ain't made me mind up about that yet. All I *am* sure of at the minute is that it ain't the baby's fault. He or she didn't ask to be born so I'll do what I think is best for it.'

'Well, I have to admire you for that at least,' David eventually told her, but Jo thought she detected a note of contempt in his voice. She didn't really much care what he thought of her at the end of the day. Her loyalties lay with Maggie, and there was nothing she wouldn't have done for her, which is why she couldn't allow her to lie on her behalf.

Maggie felt a measure of relief now that everything was out in the open and looked at David appealingly. 'Please don't judge her too harshly,' she said. 'There were extenuating circumstances that made her do what she did. It wasn't from choice, I assure you.'

Pushing himself from the chair with his one good arm, David shrugged. 'It's really nothing to do with me, is it? But thanks for being so truthful, Jo. I don't suppose it was easy for you.'

Eager to change the subject, Beryl piped up, 'Right, now that's all out in the open, can we get back to what's important? When were yer thinkin' o' goin' to see those children o' yours, Maggie?'

David bowed his head as he thought back to the conversation he'd had with Maggie in the small hours of the morning. He had been a father, yet had never known it for sure, until it was too late. The twins were still alive though, so it was important that Maggie saw them as soon as possible.

'I think you ought to go tomorrow, for what my opinion's worth,' he stated as he headed for the stairs door. 'And now if you'll all excuse me, I'm going up for a lie-down.'

The second he'd disappeared up the stairs, Beryl shook

her head wearily. 'I don't know. I've got me lad back, an' yet he ain't me lad, if yer know what I mean? He just seems so . . . bitter.'

Maggie nodded sadly. 'The war has changed us all, Beryl. No doubt he's seen things that no one should ever see. But give him time. He'll come through it in the end. I do think he was right, though – about going to see the twins as soon as possible, I mean. I'll go to the station this afternoon and book a ticket for next Monday.'

'Good for you,' Beryl told her approvingly. 'But why wait until Monday? What's wrong wi' tomorrow, as David suggested? There ain't no time like the present. At the minute, none of us knows what tomorrow might bring.'

Although the thought of just disappearing off was appealing, Maggie shook her head. 'No, I'm going to write to them today to tell them when to expect me. I can post it on the way to the station. It doesn't seem fair on the people who are caring for them to just turn up out of the blue, does it? At least this way they'll know exactly when I'm coming. To be honest, I'm hoping someone will offer to put me up for the night. That way, I needn't come straight back the same day and I'll get to spend a bit more time with them. I can't really afford to stay in a hotel.'

'Well, there is that to it,' Beryl admitted grudgingly. 'You'll find some paper and a pen in that drawer over there.'

Maggie smiled at her gratefully and was soon sitting at the table busily penning a letter to the twins telling them when they could expect her.

Upstairs, David lay on his bed with tears trickling down his face to soak into the pillow. Nothing seemed the same any more, not even Maggie. She had changed, but then it was hardly any wonder, with all she'd gone through since he had been away. He wondered how she would feel if she knew that Sam had caused him to lose his arm. He shuddered at the thought; he hadn't accepted it himself, yet. *Sam.* The pain in his heart increased. How could his own brother have hated him so very much? He knew that he would have to bear the burden of what had happened between them on the battlefield on his own shoulders, for he could never tell Maggie: it would destroy her if ever she found out. His thoughts moved on to Lucy as he recalled her sweet, smiling little face. Through all the long lonely months that he had been away, the thought of coming home to her and Maggie had kept him going. Had kept him sane. He'd imagined the little girl's face lighting up with innocent glee the way it had always done when she saw him. And Maggie, standing there with that special smile that she had always seemed to reserve just for him.

Instead he had come back to discover that he'd lost the only child he was ever likely to have, and to find Maggie a shadow of the vibrant young woman he remembered. But then, was it really any wonder? he asked himself. After all that had happened, he could hardly expect her to put the flags out for him. He wondered if they would ever have that special feeling between them again, for even after she had married Sam he had always known when he looked in her eye that she still loved him alone. Perhaps Sam had seen the look too? If he had, then David could understand why he had hated him so much. After all, Sam must have realised very early on in their marriage that although he had claimed Maggie as his wife he had not claimed her heart, nor ever could. It was ludicrous when he came to think about it. They were finally both free to do as they pleased now, and yet they had both changed.

'Give me the strength to go on,' he prayed, and lay there waiting for an answer. The only thing he heard was his mother singing along to Vera Lynn on the radio downstairs.

Later in the afternoon, Maggie wrapped up warmly and headed for the train station with a letter to the twins tucked deep in her pocket. She posted it in the first letter box that she came to, and then hurried on towards the station, where she purchased a one-way ticket to Pwllheli for the following Monday. She had barely ventured out of the house since moving in with Beryl, and was shocked to see that the city centre had been almost razed to the ground. The saddest sight of all was the once-beautiful Cathedral in ruins, all apart from its spire, which reached proudly up into the sky as if in defiance. The tram system was wrecked – the lines ripped from the ground or arched into the air in grotesque mangled shapes. Shops were flattened, including Maggie's favourite store, Owen and Owen. A major sewage system had been destroyed, and the smell hung in the air, making her wrinkle her nose. Thousands of people were homeless, and yet the mood of the rescuers and troops who were still digging amongst the rubble was one of camaraderie.

Only the day before, when Mr Massey had paid them a visit at Beryl's, he told them that, although twenty-seven factories had been hit, and 75 per cent of the city's war output had been seriously damaged, production had already restarted. Maggie found it incredible. It was as if the people of Coventry were saying, 'We're down, but not defeated.' She wished with all her heart that some of their fighting spirit could rub off on her, but as yet the pain of losing Lucy and her mother was still too raw.

However, the train ticket tucked deep in the pocket of her coat did make her feel slightly better as she began the homeward journey. In just a few short days she would see her children, hold them in her arms again. Right now, the thought of Lizzie and Danny was all that was keeping her going and she could hardly wait.

Chapter Thirty-Two

Eric arrived home only minutes after Danny to find him slumped in the chair, absently fondling Samson's ears.

'What's wrong with you then?' he enquired as he stamped the snow from his boots. 'You've got a face as long as a fiddle. Was the sledge no good?'

'Oh yes,' Danny hastened to assure him. 'The sledge is great. It's just . . .'

'Just what?'

Danny hung his head as Eric frowned. The boy had seemed so happy when he'd left him with Gus down in the village. What could have happened to make him so down? It suddenly occurred to him – Lizzie. Danny had been about to call for her when they parted. He didn't mind betting Mrs Evans had stopped him from seeing her again, hence the glum face.

'Look, how about we have something to eat and then do some work on that landscape you're doing?' he suggested.

Danny instantly looked perkier as he glanced towards his small easel where his latest picture was proudly displayed. It was a lovely winter scene of the forest that could be seen from the kitchen window, and was easily his best effort yet, as Eric had told him. Danny was hoping to get it finished for when his mother eventually came to visit so that he could give it to her as a gift.

Hopping off the chair, he grinned. 'All right then. I'll set the table, shall I?'

Eric nodded and set about preparing them some Spam fritters and mash. With HP Sauce, it went down a treat. They had a bit of swiss roll and evaporated milk for afters. As Eric put the kettle on for a cup of tea, it began to snow again.

'Oh dear. If this keeps up we're going to be completely snowed in soon,' he said.

'We could always dig ourselves out,' Danny suggested.

Eric laughed. 'What – all the way down to the bottom of the hill? I don't think we'd make it, somehow. Not to worry, I've got plenty of food in if the worst comes to the worst. It can't snow forever, can it?'

As Danny watched him, it occurred to him how much nicer Eric was than his own father. He thought of Sam and shivered; he'd always been afraid of him and the house in Clay Lane was a much happier place when he was out of it. For a second, the young boy wondered what it would have been like, if Eric had been his father . . .

Then he found himself wondering what it would be like to live here in summertime, with the trees green and all the open spaces to romp in. When he had first arrived, he'd found the vast hillside a little isolated and remote, yet now he had become used to the sound of the night creatures, and as for the branches that tapped at his window in the night wind – he now found them strangely soothing, rather than scary.

By the time they'd finished working on Danny's painting, darkness was falling. They'd been so immersed in what they were doing that the fire had burned low.

'Look, you get your palette and brushes cleaned while I go and fill the log box, eh?' Eric suggested as he rose stiffly from his seat. 'I might let Samson stretch his legs as well, while I'm at it. I shouldn't be more than half an hour or so. Will you be all right?'

'Course I will,' Danny said, standing back to admire his painting. It was almost finished now and he could just imagine the look on his mam's face when he gave it to her.

Eric shrugged on a thick overcoat and boots, then lifting the empty log box from the hearth he called Samson to heel and headed for the back door. An icy blast whipped into the room when he opened it and Danny shuddered.

I'm glad I ain't a tramp as has to sleep out in this, he thought to himself as he cleaned his brushes and carefully packed them away. He looked around the room. It wasn't what anyone would have classed as tidy in here. There were some very nice pieces of furniture stood against the walls, but they were dull from lack of polish and not positioned to show them off to their best advantage. A sudden thought occurred to the boy. Why not have a good tidy-up while Eric was gone? There'd be no harm in keeping in his good books.

He rushed around collecting up all the dirty cups and plates that were strewn about the room and washed them up, then he began to tidy the sofa. It was while he was doing this that he found a newspaper stuffed down behind one of the cushions. He was about to fling it on the fire when a headline caught his eye and he paused mid-step: *COVENTRY BLITZED*. Sinking onto the nearest chair, he checked the date: 14 November 1940. Feverishly, he began to read, and as his eyes flew across the lines, a feeling of panic gripped him. According to the paper, Coventry had suffered a massive raid that had smashed the Cathedral to the ground. Worse still though was the fact that it told of numerous factories, shops, restaurants, cafés and whole streets of houses being flattened too.

What if his mam's house had been amongst them? What if anything had happened to his mam or Lucy? And why hadn't Eric told him about it, instead of hiding the paper behind a cushion? Even as the thoughts were racing around in his head, the door opened and Eric appeared. He was laughing at Samson, who was covered in snow, and turned to remark on him to Danny, but one look at the lad's face made the words lodge in his throat. His eyes fell to the newspaper in his hand and he silently cursed himself for forgetting to get rid of it as colour flamed in his cheeks.

'Why didn't you tell me about what had happened back at home?' Danny asked accusingly.

Eric took a faltering step towards him. 'I wanted to,' he told him, 'but I didn't know what to do for the best. I . . . I didn't want you to worry.'

'But somethin' might have happened to me mam or Lucy.' Danny's voice was strangled with terror. 'I have to know that they're both all right.'

'Of course you do.' Eric sought about in his mind for a solution to the problem before finally suggesting, 'What about if we write to her tonight? I could walk down to the village and post it first thing in the morning then. You could come with me, if you like.'

'That's no good,' Danny shot at him. His head wagged from side-to-side, setting his fair curls, which Eric now noticed were in desperate need of a cut, dancing around his ears. 'It will take days to get there, an' then days for a reply to come back – *if* she's all right, that is. I need to know she's all right, *now*!'

To Eric's horror, tears suddenly flooded into the child's eyes and raced down his cheeks unchecked. Without stopping to think, he covered the distance between them and wrapped him in his arms.

'Oh, Danny. I'm so *very* sorry. I just didn't know what to do for the best. I'm sure that if anything *had* happened to your family, we would have heard by now.'

Danny angrily pushed him away. Crossing his arms, he turned his back on Eric as a scowl settled across his face. Somehow, he *had* to know!

The atmosphere in the kitchen was strained for the rest of the evening. Danny refused his meal and Eric was almost relieved when the boy finally declared he was going to bed, for he had no idea how he could help him.

Once upstairs, Danny stood by his bedroom window and gazed across the snow-covered trees to the sea in the distance. A silver moon was riding high in the sky and the ocean looked for all the world as if it had been sprinkled with fairy dust. It held no charm whatsoever for Danny tonight, however, for his mind was back in Coventry with his family.

It was as he was standing there that an idea occurred to him. Once Eric had retired to his room he would go and see Soho Gus. *He'd* know what to do. Hastily crossing to his bed, Danny slipped beneath the cold white sheets fully dressed, and then he waited.

At last he heard Eric's tread on the stairs. The man paused outside his room, and Danny screwed his eyes up tight, pretending to be asleep, but tonight he didn't come in. Eventually, Danny heard him move on along the landing, followed by the sound of his bedroom door opening and closing. Breathing a sigh of relief, Danny sneaked out of bed and once more crossed to the moonlit window. It looked very beautiful and also very cold out there, so he pulled another pair of socks across the pair he already had on and took his biggest, warmest jumper out of his drawer and donned that too. Creeping to the door, he inched it open and listened. When he was satisfied that all was quiet, he crept along the landing and silently descended the stairs. Once inside the kitchen he stroked Samson and yanked on his Wellington boots before struggling into his warm coat and wrapping his scarf around his neck. Then at the door he paused to look back. He suddenly felt very guilty for running off like this, but what choice did he have?

The sound of the bolt as he drew it back seemed to echo around the room and his heart raced as he listened for any sounds from above. Thankfully all was quiet so he stepped out into the bitterly cold night, drawing the door to behind him. It closed with a loud click. The freezing air seemed to slap him in the face and his breath floated in great lacy plumes in front of him as he stole around to the front of the house. He looked back just once when he reached the lane that led downhill and was filled with sadness as he saw the light in Eric's bedroom window shining out into the darkness. He had already made his decision. Somehow, he was going to make his way back to Coventry. Gus could come and tell Eric where he had gone in the morning. At least that way, Eric would know where he was.

Pausing, he suddenly realised that he should have brought some money with him. Would the measly amount he had saved be enough for his train fare home? He doubted it, and anyway, to go back now might be pushing his luck and might lead to him being caught out. Shrugging his shoulders he moved tentatively on, glad of the moon that momentarily lit the way when it sailed from behind the clouds. More than once he missed his footing and went headlong into the frozen snow, but he was a determined child, and now that he'd made his mind up, there was no going back.

By the time he reached *Derwen Deg*, Danny was breathless and frozen through, but his determination never wavered for a second, nor would it now until he knew that his mam and his baby sister were safe.

The farmhouse was in darkness as Danny crept around to the back of it, praying that the dogs wouldn't bark. Luckily, they knew him now and came from their kennels to lick his hand as he stroked them. Gazing up at the dark windows, Danny tried to remember which one was Gus's.

'I'm forever crackin' me bloomin' 'ead on the beam in my room,' he recalled Gus saying, which meant he was probably in the end one. 'An' the soddin' pigs keep me awake half the night wiv their snufflin'.'

The end one overlooked the pigsties. Danny moved across the yard like a ghost, his eyes sweeping this way and that until at last he was beneath the window that he hoped was Gus's. Now another problem faced him: how was he going to alert Gus without waking the whole house?

Bending, he scooped some snow up and, after forming it into a neat snowball, he tossed it up at the window. It hit the glass but slithered down it almost soundlessly. That was no good. Looking around, he saw a large, long handled pitchfork leaning against the barn wall. He discovered that, if he stood on tiptoe, he could just about reach up and tap the glass with it. His first attempt went pathetically wrong; he overbalanced and landed in an undignified heap in the farmyard. Struggling back to his feet he brushed the worst of the snow from his clothes before trying again, and this time he succeeded in tapping on the window.

Within seconds a light clicked on in the room beyond, and the next moment, Gus's sleepy face appeared through a crack in the curtains. When he made out Danny standing in the yard, his mouth gaped open in amazement.

Lifting the sash-cord window as quietly as he could, he leaned out and hissed, 'What the bleedin' 'ell are you doin' 'ere at this time o' night?'

'Come on down – I need to talk to you,' Danny whispered urgently. The window closed and Gus disappeared as Danny stood there shivering with his arms wrapped around himself.

Moments later, Gus appeared around the side of the farmhouse and taking Danny's elbow he led him into the barn, where the cattle were sleeping. 'Right then, spit it out. It must be somefing bad fer yer to be up an' about at this unearfly 'our, mate.'

'It is.' Danny solemnly told him of the newspaper report as Gus listened attentively. When he'd done, the other boy let out a low whistle.

'So, what yer intendin' to do about it then?' he asked.

'I'm goin' back to Coventry to check that me mam an' Lucy are all right.'

'Oh yes? An' how are yer plannin' to get there at this time o' night?' Gus scoffed.

'I thought I might sneak onto one o' the goods trains that leave Pwllheli durin' the night.'

Gus was shocked when he saw that Danny meant every word he said and was filled with a grudging admiration. It took guts to embark on a journey like that.

'The reason I've come here is 'cos I need you to do me a favour,' Danny explained. 'In the mornin', I want yer to go an' see Eric an' tell him where I've gone, so he won't be worried. By then it will be too late fer him to stop me anyway.'

Gus eyed him silently for a moment before suddenly telling him, 'Sorry, mate, I can't do that.'

'Why not? I thought yer were me friend!' Danny exclaimed.

'I am, which is why I'm comin' wiv yer. Yer don't fink I'd let yer go off all on yer tod, do yer? But you'll 'ave to 'ang about while I go an' get properly dressed an' fetch Albert. While I'm upstairs I'll scribble the missus a note, an' no doubt she'll let Eric know where we've gone.'

'Are you sure you want to do that?' Danny asked uncertainly, and a big grin split Gus's face.

'You bet. Now wait 'ere while I go an' get ready, will yer? It'll be mornin' before we get goin' if we stand 'ere gabbin' fer much longer.'

A smile spread across Danny's face as he watched Gus disappear through the barn door, and for the first time in his young life he understood the meaning of a true friend.

As promised, Gus appeared minutes later with Albert peeping out of the pocket of his coat.

'I've brought us some grub in case we get 'ungry on the way,' he informed Danny, and Danny saw that Gus's other pocket was bulging with apples and any other food that he had found lying about.

Side-by-side, the two boys crossed the yard and were soon on the lane that led to the village. The snow started to fall again in great white flakes that covered their footsteps, and Gus cursed. 'Bleedin' 'ell. We'll be frozen stiff before we even get to the station at this rate – that's if we make it to the station. Yer do know that some o' the roads are impassable, don't yer?'

'Only to cars,' Danny replied defiantly. 'We'll be able to find our way through the drifts if we're on foot.'

'Huh! Let's 'ope yer right,' Gus mumbled as he thought of the cosy bed he'd just left, back at the farmhouse.

Thankfully, they could just about see where they were going, for the snow was so bright that the lane stretched out before them like a silver ribbon as it snaked its way down the hillside. Even so, it was heavy going, and by the time they'd reached the bottom of the hill they were both panting. Their breath floated in front of them, like steam from a kettle and the sheer effort of having to keep lifting their feet high was exhausting.

Afraid of being seen, they kept to the shadows of the buildings as they made their way through the village. The streets were deserted, although the odd light still shone from certain windows, which told them that some people had not yet retired to bed.

'I ought to tell Sparky where we're headin',' Gus whispered as they approached the house where he was staying.

Danny shook his head. 'Best not to. If the grown-ups get wind o' where we're goin' an' we've told Sparky, he might get into trouble.'

'I s'pose yer right.'

Glad of the carpet of snow that masked their footsteps, they moved on, and soon they were adjacent to the blacksmith's cottage.

Gus saw Danny pause to stare at the windows of *Ty-Du* as they passed. Reaching out, he squeezed his friend's hand. 'Yer can't tell Lizzie either,' he told him regretfully. 'She'd be bound to want to come wiv us, an' that would only complicate fings.'

Danny nodded. Gus was right. It would be far better for Lizzie to stay where she was for now. Just until he was sure that their mam was safe at least.

When the lights of the village were left behind and he found himself in unfamiliar territory, he was suddenly very glad that Gus had offered to come with him, for he wondered now if he would ever have found his way alone.

Gus stopped to catch his breath and get his bearings. 'It'd be much quicker if we were to cut across the fields,' he remarked. 'Trouble is, there's all those disused mine-shafts that way. They're bad enough in the day so I'm not sure it would be safe to go that way at night.'

'Let's stick to the road,' Danny told him, trying desperately hard to keep the tremor of fear from his voice. 'There's no chance of anyone comin' along an' findin' us, so even if it takes us a bit longer, it don't really matter, does it?'

Heads bent, they battled on, and after a time Danny began to wonder if this had been such a good idea after all. They seemed to be in the middle of nowhere, with nothing either in front or behind them. The snow was coming down so fast that they could barely see more than a yard at a time in front of them, and without thinking he reached out and linked his arm through Gus's.

'Are you quite sure we're goin' the right way?' he said as they reached the top of a hill.

'Yep. If you look down there yer can just see the lights o' the town – look. But are you quite sure there'll be a goods train passin' through?'

'Oh yes,' Danny replied confidently. 'I remember Eric tellin' me one day that there were more goods trains than passenger trains passin' through the station since the beginnin' of the war.'

Danny's eyes became slits as he peered through the snow, and sure enough, there below him were the faint lights of Pwllheli. The sight seemed to spur them on as slipping and sliding, the boys began to descend the steep hill. The drifts were deeper here, and soon their Wellington boots were full of snow and their feet felt as if they didn't belong to them.

'Are yer *quite* sure this is what yer want to do?' Gus asked, and for the first time, Danny heard a note of uncertainty in his voice.

He nodded vigorously as he thought of his mam, and a little feeling of excitement fluttered to life in his stomach. If he arrived in Coventry to find her safe and well, which he prayed he would, then he would soon be in her arms again, smelling that wonderful smell that belonged to her and her alone. He realised in that moment just how very much he had missed her, and the thought made him renew his efforts. So much so, that Gus had to struggle to keep up with him.

At last they reached the cobbled streets of the town and began to tramp towards the railway station. They were almost there when Gus pulled Danny to a halt.

'Slow up, matey. We don't want to be seen hangin' around here, do we? We need to go furver on an' see what trains are comin' through. Look, we could sneak in through that fence there. That way we won't 'ave to go onto the platform.'

Seeing the sense in what his friend said, Danny followed him past the main entrance to a fence that had some of its panels broken. After squeezing through they found themselves amongst an assortment of engines and stationary carriages, from which hung sooty black icicles. Any train that entered the station would have to pass by them and Gus smiled with satisfaction as he crouched in the darkness. To the right of them, the dim lights on the platform chased the shadows away, revealing a couple of figures sitting huddled on a bench, suitcases at their feet.

'So what do we do now?' Danny whispered, his teeth chattering with cold and excitement.

'We wait. It can't be that long till a train comes, an' then we'll hop into one o' the goods vans at the back end of it,' Gus whispered back. At the sound of his master's voice, Albert popped his head out of Gus's pocket and looked about, then with a twitch of his whiskers he shuddered and burrowed back down.

Nodding, Danny nestled into his friend's side and settled down on the frozen track to wait.

The first two trains that went past whistled through the station without even slowing, sending flurries of snow all over them. By now, Danny was sure that he had never been so cold in the whole of his life.

'P'raps this weren't such a good idea after all,' he muttered miserably as he hugged his knees to his chin.

Gus, who was standing in the middle of the track peering along the line, turned to glare at him. 'It's a bit late to be changin' yer mind now. The way the snow's bin comin' down we'd never get back to the village anyway. Just keep yer pecker up, there's bound to be another train along soon.'

The words had barely left his lips when the stationmaster marched on to the platform and the track beneath them began to tremble.

'Birmingham train!' the stationmaster shouted, and Gus's face dropped.

'That's near enough,' Danny assured him. 'Birmingham ain't so far from Coventry as the crow flies so we can hop on another train into Coventry from there. Me mam used to go to the rag market in Birmingham on the train sometimes so that's how I know.'

Gus laughed triumphantly. 'In that case, stand well clear o' the track then, an' let's hope this one stops.'

In no time at all a train appeared out of the snow and began to slow as it approached the station. The boys held their breath as they watched a guard appear who began to load what appeared to be mailbags into one of the carriages at the back. He was so close to them that had he looked round, he would surely have seen the two lads, but luckily he was too intent on getting his job done and getting back to the warmth of the office where a nice hot pot of tea was mashing.

The second he began to walk away, Gus hissed urgently, 'Right, foller me an' don't make a sound else the game will be up.'

With his heart in his throat, Danny did as he was told. Gus sprinted across the platform and, after sliding the carriage door partially open, he climbed aboard and bent to offer Danny his hand. After hauling him in after him, he shrank down in the darkness clutching hold of the carriage door, not daring to slam it. They waited, hearts beating fast. Slowly, the train began to chug away.

'There yer go!' Gus laughed exultantly. 'We're on our way, matey. Now let's see if we can't make ourselves comfy an' try to 'ave a kip. Look – if we shove some o' these sacks togevver, we could lie on 'em. Be like a nice fevver bed, then, won't it?'

Danny nodded as they heaved some of the mail sacks together. It was certainly not the most comfortable of mattresses they had ever slept on, but even so they had barely left Pwllheli behind before both boys had fallen into an exhausted sleep.

Chapter Thirty-Three

A sharp dig in the ribs brought Danny springing awake. 'Ouch!' he grumbled as he stared at Gus who was standing over him with a deep frown on his face.

'Come on, wakey wakey. I don't know what's goin' on but the train seems to be slowin', though I can't see no sign of a station ahead.'

Danny yawned and stretched stiffly, almost overbalancing as the train suddenly slewed to an abrupt halt. The change of trains at Birmingham had been amazingly easy, as the platform there had been almost as deserted as the one at Pwllheli.

'What the bleedin' 'ell is goin' on?' Gus sounded concerned as he peered through the slight gap in the door.

Crossing to join him, Danny suddenly gasped and pointed at the sky. It was dark with aeroplanes that seemed to be heading for the city beyond. Suddenly the sky lit up with searchlights and the sound of bombs dropping not too far away reached them.

'Jesus Christ. It looks like we're arrivin' in the middle of an air raid. That's probably why they've stopped the train from goin' into the station, in case they target that.'

Fear swelled in Danny's throat. 'What are we goin' to do?'

Squaring his slight shoulders, Gus inched the door a little wider. 'Well, I ain't gonna stay 'ere like a sittin' duck, that's fer sure. Come on – let's make a run fer it. I reckon we'll be safer takin' our chances out there than squattin' 'ere.'

As Gus swung himself down from the carriage, Danny reluctantly followed him, surprised to see that although there was a sharp frost here, there was no snow.

Keeping their heads down, the two friends sprinted across the tracks and ran until they pushed their way through a hedge and found themselves in what appeared to be a park of some sort.

Glancing around him, Danny suddenly declared, 'I think I know where I am! Me gran used to bring me an' Lizzie here sometimes to feed the ducks.'

'So we *are* in Coventry then?'

Danny nodded as they began to walk across the frozen grass. In the centre of the park was a lake that was frozen over. The moon was shining down on it, making it appear like a sheet of polished glass, but neither of the boys were in the mood to appreciate it tonight.

They trudged on until they reached the entrance gates where Gus demanded, 'So which way do we go now then?'

Peering this way and that, Danny tried to get his bearings. The streets were dark and deserted, save for the searchlights that swept the sky, and it was hard to judge.

'I reckon it's that way,' he told his friend, nodding towards the area where the bombs were dropping thick and fast.

Gus shuddered but turned in that direction all the same. Keeping close to the shadows of the buildings they crept along, their eyes fearfully watching the sky overhead. The closer they got to the city centre, the louder the noise became until they had to shout to each other to make themselves heard.

'I reckon we should try an' make our way to a shelter,' Gus roared as a bomb dropped dangerously close to them. Danny almost jumped out of his skin and threw himself face down on the ground. Only yards away from them, a wall suddenly collapsed with a sound like thunder, and the ground beneath them shook. He could see the city centre ahead of them now, but it was nothing like he remembered it to be. The Cathedral, all apart from its spire, seemed to be flattened, and well-known shops were no longer there.

His lip trembled as he tried to be brave. Just twenty more minutes or so and they would be home. But could they make it? Lifting his head, he peered up at the sky through his fingers, and the sight that he saw made him suck his breath in. Multi-coloured incendiary bombs were drifting gracefully to earth on tiny parachutes, but the second they hit the ground the sound of the explosions they made was deafening.

'On second thoughts, we'd 'ave bin better off to wait back there wiv the train,' Gus shouted to him above the noise.

Danny nodded, but it was too late to do anything about it now. Bombs were dropping all around them, so they would be in as much danger if they tried to retrace their steps as go forward.

'I'm so sorry I dropped you in all this mess, Gus,' he muttered miserably. Gus's cold fingers snaked across the ground to squeeze his hand encouragingly.

'Don't be daft. We're best mates, ain't we? An' mates stick together through thick an' thin.'

Danny felt his heart swell, but now was not the time for expressing their feelings so they rose and started off again. They found themselves tramping across piles of rubble, and now the plaintive cries of people who had been hurt could be heard. They saw a terrified woman clutching a baby in her arms suddenly run out of a house into the street ahead of them, and even as they watched in horrified fascination, a bomb landed within feet of her, and tossed her into the air as if she weighed no more than a feather. The baby was thrown from her arms and landed like a little rag doll on a heap of broken bricks that had once been someone's home.

Danny's hand flew to his mouth as he stopped in his tracks, unable to take in the sight he had just seen. Fires were springing up all around them, and the streets were full of terrified people running this way and that.

He turned to say something to Gus, who was no more than a few yards behind him, just in time to see a bomb hurtling towards him. Panic set in. He opened his mouth to scream a warning but the words stuck in his throat, and suddenly everything seemed to be happening in slow motion.

Gus smiled at him then suddenly the bomb exploded and he seemed to be flying into the air. Albert fell from his top pocket and Danny watched in horror as the little creature plummeted towards the ground, to land with his head at an unnatural angle. Gus fell within feet of him and Danny raced across the debris to kneel beside him.

'A . . . Albert . . .'

With tears streaming down his dirty face, Danny scurried over to the tiny creature and carried his lifeless little body back to his master. Laying him on Soho Gus's chest, he sobbed as he saw a single tear slide from the corner of Gus's eye.

'Oh, Soho Gus, I'm so sorry I got you into this.'

Gus struggled to say something, but instead of words, blood spurted from his mouth when he opened it to speak. As Danny clutched his hand, the other boy tried to smile, but then his eyes suddenly became frantic as he stared at something behind Danny. Turning, Danny saw yet another bomb plummeting towards him and then suddenly the pain in his heart was gone and a comforting darkness enclosed him.

Earlier in the night, when the sounds of the sirens had pierced the air, Beryl had cursed, 'Oh, God love us! Not *another* bloody raid.' She'd almost fallen out of her brass bed and fumbled in the dark for her faded old dressing-gown.

Doors opening and shutting on the landing told her that the siren had woken the others too. Emerging from her bedroom, she'd found Jo propped against the landing wall. Her face was ashen and she looked as if she were about to throw up at any minute. Beryl had ushered her towards the top of the stairs. 'Go on down, love,' she'd urged. 'Get yerself as comfortable as yer can in the cupboard under the stairs. I'll be down to join yer when I've rounded Maggie an' David up.'

Jo had lurched away, gripping her stomach as David stumbled from his room, swiping the sleep from his eyes with his one good hand. He'd shot her a withering glance as she'd stepped past him and then she was gone, her footsteps making almost no sound at all on the worn stair-runners. Beryl had been concerned to see that he didn't look much better than Jo, and she cursed the Jerries under her breath. Why did they have to choose tonight of all nights? Her poor son looked as if a good night's sleep would have done him a power of good. Within seconds, Maggie had appeared too and Beryl had begun to push them along the landing.

They had only gone a few steps when David suddenly stopped dead, causing Maggie to bump into the back of him.

'You two go on down,' he told them, as sweat stood out on his brow. 'I'm going to take my chances up here.' He was too ashamed to admit that he couldn't face the close confines of the cupboard under the stairs.

Sensing his panic, Maggie turned to Beryl and told her, 'You go down to Jo. I'll stay here for a while with David.'

Beryl had opened her mouth to protest but something about the set of Maggie's mouth made her shuffle away to do as she was told. She had barely disappeared down the steep stairwell when David had begun to shake like a leaf.

Taking his good arm, Maggie calmly led him back to his room where she pressed him down onto the bed and sat close beside him. 'It's all right,' she muttered soothingly. 'I'll stay with you.'

His face when he turned it to her had brought tears stinging to her eyes. He'd looked so old suddenly, and nothing like the handsome man who had gone away to war.

Deeply ashamed, he'd hung his head as the sound of the first bombs dropping reached them through the walls of the house. It was almost pitch black with the blackout curtains closely drawn, but even so Maggie sensed that he was crying and her heart went out to him. What terrible sights he must have seen, she'd thought to herself as she gently stroked his hand and uttered words of comfort. They'd sounded inadequate even to her own ears, so eventually she fell silent and they sat shoulder to shoulder listening to the devastation that was going on all around them. Very soon the smell of burning reached them and Maggie had to suppress a shudder. What would they find when they emerged from the house this time? *If* they emerged, that was.

Downstairs, crouched in the cupboard under the stairs, Jo hadn't been feeling much better as she saw in her mind over and over again the way David had looked at her on the landing. As if she were nothing more than something dirty stuck to the sole of his shoes. But then, could she really blame him? She *was* dirty, to all intents and purposes. An unmarried mother; a former prostitute not even aware of who the father of her unborn child was. Feeling her shudder, Beryl had wrapped an arm about her slim shoulders.

'Don't worry, love. It'll all be over again soon, an' then happen we can get back to us beds.'

Her sympathy had the opposite effect to what she'd intended, for Jo had suddenly burst into heartbroken sobs.

'Do yer know somethin', Beryl, I ain't much bothered one way or the other at the minute. I mean, *look* at me . . . David thinks I'm scum, an' happen he's right.'

Beryl had been appalled as she rocked her to and fro. 'My son doesn't know the half of why yer did what yer did, me gel, so let's hear no more o' that silly talk, eh?'

Jo had fallen silent. The bottle of castor oil she had drunk earlier that night was beginning to make her feel even queasier than usual now. She could still taste the grease on her lips, imagine the sliminess as it had slipped down her throat, but would it have the desired effect?

Up until the last couple of weeks when she had started to show a little she'd thought she could go through with it, but now she wasn't so sure. After all, what life would she have after it was born – or the child, for that matter?

She would always be known as a loose woman then, and the child would be branded a bastard. No, it would be far better if the castor oil worked and she lost it. At least then she would have some chance of living a normal life. Only the week before, she'd boiled some copper pennies up in a saucepan and then somehow managed to drink the water. She had heard somewhere that this was a surefire way to get rid of unwanted pregnancies, but all it had done was make her be twice as sick as she normally was.

Just the thought of it now made vomit rise in her throat, and pushing Beryl aside, she had crawled towards the door.

'Where the bloody 'ell do yer think *you're* goin'?' Beryl had gasped as Jo thrust the door open. Jo's only answer had been a strangled groan as she clamped her hand across her mouth and made a dash for the yard.

Once again, the bombing had seemed to go on forever. Somehow, Maggie found herself curled into David's side as the pair of them finally lay down on the bed. And yet, for all their closeness they were both aware that nothing was as it had been between them. The old attraction had gone. Perhaps it's because neither of us are the people we were any more, Maggie pondered. Far too much had happened, and they both knew it. Sam was dead now, and yet strangely, they could both feel his presence far more strongly than they ever had when he'd been alive. He was still there between them, and Maggie suspected that he always would be.

David had thought of his twin brother too, and his heart was breaking. How would Maggie feel if he were ever to tell her that Sam was the cause of him losing part of his arm? He'd stared up at the ceiling, his eyes heavy with unshed tears. She must never know, even though he had longed for moments of closeness like this.

He was no longer the man he had once been, and never would be again. Maggie deserved someone better than him. Not half a man; a helpless cripple who would never even be able to hold down a proper job.

The tears had spilled silently down his cheeks then, at the injustice of it all. He had loved Maggie for as far back as he could remember, yet now their beloved daughter was dead, and it seemed they were destined never to be together.

Silently they lay, a breath apart, each locked in their own secret agony.

The next morning, after the all clear had sounded, the people of Coventry emerged from their homes to survey the damage. Bewildered and tired, they looked at the latest devastation the bombs had caused, and their hearts broke a little bit more. Flames licked up into the sky, and many more homes were gone, changing the landscape yet again. But still they were not defeated and the rescue operations began all over again as Union Jacks appeared amongst the rubble.

'Eeh! I don't know. It makes yer wonder what will become of us,' Beryl muttered as she pushed the kettle into the heart of the fire. Once more the gas and electric were off, but that was the least of their worries. At least their home was still standing, which was a lot more than could be said for other unfortunate souls.

'What are yer goin' to do now, about goin' to see the twins, I mean?' she asked as she wiped the dust from the cups. The windows had blown in yet again with the force of the blasts during the night, and everywhere was coated with thick, unwholesome dust.

'I'm still going. That's if the station hasn't taken a hit and the trains are still running,' Maggie declared with quiet determination.

David opened his mouth to speak but then changed his mind and hung his head as his mother stared at her admiringly.

'Well, yer've got guts. I'll say that fer yer, gel.'

'I need to see my children,' Maggie told her quietly. 'But are you quite sure you'll all manage without me?'

'Course we will. You go an' do what needs to be done. Lizzie an' Danny need to know what's gone on,' Beryl told her with a tremor in her voice. She certainly wouldn't have fancied having to tell the children that their father, grandma, baby sister and home were all gone.

Maggie glanced across at Jo, who was huddled in a chair at the side of the fireplace with a look of abject misery on her face. Despite all her endeavours to rid herself of her problem, the child was still growing within her and Jo was now having to face up to the fact that it would soon be too late to do anything about it. The only option left open to her now was a visit to Old Lady Moon on Temple Road, and Maggie shuddered at the thought. It was a well-known fact that many of the girls who had gone to her had ended up in hospital after she'd done her worst on them with a knitting needle, and not always a clean one at that.

Feeling Maggie's eyes burning into her, Jo flashed her a weak smile. 'We'll be fine, Maggie. I ain't goin' into work today. I might not be goin' into work ever again if the shop ain't still there. I'll go an' have a look after dinner. I could walk part of the way to the station wi' yer then.'

The sound of men hammering pieces of wood across the broken windows stopped the conversation from going any further and turning about, Maggie dragged herself upstairs to start packing a small suitcase.

After lunch, which was bread and dripping due to the fact that there was still no power to cook with, Maggie said her goodbyes. She'd decided to walk to the station as word had it that yet more of the buses had been destroyed in the bombing the night before, and a lot of the roads were closed. Beryl hugged her tightly, with tears in her eyes.

'Now you mind how yer go, eh? This family has seen enough grief in the last few weeks to last it a lifetime, so we don't want nothin' happenin' to you.'

'I will.' Maggie returned the hug and planted an affectionate kiss on her mother-in-law's wrinkled brow. 'I shouldn't be gone for more than a few days at most.'

Turning her attention to David, she felt colour warm her cheeks. 'I'll er . . . see you soon, then,' she said awkwardly.

'Yes. As Mam said, mind how you go and give the twins my love.' He seemed as ill-at-ease as she was, and Beryl's heart broke as she observed the distance between them. The woman had been forced to stand back and watch them over the years, knowing all the time, deep inside, that they should have been together. She'd hoped that once David returned and there was no longer an obstacle between them, that they would get back together, but up to now there was no sign of that happening. Still, she consoled herself, it was early days yet and they still had a lot of grieving to do before they could look to the future.

She waved Maggie and Jo off from the front doorstep and then scurried away to try and get the house back into some sort of order again.

*   *   *

As Maggie and Jo walked towards the centre of the city, they were appalled to see the extent of the latest devastation. Areas were cordoned off as troops worked on unexploded bombs. Their journey took twice as long as it should have done as they clambered over piles of rubble and followed the Diversion sign, glad to be wearing warm coats and flat shoes, but at last the station came into view.

After making enquiries, Maggie was relieved to be told that, although many of the trains had been cancelled, there was one to Wales due within the hour. Turning to Jo she told her, 'You get yourself home as soon as you can. There's no point you standing about here.'

'Well, all right then, if yer sure.' Jo suddenly clung to her as if she was never going to see her again. Maggie had kept her going, body and soul, over the last few months and she could hardly bear to let her go. She was all the girl had left now.

'Now come on, less of that,' Maggie told her, and there was a catch in her voice too. 'If you start blartin' you'll set me off.'

'Sorry.' Jo dragged a large white handkerchief around her pale face and managed a false smile. 'I'll see yer when yer get back then.'

'You certainly will. Now go on, and make sure you look after Beryl and David for me while I'm gone.'

She watched Jo walk away and then, lifting her small suitcase, she settled on the platform to wait.

'Danny, come on! Your breakfast is on the table. Don't let it get cold now.' Eric stared up the staircase, waiting to hear the sound of movement, but when none was forthcoming he sighed and began to mount the stairs. The boy must still be sulking.

Pushing Danny's bedroom door open, he opened his mouth to speak but then closed it abruptly. The bed was neatly made and there was no sign of the child. Thinking that perhaps he'd gone out to play in the snow for a while, he closed the door and made his way back downstairs. After hastily pulling his boots on he opened the back door and Samson frolicked out into the drifts. Apart from Samson's paw-prints the snow outside was untouched, which told him that wherever Danny was, he must have been gone for some time.

Returning to the kitchen, he checked the hook on the back of the door. Danny's warm coat was gone, as were his Wellington boots, hat and scarf. Eric was beginning to feel anxious. It wasn't like the boy to just disappear. Lately he'd been very good about telling Eric where he was going, and he'd certainly never ventured out of the house this early before, even on a school morning. The lad wouldn't have missed his breakfast.

Making a hasty decision, Eric began to drag his outdoor clothes on. Perhaps Danny had gone to call for Gus? There was only one way to find out so after quickly throwing some logs onto the fire, and taking the bacon off the range, he set off in the direction of *Derwen Deg*.

Olwen Thomas opened the farmhouse door on his first knock and glared at him. The plump, ruddy-faced woman was known for being outspoken, and now she lived up to her reputation as she barked at him, 'Is Gus with your Danny? I cooked him a lovely breakfast but he's nowhere to be found, the little imp. I'll tan his arse for him when he decides to come back, so I will. All that good food gone to waste.'

Eric shook his head. 'I'd actually come to see if Danny was here,' he told her, trying to keep the concern from sounding in his voice. 'It doesn't look like his bed has even been slept in, so where do you think they could have gone?'

'I've no idea,' Olwen replied. 'There's no saying what those two might get up to when they're together. I wonder – might they have gone down into the village to see that sister of Danny's.'

Eric thought it highly unlikely at that time of the morning, but having nothing better to go on, he decided to go and find out.

'You just tell that little devil he'll be in trouble when he does bother to show his face,' Olwen shouted down the path after him. 'I had a list of jobs as long as your arm ready for him to do, which is probably why he's decided to clear off.'

Too worried to be amused, Eric began the treacherous descent down the hillside. The fresh fall of snow on top of the frozen stuff had made the path dangerously slippery, so by the time he reached the village, he was frozen through and irritable. Nevertheless, he set off through the streets until he reached *Ty-Du*, where a plume of smoke was snaking up into the eerie grey sky from the cottage chimney.

Blodwyn must have seen him coming, for she opened the door before he had the chance to knock. 'What do you want *now*?' she demanded, and for a moment he was at a loss for words as he stared back at her. Her grey hair was unkempt and there was a strange look in her eyes. He noticed that the buttons on her cardigan were done up wrongly and she had odd slippers on her feet.

'I er . . . was wondering if Danny was here?' he dared to ask.

She frowned. 'And why would Dannybright be here? Is it not you he should be staying with?'

'Yes – yes, it is. But the thing is, he went out earlier

without telling me where he was going so I'm just looking for him.'

'Huh! Well, you're looking in the wrong place. Now, I'll wish you good day.' And with that she closed the door in his face.

Eric scratched his head in bewilderment as he stared up and down the deserted street. It was now fairly obvious that Gus was missing too, so he could safely assume that wherever they were, they would have gone together. But where?

After a time he decided that the best thing to do would be to go home and wait for Danny to show up. But first, whilst he was in the village, he might as well pay a visit to the post office and check if there was any mail for them.

With a smile, the postmistress handed him a small brown envelope addressed to Danny and Lizzie. After thanking her, Eric ventured out into the bitterly cold streets again. He supposed that the letter would be from their mother, and if it was, there would probably be one for Lizzie tucked inside the envelope. Pausing, he wrestled with his conscience. He had never opened anyone else's mail before, but it made sense to give Lizzie hers while he was down in the village. Otherwise it would mean yet another trek down the hill when Danny eventually returned.

He quickly slit the envelope open and just as he'd thought, found a sheet of paper with Danny's name written on it and another sheet addressed to Lizzie.

As he once again approached *Ty-Du*, his steps slowed. He had no wish to have yet another confrontation with Blodwyn, so taking the coward's way out, he slipped the paper through the letter box and hurried on his way.

Lizzie was in her bedroom when the letter arrived but

Blodwyn heard the rattle of the brass letter box, and hurrying across to the doormat, she lifted the sheet of paper and stared at it. It was addressed to Lizzie – but who could it be from?

Glancing towards the stairs door she made sure that Lizzie was out of the way as her eyes began to race across the page, and as they did, her stomach dropped into her shoes. It was yet another one from the child's mother telling her that she was coming to see her on Monday. Monday! Panic set in as she realised that it was Monday today.

If the woman came, she might well decide to take the child home with her. But Blodwyn couldn't allow that to happen. Megan was *her* child and no one would take her from her, not now that she had found her again.

With a quiet determination she thrust the letter deep into the pocket of her pinny and climbed the steep stairs, calling out to Lizzie as she went. There was no time to be lost. Her mother might appear at any moment.

'Megan! Collect your warm clothes together, there's a good girl.'

Lizzie appeared in her bedroom door, her face pale and frightened. Mrs Evans never called her by her own name any more and the girl was by now more than a little afraid of her.

'What do I need warm clothes for?' she asked nervously.

'Because I've decided we both need a little holiday, and what better time than the present?'

'But I don't *want* to go on holiday,' Lizzie protested feebly.

'Nonsense, *cariad*. You'll love it, so you will, once we get there. Now come along. There's not a moment to be lost.'

'But where are we going?'

'Somewhere no one will find us,' Mrs Evans told her, and Lizzie felt alarmed. However, she had no time to argue even if she had dared to, for the big woman had already bustled past her and was bundling an odd assortment of clothes into her small suitcase. Lizzie watched her silently. What would Danny think if he came to see her and she wasn't there? And how long would they be gone?

The questions stuck in her throat as she saw Blodwyn snap the lock shut.

'Now you go downstairs with this, get your warm things on and wait by the door, there's my sweet girl. We'll be off in no time, so we will.'

Lizzie miserably lifted her small case and went down to stand by the door as she was told.

Chapter Thirty-Four

'Now then. Wasn't this a good idea, eh?' Blodwyn grunted as she hauled Lizzie along behind her through the village streets.

Lizzie didn't answer. With every step they took her anxiety grew, but there was nothing she could do about it. They went past the village school, locked up and deserted, and Lizzie was confused to see that Mrs Evans was leading her towards the clifftops.

'Aren't we going on a bus or a train?' she ventured breathlessly.

Mrs Evans shook her head. 'No, *bach*. We'll have no need of buses or trains where I'm taking you.'

It was at that moment that Lizzie spotted Sparky, who was halfway through building a snowman. He waved as she drew closer and looked curiously at the small suitcase she was clutching.

'We're going on holiday,' she shouted to him as Mrs Evans dragged her past.

Sparky chewed on his lip. Why would they be heading for the hills if they were going on holiday? There was nothing up there but some derelict miners' cottages that hadn't been lived in for years. And why had Lizzie looked so frightened?

Waiting until they were some way ahead, he began

to follow them, keeping to the shelter of the trees and bushes so that he wouldn't be seen if Mrs Evans should chance to look behind her.

By the time the train pulled into the station at Pwllheli, it was late afternoon. Maggie was exhausted and darkness was falling. The train had been forced to stop numerous times and had also been diverted more often than she cared to remember, which had put hours on the journey, but at least she was here now.

Throwing her case onto the deserted platform she climbed stiffly down from the carriage and looked around her. Eventually she spotted the stationmaster, who was just about to disappear back into his warm office, and hurrying across to him, she asked, 'Could you tell me where I might get a bus to Sarn-Bach, please?'

Scratching his head, he frowned back at her. 'Why, you'll get no buses there tonight, madam. Nor tomorrow, if it comes to that. The village has been cut off by snowdrifts. But I *could* tell you where you might get lodgings in Pwllheli for the night, if you'd like me to.' He could have added that he would direct her to his sister-in-law's boarding-house, which had been sadly lacking in holidaymakers since the beginning of the war, but of course he didn't.

Maggie shook her head, setting her fair curls dancing around her pale face.

'Thank you very much – it's very kind of you, but if there are no buses then I shall have to walk. My children were evacuated to Sarn-Bach a few months ago and I'm desperate to see them.'

His face became sympathetic as he told her, 'I can well understand the need to see your children but you'll never make it to Sarn-Bach on foot, especially in the dark. There are six-foot-deep drifts along the way.'

'That's as may be,' Maggie replied, becoming cross now. 'But I'll have to take my chance, won't I? Because one way or another I *am* going to see my children tonight! Now, would you kindly give me directions?'

He shook his head, thinking that she must have taken leave of her senses, but then, that was the English for you. Walking to the exit of the station with her he pointed ahead. 'Now then, follow this road through the town and eventually you'll come to . . .'

His voice droned on as Maggie listened attentively, and when he had finished she thanked him and lifted her case.

'Good luck!' he shouted, and as he turned away he muttered beneath his breath, 'You'll need it.'

She walked through the unlit streets, glancing at the windows of the houses as she passed. There was hardly a light to be seen, and she felt as if she was walking through a ghost town. When she neared the end of the main street, the ocean could be heard crashing onto the beach, and as she had been instructed, she turned and began the long climb up the steep hillside. Just as the stationmaster had told her, the snow was so deep here that every now and again she found herself up to the waist in it and forced to drag her case along behind her. But Maggie was a determined woman when she set her mind to something, and right now she was determined to see her children.

She didn't become really afraid until she turned a bend and left the village behind her – and then suddenly she realised that she was in the middle of nowhere. She had been told that it was a two-mile walk to Sarn-Bach but felt as if she had done ten already. Added to that, the weight of her case was making her arm feel as if it was dropping off. She was very aware that the path ran danger-ously close to the edge of the cliffs, and with every step she took, she expected to feel herself hurtling to the beach far below. And yet, with a picture of Lizzie and Danny in her mind she kept doggedly on until at last she crested the hill and saw the outline of a small village in the valley far below her. The descent was almost as precarious as the climb and she slipped and slithered her way down the other side of the hill to land in an undignified heap at the bottom. She was on what appeared to be the main road through the village and by now her fingers were so cold that she could scarcely feel them as she fumbled in her pocket for the scrap of paper with Lizzie's address written on it. When she did find it, she had to peer at it closely, for the street was deserted and unlit. *Ty-Du*, The Green, Sam-Bach, that was it. Lifting her case again she set off with a spring in her step now. Within minutes she would see her beloved Lizzie.

She saw the green in front of her as she slithered across the frozen cobbles, and then there was the cottage directly in front of her. A smile lit her face as she skidded up to it and rapped sharply with the brass doorknocker. She kept her eyes fixed expectantly on the door, but there was nothing, only the faint sound of the waves crashing on the beach some way away.

Lifting her hand she tried again, more loudly this time, but again only silence answered her knock. Frowning now, she glanced about her hesitantly, wondering what she should do. She wasn't sure exactly what time it was, for it was too dark to make out the face of the cheap wristwatch on her arm, but she guessed that it must be getting late now. Certainly far too late for Lizzie to be out, so where was she?

Reluctantly walking away, she spotted a man with his

head bent walking towards her and hurried across to him.

'Excuse me.'

He started and looked at her suspiciously.

'I was wondering, would you happen to know where Mrs Evans from the blacksmith's cottage might be?'

'And who might be asking?'

Keeping her patience as best she could, Maggie told him, 'I'm Maggie Bright. My daughter, Lizzie, is staying with Mrs Evans.'

'Ah, I see.' He seemed to relax a little as he stared at the dark windows of the cottage. 'Is Blodwyn not in then?'

Maggie swallowed the hasty retort that sprang to her lips. Surely he had enough brains to realise that she wouldn't be asking, if Blodwyn were? Fixing a smile to her face, she shook her head.

He shrugged. 'Then I have no idea where she might be. It's not like Blodwyn not to be in of a night, unless there's something on at the church, that is. But I'm pretty certain there's nothing happening tonight.'

'In that case, perhaps you would be kind enough to direct me to *Tremarfon* then? My son, Danny, is staying with a Mr Sinclair there.'

He nodded, obviously knowing who she meant. 'You'll have to go back through the village and take the road up the hill. You'll pass *Derwen Deg*, a farmhouse on the way. *Tremarfon* is about a quarter of a mile further on. But I warn you, you have quite a hike in front of you.'

Maggie's shoulders drooped despondently. She was so tired now that she felt just like lying down in the snow and going to sleep. And oh, what she wouldn't have done for a nice cup of hot steaming tea. She realised with a little jolt that she'd had nothing to eat or drink since leaving home that morning, so now she was hungry as well as being tired. Still, she reasoned, she was on the last leg of the journey now and she could always come back and see Lizzie tomorrow. Nodding her thanks, she turned and tramped wearily back the way she had come.

When she finally arrived at the foot of the hill he had described, she felt like weeping. It seemed to stretch up and up forever, and she wondered if she had the energy left to tackle it. But then she thought of Danny and renewed her efforts. She had just begun the climb when, to add to her misery, the snow started to come down again. It began as soft white flakes that fluttered gently around her, but within minutes it was coming so thick and fast that she could scarcely see more than a few feet ahead of her. Cursing loudly, she hoisted her suitcase higher and ploughed on. After what seemed an eternity she saw a faint light shining in front of her. As she drew nearer she peered at the gate that led to what appeared to be a large farmhouse to the right of her. Swiping the snow from the brass plate screwed into it she saw the name *Derwen Deg* inscribed on it and sighed with relief. If what the villager had told her was right, *Tremarfon* should be just a little further on.

Each step was an effort now so it was a huge relief when some minutes later she saw yet another light ahead shining out into the darkness. This must be *Tremarfon*. Skirting the house and a large outbuilding, she stopped in front of what appeared to be a kitchen door. She had no need to knock, for suddenly the sharp barking of a dog pierced the air and she heard footsteps approaching on the other side of the door. It swung open and a horribly disfigured man with a black eyepatch across one eye peered out at her, sending her heart plummeting into her boots.

'Are you Mr . . . Mr Eric Sinclair?' she asked falteringly.

He frowned and nodded, then seeing that she looked fit to drop he swung the door wider and ushered her inside.

Dropping her case onto the dull red tiles she looked about her. She had no doubt that the kitchen she found herself in would be almost the size of Beryl's whole house put together, but there was nothing welcoming about it. Dragging her attention back to the man, who was watching her intently, she told him, 'I'm Danny's mother, Maggie Bright. I'm sorry to descend on you like this, but I have to see him. I did write to let him know that I was coming. Did he tell you?'

To her horror, he shuffled from foot to foot, avoiding her eyes, saying merely, 'You look absolutely worn out, Mrs Bright. Why don't you come over by the fire while I make you a nice hot drink. You certainly look as if you could do with one.'

Smiling her gratitude, she crossed to the fire and held her hands out to the comforting blaze. While he filled the kettle and set it onto the range to heat she slipped out of her sodden coat and slung it across the clotheshorse standing at the side of the fire, where it began to steam.

Next she peeled off her wet boots and stood them on the hearth, and all the while she was aware of him watching her, though he said not so much as a single word. There was a huge tabby cat curled up on the fireside chair and she found herself smiling. Danny had always wanted a pet so no doubt he would love the cat *and* the huge Labrador dog that was also watching her every move from soulful brown eyes.

'The cat is called Hemily and the dog's name is

Samson,' Eric told her as he saw her looking at them. 'I'm afraid Hemily has taken to sleeping on Danny's bed.'

When she smiled, it struck him like a slap in the face how very much like Danny this woman looked, and how beautiful she was, despite the ravages of the weather. She reminded him so much of someone he had known, but that path was too painful to take so he pulled his thoughts back to his visitor. She looked at the end of her tether.

'Is Danny tucked up in bed?' she asked, longing to see her son. Thankfully the kettle began to sing on the hob at that moment and he was saved from having to answer as he hurried across to mash the tea. Finally the moment he had dreaded arrived and he could put off the inevitable no longer.

'I err . . . I'm afraid I have something to tell you,' he admitted as he handed her a steaming mug. She looked up at him from beneath long eyelashes and his stomach did an unfamiliar cartwheel.

'The thing is,' he went on, realising there was no easy way to soften the blow, 'Danny has er . . . gone missing.'

'What do you mean, *Danny has gone missing*!' Tea spilled across the arm of the chair and Hemily leaped indignantly out of the way. Eric spread his hands helplessly as she glared at him in horrified disbelief. 'Just when did he go missing? And why?'

Falteringly, he told her of Danny finding the newspaper that reported the Blitz on his home city and the effect it had had on him. 'He was beside himself with fear that something might have happened to you,' he finished lamely. 'And I have an awful idea that he might have tried to get home to check that you were all right.'

Maggie fought back tears as she tried to take in what he was telling her. 'But he's just a child,' she said shakily.

'How on earth would he manage to get all that way on his own?'

'I don't think he is on his own,' Eric confided. 'I called down to *Derwen Deg* this morning when I realised he wasn't here and it appears that Soho Gus, a friend of Danny's, is missing too. I've already spoken to the local police and reported them both missing, then I spent the rest of the day trailing round all the local places where I thought they might be, but other than that I don't know what I can do. It's just as if they've both vanished off the face of the earth.'

When Maggie stood up and began to pull her sodden coat back on he frowned. 'What are you doing?'

'Well, I can't just sit here, can I?' she declared angrily. 'I'm going out to look for my son, of course.'

Eric glanced towards the window where he could see that the snow had turned into a blizzard. 'There really isn't much point tonight,' he told her. 'It would be like looking for a needle in a haystack in this and I've already searched all the places where they were most likely to be. Why don't you have something to eat and a good night's rest – then we'll start to hunt for them again, first thing in the morning.'

She seemed to shrink in front of his very eyes as she saw the sense in what he said.

'All right,' she said grudgingly as he hurried away to warm up some stew that he'd cooked earlier. All the while he was pottering about, her eyes stayed firmly fixed on the window. After all that she had endured over the last few months, this was the final straw and she felt as if her heart was breaking. Danny was such a little boy and he was out there somewhere at the mercy of the elements. How would he ever survive?

In no time at all, Eric had her seated at the table with

a large bowl of stew in front of her, but somehow her appetite had disappeared and she could do no more than pick at it as she thought of Danny's plight. Deep inside she was seething. How could the stupid man have allowed Danny to disappear like that? Even so, she was aware that he needn't have offered to let her stay, so she supposed that she should be grateful to him for that at least.

Had she whipped him with a stick she couldn't have caused Eric any more pain than he was already feeling, but of course, she had no way of knowing that as, an hour later, she followed him up the impressive staircase. On an impulse, she suddenly asked, 'Would you mind if I saw Danny's room?'

'Of course,' Eric said. Throwing a door open, he told her, 'This is where your son sleeps.'

Stepping past him, she entered the room, and the first thing she saw was the family photograph she had slipped into Danny's case on the day he'd left home. It was standing in pride of place on a small chest of drawers at the side of a neatly made bed. The breath caught in her throat as her hand flew to her mouth, and she almost choked on the sob that was swelling there.

'It's funny, isn't it,' she said. 'I was dreading coming here in one way because I have to tell the twins that their father, their grandma and their baby sister are all dead. Their home is gone too and I'm living with my mother-in-law now, as you probably gathered from the address on Danny's last letter telling him I was coming. And then on top of all that, I arrive here to find that Lizzie is out somewhere with Mrs Evans, and that Danny has run away. Dear God in heaven – it's like a nightmare.'

Eric lowered his head as he saw her pain, and silently withdrew to stand on the landing. Everywhere she looked, Maggie could see evidence of her son. His presence was so tangible that she expected him to appear at any minute. But he didn't, and after a few moments she slowly turned and closed the door behind her.

Eric led her further along the landing to a slightly larger room that boasted a sea view in the light of day. She nodded at him and he quietly left her standing there with her suitcase at her feet and a bleak expression in her eyes.

Once he reached the bottom of the stairs, Eric paused before going into the little-used dining room where he switched on the overhead light. The woman's portrait seemed to reproach him as he stared up into the beautiful face that he had captured for all time on canvas, and he lowered his head and wept. In his mind's eye he could see the shudder of revulsion that had crossed Maggie's face as she saw him for the first time. But then he was used to that, for didn't everyone react that way?

He cursed himself for not being stronger when Miss Williams had approached him about taking in an evacuee. If *only* he'd stuck to his guns and refused, none of this sorry mess would have happened and he would still be enjoying his reclusive life. But it had happened, and now it was up to him to try and put things right again.

With a last regretful glance at the hauntingly beautiful face in the picture he quietly turned and left the room. First thing in the morning he would start the search for Danny again – and this time he swore he wouldn't rest until he had found him.

Chapter Thirty-Five

'I don't like it here,' Lizzie fretted. 'When can we go back home?'

Turning to her, Mrs Evans smiled reassuringly. 'Why, *bach*, it isn't so very bad. At least there's a roof on this room to stop the snow from coming in – and haven't I managed to make us a nice warm fire? Now eat your food and stop moaning, Megan, there's a good girl.'

Lizzie shuddered as she pulled the thin blanket more closely about her. This derelict cottage high in the Welsh hills wasn't her idea of a holiday at all, as she had told Mrs Evans earlier in the day when they'd finally arrived there. The journey through the thick snow had seemed to take forever, and as they'd climbed and climbed, Lizzie's ears had started to pop, which had made her cry. When the row of tumbledown cottages had come into view and Mrs Evans had told her that this was where they would be staying, Lizzie had gasped incredulously.

'But . . . they're falling down!' she said.

'Nonsense. Some of the rooms still have roofs on them, look. We'll soon make ourselves comfortable, you just wait and see. And won't it be nice to be just the two of us with no one else to interfere now?'

Eventually, Mrs Evans had decided on the room they

were in now, for not only had it still got a roof on but a door as well, although the bitter wind was rattling it in its frame now. The candle she'd lit was throwing dancing shadows all across the walls and the floor was cold and damp. Lizzie was frightened. Mrs Evans seemed to be acting even more strangely than she usually did, and the child had thought of running away from her and back to the village. The trouble was, the snow was very deep and she had lost all sense of direction on the way so she was too afraid to attempt it.

When she saw something with a big fat tail scurry across the room in the far corner, she swallowed the cry of terror that rose in her throat, and tried to pretend it was Albert. She was trying her very best to be brave, but despite her best efforts, a big fat tear slid from her eye and rolled down her cold cheek.

'Eeh, *cariad*. Whatever is the matter?' Mrs Evans crooned as she crossed to take her in her arms.

Without being able to stop herself, Lizzie sobbed, 'I want me mam.'

A cold light shone in Mrs Evans's eyes as she shook the child roughly. 'Wash out your mouth now. Haven't I *told* you that from now on, *I* am your mother? Now shush. It's time we were getting some rest.'

Without any warning, she suddenly blew out the candle and Lizzie found herself in pitch darkness. Huddling down into a heap on the cold damp floor she lay there shivering until she eventually cried herself to sleep.

Maggie was wakened by the sound of someone hammering on the door. She threw herself out of bed and flew across to the window. It was barely light, but as she looked down she could just make out the shape of a policeman standing at the front door. Her heart missed a beat as she slipped her arms into the dressing-gown she had put across the end of the bed, and ran along the landing. Perhaps he'd come to tell them that they'd found Danny? The hope lent speed to her bare feet as she fled down the stairs. Her hopes were dashed, however, when she emerged into the hall to hear him having a muttered conversation with Eric.

'So as I said, we've phoned through to the police in Coventry and they'll be keeping a look-out for Danny and Gus.'

As they heard her coming towards them, both men turned in her direction and she saw the worry etched on Eric's face.

'You haven't managed to find him yet then?' She addressed the policeman and he shook his head sadly as he hastily took off his helmet.

'No, we haven't, ma'am, although we now know where the boys have gone. Young Gus left a note for the lady who looks after him down the hill, and apparently the two lads were heading to Coventry to see *you*, ma'am.' While Maggie was absorbing this piece of news, he went on. 'The note had dropped down by the bed, that's why she didn't spot it before. But I'm afraid that's not all I've come to tell you.'

'What do you mean?' she asked in bewilderment.

The portly policeman cleared his throat before telling her, 'I'm afraid it looks as if your Lizzie has gone missing too.'

Maggie felt suddenly faint, and she reached out to Eric to steady herself. She managed to croak, 'Do you think she's with Danny?'

'No, I'm afraid not. It seems that Mrs Evans got wind of your visit and she's taken Lizzie off somewhere.'

'But why would she do that?'

'Because . . .' The policeman cleared his throat again. 'It appears that Mrs Evans is having some sort of breakdown following the death of her husband. Somehow, she's got it into her mind that Lizzie is the little girl she lost a number of years ago. The vicar's wife has had some concerns about her for some time. In fact, only recently she tried to persuade Mrs Evans that it would be better for all concerned if Lizzie were to be placed somewhere else for a while. I believe that Mr Sinclair here offered to let her come and stay with Danny and himself, but Mrs Evans wouldn't hear of it.'

'Oh my God!' Maggie clapped her hand across her mouth.

'Anyway,' the policeman went on, 'this morning, the vicar and his wife paid Mrs Evans an early-morning call only to find the cottage door unlocked. When they couldn't make anyone hear them, they took the liberty of letting themselves in to make sure that all was as it should be, and that's when they found your letter discarded on the chair. The child's case was gone, as were some of her clothes, so we can only assume that Mrs Evans has taken her off somewhere.'

'Is she likely to hurt her?' Maggie asked brokenly.

He shook his head. 'That is highly unlikely, especially as she thinks the child is her own daughter. Even now I have men scouring the area for them. There's no record of them taking a train anywhere so we have to presume that they're still in the area. As for Danny, the police have already traced your mother-in-law in Coventry, and been to visit her, and as yet there's no sign of him, or his friend, Gus. As soon as there is, I assure you they'll let us know.'

Maggie sank weakly down onto the bottom step as

despair engulfed her. Now she looked in grave danger of losing the twins too, and if she did, she didn't know how she would find the strength to go on. They were all she had left to live for now.

'Should I get back to Coventry?' she asked the sober-faced officer.

He shook his head. 'I think perhaps it would be best if you stayed here until we've located Lizzie. Then, when we know she's safe and sound, we'll decide what's best to do about your son. For all we know, he could be around here somewhere too.' Turning his attention back to Eric, he asked, 'Will it be all right if Mrs Bright stays here for a while, sir?'

'Yes . . . yes, of course it will,' Eric replied quickly. It was the least he could do until there was some resolution to this dreadful affair.

Once the officer had left, Maggie began to pace up and down the kitchen like a caged animal. She felt as if she was being torn in two, for half of her wanted to get home to Coventry in case Danny showed up there, and the other half wanted to stay here until Lizzie was found.

Eric was on tenterhooks too, and eventually he rose and began to put on his outdoor clothes.

'I think I might just go and have another scout round,' he told her as he struggled into his boots, which were still sodden from the night before.

'I'll come with you,' Maggie volunteered immediately, but he shook his head.

'No – it might be best if you stayed here in case there's any news about either of them. Just help yourself to anything you want while I'm gone. I'm sure you'll soon find your way about.'

'Thank you. It's . . . very good of you to let me stay.' She still found it hard to look at him when she addressed him, for the scars on his face were hideous. He was obviously aware of the fact and all the time he was talking to her he self-consciously turned his head so that only the unscarred side of his face showed.

When she realised this, a tremor of sympathy ran through her and she tried to look at him differently. In fact, she realised that, had it not been for his disfigurement, he would actually have been a very attractive man. His hair was thick and as black as coal, and the one visible eye was a deep sapphire blue. She briefly wondered what might have happened to him to cause the scars, but her mind was too full of her children's plight to dwell on it for long and she was soon pacing again as she nervously chewed on her nails. As he moved across the room she suddenly asked, 'Did you get on well with Danny?'

'Danny and I got on very well when we came to know each other,' he replied quietly, 'but I'd better get on. I'll er . . . I'll see you later.' Calling Samson to his side, he yanked the door open.

When the door closed behind him, the silence seemed to close in on Maggie and panic started to get a grip. It was so quiet here. She was used to the noise of traffic, having lived in a city all her life, so this remote house was difficult to get used to. It was so isolated and so . . . she searched in her mind for the word she was looking for. Sad! That was it. This was a sad house in all ways – as if the owner's grief had somehow rubbed off on it. Somehow she sensed that Eric *was* sad – and not just because of Danny's disappearance. There was something about him that told her he was lonely. Perhaps she could see it because she had been lonely herself. She had been trapped for years in a loveless marriage, and deep down she had always yearned for David, who had been the first love of her life. As she thought of him now, a great well of sadness opened up inside her. They were both free now, yet life had changed them, and the closeness they'd once shared seemed to have vanished as if it had never been.

Sighing, she looked around the room. It was reasonably clean, and yet somehow it looked unloved. That was it – sad and unloved. Maggie was very tired but unused to being idle so she decided to tidy up a little. It would give her something to do and make her feel that she was earning her keep, as well as keeping her mind off what was happening.

After rummaging around behind the curtain that hung beneath the sink, she managed to find some polish and old rags, and crossing to the heavy oak table, she began to clean it. Then, systematically, she worked her way around the kitchen until every single piece of furniture shone. Next she turned her attention to the huge sash-cord windows. A drop of vinegar in water would soon sort *them* out. Very soon they were shining too, so now she began to rearrange the pieces of furniture that she could manage to move. Hands on hips, she stood back to survey her handiwork and smiled as she saw that the room was beginning to look cosy. The floor was the next thing to get her attention, though that took slightly longer for it was enormous compared to the small kitchen floor she was used to back at home. By the time she was done, she was breathless and some of her hair, which she'd tied into a ponytail with a pretty red ribbon, had escaped into little wispy tendrils that framed her heart-shaped face. Unable to find an apron, she had popped a huge artist's smock on, and now as she caught sight of herself in the mirror that hung above the mantelshelf she couldn't help but grin. She certainly looked a sight and was glad there was no one there to see her.

As she turned, her eyes were drawn to the small easel with a picture propped up on it. Crossing to it, she gazed at it admiringly. It was so lifelike that she felt she could almost hear the wind in the trees that swept down to the sea.

'It's beautiful, isn't it?'

Maggie had been so absorbed in the painting that when the voice sounded at the side of her she almost jumped out of her skin. She turned startled eyes to see Eric looking past her at the painting. Very aware of what a state she was in, she hastily tried to scrape her hair back into its ponytail.

'Sorry, I er . . . I didn't hear you come in,' she said as colour crept into her cheeks, and she was shocked to see that it was almost lunchtime.

Eric saw the question in her eyes and said, 'I'm afraid there's no news on either of them as yet, but try not to worry. The village men are out scouring the country-side for Lizzie and I've no doubt the police in Coventry will be doing the same for Danny. We're bound to find them soon. I've taken the liberty of asking the police to let your mother-in-law know that Lizzie is missing too and that you'll be staying on here until she's found.'

Maggie's shoulders sagged as she walked despondently to the window. It was such a vast expanse out there. How would they ever find such a little girl in all that space? And where was Danny? What if he'd arrived home while Coventry was being bombed? Had he been caught in the air raid? Was he lying dead somewhere?

Turning quickly away from the window she was just in time to see Eric staring around in astonishment.

'Good grief! How did you ever manage to make the place look like this?'

'Elbow grease,' she told him. 'After you went out I

423

needed something to do to keep me occupied so I set to. I hope you don't mind? I thought perhaps it would show my appreciation for you letting me stay here.'

'You didn't have to,' he told her. 'But as for minding . . . well, of course I don't mind! Everywhere just looks so . . . so homely. I have to admit, I'm not the best when it comes to prettying the place up. But you've done wonders. You must be worn out, Mrs Bright. How about I make us some dinner now as my way of saying thank you?'

'I'll tell you what. How about we do it together?' she said shyly. 'I actually quite enjoy cooking and I'd like to stay busy.'

He nodded in agreement and soon they were standing side by side at the sink peeling potatoes and carrots. Slowly, the atmosphere became less strained as he told her about some of the things he and Danny had been doing together during her son's stay with him.

She found herself smiling as he told her about Soho Gus and Sparky, and the mischief the three of them had got up to. It also struck her that he was speaking of Danny with genuine affection.

'I didn't want to take an evacuee,' he admitted, 'but Miss Williams who was organising all the billets is very hard to say no to. Until Danny came I rarely ventured down into the village unless it was to take a trip to the post office or buy supplies.'

Peering at him, she asked, 'Don't you get lonely, stuck up here in the back of beyond all by yourself?'

He shook his head. 'Not at all. In fact, that was the reason I bought this place. So that I could be on my own.'

Maggie frowned. It seemed that her earlier assumption had been right then. Eric *was* lonely – from choice, it seemed. But something must have happened in his past to make him feel that way.

'Have you lived here for long?'

'About seven years or so now.'

'And where did you live before?'

He threw the paring knife into the sink. 'I reckon it's about time I filled the log basket,' he told her shortly, and turning on his heel he marched away.

Maggie sighed, wondering when she would ever learn to keep her big mouth shut. What business was it of hers what he'd done in his past anyway? Lifting the knife, she finished preparing the vegetables. From now on she would try to be more careful. She might only be here for a few more hours or days. Then again, it could be longer so the least said about his personal life the better. He was obviously a very private person and she would have to learn to respect that.

Lifting the heavy pan, she carried it to the range then hurried upstairs to tidy herself up.

The next four days were the longest of Maggie's life. Each morning, Eric would join the men from the village as they gradually extended their search of the area for Lizzie. But it was as if she had vanished into thin air and each day he would arrive home dispirited and sad.

Thankfully, they were once again on better terms, possibly because Maggie studiously avoided asking him any personal questions.

In the time that she'd been there, she had totally transformed *Tremarfon*; the house was now warm and welcoming. She'd washed and ironed every scrap of clothing she could lay her hands on, as well as all the bedding, which had resulted in Eric coming back most days to find wet washing strung from a line on the ceiling that stretched from one end of the room to another.

'It's getting to look like a Chinese laundry in here,' he had teased her. 'If I'm not careful you'll be putting me in the copper next.'

'I don't think you'd fit in,' she smiled back, but the smile did nothing to hide the fear and heartache she was feeling and he saw through her brave front and felt her pain.

Strangely, he found that he too was missing Danny more than he could have imagined, and it came as quite a shock to him. He came home late one afternoon to find Maggie in the dining room gazing up in awe at the portrait of the fair-haired woman.

'Did you paint this?' she dared to ask.

As his eyes locked onto the portrait, he nodded.

'She's very beautiful,' Maggie said.

'*Was,*' he told her. 'She *was* beautiful. She's dead now, but . . . she was my wife.'

Maggie stared at him in dismay. 'Oh, Eric, I'm so sorry. Trust me to go and put my big foot in it again.'

She half-expected him to storm away again, but instead he slowly shook his head. 'Don't be. You weren't to know.' His eyes grew misty as he gazed at the serene face in the picture. 'Her name was Georgia,' he told her and she held her breath. 'She came from a very good family and they weren't altogether thrilled when she took up with me. I think they had set their sights higher for her. But you know what it's like when you fall in love. We would have eaten beans just so long as we could be together. As it turned out, she would have been better to listen to them. If she had, she'd still be alive.'

'I'm sure that's not true,' Maggie whispered, and without thinking, she reached out and gently took his hand. It was the first physical contact they'd had and she was surprised when his large fingers curled around her smaller ones. A tear squeezed out of the corner of his good eye and she suddenly had the urge to wipe it away. She controlled the feeling and feeling strangely embarrassed, slid her fingers from his.

'I think it's about time we both had a break,' she said, hoping to lighten the mood, and turning about, she hurried from the room.

It was much later that evening when she found her eyes drawn to the small easel in the corner again. 'Did you do that painting too?' she asked Eric.

The man gulped as he struggled to find the right words.

'Actually, no, I didn't. Danny did it. He has a real flair for art, as you're probably aware. It was meant to be his Christmas present to you. I promised him I'd get it framed for you when it was finished.'

'Oh!' Suddenly, Maggie couldn't hold back her pent-up emotions for another second and a strangled sob escaped her as she bent her head into her hands.

Eric was beside her in a trice and gathered her into his arms. 'Please, Maggie, don't cry,' he soothed as he rocked her back and forth. 'Danny will be all right, and so will Lizzie. You'll see.'

The time was ticking away and Maggie wasn't so sure now.

'Please, can I come with you when you go out searching tomorrow?' she pleaded through her sobs. 'I feel as if I shall go mad if I have to sit here waiting for news for another single day.'

He suddenly realised how selfish he had been, leaving her alone for hour after hour. He'd thought he was saving her from having to tramp through the bitterly cold drifts, but now he understood her need to be involved in the search for her children.

'Of course you can, if that's what you want,' he promised. 'We'll start to look for them again first thing tomorrow.'

Sighing, she nestled back into his arms, enjoying the comforting warmth of another human being.

Chapter Thirty-Six

Maggie was up at first light and wrapped for outdoors by the time Eric put in an appearance.

'You're an early worm,' he remarked as he crossed to the teapot on the table.

'Well, you know what they say. The early bird catches the worm,' she smiled. She felt much better today, now that she was finally going to be allowed to join in the search. Sensing her need to be doing something constructive, Eric gulped a cup of tea down and hastily got ready.

Within minutes they were on their way down the hillside. Thankfully there had been no fresh snowfalls for two days, but the snow that remained was hardpacked and frozen, making it treacherous underfoot. More than once, Maggie would have gone headfirst, had Eric not caught her, but she ploughed on regardless.

The village was just coming to life when they turned onto the road that led through it and Maggie saw a small pasty-faced boy leaning against a lamppost.

She smiled at him as they went to walk past and he suddenly asked, 'Are you Danny's mam?'

Maggie paused. 'Yes, I am,' she told him solemnly. 'Do you know him?'

'Course I do,' he retorted. ''E's me mate. Me name's Sparky.'

'How do you do, Sparky. Danny mentioned you in his letters.' As a thought occurred to her she asked hopefully, '*You* don't happen to know where he is, do you?'

'Nah,' Sparky wheezed, and she was troubled to see the blue tinge that had settled around his lips.

'Oh . . . Well, thanks anyway.' Masking her disappointment, she was just about to move on when Sparky piped up, 'I know where Lizzie is though.'

Maggie gripped tight to Eric's arm as she gazed at him incredulously, hardly daring to believe her ears. 'Are you quite sure?'

He nodded as he pulled himself away from the lamppost. 'I could take yer to 'er if yer liked. But I warn yer, it's a long way ter go.'

Hardly daring to believe him, she stared at Eric. By now, a few of the village men had emerged from their homes to start the search for Lizzie, just as they had every single day since she had disappeared.

One of them shook his head doubtfully. 'You're not at your best, Sparky. Perhaps it would be easier if you just *told* us where she is.'

Sparky shrugged. 'I can't tell yer the way, I can only show yer. An' I'll be all right, 'onest I will.'

The police officer who had visited *Tremarfon* earlier in the week had also joined them by now and he took control of the situation immediately.

'Very well. If the lad says he's all right to lead us, we have to take his word for it.'

One of the village men leaned towards him and whispered, 'Sparky isn't all the ticket, you know. He could be dragging us all off on a wild-goose chase.'

'You're quite right,' the policeman answered coolly. 'But do you want to take the risk of *not* checking it out?'

'I suppose not,' the small, grey-haired man muttered.

With Sparky leading, the procession began to wend its way through the village. Maggie's heart was pounding so loudly against her ribcage that she was sure the others must be able to hear it. With every step she took, she breathed a silent prayer that they would find her daughter safe and well, but she couldn't rid herself of a terrible sense of foreboding. If what she had heard was true, then Blodwyn Evans had lost her mind and could be capable of anything.

Going up the mountainside was a steep climb and extremely slippery, and before long, Sparky was gasping for breath though he kept going gamely on. The air seemed to get thinner the higher they went, and soon the whole of the silent party was puffing and panting, Sparky most of all.

On a few occasions Maggie found herself looking at him and thinking, What if he collapses before he shows us where Lizzie is? Then she chided herself for having such selfish thoughts. To the right of them was a sheer drop to the deserted beach below, where waves pounded relentlessly onto the shore.

The peak of the hill was shrouded in a thick mist, and Maggie began to fear that they would never reach the top of it. But then, just as she was beginning to despair, Sparky turned away from the steep drop and began to walk in the opposite direction. Maggie had the awful feeling that perhaps he didn't know where Lizzie was, after all. How could he, when everywhere looked the same in the snow? Nevertheless, she followed him, very aware that his steps were slowing and his breath was coming in harsh, painful gasps. He suddenly stopped dead and clutched at his side, as his shaking finger pointed to the left of him.

'You'll find some old miners' cottages a bit further on. Lizzie is in one o' them,' he wheezed.

Eric and some of the villagers began to hurry on whilst Maggie paused to look at Sparky with concern. 'Are you all right?' she asked as he sank to the ground.

He nodded weakly. 'I'm fine, missus. Now you get off an' find Lizzie, eh?'

Maggie felt torn between anxiety for the brave lad and her need to find Lizzie, but thankfully one of the village men solved her problem.

'I'll stay here with the little one,' he said kindly. 'You go and see if your girl is where he says she is.'

Maggie took off as if she had wings on her heels and in no time at all had caught the rest of the party up.

'There they are!' someone suddenly shouted, and sure enough, as Maggie peered into the mist, a row of near-derelict cottages came into view.

The policeman who had accompanied them flapped his hands at them and they all drew to a halt. 'Now,' he said quietly, 'we need to do this properly.' Leaning towards Eric, he whispered, 'If Blodwyn and Lizzie *are* here and Blodwyn hears us coming, there's no telling what she might do in the state of mind she's in.' Turning to the small party he instructed, 'You, Bill, and you, Owen, go around the back. Eric, you come with me to the front, and the rest of you keep your eyes open.'

Silently, they began to steal forward, their footsteps making no sound on the soft blanket of virgin snow. As they drew closer, they saw a small wisp of smoke rising from one of the chimneys and the policeman put his finger to his lips, demanding total silence. With her heart in her mouth, Maggie crept on, keeping as close to Eric as she could. As they approached one of the few remaining doors left intact, the policeman pointed down and they saw some fresh footsteps in the snow.

Taking his truncheon from his belt, the policeman pulled himself to his full height and then after taking a deep breath, he shouted, 'NOW!'

Plunging forward, he pushed hard on the door, sending it crashing back onto the wall behind it. An overpowering smell of damp and urine met them as they stormed into the room, but at first glance it seemed to be deserted. There was a small fire burning in the fireplace but nothing else except for a small suitcase and a bundle of old rags in a far corner.

Maggie felt tears of despair well in her eyes. But then she thought she saw the bundle of rags move. Even as she watched, a small, bewildered face appeared and she uttered a cry of relief. '*LIZZIE!*'

In seconds she had covered the distance between them and snatched the child into her arms as she covered her with kisses.

Eric felt a lump form in his throat as he offered up a silent prayer of thanks.

'Mammy . . . is that you?' Lizzie hardly dared believe it as she looked up at the face she had been longing to see.

It was as they were all standing there that a shadow suddenly appeared in the doorway. Blodwyn Evans, her arms full of twigs that she had dug out of the snow, was staring disbelievingly at them.

'*What do you want?*' she screeched as she saw Lizzie cradled in her mother's arms. 'Go away, the lot of you, and leave me and my Megan in peace, can't you? Megan – come to me, *bach*.'

When the child cowered closer against her mother, Blodwyn's face fell and the policeman took a step towards her. 'Now Blodwyn, calm down,' he whispered soothingly. 'This is *not* your Megan. It's Lizzie Bright and her mother is here to take her home. You come with me now. I can get you some help.'

Dropping the twigs, she slapped his hand away as he held it out towards her. Then she began to back out of the door, her eyes shining with madness. 'I know where you want to take me,' she screamed accusingly. 'You want to lock me up in the madhouse as you tried to, many years ago. But I won't come with you. Do you hear me?' Turning, she began to run across the frozen ground with surprising speed. The policeman started after her, his heart in his mouth as he saw that she was heading directly for the cliff edge.

'Blodwyn, *stop!*' he bellowed as he became aware of her intentions, but it was too late. She disappeared into the mist and seconds later, they all heard a bloodcurdling scream. When he arrived at the edge of the cliff seconds later, he warily peered over, and there, far below him, was the big woman's broken body, lying on the rocks. Even as he watched, the waves came in and snatched at her body and when next he looked, she had been sucked out to sea.

It was a sombre procession that wove its way back down to the village. One of the men carried Sparky, who was struggling for breath, whilst Eric carried Lizzie close to his chest, and Maggie clung on to her hand as if she were afraid to let her go.

As soon as the cottages of Sarn-Bach came into sight, one of the men ran for the doctor to see to Sparky.

Outside his home, Maggie kissed his sweating brow tenderly. 'Thank you, Sparky,' she whispered and he smiled weakly back at her. She turned to leave but then paused and asked him, 'What made you decide to tell us where she was?'

'Soho Gus came to me while I were in bed last night an' told me to,' he panted.

Maggie looked at Eric in confusion. 'Isn't Soho Gus the little boy that ran away with Danny?'

As confused as she was, he nodded. 'Yes, it is, so perhaps they're still around here somewhere too?'

'*No.*' Sparky shook his head. 'Gus told me that Danny was . . .' A coughing fit stopped him from going any further as the man who was holding him carried him over the threshhold.

'I'm sorry, but the child has had enough for now. You can talk to him later when the doctor has seen him. I'll send him up to *Tremarfon* to check Lizzie over when he's done with Sparky.'

Eric nodded his thanks and moved on, with Maggie running to keep up with him. Not another word passed between them until he had kicked the door to *Tremarfon* open and laid Lizzie down on the settee. Then, crossing to the kettle, he told Maggie, 'We need to get something warm inside her. I think she's in shock.'

Maggie nodded as she ran to fetch a warm blanket to tuck around her. Lizzie's eyes were blank and unseeing, and Maggie felt panic beginning to rise inside her.

'She'll be all right, won't she?' she asked Eric fearfully.

He nodded. 'Of course she will. But you have to understand she's been through a very difficult time, shut away up there with a madwoman.' He shuddered as he recalled the sight of Blodwyn's broken body lying on the rocks. Despite what she had done, he couldn't help but feel a measure of sympathy for her, though he doubted that Maggie would. Given what the woman had put her daughter and herself through, he could hardly blame her.

'Let's just keep her warm and quiet until the doctor

comes, eh?' he suggested. Nodding, Maggie turned her attention back to her child.

Much later that evening, as they sat by the fire sipping hot cocoa, a sudden thought occurred to Maggie.

'Didn't you find what Sparky said about Soho Gus going to see him rather strange?'

Eric eyed her curiously. 'Strange in what way?'

'Well, think about it. Sparky said that Gus had come to see him *during* the night, but if that's the case, how would he have got in? And if they're still round about here, why hasn't Danny come home?'

'Mmm, I see what you mean,' he admitted. 'But you know – you have to take what Sparky says with a pinch of salt. The child is . . .' He struggled to find a nice way to put it before deciding on, 'He's a little backward, to say the least.'

'I do hope he's going to be all right,' Maggie fretted. 'If what the doctor told us earlier was true, then the poor child is far from well.'

'He was far from well *before* today's escapade,' Eric told her truthfully. 'Sparky has a heart condition and since losing his family during a raid on London, the poor little chap seems to have deteriorated. I'm amazed that he managed to lead us all that way today. Still, we need to try and look on the bright side. At least Lizzie is safe now, and if what the doctor says is true, then she'll be as right as rain in a few days. Children are far more resilient than we give them credit for.'

Maggie looked across at the child who was still curled up fast asleep on the settee. Eric had offered to carry her upstairs hours ago, but as yet, Maggie couldn't bear to let the little girl out of her sight.

'I suppose now that I know she's safe, I *should* be

thinking of getting back to Coventry to look for Danny. The trouble is, the raids are still going on there and I don't want to take her out of one unsafe situation just to put her straight back into another one.'

'Then you have a couple of options, don't you? One is, you could leave her here with me. The second is, *you* could stay a while longer too. The police in the village are keeping in constant touch with the force back in Coventry, and as soon as they have any news at all they've promised to let us know. They will call round to your mother-in-law's to inform her that Lizzie is safe, and tomorrow you'll need to break the news about her family being dead to her. It isn't going to be easy for the child.'

Maggie nodded in agreement, and as she looked across at Eric she suddenly wondered how she could ever have considered him unattractive. The scars were still there, as plain as day, and yet now that she'd looked beyond them and pierced the hard front that he wore like a suit of armour, she saw a very different Eric. With the firelight playing on his thick mop of black hair he looked almost attractive, and her heart gave a funny little lurch.

Blushing fiercely, she dragged her eyes away from him to stare into the fire.

'I really don't know why you've been so kind to us all,' she muttered. 'All I can say is, thank you. I would have thought you'd be glad to see the back of all of us by now, after all the trouble we've brought to your door.'

Eric was temporarily at a loss as to how to answer her. Just a few short weeks ago he had hated having to take a child into his home, and yet now he missed Danny more than he could ever have dreamed. And Maggie; since she'd been staying with him he had started to enjoy coming home to a friendly face and a cosy house. He realised with a little jolt that he would miss her terribly

437

when she left. The realisation angered him. What sort of silly game was he playing anyway? Hadn't he seen quite clearly the look of revulsion that had crossed her face the first time she saw him? Why should she think any differently about him now? He had promised himself that he would never allow himself to love anyone ever again, and yet here he was, letting his heart rule his head.

'Well, think about what I've said,' he told her, rising abruptly. 'I'm off to bed. Would you like me to carry Lizzie up for you?'

'Yes, please.' Maggie had the strangest feeling that she had somehow upset him, but had no idea how. Eric was a very hard man to understand, as she was discovering. Warm as a blanket one minute and then cold as ice the next.

Sighing, she followed him to the settee where he lifted Lizzie, who didn't even blink, into his arms. Maggie ran up the stairs ahead of him and opened her bedroom door, then crossing swiftly to the bed she threw the bedclothes back and asked him, 'Would you put her in here? I'd like her in with me tonight, if you don't mind.'

He laid the child down as if she was made of china, and then backed towards the door. Pausing with his hand on the door handle, he looked at mother and daughter, and the sight of Maggie tenderly tucking her child in touched him deeply. It seemed such a very long time since anyone had looked at him with love shining from their eyes. Closing the door softly, he made his way along the landing to his lonely room.

Deep into the night, Eric tossed and turned as sleep evaded him. Eventually, he slipped out of bed and pulled his trousers on before quietly creeping along the landing and down the stairs. Samson stirred from his place in front of the fire when Eric entered the kitchen, but when he saw his master he laid his head back on his paws and went straight back to sleep.

Moving to the kitchen window, Eric stared out into the black night. The wind was howling through the trees, making them appear as if they were involved in some twisted macabre dance. He found himself thinking of Danny, hoping desperately that he had found shelter somewhere.

Strangely restless still, he padded across the hall and into the dining room. After clicking on the light he again stood in front of his late wife's portrait. Staring up into her lovely face, a great sadness overwhelmed him and he felt the urge to cry.

'You must miss her very much.'

Spinning around, Eric found Maggie watching him with a look of deep sympathy on her face.

He opened his mouth to tell her to mind her own business, but then snapped it shut again. He was tired of always being on his guard; tired of the guilt that gnawed away at him like hungry maggots day and night. Maggie of all people must know how he felt. After all, she had lost her own husband not so long ago. He wondered if she hurt as he did.

Suddenly realising that he wasn't wearing his eyepatch, his hand instinctively flew up to cover the empty socket where his eye had once been.

'You don't have to do that in front of me.' Her voice was kind. 'In fact, I think you look far nicer without it.' She led him to the door and, after clicking off the light, ushered him towards the kitchen where she sat him down in a chair.

'Now,' she told him, 'I'm going to spoil *you* for a change. I'm going to make us both a nice hot drink, with some of that shortbread I made the other day, and then we're going to talk. I think it's time – don't you?'

He watched as she bustled about the room rattling cups and spoons and looking for all the world as if she belonged there. When she eventually joined him, she sipped at her cocoa and looked at him solemnly over the rim of her mug. She said not a word, and the only sound to be heard was the ticking of the clock on the mantelpiece.

It was Eric who eventually broke the silence when he asked, 'Do you miss your husband?'

'Not really.' Somehow Maggie felt that she could be truthful with Eric. 'Our marriage was never a bed of roses, if I am to be honest, and I'd be a hypocrite to say it was. But it wasn't his fault – not really. I think I have to shoulder the worst of the blame.'

When his eyebrows rose in confusion she slowly began to tell him of her life. She told him about how she had fallen in love with David, and the way she had betrayed him, albeit unknowingly, with his twin brother. And as the sorry tale unfolded, the tears slid unchecked down her cheeks.

Eric listened in silence and thought he had never heard such a sad tale in the whole of his life. 'But David is home again now, isn't he?'

She nodded. 'Yes, but he's not the David I knew any more. Too much has happened to him – to both of us, if it comes to that. All I care about now is being reunited with Danny, then I'll find somewhere for us to live, and we'll get on with our lives again.'

'That might be easier said than done.'

She stared at him. 'What do you mean by that?'

'I mean that things don't always work out as we'd like them to. I'm a prime example. After Georgia died I bought this place and thought I could leave the heartache and the guilt behind. But I couldn't. It has a habit of following you.'

'But why should *you* feel guilty?'

For a moment Maggie was sure that he was going to shut down again as he normally did whenever he spoke of anything personal. Then he took a deep breath and told her, 'If my wife hadn't married me against her family's wishes she would still be alive today.' His mind began to skip back over the years, and suddenly all the feelings he had bottled up inside for so long poured out of him.

'Georgia was very upper class compared to me. You know – born with a silver spoon in her mouth and all that. I met her at an art exhibition in London, and from the moment I set eyes on her, I knew she was the girl for me. The biggest shock was that she felt exactly the same way about me. I could hardly believe my luck. I was a struggling young artist living in a dingy basement in the Charing Cross Road, but she didn't care. Neither of us did, as long as we could be together. The problem was, her family had other ideas. She had a cousin who was an up-and-coming barrister, and it seems that from when he and Georgia were young, the families had earmarked them for marriage. They were totally appalled when Georgia announced that we wanted to get married. "What can he offer you?" they asked her. She just laughed and said that as long as we could be together, she'd be happy to live on dry bread. They then told her that if she went ahead with what they called "this foolhardy idea", they would stop supporting her. So – to cut a long story short – we went ahead and got married, and that's exactly what they did.' His eyes had taken on a faraway look as Maggie waited for him to go on.

'We lived in that little flat for three years and at first it was really hard. Georgia had to go out and get a job to make ends meet. I told her that I'd do it but she wouldn't let me. "You're going to become a well-known artist one day," she told me. She believed in me, and sure enough, slowly my paintings began to sell. After a time I told her we could afford to move to somewhere better, but by then she was quite happy where we were. She had the knack of making a home out of nothing, a bit like you, I suppose, so we decided to stay where we were for a while longer and save every penny we could. My big break came when I began to do illustrations for children's books. That's how I earn my living now. I post them off to London each week and at the end of every month I get a cheque. Anyway, one night I was a bit behind with my work so I decided to stay up late and carry on. The light in the flat wasn't very good, especially at night, so when Georgia went off to bed I lit some candles and stayed up at my drawing-board. I was tired and must have fallen asleep. The next thing I know, there's someone hammering at the door and the flat is full of smoke. One of the candles must have fallen over and set fire to the drawings I was working on, and the whole place went up like a box of kindling.' He paused and had to take a deep breath before going on. 'By the time the firemen had broken the door down I'd headed off to the bedroom to try and get Georgia out . . . and that's the last thing I remember until I woke up in hospital the next day.' His eyes were so full of raw pain that Maggie could almost feel it.

'I got these.' He touched the scars on his face. 'But Georgia didn't make it. She died from smoke inhalation.'

'Oh, Eric, how *awful*. But you shouldn't blame yourself. It was an accident.' Maggie's heart went out to him as she tenderly wiped the tears from his cheeks, and suddenly he was sobbing in her arms as she cradled him against her chest.

In that moment she felt closer to him than she had ever felt to anyone in her whole life. Probably because they had both suffered so very much and were continuing to suffer.

Chapter Thirty-Seven

The next morning, Lizzie developed a raging temperature. Maggie was almost beside herself with worry as she mopped the child's sweating brow again and again with a cool flannel. Eventually, Eric decided to walk down into the village and get the doctor to come back up to *Tremarfon* to look at her.

She flashed him a grateful smile, very aware that they were causing him a great deal of trouble.

'It's really kind of you,' she told him for at least the dozenth time. He waved aside her thanks. In actual fact, he was glad of an excuse to get down to the village, for as he'd lain in bed and relived the episode of the day before, something had come back to him. It was something Sparky had said when they arrived back in the village. Eric remembered commenting that if Gus had visited Sparky in his bedroom, then perhaps both boys were still somewhere close to the village? Sparky had denied it and had begun to tell him that, 'Danny was . . .' then a coughing fit had stopped him from going any further. Perhaps he'd been about to tell them where the boys were?

Not wishing to raise Maggie's hopes, he decided to call in and see if the child was well enough to talk to him. But first he would call on the doctor and arrange for him to visit Lizzie.

Nodding his goodbyes to Maggie and Lizzie, he turned to set off.

'Oh, just a second. Could you pick these up for me from the village shop while you're down there?' Maggie asked. 'It's just a few bits we're running short of and something for dinner.'

He smiled wryly as he tucked the list into his pocket. He was beginning to feel like an old married man, which would be quite funny if it weren't so frightening. After reaching the village, he collected the supplies first then headed for the doctor's house.

Luckily the doctor was in when Eric arrived and he assured Eric that he would call in at *Tremarfon* later in the day. 'It's been a bad business all the way round!' he exclaimed sadly as he shook his head. 'Let's just thank God that Lizzie came out of it as well as she did. It's a pity that Sparky didn't fare so well though, the poor little soul.'

'What do you mean?' Eric demanded.

The other man sighed. 'I'm so sorry, Mr Sinclair. Of course, you couldn't have heard, could you, stuck up there in the hills. Sparky died last night. It wasn't totally unexpected, I have to say, so I don't want you or Mrs Bright to blame yourselves. Sparky had been a very poorly little boy for a very long time. To be honest, I'm amazed that he lasted as long as he did. He had a very severe heart condition, and in the end his heart just gave out. His ending was very peaceful though, which is something we should be thankful for, I suppose.'

Eric leaned heavily against the doorframe as shock overcame him. So the poor little chap had passed away. At least he had died a hero, but now he wouldn't be able to tell him where Gus and Danny were.

Mumbling his thanks, he stumbled out of the doctor's

and began to make his way home. How would Maggie take the news when he told her? He shuddered to think, as he moved along on feet that felt as heavy as lead.

As he neared *Tremarfon* he saw Maggie looking out of the window for him with a wide smile on her face. When he walked into the kitchen, frozen to the bone, he soon saw why. Lizzie was propped up on cushions on the settee sipping hot milk and looking much better.

'I think it's just a heavy cold,' Maggie told him as she took the supplies from Eric and helped him out of his coat. He smiled with relief as he went to hold his frozen fingers out to the warmth of the fire.

'Well, that's good to hear. If she's come out of all this with nothing worse, then I think she's been extremely lucky. The doctor will be calling round later on, just to make sure. Meantime, is there any tea left in that pot? I'm dry as a bone. It's absolutely bitter out there.'

'Of course.' Maggie hurried away to fetch a cup and as he stood there he wondered how he should tell her about Sparky. Knowing what a soft heart she had, she was bound to take the news badly.

Once he'd drained his cup, he gently took her elbow and led her towards the deep stone sink, out of earshot of Lizzie. 'Maggie . . .' he began hesitantly. There seemed no easy way to tell her the terrible news so he ended up just blurting it out. 'I'm afraid Sparky died last night. According to the doctor it was only a matter of time. His heart condition was very severe.'

'I see,' she said softly as tears filled her eyes. She seemed to have shed so many tears over the last few months that it was always a shock to her when more came that she had any left to cry. 'Then may God bless his soul. Without him, we would never have found Lizzie.'

Heads bowed, they both thought of the brave little boy. The world would be a much sadder place without him. They could only pray that somewhere he would be reunited with his family again.

It was as they were still standing there that Eric said quietly, 'Have you broken the news to Lizzie yet about Danny being missing, and about everything else?'

Maggie shook her head, her eyes full of fear at the prospect, yet she knew that she could put it off no longer. 'I'll go and do it now,' she said, and Eric left the room. Eventually, he heard Lizzie begin to sob. As the sound tore through him he squeezed his eyes tight shut and turning about, he walked swiftly away.

'Eeh, I really don't know how much more o' this I can take,' Beryl fretted as she sat at the kitchen table. She was stiff and sore from yet another night spent huddled in the cupboard under the stairs. The bombing just seemed to be going on and on, and now she was weary of it.

'If the buggers start up again tonight I'm stoppin' in me own bed an' takin' me chances,' she declared as she sipped at the hot sweet tea Jo had made her.

Grinning, Jo handed a cup to David, who grinned back at her. The look that passed between them was not lost on Beryl, and she sighed. Those two were getting on like a house on fire these days. The week before, they had been subjected to yet another terrible raid that had lasted almost all night, and David had reacted badly to it. Jo had insisted on staying in his room with him, talking to him soothingly and holding his hand, and ever since then she seemed to have taken on the role of his carer. If he cried out in the night, in the grip of some terrible nightmare, as he frequently did, it was now Jo who would go to him and comfort him. She would cut his meal up for him and pander to his every whim, which was all very well from where Beryl was standing, but what would happen when Maggie got back home? She had always seen David and Maggie as a couple despite the fact that Maggie had married Sam, but now . . . Narrowing her eyes, she watched them. Perhaps it was just her reading too much into the way they were together. After all, she had to admit, Jo was a kind-hearted girl and would probably have shown the same care and concern for anyone in David's position.

When a sharp rap came to the front door she started.

'I'll get it,' Jo offered, jumping up from her seat at David's side. 'I bet it's the police again, come to give us an update on the search for Danny.'

Beryl nodded in agreement. 'Happen yer right an' God willin' they'll be bringin' us *good* news fer a change.'

The weary stoop of Jo's shoulders told their own story when she next came back into the room. 'No word on Danny as yet,' she told them, 'but thank goodness, Lizzie has been found safe. The policeman told me that Maggie is going to stay with her as the little one isn't too well at present, then no doubt she'll come back to wait for news of Danny.'

'Aw well. Thank the Lord *one* of 'em is accounted for,' Beryl muttered, tears of relief in her eyes, but where in God's name could Danny be?

That night, Beryl Bright simply couldn't get off to sleep, which was surprising, because after all the disturbed nights she'd suffered recently, she was tired out. Eventually she slipped into a restless doze, and it was then that the strangest thing happened, for suddenly she became aware of someone standing at the side of the bed. She rolled over to find herself looking at a little boy with startling red hair who was holding what appeared to be a large white mouse or rat in his hand. She felt no fear. In fact, it seemed like the most natural thing in the world that he should be there.

''Ere, are you Danny's nan?' he asked, with an unmistakable cockney accent.

'That I am.' Beryl's head bounced eagerly on her shoulders at the mention of her grandson. 'Why, who's askin'?'

'It don't matter who I am,' he told her cheekily. 'I've come to tell yer where Danny is.'

'Oh yes, an' how would you know that then?'

'Let's just say I do.' He tapped the side of his nose knowingly. 'Now, do yer want me to tell yer or what?'

'Of course I do,' Beryl snapped as hope grew in her heart. 'I just hope this ain't some sort o' cruel joke though, 'cos we've been goin' out of our heads wi' worry about him.'

'Right. Well, you'll find 'im in the Coventry an' Warwick Hospital.'

Rolling over, Beryl immediately slipped back into a deep sleep.

Both Jo and David remarked on how quiet she was the next morning at breakfast and eventually she told them, 'Do yer know, I had the weirdest dream last night. I dreamed this little boy was in my room. He said that our Danny was in the Coventry an' Warwick Hospital.'

'Dreams can be funny things,' Jo said as she scraped some marge onto a slice of toast.

'Yes, I know that,' Beryl said in a state of great agitation. 'But it was so real, almost as if he was really there.'

'But we've already checked all the hospitals, Mam,' David pointed out.

'I know we have,' Beryl agreed, 'but all the same I

449

feel as if I ought to check again. Come on – let's get us coats on. It can't do any harm, can it?'

Realising that they would get no peace until they'd done as she asked, Jo and David put their coats on, and in no time at all, they had all set off through their fallen city. David peered up at the spire of the once-magnificent Cathedral and silently cursed the war that had caused it to fall. But his heart was lighter than it had been for some time, now that he knew at least Lizzie was safe, and he tried to concentrate on what they were doing.

The hospital was in total chaos from the casualties that had been brought in. People were lying on stretchers in corridors, and harassed doctors and nurses were running to and fro.

Beryl lifted her handbag higher and purposefully approached the reception desk. 'I've been told me grandson is in here,' she told a ferret-faced receptionist.

'Name?' the woman asked impersonally.

Controlling her temper, Beryl snapped back, 'Daniel Bright!'

'Age?'

'Ten years.'

The woman began to run her finger down a seemingly endless list of patients as Beryl tapped her foot impatiently.

Eventually the receptionist shook her head. 'I've no one of that name listed here.'

'You *must* have,' Beryl insisted, and when the woman saw that she wasn't going to budge, she sighed.

'I'll pass you on to someone who might be able to help you,' she told her eventually. 'We do have a ward full of people who had no identity on them when they were brought in, so there is a *faint* chance that he could be amongst them.'

Beryl nodded grimly as the woman rose from her seat and bustled away down a corridor. Some minutes later, she returned with a young nurse who looked fit to drop.

'Would you like to follow me?' she asked tiredly and they all nodded. They seemed to walk for a long time through corridors that smelled of whitewash, stale disinfectant and death. At last she stopped at some doors that led into a ward.

'How old did you say your grandson was?' she asked. 'Danny is ten.'

'Mmm . . . Well, I don't want to raise your hopes, but it just so happens that we *do* have a little boy of about that age in. I'm afraid the shock of his injuries and what he must have gone through have made him lose his memory. But if he is your grandson, seeing you might be just the medicine he needs. Would you like to come with me?'

Beryl could only nod numbly as fear blocked her throat. The nurse pushed the double doors open and they found themselves in a long ward. On either side were neatly made beds full of people of all ages, shapes and sizes.

'This way,' the nurse told them, and they all silently trailed after her. About halfway down the ward she pointed to a bed that had curtains pulled around it.

'The only one we have remotely answering your description is the child in there,' she told them. 'I'm afraid if he isn't Danny, then I can't help you. Are you ready to go in?'

Jo slipped her hand into David's and squeezed it as Beryl solemnly nodded. Swishing the curtain aside, the nurse waited for Beryl to step past her. She found her eyes focused on a large metal cage that completely covered the child's legs. Then they slowly travelled up the bed and there was Danny, looking very pale and ill, but it was Danny all the same.

'*Oh, thank the Lord!*' Beryl exclaimed, and as she fell on her grandson, tears of joy began to rain down her face.

'Right, how about you joining me in a glass of wine then? I picked it up on impulse while I was down in the village and I don't much like drinking alone.'

Maggie chewed on her lip. She'd never been much of a drinker, but then a couple of glasses couldn't hurt, could it?

'All right then,' she agreed as Eric scrabbled around in the kitchen drawer for a corkscrew. Lizzie, who was getting better every day, was fast asleep upstairs, and Maggie decided it might be nice to unwind a bit.

Eric turned the wireless on and the haunting strains of Vera Lynn floated around the room. By the time she was halfway down her glass, Maggie felt herself relaxing a little for the first time in weeks. The room was warm and cosy and the light from the fire was making her feel sleepy.

As Eric topped up her glass, he noticed the way the firelight was turning her hair to the colour of spun gold and his heart began to hammer. She was so beautiful that it hurt him to look at her. But her beauty was not just on the outside. Maggie Bright was beautiful on the inside too, as he'd discovered over the time she had been staying with him.

When their hands accidentally touched, he felt an electric shock pass through him and he knew that she had felt it too, for her eyes suddenly opened wide as she looked up at him.

Dropping onto the seat beside her, he muttered, 'I shall miss you when you go, Maggie.'

'I shall miss you too,' she said wistfully, and she meant it, for she knew now, without a shadow of a doubt, that she was falling in love with him. Oh, she knew it was foolish and that nothing could ever come of it, but Eric was like no man she had ever known. Not even David. But Eric was still in love with his late wife – he'd made that abundantly clear – and soon she would be gone from him forever and he would be left with his memories.

The thought brought tears to her eyes, and as he saw them trembling on her lashes he hesitantly reached out to wipe them away. When her hand came up to caress his, their eyes locked and then suddenly they were in each other's arms.

'Oh, Maggie.' His voice was strangled with emotion as they fell back in a heap on the settee, and then their lips were joined and a million fireworks exploded behind her eyes.

His hand was roving over her, leaving trails of fire, and she recklessly gave herself up to the pleasure of it, then somehow they were on the hearthrug with their clothes discarded in a heap, and feelings that she'd never known she had sprang to life as they tenderly made love to each other.

When it was finally over she lay in his arms, knowing that, whatever happened in the future, she would cherish this memory until the day she died.

At some point they both drifted off into a contented sleep, and only the sound of heavy pounding on the door brought them springing awake.

Eric jumped up and began to pull his clothes on, and suddenly embarrassed, Maggie did the same. Buttoning his flies, Eric disappeared into the hallway, and as she was running her fingers through her wild hair, Maggie heard voices at the door. Seconds later, Eric reappeared, closely followed by the policeman from the village who was gripping his helmet tightly in both hands.

Her embarrassment fled, to be replaced by fear.

'You've got some news about Danny, haven't you?' she whispered.

His head bobbed. 'Yes, ma'am. We took a call from Coventry this morning. Your son has been found in the Coventry and Warwick Hospital.'

'Why is he in hospital?' Her face had paled to the colour of putty, yet overriding her fear was relief that he was alive.

The portly policeman shrugged. 'They didn't say what his injuries were. Only that he was in the hospital.'

'What about Soho Gus?' Eric asked.

Taking his notebook from his pocket, the man flipped through his notes. 'It appears that when Danny was found, there *was* another child with him. It seems that the poor little lad didn't make it. As he had no identity disc on him he was buried in the communal grave in the London Road Cemetery.'

Maggie shook her head in denial. 'That can't be right. Sparky told us that Gus had been to see him on the night before we found Lizzie.'

Again the policeman shrugged. 'I don't know about that, ma'am. All I know is what the police at Coventry have told us.'

Maggie shuddered. 'I have to go to Danny,' she said hoarsely.

A feeling of loss settled over Eric like a heavy weight. Once she got home, Maggie would resume her relationship with David and would be lost to him forever. But then, had he really ever expected her to stay?

'You're right,' he said flatly. 'Danny needs you. You should go to him.'

Maggie thought that she heard a note of regret in his voice but then dismissed the idea. He was probably just glad to get rid of her after what had happened between them last night.

'But what about Lizzie?' she said suddenly. The child was growing stronger by the day but was nowhere near well enough to face the journey home yet.

'Lizzie can stay here with me for as long as you like,' Eric assured her. 'Now you just go and pack your case. The officer here can help you down the hill with it and see you get to the train too, no doubt.'

'Of course I will, sir,' the policeman told him respectfully as Maggie slowly turned away.

Within half an hour she had packed her case, washed and tidied herself and was ready to go. Lizzie was tearful but happy enough to stay with Eric, which was one weight off her mind at least.

At the door she held her hand out awkwardly. 'Thank you so much for all you've done. I'll be sure to write as soon as I've seen Danny, to let you know how he is. And to make arrangements about Lizzie, of course.'

They shook hands, like a pair of strangers, and as Maggie turned away she felt as if her heart was breaking.

Chapter Thirty-Eight

She noticed the change the second she walked through the door, yet couldn't quite put her finger on what it was. Beryl fussed over her, and Jo and David both seemed delighted to see her, and yet . . . something was different.

The journey back had seemed to take forever, for once again, the train had been diverted countless times due to damage to the tracks. Maggie was feeling absolutely worn out, but nevertheless she was determined to see Danny that very night, as she told them within minutes of getting home.

She saw them exchange a worried glance and knew instinctively that something was very wrong. 'So what exactly is the matter with him?' She didn't want to know, yet was aware that she had to face whatever it was.

Beryl fished in her pinny pocket for a huge white handkerchief, which she noisily sniffed into while Jo looked at David imploringly.

'The thing is, Maggie,' David began awkwardly, 'Danny is actually very lucky to be alive, but . . .'

'But what?' Her nerves were stretched to the limit and there was murder in her eyes as she glared at him across the table.

'The boys were near a building that took a direct hit, and Danny's legs were trapped under falling debris . . .'

David took a deep gulp before finishing, 'He's lost both of his legs.'

'No! Oh, dear God, no!' Maggie was almost beside herself with grief. After all she had gone through, this latest tragedy was just too much to bear.

Openly sobbing, Beryl ran around the table and hugged her daughter-in-law's shaking frame to her. 'Be thankful fer small mercies, love. At least he's still alive, which is more than can be said fer the poor little bugger that came with him.'

Maggie thought of Sparky and poor Soho Gus. As Beryl had quite rightly pointed out, Danny was alive, which was more than could be said for those unfortunate little souls.

'I'd better get off to the hospital.' She made to rise from the table but Beryl pressed her back into her seat.

'There ain't no point in rushin' off nowhere. The Matron at the hospital is like a bloody Sergeant Major. You stand no chance o' gettin' in till it's the proper visitin' time. So you just sit there an' try an' rest while I dish the dinner up. Me an' Jo have it all ready so we can have it on the table in a jiffy.'

Reluctantly, Maggie did as she was told while Jo and Beryl hurried away to serve the meal.

Once it was on the table, Maggie noticed the way Jo cut David's food up for him and the warm smile he gave her. It dawned on her then what the difference was. They were acting almost like a married couple. David seemed to have regained some of his former spirit, and Jo finally had the bloom of pregnancy in her cheeks. She'd gained a little weight, and her eyes, which had been dull and empty, were shining.

David suddenly noticed her watching them and blushed furiously, and in that moment, Maggie knew that she was right. There *was* something growing between them, even if they hadn't openly acknowledged it yet; it was there for all to see.

Lowering her eyes to her plate, she considered this latest development and asked herself how she felt about it. And after a moment it struck her with frightening force that she was glad for them! For so many years she had thought that somehow she and David would be together one day, but that had been before she met Eric . . . Just the thought of him was enough to make her tremble, and she knew now without a doubt that she loved him with all of her heart. Of course, she accepted that there could never be a happy ending for them. But if Jo and David wanted to get together, then she would give them her blessing.

Later that evening, Beryl and Maggie set off for the hospital through the darkened streets of Coventry, praying that another raid wouldn't start while they were on their way. It was bitterly cold, and the pavements were thick with frost, which had Beryl cursing loudly with every step she took.

Jo and David had decided to stay at home as the Matron was very strict about allowing no more than two visitors to a bed.

As they neared the hospital, Maggie's stomach began to do somersaults. Her poor boy! How would he feel about losing his legs? He'd always been such an energetic child, but now . . . She stopped her thoughts from travelling the road they were taking. The last thing Danny needed was for her to turn up in floods of tears. She would have to be brave for him and together they would learn to take each day one at a time.

She followed Beryl along a labyrinth of corridors until

they reached Danny's ward. There, Beryl hovered uncertainly, like a little bird about to take flight.

'Perhaps it would be better if I let yer have the first minutes alone wi' him, eh?'

Maggie nodded gratefully, then taking a deep breath, she pushed the double swing doors open and began to walk between the neat rows of beds. She spotted Danny almost immediately, and in that moment she knew that they would come through this. He was still her boy and he was alive, which was all that mattered.

When he turned his head as he heard her heels tapping towards him, he held his arms out to her and cried, 'Oh, Mam. I *knew* yer'd come.'

He looked dreadfully pale, and the metal cage that covered the place where his legs should have been made it awkward to cuddle him, but still she managed it. It would have taken far more than a cage to stop her.

'How are you feeling, darling?' she whispered into his hair. In actual fact he looked much better than she had expected him to. At least he knew her, which was a relief, for she'd feared that he wouldn't remember her.

'Better, since Soho Gus came to see me earlier on,' he told her.

The hairs on the back of Maggie's neck stood to attention as she stared down at him. '*Soho Gus* came to see you?'

He nodded joyfully. 'Yes – earlier on today. He told me you were comin' and I'd got to shape meself up so as not to upset yer.'

'Danny . . .' She struggled to find the words to tell him the terrible news. She had never knowingly lied to him in the whole of his life, and had no intention of starting now, even if what she had to say was going to be painful for him. Far better to get it over with. 'I'm afraid he couldn't have. You must have imagined it. You see, Gus was killed on the night you arrived in Coventry.'

She expected tears and tantrums, but instead he just gazed at her calmly. 'I know he was. He told me so. But yer see . . . Well, he was me best mate, an' like he told me – he'll always be here to watch over me.'

Maggie swallowed the painful sob that rose in her throat. Danny was obviously imagining things, but if it brought him comfort then she wouldn't argue with it.

'They come to measure me up fer a wheelchair today an' all,' Danny told her matter-of-factly. 'So as soon as I've got it, we can go back to Wales an' I can get on wi' me paintin'. Eric says I have a talent, an' like Gus said, yer don't need legs to paint, do yer? So all in all, I reckon I've come out of all this all right.'

Maggie was so shocked that she was rendered temporarily speechless. Never for one minute had she imagined taking him back to Wales, yet she supposed it *did* make sense – until the war was over, at least. If Eric would have them, that was.

When Beryl joined them, she beamed to see Danny looking so much brighter. 'Why, lad, yer look the bee's knees. Yer had me worried fer a time there.'

'He reckons his friend came to see him earlier on,' Maggie told her.

Beryl frowned. 'What friend would that be then?'

'Soho Gus,' Danny answered promptly.

'Oh yes? An' what does this here Soho Gus look like?' Beryl asked as a thought occurred to her.

'Well,' Danny frowned in concentration as he thought how best to describe him. 'He's about the same size as me an' he's got a mop o' bright gingery-red hair. Oh, an' he never goes nowhere wi'out Albert. That's his white rat. He lives fer most o' the time in Gus's top pocket.'

His grandma visibly paled in front of their very eyes. 'I think I know the lad,' she declared. 'That were the one I dreamed about, who told me where you were, bless him . . .' She got no further, for she was too busy rushing around to the other side of the bed to help Maggie, who had fallen in a dead faint onto the polished floor.

Two weeks later, the Sister at the hospital informed them that Danny was going to be allowed to go home.

'We wouldn't normally discharge him this quickly,' she told Maggie sternly, 'but with the way things are, the beds are in very short supply, so if you think you can manage . . .'

'Oh, I can manage all right,' Maggie hastened to assure her, and so the very next day Danny was delivered by ambulance back to his grandma's.

It was only then that Maggie broke the news to him about the deaths of his father, grandma and Lucy. He cried, but took it far better than she had expected him to, for as he told her, he'd already guessed that something was wrong when none of them visited him in hospital.

Leaving him alone with his grief for a while, Maggie then wrote to Eric, asking if she and Danny could go back to stay with him and Lizzie at *Tremarfon* whilst Danny recovered. His reply came back by return of post, saying that he would be delighted to have them, and so it was arranged. The days before they left were difficult, for Beryl's house was small, and not easy for Danny to manoeuvre his wheelchair around in. It almost broke Maggie's heart to watch him as he struggled to master the art of moving himself around.

'No, Mam, don't help me. I want to learn to get about on me own,' he would tell her if she so much as made a move to help him. His courage made her heart swell with pride and she knew that they were going to come through this.

David was endlessly patient with his nephew and went out of his way to find things to entertain him. It was almost as if, now that Danny too had suffered the loss of a limb, in fact, two limbs, there was some unspoken bond between them and David could finally face up to his own injury. In truth, he was humbled to see this young boy's bravery and determination to cope, and while he watched admiringly, his own healing process finally began.

Maggie meanwhile watched the love between Jo and David grow, and wondered when they would recognise what was happening themselves.

She and Beryl took Danny out for a walk around Swanswell Park one crisp bright afternoon, and returned to find David and Jo positively glowing.

'Maggie, I er . . . I wonder if I might have a word with you in the front room?' David asked as Jo blushed to the roots of her hair.

'Of course.' Maggie drew off her gloves and tossed them onto the table as she followed him into the small front parlour. He closed the door and then stood staring at her, looking highly embarrassed.

'Maggie, I felt it only right to speak to you before we said anything to Mam, because . . . Well, you and I go back a long way. I'll admit I always considered you to be *my* girl, even after you married Sam. But the thing is – the war has changed us all, and I . . .'

When he faltered, she laughed and decided to put him out of his misery. 'What you're trying to tell me, David, is that you and Jo have fallen in love and you want me to give you my blessing.'

'But . . . how did you know?' he asked incredulously.

Maggie giggled. 'A blind man on a galloping horse could see how you two felt about each other. I think I saw it the first day I came home, even before you two did. And if you're asking me how I feel about it, well – all I can say is I'm delighted for you both. You look right together and I hope you'll both be very, very happy. Jo is a lovely girl, David. Don't you ever forget it – you're a very, very lucky man.'

Relief washed over his face as he hastily hurried to her and planted a kiss on her cheek. 'But what about you, Maggie?'

She smiled reassuringly at him. 'Don't you get worrying about me. I've got Danny and Lizzie to worry about, thank goodness.'

As he took her hand in his, his eyes were full of tenderness. 'I reckon you and I were never meant to be, don't you?'

She gently stroked his cheek. 'Everything happens for a reason. Let's just leave it at that, eh? And be grateful for what we've got. Now come on, let's go and put Jo out of her misery and tell your mam the good news.'

With his arm about her shoulder, they went to do just that.

The following week, Jo and David were married by Special Licence at the register office. It was a simple wedding, with only Beryl, Danny, Maggie and two strangers they dragged in off the street to act as witnesses attending, but even so, the love that shone between Jo and David as they took their vows brought tears stinging to Maggie's eyes. Jo looked beautiful in a suit that Maggie had hastily run up for her on Beryl's sewing-machine, and she carried a tiny posy of snowdrops. David managed to look handsome in the only suit he possessed, which was now far too big for him, and looked proud and happy. Once outside, Danny threw confetti over them as David lovingly stroked the tiny person growing inside his new wife's stomach.

Maggie was content in the knowledge that she was witnessing a coming together of souls.

The next morning, bright and early, Maggie called at the florist's in Gas Street, and after buying a pot containing a bright red Christmas Rose, she wheeled Danny to the London Road Cemetery. Two large communal graves were a harsh reminder of the war that was raging all around them.

Danny's eyes filled with tears as he stared at the huge unmarked grave. Somewhere in there lay the best friend he had ever had.

'Just try to think that he's in a better place now, love,' Maggie soothed him.

Danny nodded. 'Do yer suppose there's any chance that he might meet up wi' our Lucy an' me gran?'

Maggie was aware that Danny hadn't mentioned his father but wisely chose not to comment on it. Danny had more than enough to come to terms with at the moment. 'I think there's every chance. The angels look after their own.'

Leaning over the side of his wheelchair, Danny laid the plant on the edge of the enormous grave.

'Goodbye, Soho Gus . . . I'll never forget you,' he whispered.

Turning the wheelchair about, Maggie steered him home.

'How much longer now, Mam?' Danny asked for the

hundredth time as he gazed from the train window. The nightmare journey he had made back from Wales to Coventry on that fateful night a few short weeks ago, seemed so remote.

'We'll soon be there,' Maggie assured him. 'Look, you can see the Welsh hills in the distance. We'll be in Pwllheli in no time, and Eric has promised to be there to meet us.'

Her heart pounded at the thought of seeing him. He'd written to say that he'd meet them at the station, but was it merely because he felt he had to? She would know soon enough so she settled back in her seat to watch the Welsh countryside flash past the carriage window.

As they drew into the station, Maggie began to gather their cases together and she manoeuvred Danny's wheelchair into the corridor. His face was alight at the thought of seeing his sister and Eric again, and her heart swelled with pride. Her son had been through so very much, yet had come out of it all with a smile on his face. He truly was a shining example to them all.

The train finally lurched to a standstill, and somehow Maggie managed to roll the wheelchair along the narrow corridor to the door. The platform was misty with smoke from the engine as she clambered down, dragging their cases behind her. She then turned to lift the wheelchair with the help of a friendly porter who had seen her struggling.

'Thank you very much.' After delving into her purse, she slipped some coins into his hand, then peered along the length of the platform. It was then she heard a familiar voice and her heart began to sing.

'Mammy!'

Spinning around, she saw Lizzie pounding towards her, her beautiful hair flying behind her like a golden cloud.

And then she was in her mam's arms and they were laughing and crying all at the same time. Within seconds, she had disentangled herself from Maggie and flung herself at her brother, almost climbing into the wheelchair with him in her excitement. Maggie felt tears prick at the back of her eyes. She had wondered how Lizzie would cope with seeing her brother in a wheelchair, but she needn't have worried. He was still her brother, and the fact that he no longer had any legs had done nothing to change that.

'Hello, Maggie.'

Turning quickly, she now found herself looking up into Eric's face. His eye-patch was gone, and somehow the scars on his face looked nowhere near as disfiguring as she had once thought them to be.

He touched his face self-consciously. 'I er . . . decided not to wear the eye-patch any more,' he told her. 'Lizzie said it frightened her.'

Suddenly shy, she held her hand out to him. All the way there on the train she'd rehearsed what she would say to him, but now the words died on her lips. She wanted to fling herself into his arms and tell him how much she'd missed him, but she knew that she mustn't. It wouldn't be fair to compromise him when he'd done so much for them all already.

Sensing her embarrassment, he turned his attention to Danny.

'So – how are we feeling then?' His obvious delight at seeing him brought an answering smile from Danny.

'I'm all right,' he replied with a cheeky grin. 'All ready fer me next art lesson now.'

'I'm glad to hear it.' Eric ruffled his hair affectionately before bending to lift the cases. 'Let's get cracking then, shall we? Lizzie and I have done you a nice dinner all ready for when we get home.'

Lizzie grasped the handles of the wheelchair and hurried after Eric. Maggie could hardly take her eyes off the child. She'd put on a little weight and her cheeks were glowing, due to the combination of fresh air and good food she had received. Suddenly she felt guilty. Beryl and David had ensured that she left Coventry with some money in her pocket, but it wouldn't last for long and she couldn't expect Eric to house and feed them all for nothing. Her pride would not allow it. Perhaps there might be a part-time job she could do somewhere whilst the children were at school – when Danny was fit enough to return to school, that was.

She promised herself that as soon as the children had settled in she would talk to Eric about it. At least then he would know that she wasn't intending to take advantage of him just because of what had happened between them.

Outside the station, Eric lifted Danny and gently placed him on the back seat of the car with Lizzie, then folding his wheelchair up, he put it in the back with the cases before opening the front passenger door for Maggie.

'Ma'am.' There was a twinkle in his eye as Maggie shyly squeezed past him.

All the way back to *Tremarfon* the car was filled with the excited chatter of the children, which was just as well, for Maggie was struck dumb, and was already wondering if this had been such a good idea, after all. It briefly crossed her mind that she might be able to find somewhere in Wales for her and the children to live until after the war was over – if she could find a job, that was. But then, how would Danny cope with her at work? He now needed a fair amount of help with even ordinary everyday things.

All the way back she pondered on her situation until

at last, Eric drove into Sarn-Bach. Danny suddenly fell silent as they drove past the house where Sparky had lived. Maggie had been forced to tell Danny what had happened to him. Just thinking back to it now made her eyes well with tears.

Lizzie squeezed his hand, feeling his pain as she always did. 'Try not to get upset,' she told him softly. 'Sparky probably saved my life an' Eric says he was a hero.'

Danny nodded, but his chin sank to his chest as he thought about his little friend. At last they turned up the lane that would lead to home and Danny gazed at *Derwen Deg* as they passed it. He missed Soho Gus more than he could say, and yet he still felt as if he were somehow close.

'He came to see me when I were lyin' in the hospital, yer know,' he told Lizzie. 'I hardly knew what day it was, or *where* I was, fer that matter, but Gus soon put me straight. "Pull yerself together an' get on wi' things," he told me. I were feelin' really sorry fer meself 'cos me legs had gone, but it's like he said: "Yer've still got yer arms, ain't yer?" That got me to thinkin'. At least I'm still here, ain't I? An' then Mam came back an' I knew things were goin' to work out all right. When me stumps have healed a bit they reckon they can make me some pro . . . prosth . . . Oh, I can't remember the posh name, but it means pretend legs. Yer can learn to walk again an' everythin' on 'em.'

Lizzie gazed at him admiringly. In her eyes, Danny was a hero too. But then he always had been, and nothing would ever change that.

The car slithered on up the slippery slope and then at last there was *Tremarfon*. Maggie experienced a strange sense of home coming as Eric drew the car to a halt and hurried around to the back of it to get Danny's wheel-chair out.

Samson bounded out to meet them, almost knocking the small wheelchair over in his excitement when he saw Danny.

'I shall *have* to get them legs fitted now, won't I?' he laughed. 'So I can take Samson for a walk again.'

When they entered the kitchen, Maggie gasped with surprise. Bright scatter rugs covered the floor, and pretty cushions were arranged on the chairs and the settee. There were shiny brass candlesticks on the mantelshelf and a bowl of marigolds standing in pride of place in the middle of the table.

'Why, it looks lovely,' she gasped.

Lizzie giggled. 'Soon as Eric knew you were coming home, he said he thought we ought to make the place a bit more homely, so we went shopping. I helped him to choose everything. Do you like it, Mam?'

'I love it,' Maggie declared, then turning to Eric she told him, 'Thank you.'

He shrugged as he dropped the suitcases onto the floor, and Danny wheeled himself across to stroke Hemily.

'The place was overdue for a bit of refurbishment,' he mumbled, then scurried away to put the kettle on as Maggie stood gazing around at his handiwork.

Danny winked at Lizzie and she giggled as she too stroked the huge fat cat asleep in the armchair. From now on, things were going to get better – the twins were sure of it.

Chapter Thirty-Nine

They had been back at *Tremarfon* for three days and things were beginning to fall into a pattern. Lizzie had returned to the village school, but Maggie didn't yet feel that Danny was ready for it, so he got to stay at home with her as they began to plan Christmas, which was only weeks away now.

'Can we have a Christmas tree?' Danny asked Eric one night as they all sat at the table having sausage and mash, with tapioca and homemade strawberry jam to follow.

'I certainly can't see any reason why we shouldn't,' Eric replied. 'Although I have to admit I've never had one here before.'

Danny smiled with satisfaction as he gazed across at his painting. He'd finished it earlier in the day, and Eric had promised to take it into a shop in Pwllheli to get it framed for him so that he could give it to his mother for Christmas.

He loved being back at *Tremarfon*. The only thing he didn't love was the way Eric and his mother were behaving towards each other – as if they were polite strangers. He'd remarked on it to Lizzie the night before as they were lying in bed and she'd agreed with him.

'What do yer reckon is up with 'em?'

Lizzie pursed her lips. 'I ain't got a clue. They seemed to get on really well when she came here the last time.' Suddenly leaning up on her elbow, she now asked him, 'Danny, what's it feel like to have no legs?'

Danny frowned as he thought how best to answer her. 'It's strange really,' he told her eventually. 'What I mean is, apart from the fact I can't get about like I used to, it don't feel no different now that the pain's gone. In fact, sometimes I think they're feelin' itchy but when I lean down to scratch 'em they ain't there any more.'

Content with his explanation, Lizzie's thoughts moved on. Smiling dreamily, she gazed beyond the window at the wind whispering through the trees. 'Wouldn't it be wonderful if we could stay here forever?'

'What . . . like a real family, do yer mean?'

Lizzie nodded in the darkness. 'Yes. We ain't got nothing to go back to Coventry for now, have we? We ain't even got a house there. An' Gran won't have room for us, with Jo and David living there now. An' Jo will have a baby soon.'

'I hadn't thought of that,' Danny sighed, but then he brightened again. 'Let's not worry about it fer now, eh? Yer know what Soho Gus told me. Everythin' 'appens fer a reason.'

Sighing with contentment, Lizzie nestled down into the warm bed, and very soon both of them were fast asleep.

Downstairs in the kitchen, the atmosphere was nowhere near as relaxed as Maggie wondered how to approach what she wanted to say to Eric. He was sitting reading the newspaper in the chair at the side of the fire, with Hemily on his lap and Samson curled up at his feet.

Lifting her knitting, she went and sat in the opposite

chair to him, then tentatively she asked, 'Eric, I was wondering – could I have a chat to you about something?' The knitting needles clicked furiously as her nerves ran out of control.

Laying the paper down he gave her his full attention. 'Of course. What's troubling you?'

'Well, there's nothing *troubling* me exactly. It's just that I'm very aware that you're now keeping the three of us, and it doesn't feel right.'

'Oh, I see. So what are you saying then? That you'll soon be shooting off back to Coventry?'

Her mouth dropped open in astonishment. 'No, of course that's not what I was going to say at all! I wouldn't dream of leaving Danny as he is, or Lizzie for that matter. What I *was* going to say was that I've been thinking of getting a job and I wondered if you might know of any going?'

She thought she detected a look of relief cross his face, but it was so fleeting that she assumed she must have imagined it.

Steepling his fingers, he stared thoughtfully into the flames of the fire, as she rushed on, 'I know it would mean putting a lot more work on to you, what with having to help Danny and everything. But at least I could pay our way then, and I *would* do my share of the work when I got home,' she added hastily.

'Don't you think you do more than enough already?' He was looking at her now, and her stomach was churning as it always did when she was close to him.

'What you have to remember is, I already get paid a small amount for looking after evacuees. And you . . . well, just look at the difference you've made to this place! I've hardly lifted a finger since you came back. Maggie, you don't owe me a single penny. *I* should be paying *you*

472

actually for taking such good care of the place. Unless you need some money to get back to David in Coventry, that is?'

So that was it. Tears of humiliation stung at the back of her eyes. He was trying to get rid of her and using David as the excuse. Well, she certainly wouldn't enlighten him to the fact that David was now a married man. Let him stew. Why couldn't he just be man enough to tell her that what had happened between them had been a mistake?

'I have absolutely no intention of going back to Coventry until the war is over,' she told him primly. 'And now, if you'll excuse me, I think I'll get an early night.'

The following morning as they all sat at the table having breakfast, Eric asked Danny, 'Do you fancy coming into Pwllheli with me for a ride today? I thought we could drop your painting off at the picture-framer and do a bit of Christmas shopping. Lizzie, you can come as well if you like.'

Both the small heads nodded eagerly as Maggie stared fixedly at her plate. She would have liked to go too. Christmas was getting uncomfortably close and as yet she hadn't bought so much as a single gift. She wouldn't ask him if she could go with them, though. Instead she rose and began to clear the dirty pots from the table, letting them clatter into the sink to relieve her frustration.

Damn and blast Eric! Why didn't he just ask her to leave, if that was what he wanted? Perhaps it wouldn't be such a bad idea to move back to Coventry, after all? The twins glanced at each other apprehensively as they picked up on their mam's mood. She was slamming about with a face like a bulldog sucking on a wasp, though they had no idea why.

Half an hour later, they were all ready to go. Maggie walked to the car with them while Eric packed Danny's wheelchair and his painting in the back.

'Have a good day then,' she told them, forcing a smile to her face as she leaned through the car window to kiss them goodbye. 'Eric, drive carefully, won't you?'

'Of course I will,' he told her shortly as he clambered into the driver's seat. He started the engine and then they were off and the children were waving furiously to Maggie as the car started the downhill slide. She watched until they were out of sight, then shuddering, she drew her cardigan more tightly about her and hurried back into the house. A few downpours of rain had shifted much of the snow that had been lying, but now it was muddy slush underfoot. Shutting the kitchen door firmly behind her, she rushed over to the fire and held her hands out to the dancing flames.

'Bloody men!' she muttered.

The children were highly excited when they got home late that afternoon, and Lizzie shot off up the stairs with two parcels gripped under her arm.

Danny grinned at her innocently. 'Just a couple o' things we picked up fer Christmas,' he told her as he saw the question in her eyes.

Eric winked at her as if to say, 'Ask no questions,' so she hurried away to put the kettle on instead.

When Lizzie reappeared, Maggie nodded at an envelope propped up on the mantelpiece. 'A letter came for you two today. It looks like it's from your gran.'

Lizzie handed it to Danny. 'Go on, you read it out to me,' she told him eagerly.

Danny slit it open with his thumb, and as he withdrew the sheet of paper inside, two ten-shilling notes fluttered to the ground. Whooping with delight, Lizzie pounced on them and told him, 'Well, go on then.'

Slowly he began: *'Dear Lizzie and Danny, I hope this letter finds you both well and looking forward to Christmas. I have put some money inside for both of you, as it's unlikely that I shall see you. Buy yourselves something nice with it from me. I hope you are both settling down there and behaving yourselves for your mam. Everything is fine here. Jo is getting bigger every single day and she and your Uncle David can hardly wait for the baby to come now . . .'*

Danny continued to read the letter aloud as Maggie glanced across at Eric. He was frowning and his eyebrows had disappeared into his hairline. He looked at her as if for an explanation, but she merely looked away. Let him think what he liked. It would serve him right for jumping to conclusions.

As she laid the tea on the table he was unnaturally quiet, though the twins more than made up for it with their excited chatter. They'd spent a wonderful day in town and then come home to a letter from their gran, which was the icing on the cake. On top of that, they now had ten whole shillings each to spend on anything at all they liked!

The mood was light as they shot ideas as to just what they should spend it on across the table at each other.

'Why don't you save it?' Eric suggested.

Maggie laughed. 'You *must* be joking. It would burn a hole in their pockets.'

'We could buy a little present for the baby when it comes from both of us, with some of it,' Danny suggested through a mouthful of homemade bread and jam.

Lizzie pondered. 'Wouldn't it be better to wait till it's born? That way we could buy it something pink or blue,' she pointed out.

475

Danny shrugged. 'I reckon I'll leave that to you then. I ain't much good when it comes to baby things.' His eyes grew dark as a picture of Lucy flashed in front of his eyes. He still missed his baby sister every single day. Maggie saw the look and her heart ached too. There was a great hole inside her that no one could fill since she had lost Lucy and her mother, but she knew that she had to go on for the twins' sake. They'd all been through so very much, but they still had each other and that was what kept her going.

Suddenly the mood had changed and silence hung over them.

Sensing their sadness, Eric suddenly asked, 'So why is your Uncle David so excited about Jo's baby then?' He'd been longing to ask ever since Danny had read his gran's letter aloud. He had promised himself that he wouldn't, but now his curiosity had got the better of him and it was too late to take the question back.

''Cos it's their first baby, I suppose,' Danny told him. 'They kept talkin' about what they might call it when it was born, after the weddin'. Didn't they, Mam?'

Maggie felt her cheeks burning as Eric scratched his head in confusion.

'After *whose* wedding?'

'*Their* weddin', o' course,' Danny grinned. 'They're livin' wi' me gran fer now but once the baby's born an' the war's over they're goin' to get somewhere of their own to live.'

Eric looked totally shocked and stared at Maggie as if for confirmation of what Danny had said.

'It's true,' she muttered. 'David and Jo got married a few days before Danny and I came back here. They make a wonderful couple. I think they'll be very happy together. At least I hope they will.'

'But I thought you and . . .' Eric forced himself to stop

from going any further. The twins were watching him closely and he didn't want to say too much in front of them. There would be time to talk to Maggie about this when the youngsters were safely tucked up in bed.

By the time they said goodnight, Eric was almost bursting with curiosity. Why hadn't Maggie told him that David had married her friend? He'd assumed after she told him her life story that she and David were destined for each other, so how could she be happy about him marrying someone else?

When she came back down the stairs after seeing to the twins he was waiting for her.

'So, how about you tell me just what's been going on then?' he demanded, the second she closed the door behind her.

'There's nothing more to tell other than what Danny's already told you,' she said sharply. 'When I got back home I saw immediately that David and Jo had fallen for each other. To be honest, I think I saw it even before they did. Obviously, I was very taken up with visiting Danny in the hospital, and then one night I got back and David told me how he felt about her.'

'And what did you tell him?'

'I told him not to waste time; gave them both my blessing. If there's one thing that this war has taught me, it's that time is short. None of us know if we are even going to be here tomorrow, so every moment is precious. Just a few short months ago, I had a mother, a husband and a beautiful baby girl. Danny had two very special friends. Now they're all gone and they won't be coming back. Somehow we have to go on and make the best of what we have. So now, if you don't mind, I'm really tired and I'm going up to bed. Goodnight. I'll see you in the morning.'

477

'Maggie, wait . . .' His only answer was the sound of the door closing behind her and for a while he stood there staring off into space. So much of what she had said made sense. Slowly he made his way to the dining room where he clicked on the light and stared up into the face of his late wife. Was he imagining it, or did he see a great sadness in her eyes? His shoulders sagged as he turned about and slowly climbed the stairs to his lonely bed. What was it Maggie had said? *Time is short.*

Overnight, the snow began to fall again as it was prone to do in the Welsh hills, and Lizzie and Danny shrieked with excitement when they managed to rub off a small patch on the ice that had formed on the inside of the bedroom window and peep through it.

Everywhere looked clean and fresh again.

'Come on, let's go and tell Mam an' Eric!' Danny exclaimed as he manoeuvred his wheelchair towards the bedroom door.

Lizzie thumped off down the stairs ahead of him and within seconds came back with Eric, who carried him downstairs.

Maggie grinned at him. She was standing at the sink and, knowing how much Danny loved the snow, she had guessed that he would be thrilled to see it again. The snow here seemed to be completely different to the snow they got back at home in Coventry. Within minutes of it falling there, it was turned to dirty grey slush from the many footsteps that trooped through it. But here it made everything look crisp and bright.

'This is goin' to be the *best* Christmas ever,' Danny declared as he stabbed his fork into a fat juicy sausage.

'Oh yes, and what would you *really* like for Christmas then, if you could have anything in the world you wanted?' Eric asked him with a twinkle in his eye.

Danny suddenly became solemn as he looked at the faces gathered around the table. Glancing at Lizzie he said quietly, 'What Lizzie an' I would both like more than anythin' in the world would be fer us both to be able to stay here at *Tremarfon* forever.'

Maggie almost choked on the piece of bacon she'd just swallowed and Eric had to jump up and thump her on the back as she turned a frightening shade of red.

Lizzie and Danny grinned at each other and then nonchalantly carried on with their breakfast.

Once the table had been cleared, Eric lifted Danny onto the sledge he had made for him and Soho Gus. 'Are you quite sure you can manage to drag him along?' he asked Lizzie.

She gave him a smile that was so like her mother's it made his heart skip a beat. 'Of course I can,' she informed him scathingly. 'I'm only dragging him as far as the garden anyway, an' then we're goin' to build a snowman, ain't we, Danny?'

Danny grinned enthusiastically and suddenly, Eric felt ashamed. This poor child had lost both his legs and yet he had displayed more courage in the last few weeks than he himself had in years. Lizzie too had suffered a terrible ordeal at the hands of a woman who was demented, and yet as soon as it was over she had got on with her life. Maggie had lost her husband, her home, her baby and her mother all in the space of a few short months. But rather than let it beat her she was now fighting to build a future for herself and the twins.

Since the accident that had caused him to lose his eye and his wife, he had hidden behind his scars and shut himself away in a world where no one could reach him. Lost in his own self-pity. Turning away from the children, who had already forgotten he was there, he squared his shoulders. It was time to put things right. If it wasn't too late, that was.

Maggie glanced up from the sinkful of dirty crockery she was washing when he entered but then turned her eyes back to the task at hand.

He hovered by the door, drinking in the sight of her. Her clothes were shabby and her hair was tied into a ponytail, which made her look almost like a young girl. And yet, to him she still looked beautiful. Maggie didn't need fancy clothes and expensive hairstyles. She had an inner beauty that shone through.

'Maggie, why didn't you tell me that David was married?'

A flush spread up her neck and into her cheeks as her hands became still in the soapy water. 'You didn't ask,' she told him dully.

He crossed to stand right behind her, so close that she could feel his breath on the back of her neck and her heart began to thump painfully. Her eyes focused on the children playing out in the garden through the window.

'Maggie Bright. Will you *please* turn around?'

Slowly drying her hands on the thin towel at the side of the sink, she then turned to look up at him, thinking how much better he looked, now that he no longer wore the ugly eye-patch.

Tenderly, he took her hands in his and asked her, 'Will you answer a question truthfully for me?'

She nodded numbly as he took a deep breath. 'Maggie – do you still love David?'

The look on her face answered his question before she even opened her mouth.

'Of course I don't. To be honest, I wonder now if I

ever did. David has found his soulmate in Jo and I couldn't be happier about it.'

'Good, now one more question. Do you think you could ever love *me*?'

Shock robbed her of the power of speech.

He grinned. 'Maggie, before you answer that, perhaps I should tell you something.' There was no going back now so he hurried on. 'I think I've loved you from the very first second I set eyes on you, but I didn't dare to believe that there was a future for us. For one, I never thought you'd entertain someone who looked like me when you could have any man you wanted. Secondly, I thought you were still in love with David. But earlier on, when Danny told us he'd like to stay here at *Tremarfon*, it got me to thinking. I want you to stay, Maggie. On any terms you want. You can be my friend, my live-in lover, or better still . . . my wife. I know you don't love me, but—'

'Ssh . . .' She started to giggle as she launched herself into his arms. 'Who said I didn't love you? Did you think what happened between us before happened just because I'd had a drink? You silly man, I fell in love with you within days of being here, but I thought you were still in love with your dead wife.'

A look of pure joy lit up his one good eye, and her heart took flight as he sank dramatically down onto one knee. 'In that case then, Maggie Bright, will you do me the *very* great honour of becoming my wife?'

She laughed, a gay laugh that echoed around the room. 'Mr Eric Sinclair, nothing would give me more pleasure. Yes, I will.'

She would have said more but he sprang up and pressed his lips to hers, and suddenly words were unimportant.

Lizzie, who had just come in at the back door, gazed at them speechlessly, then with a whoop of joy she bounded across the snow to Danny again.

''Ere, Danny,' she gasped. 'You'll never guess what. Yer know what yer were saying earlier on about us wanting to stay here at *Tremarfon* forever? Well, I reckon we're about to get our wish!'

Epilogue

Coventry, May 1945

From the doorway of Beryl's little terraced house in Gas Street, Maggie watched as people hung out of their bedroom windows, putting out flags and *Welcome Home* signs for the loved ones who would soon be returning. Today, they would try very hard not to think of the ones who would not be coming home. Red, white and blue bunting was strung between every available lamppost, and stretched for as far as the eye could see, turning the drab little street into a sea of colour. Men were erecting trestle tables all up the middle of the street. At last the war was over.

Eric came to stand behind her and put his arm around her swollen waist. The child inside her kicked lustily as if it sensed the presence of its father. Back in the kitchen, they could hear Lizzie teasing her harassed grandma as they buttered yet another loaf.

'Crikey, Gran. At this rate there'll be enough to feed the whole o' Coventry, let alone the street,' she laughed.

'Better too much than not enough,' Beryl rejoined. 'If we're goin' to have a party then let's make it a good 'un, that's what I say! It's certainly been bloody long enough in comin'. Six long years.'

Eric grinned, before bending to lift his two-year-old daughter, Katie into his arms.

'Hello, sweetheart.' He laughed as he saw the icing that was caked into her dark curls. Katie was a tiny carbon copy of Lucy, and he and Maggie absolutely adored her. 'Gran been feeding you fairy cakes again, has she?' Glancing back at Maggie he saw the look of sadness that had settled across her features and instantly guessed why. 'Missing Danny, are you?'

She nodded. 'Yes. It doesn't seem right, us all being here without him.'

Gently placing Katie back down, he turned her to face him. 'You know this is an important time for him,' he pointed out. 'He was so lucky to get that place at art school in Chelsea. If it hadn't been for the fact that he was in the middle of exams, heaven and earth wouldn't have kept him away. Though I have to admit I'm not altogether sure that was the *only* reason he chose not to come. I don't think he wants you to see him on his prostheses till he's mastered the art of walking properly on them.'

Maggie nodded in agreement; she had thought much the same. Like everything else that life had thrown at him, Danny was struggling with his new legs with a courage that made her heart swell with pride. She was proud of both of the twins, for Lizzie could now speak fluent Welsh and was the star pupil back at the school in Sarn-Bach. Already she'd decided that she wanted to become a teacher, and Miss Williams had every intention of making her dream come true. Maggie didn't have time to ponder on it though, for just then, David and Jo turned the corner of the street and waved at them. Jo was pushing a pram with their three-month-old daughter inside, whilst David clung on to the chubby hand of four-year-old Jonathan, who was straining to get to his Cousin Katie.

Maggie's face lit up at the sight of them. They made

such a lovely family and looked so happy that it did her heart good to see them.

'How's the new house coming along?' she asked Jo after they'd all had a hug.

Jo pulled a wry face. 'Not too bad. It would be much easier though if Jonathan didn't keep stripping off every bit of wallpaper as fast as I put it on. I've asked David to talk to him, but you know what a big softie he is with the children.'

They almost had to shout to make themselves heard above the clatter in the street. Women had appeared now and were throwing huge white sheets across the tables as fast as the men could assemble them.

'Come on,' Maggie grinned, taking Jo's arm. 'Let's go and scrounge a cup of tea off Beryl. She's been hard at it since six this morning.'

'How long are you here for?' Jo asked as they stepped from the pavement into the tidy front parlour.

'Just till the end of the week. Eric is doing a big contract for a children's publisher's in London so he doesn't want to get behind with it.'

They strolled into the kitchen arm-in-arm and Jo looked at fourteen-year-old Lizzie in astonishment. 'Good grief! You've turned into a young lady, and a beautiful one at that since the last time I saw you. I bet your dad is having to beat the boys off with a stick.'

Lizzie flushed. She was very aware of her fast-blossoming figure and didn't as yet quite know how to handle it.

'Leave her alone,' Beryl scolded. 'You're embarrassing the poor girl.'

Turning her attention back to Maggie, Jo asked, 'So how much longer before this little one puts in an appearance, then?'

Maggie gently stroked her swollen stomach. 'Not long now, thank goodness. I'm sure this one is going to be a boy. It never keeps still. I think it's going to be an athlete.'

At that moment, Katie and Jonathan toddled into the kitchen and immediately began to attack the plate of fairy cakes.

'Get off, the pair o' yer!' Beryl shouted at them, but there was a wealth of affection in her voice. 'There won't be a single one left at this rate by the time they're due to go out on the table.'

David and Eric appeared in the doorway. They were laughing at the antics of the local children who were erecting an enormous bonfire at the end of the street on the common.

'Little sods have been at it since early this mornin',' Beryl announced. 'They've given 'em two days off school to celebrate, an' don't we know it! I tell yer, they're getting that carried away I'm scared to leave me door open in case they whip it off its hinges an' chuck that on the bonfire an' all. Anyway, that's enough chat fer now. Help me to get some o' this stuff out on to the table, would yer? I've still got to get me curlers out an' make meself look respectable before the party starts.'

They all grabbed a plate each and piled out into the street where the tables were beginning to groan beneath their weight of food. There were sandwiches with all manners of fillings, wobbly jellies that reflected the light of the bright May sunshine, cakes of all shapes and sizes, and dishes loaded with homemade pickled onions.

At the other end of the street a band was tuning up and Beryl sighed with satisfaction. 'Looks set to be a good night.'

As darkness fell, the party got into full swing. Barrels of beer had been placed at either end of the tables and everyone was in high spirits. Sticky-faced children sat on doorsteps with their plates loaded with food. Fireworks exploded in rainbow colours in the sky above them. The band was belting out merry tunes and as the beer flowed like water, people took to the street and began to dance around the tables.

Maggie stood quietly, thinking back over the last few years. They had not all been easy. Her eyes settled on Katie; she was so like Lucy that sometimes it was painful to look at her. She thought of her mother and Sam, and a great feeling of sadness descended on her, but then Eric was there with his arm thrown protectively about her shoulders.

'All right, sweetheart?'

She nodded tearfully as she realised how lucky she was. The war had taken its toll on all of them, but they had come through it and now they could gradually rebuild their lives. Life was for the living.